S0-BRV-437

"Has any man ever taken your clothes off item by item?"

Honor didn't reply, for the simple reason that she was speechless.

"Have *you*," Ryan Bailey continued, after waiting politely for a moment, "ever tried to tempt a man unbearably? Other than just by being your cool, immaculate self?"

"*Mr.* Bailey!"

Ryan looked ironically into her blazing eyes. "That's what we could achieve, Miss Lingard—the resolution of some or all of those matters."

LINDSAY ARMSTRONG was born in South Africa, but now lives in Australia with her New Zealand-born husband and their five children. They have lived in nearly every state of Australia and tried their hand at some unusual, for them, occupations, such as farming and horse training—all grist to the mill for a writer! Lindsay started writing romances when their youngest child began school and she was feeling a loose end. She is still doing it and loving it.

A Careful Wife

LINDSAY ARMSTRONG

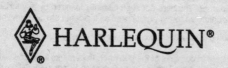

HARLEQUIN®

TORONTO • NEW YORK • LONDON
AMSTERDAM • PARIS • SYDNEY • HAMBURG
STOCKHOLM • ATHENS • TOKYO • MILAN • MADRID
PRAGUE • WARSAW • BUDAPEST • AUCKLAND

If you purchased this book without a cover you should be aware that this book is stolen property. It was reported as "unsold and destroyed" to the publisher, and neither the author nor the publisher has received any payment for this "stripped book."

ISBN 0-373-80521-7

A CAREFUL WIFE

First North American Publication 2001.

Copyright © 1996 by Lindsay Armstrong.

All rights reserved. Except for use in any review, the reproduction or utilization of this work in whole or in part in any form by any electronic, mechanical or other means, now known or hereafter invented, including xerography, photocopying and recording, or in any information storage or retrieval system, is forbidden without the written permission of the publisher, Harlequin Enterprises Limited, 225 Duncan Mill Road, Don Mills, Ontario, Canada M3B 3K9.

All characters in this book have no existence outside the imagination of the author and have no relation whatsoever to anyone bearing the same name or names. They are not even distantly inspired by any individual known or unknown to the author, and all incidents are pure invention.

This edition published by arrangement with Harlequin Books S.A.

® and TM are trademarks of the publisher. Trademarks indicated with ® are registered in the United States Patent and Trademark Office, the Canadian Trade Marks Office and in other countries.

Visit us at www.eHarlequin.com

Printed in U.S.A.

CHAPTER ONE

RYAN BAILEY was never an easy man to deal with but in a cold rage, as he undoubtedly was now, he was impossible.

Honor Lingard reflected on this from a corner of his large, luxurious office where she was seated upon a beige leather Barcelona chair. She was well out of the immediate arena, thankfully.

Her black velvet Chanel-style suit, worn with a white silk blouse, was immaculate; her long legs, clad in the sheerest nylon and elegant suede shoes, were crossed neatly at the ankles; a notebook reposed in her lap but her hands were folded on it and her dark eyes were downcast as she listened to the fireworks a little wryly…

'That's the third tender we've lost in as many months, and lost to the same company,' Ryan was saying to the two men in front of his desk. 'What the hell is going on? What, precisely, am I paying both of you small fortunes to achieve—the *destruction* of Bailey Construction? Forgive me for cherishing these doubts but—'

'We tendered exactly according to the guidelines you yourself set, Ryan,' Bill Fortune said hastily.

'And it didn't occur to you,' Ryan said icily, 'when it happened twice, let alone three times, to smell a rat? No, apparently not.' He answered his own question scathingly. 'You simply sat back like a couple of Boy Scouts at a tent-erecting contest!'

'Well, you were overseas and—'

Ryan stood up and towered behind his desk. 'Do I have to do everything? Would you like me to hold your hands when you go to the bathroom? Don't you know damn well that no one could have undercut us unless it was with vastly inferior materials or unless,' he said significantly, 'there was a bit of bribery and corruption going on?'

'Ryan,' Bill said placatingly, 'yes, I did wonder, but we don't quite have your way of—' he shrugged '—dealing with things like that.'

'Then I suggest you acquire it,' his boss said in the coldest, most cutting way, 'or you're fired, both of you. That'll be all.'

The two men left, but not before re-registering Honor's presence with a degree of embarrassment—she had arrived in the office only moments before them and been told curtly to sit down in the interim. She didn't rise immediately as Ryan sat down himself, banged a folder closed and barked an order to his secretary via the intercom. Instead she took those few moments to study him discreetly...

Ryan Bailey was forty—a tall, dark, rugged man who could not be described as handsome but nevertheless had a commanding, even electrifying presence. He also had a pair of smoky grey eyes that could cut you out and pin you to the wall and, in the case of a lot of women, for reasons best known to themselves, did strange and exciting things to their composure.

He was divorced and had made himself a fortune, initially out of Bailey Construction—he was a civil engineer—but he had diversified over the years. He had also been overseas for most of Honor's period of employment but she had heard enough about him to know that he was a complex, surprisingly sophisticated man when he was not riding over people like a steam-shovel, and she was reflecting on that, her gaze resting on him unseeingly, when he spoke.

'And what are you looking so superior about, Miss Lingard?' he drawled.

Honor narrowed her eyes. 'I was merely wondering,' she said smoothly, 'whether it was quite diplomatic or indeed necessary to include me in that little scene.'

'Then may I say that despite your degrees, your experience with Sotheby's, your undoubted *savoir-faire*, your super if not to say overly cultured aura, et cetera, it was as just another employee that I hired you to be curator of my art collection?'

'And may I say, Mr Bailey,' she returned evenly, although a little pulse beat rapidly at the base of her throat, 'it was not on my account that I expressed that opinion? Were I employed in a fish and chip shop I would still expect my employer to behave reasonably.'

'You think I was being unreasonable?' he shot back. 'Then look upon it like this—with no Bailey Construction there would be no art collection for you to "curate".'

She stood up and smoothed her skirt. 'Perhaps you could give me a call when you are in a less argumentative frame of mind, Mr Bailey? I don't see that we can achieve anything at the moment and—'

'Ah, but you're wrong there, Honor.' He lay back in his chair, formed a steeple of his hands and gazed at her meditatively. 'Has any man ever taken your clothes off item by item? Or slid his hands beneath your skirt and cradled your hips?'

She didn't reply for the simple reason that she was speechless.

'Have *you*,' he continued, after waiting politely for a moment, 'ever tried to tempt a man unbearably? Other than just by being your cool, immaculate self, which I have to say is a bit of a temptation on its own. The thought of you letting your hair down, speaking metaphorically, and allowing your tall, beautiful body to move freely and wantonly—'

'*Mr* Bailey—'

'Is quite mind-boggling,' he overrode her, and continued lazily, 'You know, I have the feeling that black lacy underwear would become you almost—unbearably well. So—' he paused and looked ironically into her blazing eyes '—that's what we could achieve, Miss Lingard— the resolution of some or all of those matters.'

Honor did the only thing possible other than making a fool of herself in an ungovernable show of anger—she turned on her heel and strode out, slamming the door and ignoring the startled look of Pam Myer, his secretary.

Honor's office in Bailey House—a tall building on the waterfront—overlooked the Brisbane river. Bailey Construction and associated companies occupied three floors and some of the Bailey art collection was housed in the reception areas as well as in Ryan Bailey's suite of offices.

For the first time Honor marched past the McCubbins, the Streetons—her personal favourite—a Tom Roberts and the Absaloms without a look. Nor did she spare a glance for the river in the late afternoon sunlight as she closed herself into her office and leant back against the door, her mouth set grimly, her dark eyes still smouldering while she dwelt on the greater and lesser insults that she'd just received.

Then she pushed herself away from the door and picked up her phone just as it rang. '*Yes*?' she said through her teeth.

'Honor, it's Pam. I—er—that is, Mr Bailey asked me to—'

'Pam, please do me a favour and tell him to go to hell,' she said tersely into the phone.

'Honor,' Pam replied reproachfully, 'I don't think I should do that; it just makes him all the more difficult.'

'Difficult! The man is unbelievable,' Honor said furiously.

'Well, I tend to disagree; he's been so very good to me, you see—'

Honor sighed and held the phone away from her ear for it was a well-known fact that Pam had worshipped Ryan Bailey since her elevation from the typing pool and since he'd apparently helped her extricate herself from a violent relationship.

She put the phone back to her ear and cut across Pam's rhetoric abruptly. 'All right, just tell me what he wants. Then I'll be able to tell you that I won't be doing it.'

'The thing is, we've had to arrange a last-minute reception for a government delegation from Papua New Guinea this evening; there's some possibility of a contract to build a bridge over there *and*…he would like you to be at the reception,' Pam said rapidly.

'I know nothing about building bridges and very little about Papua New Guinea,' Honor said. 'More-over—'

'He would like you to be there in your capacity as curator of his collection. The minister is apparently very keen on Australian art, particularly aboriginal art. He's also an avid collector of ancient Papuan artefacts. Honor—' Pam took a breath '—please?'

Why did I do that? Honor asked herself as she put the phone down. Why did I not just hand in my resignation and walk out of this building this very afternoon?

'Because I'd like to show Ryan Bailey a thing or two,' she answered herself through her teeth, then sat back with a sigh and considered things more realistically.

It *was* one of the more important private collections in the country and there was not only art but a quite significant stamp and medal collection; it was, compared to working at the National Gallery or a similar state-run institution, a magnificent opportunity to have a fairly free rein.

Which was not to say that Ryan had given her carte blanche or that he didn't have very decided opinions about what he should or should not acquire, but they had discovered that they had similar judgements, and he'd appeared to receive her ideas to build his collection into a major one favourably.

Until now, she thought irritably, and drummed her fingers on a catalogue. He's been away most of the time—how could I possibly work with a man who thinks like that? Well, she thought bitterly, don't all men think like that? So what should she do—hide away in a nunnery? No, for they don't all tell you what they're thinking; they don't, thankfully, all use that sordid kind of talk to reduce you to size. Unless—

She got up suddenly and walked over to the window. A few minutes later she turned back to her desk, picked up her bag and took herself to the powder-room, where, as she rinsed her hands and started to repair her makeup, she found herself studying her reflection a little narrowly.

She was tall—five feet eleven in her bare feet—and slender, which was undeniably an asset when it came to clothes. Her father had once commented that she was 'elegantly constructed' and should never regret that she wasn't conventionally pretty. Far better to have good bone-structure and an individual kind of face, he'd said.

Was it so individual? she wondered as she got out her lipstick but didn't start to apply it immediately. She certainly had a fairly square jaw and a finely chiselled nose and mouth, a faint dusting of freckles on a pale skin, dark hair that she wore short but beautifully cut and, normally, cool dark eyes.

The column of her neck was smooth and she had straight shoulders, narrow hands and feet, short nails, well-manicured but unpolished, and she only ever wore an unusual gold signet ring on the little finger of her left hand.

At twenty-eight she was usually assured and poised. It struck her now that she'd never considered the matter much but she'd certainly had an eclectic upbringing, especially with her mother dying when Honor was very young.

Her father had been a Supreme Court judge, a man of taste and discrimination; he was dead now too, but had undoubtedly been a favourable influence on her, as well as leaving her quite substantial private means.

She'd also travelled widely during and after her school days—as a scholar she'd been on a year's Rotary exchange programme to Japan and as a result spoke Japanese fluently. She'd studied for years on her chosen subject and was confident of her reputation in the art world.

But, she mused, has all this quite unwittingly led me to project a 'super if not to say overly cultured aura'?

'Well, no,' she murmured. 'The thing is, Honor, not to let the man get to you—that's all.'

'I suppose the most famous Australian impressionists are from what we call the Heidelberg School, Minister, although they weren't precisely impressionists and Heidelberg is a suburb of Melbourne where they gathered at times, not Heidelberg, Germany. But they certainly were the first concertedly nationalistic painters other than the Aborigines, whose work was ignored in those days, unfortunately.'

'Which is to say,' the minister, who was a huge black man with a particularly sweet smile, said, 'they didn't paint Australia to look like Europe.'

'Exactly.' Honor smiled back. 'Mr Bailey is lucky enough to have some fine examples of their work.'

'And I would say, Miss Lingard, that Mr Bailey is very lucky to have you,' he replied courteously. 'Would I be mistaken in thinking that I address Judge Lingard's daughter?'

'No, sir, you would not,' she said warmly. 'Did you know my father?'

'Quite well, as it happens. A fine man. Do let us continue our tour, Miss Lingard; I am most interested.'

Which was how it came about that the minister stayed at her side for nearly an hour, a fact that was viewed with considerable appreciation by some members of the staff.

'Thank God for you, Honor,' Bill Fortune said into her ear when she'd finally surrendered the minister back to his entourage, some of whom were deep in discussion with Ryan Bailey as the champagne flowed, the canapés circulated and the beautiful flower arrangements glowed softly beneath the discreet lighting. 'If we get *this* contract he might just forget about the three we lost while he was away.'

She accepted a glass of apple juice, viewed it with a touch of cynicism and said, 'I doubt it, Bill. I've got the feeling he's got a memory like an elephant. How do you put up with him?'

Bill cast her a curious look, opened his mouth, closed it, then said simply but with a strange undertone, 'He's the best in the business.'

'Oh, well, they say it takes all kinds,' she murmured. 'But I wouldn't bank on me swinging any kind of construction deal either, Bill.'

'He looked most impressed. With you and the art!'

'He knew my father, that's all, and he's genuinely interested in art.'

'Honor, sometimes the world turns on those little things,' he assured her.

Later that evening when she descended to the underground garage Honor found her racy little Ford Capri sitting at a drunken angle.

She swore beneath her breath as she inspected the flat tyre, opened the boot, and swore further to discover that her spare, which she had never given a second thought to, was also conspicuously limp in appearance. She slammed the boot as she decided she'd just have to take a taxi home.

It was in the moments later as she debated whether to go back upstairs to the office to ring for one or try her luck on the street that Ryan Bailey stepped out of the lift, swinging his car keys.

'A problem, Miss Lingard?' he drawled as he approached. 'Do tell me what I can do to help.'

She considered the fact that they'd circled each other during the evening with, on her part at least, deliberate, distant formality, and said wearily, 'I might have known it would be you.'

He smiled. 'The last person on earth you'd consider asking for help? How irritating,' he said gently.

She threw her keys into her bag and snapped it shut. 'Yes, it is. But I don't need help; I'll get a taxi and get someone to fix my car in the morning.'

'I could always change the tyre for you,' he suggested.

'No, you couldn't; the spare's flat too.'

He raised an amused eyebrow. 'Dear me, you are having a bad day, Miss Lingard. But there's no need to get a taxi; I'll give you a lift.'

'No, thank you, Mr Bailey,' she said coolly. 'You're also the last person I would accept a lift from. I don't know why but I have this aversion to being in close contact with men who take it upon themselves to discuss my underwear.' And she turned to stride away.

He only laughed quietly.

But once on the street she found that there was a dearth of taxis, and as she hesitated at a corner a blue Lamborghini slid into the kerb beside her and Ryan leant across to say drily, 'Get in, Honor. You're in far more danger of being mugged if you roam around here on your own for much longer than you are of anything you might encounter from me.'

She gritted her teeth, made the mistake of looking around and, observing a group of loitering youths, slid into the car with a frustrated sigh.

'Where would you like to go?'

'Home,' she said flatly. 'Or if you could find a taxi

rank, that would do fine; I wouldn't want to take you out of your way.'

'I've got a better idea,' he said briskly, and cast her a scathing look as she tensed visibly. 'I know a place that stays open late and would provide a decent meal—I don't know if you can live on canapés but I can't. It's a place where you would be quite safe and at the same time we could discuss why you're still working for me, how long you plan to continue working for me, and why you haven't even called me some unprintable names.'

'Look here—'

'No, you look here, Honor,' he said impatiently. 'Either we sort this out now or we come to a parting of the ways.'

'I...you...there would be nothing *to* sort out if you hadn't made those remarks,' she said angrily.

He shrugged. 'I was not, at the time, having a very good day myself. We're here,' he added briefly.

There were quite a few other late diners in the white-washed, low-ceilinged restaurant of his choice. There were comfortably padded banquettes with decent-sized tables that allowed them to sit opposite each other without being cramped but with some privacy. There were yellow tablecloths and napkins, and yellow candle-glasses which meant that the light was dim and flickering but warm—and there was the most marvellous aroma of food that made Honor realise she *was* hungry.

She chose a pepper steak and vegetables, a choice Ryan signified his approval of by ordering the same for himself. He also ordered a bottle of wine and didn't commence any conversation until it had been poured.

And then he only said, 'Well?' with a faint smile lurking in his remarkable grey eyes as he raised his glass in a silent toast.

Honor sipped her wine. 'Well what?' she said coolly, one black velvet-clad elbow on the table, her long-fingered hand curved around the stem of her glass as she just as coolly studied his unhandsome face, which was redeemed by those eyes and a curiously sensitive-looking mouth.

She observed his strong neck and front-row-forward shoulders beneath a beautifully tailored dark grey suit, worn with a pale grey shirt and maroon tie, and the thick, nearly black hair with strands of grey in it...

'Would you care to unburden yourself first or should I?' he said, with a quizzical little look.

She refused to be put out. 'I would have thought that's exactly what you did this afternoon.'

He grimaced. 'My apologies, then.'

'Accepted,' she murmured despite the jolt of surprise she felt.

His eyes narrowed. 'Is that all?'

'Yes.' She raised an eyebrow. 'What did you expect?'

He considered. 'Some sort of harangue, I guess, or—'

'I don't go about haranguing people, Mr Bailey.'

'You were—' he paused and studied her '—furious with me at the time, however.'

She allowed a faintly reminiscent smile to play on her lips. 'Yes, I was. But I sat down and had things out with myself and it turned out that your job still interests me so, provided of course there are no more incidents of that nature, that's how things stand.'

'And this evening in the garage?' he reminded her, with a wry little glint in his eyes.

'Ah, yes, I slipped up a bit there,' she conceded equally wryly. 'It could be that from time to time I may not be as…equitable as I'd like but the solution to that, Mr Bailey, is for us to limit ourselves strictly to business.'

'You're good, Honor, very good,' he drawled, and waited with an attentive look as her mouth hardened. Then she forced herself to relax before he went on, 'You've also got me a bridge to build in the wilds of Papua—how does that affect you?'

Her eyes widened. 'Surely—not?'

'Surely yes.'

'I mean all I did—'

'Was very little,' he agreed, and grinned as she grimaced. 'But it might just have swung the balance our way. My compliments,' he added.

She blinked and sipped her wine and he took advantage of her slight bewilderment to say, 'Why don't you confess that you're still fighting mad with me? I think I'd like you better for it.'

A faint tinge of colour crept into her cheeks but she narrowed her eyes and forcibly restrained herself from telling him that she couldn't give a damn *what* he liked. Instead she put her head on one side, considered, and finally said reflectively, 'Why should I?'

'It doesn't seem normal to be so contained,' he said drily.

'Your idea of normal and mine must differ, then— thank you,' she murmured as her steak was placed in front of her.

They ate for a while in silence, until he said, 'In this day and age women are extremely vocal and particularly about things like that.'

She cut a piece of steak—it was delicious—but toyed with it for a moment. 'My father,' she mused, 'taught me to be wary of any jargon, be it feminist, communist or whatever, if that's what you mean. He also taught me to be wary of generalising.

'So I suppose while you did make me very angry you didn't alter my perception that you are only one man. Nor—' she paused and looked at him coolly '—more importantly did I lose sight of the fact that I didn't want to discuss the matters you raised, even in anger. Much as that disappoints you,' she added pointedly.

'I see.' Ryan put his knife and fork together and pushed his plate away. 'Is that your way of telling me that you'd never wondered about me the way I had about you?'

'Look here,' she said crisply and pushed her plate away, unfinished. 'I—'

But he raised his hands and said wryly, 'I'm just trying to establish certain things. From the moment I first met you I thought you quite magnificent. I had not intended to tell you that the way I did but the truth of it remains. It seems to me that we'd be rather well-matched, Miss Lingard. However, I don't intend to press the point if you're so determined to be—unimpressed.'

'Well, I am,' she asserted shortly, and couldn't for the life of her have said why, in all her seething emotions, his last words should have aroused a sense of indignation in her.

'Fine.' He topped up her wine. 'Are you living with anyone?'

'No. Are you?'

He laughed. 'No. I didn't think it was likely, as a matter of interest.'

'Not likely that I would be living with someone?' She looked imperiously across at him.

'Yes.'

'Why?'

'You just don't have the aura,' he said meditatively, 'of someone who is engaged in a passionate relationship with a man.'

'Well, before I remind you that only moments ago you said you weren't going to press the point—'

'This is a slightly different point,' he drawled.

'I have to dispute that—'

'You're welcome to dispute all sorts of things, Honor,' he said wryly. 'I've got the feeling you spend a lot of your time—disputing points.'

'Will you let me finish?'

'By all means,' he murmured, and sat back with a look of polite interest in his eyes.

She said something highly uncomplimentary under her breath and looked at him exasperatedly. 'You've thrown me right off track, Mr Bailey.'

'You were about to take issue with my observation that you don't have the aura—'

'Ah, yes—two things,' she said. 'I don't particularly admire men who are such experts, or think they are, on those matters—'

'It's not a salacious kind of thing, Honor, if that's what you're trying to say.'

'Of course it is,' she countered with withering scorn.

'Do you really think so? I tend to think that it's what goes on between the sexes a lot; it's human nature, in other words, to wonder, to make certain judgements. Now, undoubtedly some people do have an unfortunate knack of—debasing human nature but, seeing as I'm *right*, I can't help feeling that I should be acquitted on that charge.'

'That's the worse piece of logic I've ever heard,' she declared.

'Ah, well.' He shrugged philosophically. 'What was your second point?'

'That I might just be the one to confound you, Mr Bailey.'

'But not right now?' he suggested.

'No, not right now,' she agreed coolly and calmly. 'But then again, what are we left with? If it's not because there's another man in my life that you aren't getting through to me, all it leaves is the plain fact that I'm just not *interested* in you.'

He laughed. 'One plain fact it certainly does confirm—that you're a worthy opponent, Honor. Anyway, now you've sorted all that out, I brought some paintings back with me. I think I'll keep them at home but they'll need to be catalogued et cetera. When would it suit you to come around?'

She drew a deep breath. 'Whenever it suits you, Mr Bailey,' she said frostily.

CHAPTER TWO

RYAN'S house was a yellow stucco Mediterranean-style mansion on the river, with a private jetty at which a large motor cruiser was tied up.

Because of all the valuables it contained there was a complicated alarm system and as Honor waited at the bottom of the driveway, before a set of remotely controlled gates, she happened to notice a brawny young man with red hair and a bushy red beard stop on the pavement to stare either at her car or herself.

It was a fine afternoon, she had the roof down and the Capri often attracted attention, so she shrugged, wondered if he had any idea that a Lamborghini lay on the other side of the gates and forgot about it when they opened smoothly and she drove through.

Ryan's middle-aged housekeeper opened the front door and led her into the library. 'He won't be long, Miss Lingard; he's on the phone,' she said. 'There they are—*more* pictures! I really don't know where he's going to put them. Excuse me if I run away but he's got guests coming shortly.'

'Not at all, Mary,' Honor murmured. 'I'll be fine.'

And indeed she was for the next twenty minutes as she examined the four paintings with interest—in the case of one even with reverence—at the same time as she registered the curiously irritating fact that if she'd been able to get her hands on them and had had the extremely considerable wherewithal she would have bought them herself.

'What do you think?' a voice said from behind her.

She swung round. Ryan was casually dressed today in khaki canvas trousers with a plain white shirt open at the throat. He looked big, brown and relaxed and they hadn't laid eyes on each other for four days.

Honor discovered that she wasn't feeling at all relaxed as his grey eyes roamed over her figure, clad in a straight, sleeveless burgundy silk dress patterned with tiny ivory dots, ivory stockings and flat burgundy suede shoes. A matching clutch bag completed the outfit.

'I'm impressed,' she said briskly to break the moment.

'So am I,' he murmured, and smiled lazily. 'But before you say, Now look here, Mr Bailey, let's get back to the paintings. I was rather lucky to stumble across this Sisley, don't you think?'

She gazed at the soft harmony of the landscape, the restricted yet delicate palette and sighed. 'How on earth did you happen to "stumble" across it?' she said wistfully.

'An English friend of mine discovered the roof of his ancestral home was leaking.'

'I wonder if he's still a friend?' she said tartly.

'Oh, I think I gave him a fair price for it. I just—' he narrowed his eyes '—don't quite know where to put it.'

'If it were mine,' she said without thinking, 'I'd have it in my bedroom. I think it would be rather lovely to wake up to.'

He raised an eyebrow. 'So you wouldn't be tempted to show off your Sisley?'

'No. Will you?'

He considered, then said gravely, 'No. I think I might

put it in *my* bedroom and think of you waking up, Honor.'

She opened her mouth, closed it, then said with what she hoped was a dry but light touch, 'Did I walk into that one? Forgive me, I didn't mean to. Um, if you've got all the paperwork I could go back to the office and start negotiating the insurance on them. This one—' she pointed to a small still life '—needs reframing. The others are in pretty good condition so far as I can tell but—'

'I'd rather you didn't go back to the office right now, Honor,' he broke in. 'I have other plans for you this afternoon.'

She stiffened and stared at him. 'What do you mean?'

'I'm taking a few guests down the river for a sunset cruise. I'd like you to come.'

'Why?'

'As my curator.'

'On a boat cruise? I think you're going round the bend, Mr Bailey, if I may say so. Don't tell me there's another bridge contract to be swung because I simply wouldn't believe you! So—'

'No, there's not, but Brad Oldfield is one of my guests.'

'So I...*Brad Oldfield!*' she said incredulously.

'Yes, you heard right,' he replied, with a faintly malicious smile twisting his lips. 'One of our foremost painters who is a renowned recluse but whom I was able to tempt out today. Will you come?'

She licked her lips and said feebly, 'I'm not dressed for boating...'

'It's not that kind of boating.'

It wasn't.

His boat, the *Sandra-Lee*, was a fifty-foot vessel with

two decks and a main salon that was the last word in luxury and comfort. There was a young man dressed in crisp white to handle her, and Mary was on board to dispense hospitality.

As they got under way Honor found herself placed on a comfortably cushioned circular bench on the back deck with a glass of apple juice in her hand and Brad Oldfield beside her. There were about sixteen other guests, and many of the women would have outdazzled a laser display with their jewellery. On the whole it was a friendly, lively gathering and they slipped down the winding Brisbane river as the sun started to sink.

The one problem was a lot of people's confusion over Honor's status, as she first discovered when Brad fixed her with a steely blue stare out of a deeply wrinkled, craggy old face and said, 'So you're his latest? Hope you know what you're doing.'

'Doing?' she said with a frown before it sank in. 'Oh! No—'

'Not an easy man to live with, as Sandra found to her cost, which is not to say that she should ever have married him—like mating a lamb to a tiger,' he said scornfully, then looked thoughtful. 'Funny he's never changed the name of the boat—she's my niece, y'know. Don't think she's ever got over him, more's the pity—'

'Mr Oldfield,' she broke in firmly. 'I'm his art curator, not—anything else.'

'What? Oh! Yes, he did tell me he'd hired someone to look after his collection. I thought it'd be a fuddy-duddy old man with round spectacles—either that or a swinging, long-haired, trendy chap.

'Well, now! I have to tell you I've never met a curator I could abide but I might just make an exception for you, so long as you don't blind me with all the gobbledegook that so-called arty people talk. I can't abide that either; I just paint what I paint and if people like it that's fine with me; if they don't that's their affair.'

'Mr Oldfield,' she said with a faint smile, 'I like your work very much but perhaps we should discuss the scenery or the weather?'

He laughed, a booming, deep laugh, and tucked his hand through her arm. 'With pleasure, m'dear. Mind you, I think Ryan's a lucky dog all the same,' he said to the gathering at large, thereby adding to the confusion.

It was quite dark as the *Sandra-Lee* commenced her return journey upstream from the mouth of the river, but as they cruised under the Gateway Bridge the lights of Brisbane began to prick the velvet darkness in ever-growing clusters.

They sailed past the New Farm wharves and Breakfast Creek with the party growing ever livelier, often with Brad Oldfield, who might have been a recluse but believed in making the best of his times out, apparently, as the focal point. He also had a decidedly naughty eye for lovely ladies but at one point declared that Honor was the loveliest of them all.

'It's just as well he doesn't get out too often,' Ryan remarked to Honor, observing the tinge of colour in her cheeks. 'You've obviously made a hit.'

'He's an old reprobate,' she said tartly, then relented. 'But you can't help liking him. I didn't realise you were related.'

'We're not—well, only distantly by marriage.' As he said it his grey eyes rested thoughtfully on her.

I know what you're wondering, she thought. Whether I have any interest in your marriage—well, no, I don't.

And to prove a point—to herself? a treacherous little voice asked—she turned away.

The party lasted for about an hour after they'd tied up at Ryan's jetty. Honor had just decided to leave as the first few people made moves to go, but found herself buttonholed by Brad, who suddenly decided to talk art. This he did indefatigably until she was the only one left, then quite abruptly he told her that he was going to bed.

'Ryan's putting me up for the night,' he confided with a wink, and, a little unsteadily, climbed off the boat and walked up the jetty towards the house.

Honor blinked then stepped into the salon to retrieve her bag, to find Ryan sitting alone with a sheet of paper covered with figures in front of him.

He looked up and put down his pen. 'Thought he was never going to let you go,' he said wryly.

'So did I.' She picked up her bag. 'Well, thank you—'

'Why don't you stay and have a nightcap with me, Honor? I'm sure that's what Brad was trying to engineer.'

Her bag slippd out of her fingers in sheer surprise and she cursed herself as she bent to retrieve it. 'Why would he want to do that?' she heard herself say curtly as she picked it up.

Ryan sat back and shrugged. 'He likes me despite what happened with Sandra.'

'I don't quite get your drift,' she said, now upright and clutching her bag in two hands.

He smiled. 'Didn't think you were obtuse, Honor, but in a man-to-man sort of way I suspect he's decided to help me along—with you.'

'What?' She stared back, her expression frowning and incredulous.

'Help my cause along sort of thing,' he explained helpfully.

'You…have you actually *told* him—?'

'I haven't said a word,' he denied.

'Then how come…? I'm speechless!'

'He must have divined it—sorry. My interest in you, I mean,' he said in a way that was a complete mockery of an apology.

'I thought we'd decided that that was not on,' she said as coolly as she was able to.

'*You* did.'

'No, you *agreed* not to press things!'

'I have yet to lay a finger on you, Honor,' he said with irony, 'even in the normal course of events.'

'There are different ways of pressing things,' she said bitterly. 'If this is what I'm going to come up against every time I'm in your company—well, it's not going to work.'

'Why don't you sit down instead of getting yourself all worked up, and tell me why? Or, even, let me tell *you* why. Champagne?' he offered. 'You've been on the apple juice all night, I noticed.'

'I loathe champagne,' she said coldly.

'Coffee, then? Mary left some.' He pointed to a flask on a sideboard. 'Do you consider yourself vastly superior to me, Honor?'

Again, surprise held her. 'No—what do you mean?'

'If you sit down I'll tell you.'

She looked around frustratedly then sank down on to a broad couch.

The salon of the *Sandra-Lee* was furnished in ivory and grey—ivory carpet, grey and ivory floral upholstery, mottled black marble lamps with jade-green shades, lined with pink so that they shed a soft glow, and grey-lined woodwork.

It was an elegant yet restful place and the couches were broad and soft. Honor found herself wondering if he often used the boat for serious cruising, and then wondered whom he took with him.

'There.' He placed a cup of coffee beside her and took his back to the table he'd been working at. 'Where were we? Ah—'

'Do I consider myself vastly superior to you, Mr Bailey?' she said drily. 'Why on earth should I?'

'You come from a long line of judges and professional men—I believe you even have a premier of Queensland in your family tree—whereas my father was a coal-miner.'

She blinked. 'I had no idea.'

'So you don't view me as a jumped-up, self-made man with cultural pretensions?'

'I don't—no!' she protested. 'Look here, you've accused me of this before!'

He smiled and linked his fingers. 'Then you didn't realise that tonight you looked a little like a thorough-bred among some nags?'

She had started to sip her coffee but she spluttered and put the cup back with a snap. 'How dare you? No such thing crossed my mind.'

'It must be unwitting, then,' he murmured, his well-cut mouth twisting wryly. 'But I distinctly saw you glance around at the display of jewellery with—distaste. I distinctly felt those women who were loaded with it cringe inwardly and long to be wearing only tiny pearls in their ears and a gold signet ring.'

'All right,' she said on a rising tone, 'I get the picture; you think I'm a raving snob—'

'You didn't—?'

'Yes, I did,' she conceded wearily, 'but it's a personal preference of mine, that's all. And it has nothing to do with how I feel about you!'

'I'm relieved,' he said, with a singularly sweet smile.

'Oh…' Honor retrieved her cup and drank her coffee disgustedly.

'I guess that leaves your physical preferences,' he said meditatively. 'In men, I mean.'

'Exactly!'

'Well, how *do* you like them?'

'I'm not going to discuss that with you,' she said carefully. 'At the risk of sounding like a raving snob, I find this whole thing distasteful and—' she tilted her head and eyed him coolly '—salacious,' she finished softly but dangerously.

'We could put that to the test,' he murmured, and stood up. 'You know, many women never *do* know how to judge a man. For example, whether I should or should not have the experience to know it, I know damn well that you are unawakened to a degree that might surprise you. Which is not to say completely inexperienced.'

For about the fourth time that night she got a shock, but this one sent a wave of colour up her throat, causing him to say mildly, 'So it's occurred to you too, Honor? Why, then, don't you test my hypothesis out—that you've chosen the wrong men up until now?'

'How—?' It came out as a husky, breathless sound and she cleared her throat and tried again. 'How can you possibly know…make a judgement like that when we barely know each other?' she was at least able to finish crisply.

He shrugged. 'Several things—your utter determination to have no truck with that kind of thing at the moment for one. I might tell you the others—one day.'

She got up abruptly to cover her confusion—confusion because, incredibly, there'd been a promise in his words that had acted strangely upon her. But what she'd planned to say died on her lips as things got worse.

They were standing about two feet apart and she was suddenly overwhelmed by his sheer masculinity, and curiosity, which made her wonder, What *would* it feel like to be in this man's arms? How would his hard strength feel against her? How would she feel if he ran his big hands down her body…?

And, to her horror, she felt a trickle of apprehension run down her spine, a dew of sweat break out on her brow—and a trickle of arousal run through her.

She swallowed and wondered wildly if he could see or guess the effect that he was having on her. But he made no move, only watched her gravely out of those worldly, sophisticated eyes.

Of course he does, damn him, she thought angrily, and said shortly, 'I'm going.'

'Yes. Goodnight, Honor. Just ask Mary to open the gates for you,' he replied quietly, but their gazes clashed until she jerked hers away—and went.

The next few days were distinctly uncomfortable for Honor. Not because she saw Ryan Bailey but because she was uncomfortable with herself, unable to settle to much and angry with herself for allowing *her* equilibrium to be disturbed by a man who was notorious for having that effect on every woman he met.

Is that why I dislike him? she wondered one evening when she was eating a solitary meal in her apartment on the other side of the river.

Her apartment was normally a source of pleasure. It was spacious and she'd furnished it with some of the remnants of the gracious home she'd grown up in— beautiful pieces which her father had acquired as a dedicated collector of antiques—and her own collection of art, which, while being nowhere near Ryan Bailey's in size or value, still afforded her much gratification.

She also enjoyed cooking, had a wide circle of friends and often gave dinner parties. She played extremely competitive tennis three times a week, gave quite a few hours of her time to a painting and drawing course for handicapped children, and had the skill and expertise— should she ever be out of a job in the art world—to make clothes for a living. As it was, she made most of her own.

Why, then, she mused, does my life feel a bit flat all of a sudden? I've got a challenging job which, if you take away the man, I love, and which allows me to travel around doing what I like best; I'm going to a heavenly Fijian island for my vacation...

She got up suddenly and rinsed her plate at the same time as she chastised herself.

'You *know* why,' she murmured. 'Ryan Bailey raised several questions that you can't seem to answer. Do you live in an ivory tower of culture that causes you to be superior, if not a downright snob? Are you lacking a man in your life to the extent that even a man such as he can...well, whatever?

'But, most unsettling of all, how the hell did *he* know that the two love affairs you've had have been disasters?'

She grimaced at her vehemence and turned the tap off. Of course he couldn't possibly know the details but he'd obviously sensed something—it was almost as if he'd put his finger right on the spot. She'd gone into both of those affairs because she'd believed she'd been in love but the expectations had never quite...what?

She sighed and turned away from the sink to consider the lowering hypothesis that she'd chosen the wrong man twice.

Which is not to say that *he* could ever be the right man for me, she reflected. I could never put up with him for one thing—that dominating, arrogant manner... Well, I just couldn't, she thought with a stiffening of her spine, but later that evening she was considerably annoyed to find herself wondering about Sandra Bailey, who'd never got over Ryan, according to her uncle.

Thus it came as quite a shock to meet her the very next day...

Honor was moving through the reception area of Bailey Construction when a fair, attractive, beautifully dressed and groomed but timid-looking woman came through the glass doors and approached the desk. The receptionist rose immediately and assumed her most deferential air.

'Good morning, Mrs Bailey. How are you? Mr Bailey asked me to show you right in—oh, excuse me, Miss Lingard, Mr Bailey also would like to see you at ten o'clock.'

Honor paused. 'What about?' she said rather tartly, whereupon Sandra Bailey turned to her and said diffidently,

'You must be Honor Lingard. My uncle, Brad Oldfield, told me he'd met you. How do you do?'

'I'm very well, thank you,' Honor said after a moment, having collected herself. 'And I very much enjoyed meeting your uncle, Mrs Bailey.'

'He's such a character, isn't he? Well, I guess I shouldn't keep Ryan waiting,' she said with a grimace. 'Goodbye.'

'Goodbye,' Honor murmured, and stared after her, thinking about lambs and tigers...

At ten o'clock she was in Ryan Bailey's outer office talking to Pam when the door to the inner sanctum opened and he ushered his ex-wife out, saying, 'Let me know, won't you?'

'Yes,' Sandra replied, and smiled up at him with her heart in her eyes.

'Come in, Miss Lingard—I believe you and Sandra have met?'

'What is it now?' Honor said particularly ungraciously as he closed the door. She wore a short-sleeved watermelon-coloured linen suit with cream alligator-skin shoes and she not only looked impatient, she felt it. And curiously unsettled.

'Perhaps you'd better tell me what *I've* done now. Sit down,' he said.

She sat and said irritably, 'Nothing. But I'm waiting.'

He raised a wry eyebrow and surveyed her quizzically. 'Is it Sandra?'

'What do you mean, "Is it Sandra?" She's got nothing whatsoever to do with me, but, just as a matter of interest, why is she still in love with you?'

'She's not—'

'Oh, come now. She looked as if she was, her uncle reckons she is—'

'Honor,' he overrode her, 'are you really asking for a detailed explanation of my marriage and my ex-wife? And, if so, why?'

Their gazes clashed, his smoky grey and highly amused, hers dark and stormy. 'Just tell me what you wanted to see me about—other than to parade me before your ex-wife,' she said angrily.

'Now why would I want to do that?'

'Because at times I'm sure you can be quite machiavellian,' she said bitterly.

He grimaced and folded his arms. 'At times I'm sure you're right. This was not one of them, however. Nor would there be any sense in parading you before my ex-wife—that I can see anyway, but perhaps you could enlighten me?'

That brought her up short and she watched him narrowly through her lashes with her mouth set for a long moment before she shrugged and managed to say more coolly, 'So?'

'I've had a request for sponsorship from a young painter—well, I presume he's young; we haven't met. I got a canvas in the mail plus a quite extraordinary letter suggesting that if I were to hang just one of his paintings I would soon be inundated with offers to buy it and that he would graciously concede to split the profit fifty-fifty with me.

'That's one thing I wanted to see you about; the other is that a television station has approached me about doing a programme on the collection.' She raised an eyebrow. 'You approve?' he murmured.

'Why not? It can only add status to your collection. Don't you approve?'

He looked thoughtful. 'On the whole, yes, although I generally shun publicity. But I'd like it to be done properly, which is to say that I'd like *you* to liaise with them and make sure it comes out right—not just as an exercise which proclaims that money can buy you great art whether you can tell the difference between Van Gogh and Constable or not.'

'You mean you'd like me to ensure that it's done tastefully and that, above all, you come out as a man of culture and discrimination?' she suggested gently.

'Yes.' He eyed her narrowly.

'I'm really surprised, Mr Bailey—you don't think I might *over*do it?' she asked with widened eyes.

'No,' he said drily.

She started to feel much better, she discovered. 'Well, then, what about the canvas you received this morning? Is it any good?'

'You can be the judge,' he murmured, and walked across the room to sweep aside a curtain behind which, against the wall, stood a large, roughly blocked canvas of a female in full frontal, unclothed splendour as she knelt in a riotous garden. 'I know it's not Sandra's taste and poor Pam got the surprise of her life when she unpacked it so I thought it might be better...veiled for the time being. Other than to your professional eye.'

She gritted her teeth and strolled forward. 'Now *that* might be perfect for your bedroom, Mr Bailey,' she said, and added before he could speak, 'It has some merit, I think. There's certainly a vitality about it but unless you wish to alienate half your staff I wouldn't hang it here.'

'Are you speaking as a connoisseur of art, Honor, or a woman?'

'I'm speaking as a woman, Mr Bailey, who only the other day read in a newspaper about a mural that depicted certain parts of the female anatomy and was on exhibition in the foyer of a building. It did just that—annoyed a lot of the women who worked on the premises.'

'Yes, I read that too,' he said amusedly. 'So you feel

I ought to recommend that this young man should approach a gallery where art is art whatever the subject?'

'Not at all—I leave that up to you. There's no reason why you *shouldn't* have it in your house or on your boat if it appeals to you,' she said sweetly. 'What's his name?'

'Mark Markham.'

'Never heard of him.'

'Neither have I.' Ryan allowed the curtain to drop. 'That'll be all, then, Honor. Pam has the details of the television programme.'

'Great,' she said brightly, although a close observer would have seen that her eyes were actually bright with anger. 'I'll get to work on it immediately.'

She had nearly a month, she discovered, to prepare for the television programme, but it was the profile that the station had requested on Ryan Bailey which gave her the most trouble.

Her request for one from him was ignored. At the same time as the station themselves asked her what she knew about his background they said that he had resolutely shunned publicity throughout his meteoric rise to riches so their information was sketchy.

'I know his father was a coalminer but that's all,' she said tartly, then bit her lip. 'But that's off the record—well, until I can lay my hands on him and find out just what he wants to have known about him.'

'Miss Lingard, we'd very much like to feature you in this programme as well,' the voice down the line said. 'How do you feel about that? We do know quite a bit about you and you would have an excellent image on television, we feel.'

She grimaced. 'Look, I'll check that out as well—no,

this time I will really get back to you with something concrete,' she vowed.

'Pam, where is Mr Bailey?'

'Honor, he's so busy at the moment that he just hasn't got time for anything else. I promise you I've passed all your memos on to him but—'

'Look, I *need* him, Pam! I can't—'

'Well, well,' a voice drawled behind them, 'that's a change of heart, Miss Lingard.'

Her nostrils flared as she breathed deeply and turned to confront Ryan with her mouth set. 'Where have you been?' she said imperiously. 'Why did you tell me to organise this thing on your collection and then carry on as if you were invisible? If this is how you run Bailey Construction I'm *amazed* it didn't crash years ago!'

Pam gasped and looked at her with hurt incredulity, causing Ryan's lips to twist with wry amusement. He said, 'It's all right, Pam. Honor is a very plain-speaking person, as well as a very arty one, and has different priorities, I guess. Uh—when am I due to be at my next appointment?'

'In about three quarters of an hour, Mr Bailey, but it's on the Gold Coast so you're running late—your car is already here.'

'Then ring ahead and tell them I'm ever so slightly delayed, Pam, and if you do need me so badly, Honor—' he turned to her blandly '—you'll have to take a little trip down to the coast.'

'But that's ridiculous,' she objected. 'I don't want to go all that way, and how will I get back?'

'Warren will bring you back; I'm staying down there overnight. And that's my last offer,' he said with a sweet smile.

She shot him a blazing look, then said tightly, 'Oh, very well!'

Warren turned out to be the young man who'd handled the *Sandra-Lee* and who doubled as gardener and chauffeur, apparently. The car was a vintage Rolls-Royce with a vast back seat complete with cocktail cabinet.

'There,' Ryan said, settling himself in one corner, 'that's not so bad, is it?'

Honor sat in the opposite corner as far from him as she could get and smoothed her skirt. Then she took a notepad and pen from her bag and said sardonically, 'I'm suitably impressed, Mr Bailey. A Lamborghini and now this, and all for one man.'

'Well, I tend to regard this as a symbol of Bailey Construction,' he said pleasantly. 'It's much more comfortable for transporting overseas clients et cetera around—incidentally, if you weren't with me it would also be very comfortable for snatching a nap on the run—and yes, it does make a favourable impression. Whereas the Lamborghini I regard as a form of pleasure.'

'I see. Would you like me to quote you?' she queried. 'And I do apologise for coming between you and your naps.'

He grinned and murmured, 'That too, Honor.'

She set her lips in a tight line and tried to keep an equally tight rein on her temper, until he said, 'Aren't you going to speak to me again?'

'I'm working on it,' she retorted.

'Then let me help you. Should we address ourselves to the subject of those increasingly impassioned memos you've been sending me?'

Look, Honor, she told herself, just don't take the bait,

will you? 'If they're increasingly impassioned it's because *I'm* receiving increasingly impassioned requests from the TV channel to help them get this show on the road,' she said with outward calm.

'What do they want?'

'Some background on you.'

'I don't see that that's necessary.'

'You may not but they do assure me that a half-hour programme needs a bit on the man as well as his collection. They also want to know…well, they've asked me to be in it,' she said coolly. 'I told them I'd check it out with you first.'

'Why not?'

She watched the road for a bit as the South East Freeway gave way to the Pacific Highway. 'OK,' she said at length, then added, 'Look, could we not just put together a limited curriculum vitae? At least then, by the sound of it, you'd get your version across, not what they might dig up or be tempted to manufacture out of sheer frustration.'

'All right,' he said lazily. 'But tell me first how you've shaped the rest of it.'

'I can't shape it completely,' she said sensibly. 'It's their programme after all.'

'But I'm sure you've made some suggestions.'

'Well, what I'd like to do is to let it be known what a comprehensive collection it is, so I've made a list of the really interesting paintings and why they are so—particularly early ones, for example, with an Australian or a historical as well as an artistic impact—unusual ones—ones with an anecdote to do with their painting or the painter or how you acquired them.' She pulled a sheet from her bag and handed it to him.

'Good thinking,' he said after studying it.

'Then I thought we could do a few of the really well-known ones, and finish off with the coins and medals or, you know, they might like to dictate the order of things, but I think that would be a well-rounded view of your collection.'

'Interspersed with bits of you and me doing a commentary?'

'Yes, but I'd be quite happy to stay out of it if you prefer.'

'Well, I think we should provide an interesting contrast in styles—you for the tone, me for the money,' he said idly.

'I thought you didn't want it to go that way,' she objected.

'I certainly wouldn't like to appear a fool—no, Honor, I was having you on—but only a bit,' he mused. 'Because I do see your expertise as adding considerable tone to my collection. In fact I regard you as nearly as good an investment as my Sisley.'

'I'm not sure if that's a compliment—'

'Oh, it is.'

Once again she stared out of the window as the big car ate up the miles in almost silent, air-conditioned comfort. 'Talking of your Sisley...' she said eventually.

'No.'

She flicked him a quizzical glance from beneath her lashes. 'All right. What about your life story, then?'

'Are you thinking along the lines of...Ryan Bailey who started out life as a coalminer's son—that kind of thing?'

She grimaced. 'I've already given them that bit,' she said honestly. 'I'm afraid to say it slipped out in the heat of the moment.'

'Did it, now?' He looked at her with nothing but wry

amusement in his eyes. 'Never mind; it's not something I'm ashamed of nor is it any secret. So use it if you like.'

'Well, what else?' she queried when he said no more.

'I'll get Pam to type something up for you—'

'Now look here, I've been down this road before,' she said irately. 'And, talking of roads, why am I taking a long, boring trip to the Gold Coast for...for nothing?'

'Not that long; we're nearly there. Boring? I've found it quite enjoyable so—'

'But you don't have to turn around and go straight back again!' she said between her teeth. 'Mr Bailey—' She stopped and then said, 'What I will do is scrape up the bare outline, which will mostly be to do with the success of Bailey Construction, I suspect, and if they don't like it they can lump it and if you don't like it you can fire me or go to hell—or do both!'

'That'll suit me fine, Honor.'

'Why didn't you just tell me in the first place?'

'It's always a pleasure to see you getting annoyed, Honor. You're extremely attractive when you do, you know— Ah, we've arrived,' he murmured as they pulled up in the forecourt of the Sheraton Mirage. 'You know, I really would like to buy you dinner to compensate for this long, boring trip you've had but unfortunately—'

'Forget it, buddy,' she said briefly, and turned her face resolutely to the window. But after a moment she swung back and said, 'And just don't plan any more of these futile jaunts while you're about it.'

'I'm suitably deflated, Honor. I'll try to be a good little—employer when I get back.'

'I wouldn't try too hard. For you I'd say it would be like trying to turn back the Red Sea.'

* * *

Nor was Honor's opinion of him much swayed when Pam revealed how benevolent he was to a variety of charities.

'So what? Why shouldn't he be?'

Pam looked reproachful. Together they were trying to work out a simple history of Bailey Construction. 'I thought you could...slip it in,' she suggested. 'I know he likes to be very private but it's just a pity more people don't know what kind of man he really is.'

'Pam—' Honor looked at her exasperatedly and sighed on seeing such heartfelt devotion in the other girl's eyes '—I couldn't do it without his approval and I doubt if he'd give it,' she said instead of what she'd been about to say.

'I don't suppose he would—oh, well, it was just a thought. Are you...are you getting on with him any better now, Honor?'

She considered how best to reply, instead of again saying what sprang to her lips. 'Provided we stick to business we're fine,' she said austerely.

'I'm sure he will,' Pam replied.

And the fact that he did, when their paths crossed over the next couple of weeks, certainly vindicated Pam, but Honor was both amazed and horrified to find that it annoyed her even more...

CHAPTER THREE

'CAN I buy you a drink?'

'Thank you, Mr Bailey, but—'

'Oh, come on, Honor,' Ryan said roughly as the television crew packed up their cameras and prepared to depart. 'We've played cat-and-mouse games with each other for weeks; just do it.'

And he took her arm and steered her towards his office, to the no doubt secret delight, she thought bitterly, of all the Bailey Construction employees who had gathered to watch the making of the programme on their boss's private art collection.

'Sit down,' he added warningly as he opened a cocktail cabinet once they were in his office.

So she sat in the same beige leather Barcelona chair as she had before, but with her mouth set mutinously as he opened a bottle of French champagne then set it down irritably. 'What the hell *do* you like to drink, Miss Lingard, other than apple juice?'

'I don't suppose you'd have Campari and soda?'

'I don't suppose I have; I might have known—yes, I do,' he said flatly, and added, 'You'll have to forgo the lemon, however.'

She said nothing as he handed her a tall glass but their eyes clashed, causing him to grimace wryly, then he sat down opposite her in a second Barcelona chair.

'I can't work out,' he said, 'what annoys you more—

to be treated like an employee or not to be treated like an employee. Cheers!' And he raised his glass in an ironic little salute.

'Well, I think you just annoy me period. Cheers!' she replied.

'I've mentioned this before—but why then do you continue to work for me, Honor?' he drawled.

'And I told you once before, when I add up the pros and cons the pros of the job win out.' She set her glass down. 'I even got some publicity out of it today.'

He watched her in silence for a moment then said, 'You were good, too.'

'So were you,' she said matter-of-factly.

'Don't you think, then,' he mused, 'that we could put this mutual admiration act to some better use?'

'Such as?'

'Such as just trying to relax in each other's company for a change.'

She tossed her head and said baldly, 'No.'

'What are you afraid of, Honor? Yourself?' he said quietly.

'Oh, look, that's got to be such an old, hoary one!' she objected.

'It's often the old ones that are true.'

She thought for a bit and wondered if he could see through her defiance to the uncertainty that lay beneath it. It was an uncertainty that had grown over the last weeks while she'd so deliberately tried to keep her distance from him, and she had been particularly annoyed to find that what had helped it to grow had been the way he'd also kept his distance since their trip to the coast— reduced their relations to a cool, employer-employee basis.

I don't *like* the man, she'd told herself often enough.

Who does he think he is, anyway, to proposition me one day then treat me like anyone else who works for him the next?

But of course the irrationality of this hadn't failed to impinge on her consciousness. Nor had the fact that while she might not like him she couldn't help being increasingly aware of him. And in a rather physical sense, she'd told herself tartly once, then wondered if she should be surprised. Obviously most of his female staff suffered from the same thing. Put plainly, Ryan Bailey was a dangerously attractive man once you got to know him, you had to admit.

And that's just it in a nutshell, she thought, with a little shiver that wasn't all disgust; he's dangerous for a start. He can demolish you with a few well-chosen words, he's damnably clever and high-handed, he's strong and big and rather splendidly made…and you just can't help wondering what it would be like to have him make love to you, she thought helplessly. But what about the other women in his life—his *wife*, the rumours of mistresses…?

She lifted her lashes suddenly and found him studying her thoughtfully and comprehensively—the way her dark hair lay on her forehead, that faint sprinkling of freckles on her skin, her mouth and nose, the V-neck of her black crêpe belted jacket, patterned with tiny white flowers and worn with a short, straight black skirt, her ankles…

She licked her lips and started to say something—anything that would break the moment and her own sudden, leaping awareness of her body, which, beneath her clothes, was clad, ironically, in black lace underwear—when the phone rang.

'Ah,' he said lazily, 'that's probably the call I'm expecting from Port Moresby to do with the Papuan bridge—this could take a while but finish your drink by all means, Honor, before you go.'

She didn't say it but the message in her eyes couldn't have been clearer: You bastard! And she simply got up and left his office without a backward glance.

Honor raged inwardly for quite a few days and, when she discovered herself playing wild, uncontrolled tennis, took herself to task—or tried to. But, try as she might, she couldn't persuade herself to leave Ryan Bailey's employ; all she could succeed in doing was regaining most of her composure. Fortunately they had hardly anything to do with each other.

Then a strange thing happened on a Saturday afternoon. She opened her door to find the brawny, red-haired and bearded young man whom she'd seen on the pavement outside Ryan's house weeks ago standing there.

'Miss Lingard?' he said deferentially.

'Yes…?'

'Miss Lingard, I'm Mark Markham; how do you do?'

Her eyes widened. 'You don't mean—'

'Yes. I painted the nude in the garden. Did you see it?'

'I…yes, as a matter of fact, but—'

'What did you think of it, Miss Lingard?'

'Well, I thought it had some merit,' she said slowly.

'Miss Lingard, could I ask an incredible favour of you? I've rigged up a sort of exhibition of my paintings—in an old boat-shed,' he said ruefully but quite charmingly. 'I've asked a few friends round tomorrow morning and I've bought a few bottles of wine. Would you come and have a look at them? Please?'

'Well, I... Mr Markham, how do you know who I am? And how did you get my address?'

'I saw you on television,' he said simply. 'And I looked you up in the phone book.'

'Ah.' She grimaced, but more because of the recollection of the acute discomfort she'd suffered while viewing herself and Ryan together on television. 'Did he send the nude back?'

'He did.' Mark grinned boyishly. 'But I'm nothing if not an optimist. And if you don't like nudes,' he said anxiously, 'there are all sorts of other subjects.'

She considered it then smiled. 'OK. Give me your address. But I must warn you that I can make no promises on Mr Bailey's behalf or anything like that.'

He produced a handwritten card and thanked her profusely. It was only when she'd closed the door that she thought to wonder what he'd been doing outside the Bailey house that day, but after a moment shrugged and forgot about it.

It was a very warm day the next day—the kind of warm, humid day that Brisbanites tended to associate with storms in the late afternoon—and Honor chose a pair of loose grey pyjama-style trousers with a long, sleeveless silk jersey button-through top in the palest apricot, rope-soled white canvas espadrilles and a jaunty raffia hat she'd made herself which had apricot and white flowers round the crown.

She also put her tennis racquet in the car, plus a small bag with tennis clothes and shoes and a change of underwear. Despite the growing heat she thought she would visit her club afterwards and reassure them that one of their star players had not run amok. She hadn't been game to go back since hitting balls over walls and serving four double faults in a row.

She set out to find Mark Markham's boathouse with more of a sense of well-being than she'd experienced for some time. It was quite a drive, being across the river and on the shores of Doughboy Creek which ran off the Brisbane river towards its mouth. But she finally found it sandwiched between a seedy-looking caravan park and a boat-building yard.

He came out to greet her, directed her to some undercover parking in a carport, then helped her to alight most politely and suggested that she put the roof up.

'Well, I'm not going to be that long,' Honor temporised.

'Ah, but around here you never can tell, and I should bring that bag in with you—and your tennis racquet,' he said solemnly. 'Just in case.'

She shrugged, looked around, then did just that.

Inside his boat-shed, which had a gallery around the concrete slipway upon which rested a small ancient cabin cruiser, his paintings were displayed in all their colourful glory on the rough wooden walls and there was a table with a white sheet over it, glasses and a carafe of wine. Honor couldn't help feeling charmed by the set-up as well as by the youthful ingenuousness of Mark Markham—she thought he was about twenty-three at the most.

It was only after she'd drunk half a glass of cheap red wine and commented upon several paintings—the best of which, she told him, in her opinion, were his boats and seascapes—that it occurred to her that she was the only guest. But when she pointed this out he said that others would be coming, rest assured.

It was about two minutes later that she began to feel most strange and swayed where she stood. She turned to him accusingly, her eyes dilating fearfully, but she was unable to speak and he caught her as she would have fallen and said earnestly just before she passed out, 'I'm *terribly* sorry, Miss Lingard, and please don't worry, but sometimes you have to do these things in the cause of your art.'

Honor awoke slowly and got the distinct impression that she was at sea, and a rough sea at that. What hit her moments later and made her close her eyes because she *had* to be hallucinating was the fact that she seemed to be at sea on the *Sandra-Lee*.

But when she opened her eyes again there was no doubting that she was lying on a grey and ivory floral couch and there was a mottled black marble lamp with a green shade on the table beside her head...

She sat up abruptly and held her head as it swam alarmingly. Then she tensed convulsively as a familiar voice said, 'Take it easy, Honor.'

'You!' she gasped, her eyes coming to rest on Ryan Bailey who was sitting on the floor, propped against a column, his long legs, in the khaki canvas trousers she remembered, stretched out in front of him, his feet bare, his dark hair unusually tousled, his yellow shirt streaked with dirt.

'How dare you do this to me?' she hissed, swinging her own legs down but deciding against standing up as the boat tilted alarmingly.

'I haven't done anything to you,' he replied a shade grimly. 'I am in fact handcuffed to this post behind me.'

Honor's eyes nearly fell out of her head as she registered the fact that he seemed not to be able to show her his hands, which were indeed around the post behind him. 'Are you crazy?' was her next reaction. 'Who's driving this wretched boat, then?' She tried to stand up but it tilted the other way. 'Now *look here*—'

He grinned fleetingly. 'I wondered when we'd get to that— Honor, do you seriously believe I would handcuff *myself* to a post? Why? So that we could indulge in some seriously kinky sex?'

She blushed vividly, which made her even angrier. 'Then why did you allow yourself to be handcuffed to a post? What is going on?'

'We've been kidnapped.'

'Kidnapped?' she said blankly.

'Kidnapped,' he agreed with irony.

'Why? Who by—do you mean Mark Markham?'

'None other. How did you get here?' he asked politely.

'I wish this boat would keep still,' Honor said intensely.

'We're riding through quite a storm.'

'Where?' she asked, going pale.

'Moreton Bay.'

'You're joking!'

'I'm not. But he seems to be handling her fairly well. How did he get you here, Honor?'

She swallowed and told him. 'He must have drugged the wine and loaded me, unconscious, on to that old boat of his and brought me here. No *wonder* he wanted me to lock the car up and bring my things out of it…' Words failed her as she looked around and her eyes fell on her bag and racquet.

'I wondered why you came equipped for tennis,' he said.

'I *didn't*. I mean—I was going to play tennis afterwards. Of all the conniving… I knew I should have asked him what he was doing loitering outside your house!' she exclaimed, and told him about that too.

Ryan smiled grimly. 'I think it would be fair to say that the young man has done a pretty thorough job of casing the joint—and us.'

'Well—how did you get here?' she said helplessly.

'I decided to take some time off. I brought the boat into the bay to do some fishing and two nights ago I was peacefully anchored off St Helena and asleep, when he slipped aboard, knocked me out and tied me up—a state I've been in one way or another ever since.'

Her eyes widened as she registered the dark bruise on his temple for the first time. 'So he's violent as well as insane!'

'Not terribly,' Ryan murmured. 'He apologised profusely. Said he was only doing it in the cause of his art—'

'That's what he said to me!' Her eyes darkened as she remembered. 'So...why exactly has he kidnapped you?'

'He doesn't call it that. He talks of it as being the only way he could get through to me. He would like me to pay him one hundred thousand dollars for all his paintings, whereupon he will release me absolutely unscathed.

'He appears to be quite sure he can talk me into this—I haven't pointed out to him that once he does release me he will immediately be arrested and charged with kidnapping—something that doesn't seem to have occurred to him.'

'Well, for heaven's sake don't!' she implored. 'But why am I here?'

He settled himself more comfortably—or tried to—and said wryly, 'That could be my fault.'

'What do you mean?'

'Well, I told him I never bought paintings without consulting my curator.'

She stared at him. 'Of all the—*lies*, if nothing else! Did you go so far as to tell him my name?'

'No, and I carefully avoided mentioning that you were a woman. What I forgot to take into account was that—'

'Television programme! How dumb can you be?' she said scathingly. 'Oh, I don't believe this!'

'Then you'd better start to, Honor,' he said mockingly. 'And, at the same time, would you mind applying your mind to getting these bloody things off me? What we need is a pair of bolt-cutters or a hacksaw and you'll find them—'

'A hacksaw?' she said faintly as the boat rolled drunkenly and a flash of lightning illuminated the salon. 'I could cut your arm off in these conditions! Why not just pay him? You have so much money! Where is he, anyway?' She looked around wildly.

'He's driving from the fly bridge,' he said grimly. 'I have never succumbed to blackmail in my life and I don't intend to start now. Pull yourself together, Honor,' he added cuttingly.

She glared at him and finally stood up. What she saw out of the salon windows nearly caused her to slump back again—a grey, storm-tossed sea, heavy rain and Mark Markham's battered little cabin cruiser wallowing along behind the *Sandra-Lee* on a long rope.

She suddenly turned to Ryan. 'A radio—you must have radios on board—I'll call for help! Just tell me how to do it.' She started towards the downstairs drive station, forward on the left-hand side of the salon, with its big stainless-steel wheel and bank of instruments.

'He's rendered them all inoperative.'

Honor took a deep, angry breath. 'And I thought he was quite charming,' she said. 'I—'

'He's as mad as a coot,' he said witheringly.

'But you said—'

'Yes, but who's to say what he *can* do? How much stability do you *expect* from a man who lured you into a trap, drugged you and brought you here, Honor?' She chewed her lip. 'The other thing is that while he seems to be pretty experienced boat-wise these are not normal conditions and I—'

'You're right,' she said abruptly. 'Tell me where to find these things.'

He explained to her how to get into the engine-room and where to find a toolbox, all of which turned out to be a terrifying experience because the engine-room—a cauldron of noise and heat—was in the bowels of the *Sandra-Lee*, which was rolling so much now that Honor had to get about on her hands and knees and was only just able to get upstairs to a bathroom before she was horribly seasick.

'This is terrible,' she muttered when, pale and clammy from the experience and not at all sure she wouldn't be sick again, she made it back to Ryan's side. But at least there was plenty of fresh air coming from the salon door, open on to the back deck, and she took some great gulps of it before she went on, 'No hacksaw and the bolt-cutters are too big but—' he swore '—I got this.' And she produced a file.

'Good girl,' he said briefly. 'Get to work.'

So she filed away awkwardly, kneeling on the floor behind him for about five minutes until he said urgently, 'He's coming down; don't let him see—'

In a panic, she hid the file by sitting on it, then could think of no explanation as to why she should be sitting on the floor right next to Ryan if it weren't to free him somehow—and did the only thing she *could* think of. Which was to wrap her arms around him and lay her head on his shoulder lovingly.

'Well, well!' Mark Markham stood in the open doorway, having come down the outside ladder from the fly bridge, his legs wide apart and braced, his red hair and beard wet, wild and woolly, his blue eyes bright and demented. 'Just came to see how you were getting on— wondered if you two weren't more than art collector and curator!

'Hey, sorry about the weather, but as you can see I'm handling things well although I'm not a hundred per cent sure where we are, but I'll get you there, never fear!' And he disappeared back up the ladder.

Honor groaned. 'Get us where?'

'God knows,' Ryan said, and added wryly, 'Nice as this is, Honor, the sooner you get me free the better.'

She leapt back from him as if burnt, glared at him, and started to file again. And she had just managed to file right through the link with a cry of triumph when there was a sickening bang, she hit her head on the column and everything went dark.

How much later she didn't know, but eventually she stirred and opened her eyes. 'Where am I?' she whispered, and wet her lips. It was dark outside and there was only one dim light on inside. 'Where—?'

'It's OK, Honor,' Ryan said quietly. 'You're all right; you hit your head, that's all.'

'All... All!' She tried to sit up as everything started to come back to her, but the world seemed to be at an odd angle and she seemed to be in his arms on his lap on the floor. 'What's *happened*?' she said fearfully.

'Lie back,' he murmured. 'You could be dizzy for a

while. What's happened?' he went on as she complied
dazedly. 'Our crazy friend has run the boat aground—
don't worry,' he said as she felt the *Sandra-Lee* lift
rhythmically then sink back, and realised that the motors
were silent although the wind and rain were still hell-
ishly audible. 'He's also left us to our fate but we're not
in any immediate danger.'

'Why did he leave us?'

'I don't know if the impact shocked him back to some
sanity or further madness but he took to his own boat
and sailed off.'

'So we're...stuck on a beach or something?' she said.
'Do you mean an island?'

'Yep. I did a bit of a reconnaissance while you were
out like a light; I was afraid it might one of the sand-
banks with which Moreton Bay is littered, but it's a
beach and we're safe for the time being,' he said quietly.

'Do you know which island?'

'No.'

Honor tensed.

'Look,' he said, 'once this storm abates I might be
able to recognise where we are; I know the bay quite
well, but in any case we'll be spotted as soon as the
weather clears, and in the meantime we have plenty of
food and water. But we are going to list right over so it
might be an idea to try to make a camp ashore. She could
also be holed; I haven't had a chance to check that.'

'Your poor boat,' she said, with sudden tears rolling
down her cheeks.

'Yes, I know, but she is insured.'

'Will anyone worry about you in the meantime?'

He took a moment to reply. 'Not unless any crisis
rears its head at work—'

She sat up excitedly and this time he didn't resist her.

'But how would they get in touch with you anyway? I mean to say the radio must be a two-way kind of thing?'

'It was,' he said a shade grimly. 'I had several radios as well as a sea-phone and a mobile phone—Markham took care of them all, including the EPIRB and flares, which I suspect he nicked and took with him.'

'What's an EPIRB?'

'A radio beacon that, when activated, beams up to any aircraft or satellites in the area and gives your position—but it's missing.'

She sank back and he put his arms around her again. 'So he's liable to be rescued but we're not. Did you see his eyes?' she whispered, with a shiver. 'How could I have been so taken in?'

'He's probably fairly normal a lot of the time.'

'I even liked some of his paintings, particulary his seascapes.'

'More than his nudes?'

She chuckled and rubbed her cheek on his shoulder. 'Much more.' Then, realising what she'd done, she sat up awkwardly. 'So what do we do now? Oh, I've had a brilliant idea! Don't you have a dinghy?'

'I did.'

'Don't tell me he stole that too!'

'He used it to get back to his boat; the rope broke.'

'So he's out there in this—serves him jolly well right if he drowns,' she said severely.

'Mmm… How are you feeling?'

'All right,' she said, and explored her head cautiously. 'What about you?'

'I've got a lump as well.'

'Did you get knocked out again?' she asked, wide-eyed.

'Not quite but I was rendered groggy enough for

Markham to get a head start on me when he decided to abandon ship in my dinghy with my EPIRB,' he said bitterly.

Despite herself Honor smiled at him almost affectionately.

'What's that supposed to mean?' he asked with a lifted eyebrow.

'I don't know—it makes you seem more human somehow.'

'Thank you,' he said gravely, then swore as the wind rose to a crescendo and the *Sandra-Lee* slewed sideways with a horrible grating noise. 'Honor, I think we will have to get off but first of all I'm going to have another look. Do you think you could, in the meantime, gather together some essentials to take ashore with us?'

She opened her mouth to protest but he outstared her calmly until finally she said quietly, 'All right.'

The news he came back with was not good.

He'd discovered a hole in the hull on the port bow, the tide was rising and might just refloat the *Sandra-Lee* and the wind was strengthening from the opposite direction and could blow her away from the beach.

If that happened and she started to take water she could sink, he told Honor. He also told her that he'd tried to secure the anchor to prevent just that happening but didn't have a lot of faith in it holding.

'So we're going to take as much food and water off as we can, Honor—we've only got a couple of hours— and anything else we can get off. I've found a fairly protected spot to camp at a little way up the beach.'

'When is it likely to abate?' she asked fearfully.

'No idea. I've got the feeling there's a whole line of freak storms passing through.'

'And I had the feeling there was stormy weather due this morning,' she said ruefully.

'You and me alike—they've probably been broadcasting strong-wind warnings et cetera for days.'

She tensed. 'There is a cyclone coming down the coast; I heard it on the radio. It's east of Gladstone but I didn't give it much thought—they don't usually come down this far, do they?'

He swore, then said, 'No, but they can whip things up a bit. OK, I'm going to rig up a pulley system so that you can pass things down to me; it's bloody hard work getting on and off the boat at the moment. Let's get going.'

It was an exhausting night—in fact Honor was crying with weariness and fear when he at last helped her down over the side in the wet, stormy darkness. The tide had turned, so it was now ebbing in the same direction as the wind, but was still high enough for the *Sandra-Lee* to be afloat and straining at her anchor chain. Honor found that she could only stand up right if she clung to Ryan.

Then, all of a sudden, a huge gust bowled them both over and with a grinding roar the boat parted from her chain and started to float away into the darkness...

CHAPTER FOUR

'This is unbelievable!' Honor heard herself say although she seemed to be asleep, then she woke up some more and groaned as she moved because her head hurt and every muscle in her body was aching.

'What's wrong?'

'I feel as if I've been through a wringer,' she said, lifting her eyelids, which seemed to have heavy weights on them.

'Well, it wasn't far off that. Hi,' Ryan said as her dark eyes focused. 'And before you say, Now look here, Mr Bailey, you wouldn't have slept nearly so well any other way.'

Close up as he was, she noticed for the first time that his smoky grey eyes had darker little flecks in them. Close on the heels of this discovery came another one— that she was cradled in his arms, that they were stretched out on padded deckchair cushions beneath an overhang of rock and that there was rain drumming down on the canvas awning which he'd erected somehow from the lip of the rock to the beach, and that there was murky daylight coming in from the open end of the canvas.

Now don't be missish, she warned herself. On the other hand—her lips curved into a faint, rueful smile— don't get to like it too much either.

'And what's *that* supposed to mean?' he asked.

'Nothing,' she murmured, and pulled free to sit up,

'other than that these are exceptional circumstances, Mr Bailey. I feel dreadful; I'm quite sure I look dreadful,' she added conversationally, 'and by the sound of it the storm or storms have not abated much.'

'No—' he sat up himself '—I don't think they have. As to feeling dreadful, a cup of coffee and an aspirin might help but you don't look that dreadful at all.'

Honor ran her hands through her hair and looked down at her pale apricot silk jersey top and pyjama-style trousers. They were both streaked with a variety of marks and were torn in places. 'Did you say coffee? How clever of you to insist on bringing a Primus.'

He grinned. 'I'll be able to set us up much more comfortably today, Miss Lingard.'

She raised an eyebrow. 'What's the time?'

'Eleven o'clock. We slept in.'

'At least the wind's not howling quite as badly. Have you looked out yet?'

'I'm about to do so right now.'

In the event they looked out together and the dark, nightmarish beach of her recollection was much less frightening, not that she could see terribly far because of the rain. But there was a low cliff behind them that ran down to a point of sand, and there was a vista of churning sea in front. There was no sign of the *Sandra-Lee*.

She said nothing as she watched him scan the hazy, leaping horizon and saw his mouth tighten. But when he spoke all he said was, 'I suggest we use that direction for ablutions; the overhang will keep you dry and there are plenty of bushes. I'll go first just to check it out.'

By the time Honor came back he had the small Primus stove going and a pot of water boiling on it, and in a few minutes he handed her a mug of instant coffee and an aspirin.

'What a way to start the day,' she said, but gratefully. 'Do you think she's—sunk?'

'Probably.' He put his mug down and started to open a can of baked beans. 'But, depending on where we are, she may be visible. Parts of the bay are quite shallow. She may even be sticking out.'

'And other parts?' she said quietly.

'Twenty metres or more. Honor—' he stopped what he was doing and looked at her levelly '—provided we're careful with the water, and there's plenty of fresh water coming down from above, we have enough food to last us for days.

'They'll also be looking for us as soon as conditions permit—when I don't get in touch with them to let them know I'm OK in this kind of weather they're bound to. So we're just going to have to sit it out, make the best of it—and not panic.'

'Who says I'm panicking?' She tilted her chin at him and her eyes were cool.

He studied her for a long moment then smiled briefly. 'That's my girl. Do you like to cook?'

'Yes.'

'Then I'll leave that side of it up to you from now on and I'll concentrate on keeping us safe and dry.'

'Yes, sir, skipper.'

'Honor—'

'No, Mr Bailey—Ryan—' she shrugged '—that's just my way of letting you know I'm on side.'

And she deliberately kept herself occupied for the next few hours, trying to make their refuge habitable. 'I nearly rebelled last night,' she told him once, 'when you insisted that we cart all this stuff off the boat, but I see your wisdom now.'

For as well as foodstuffs and water he'd unearthed several waterproof groundsheets which they'd wrapped and tied around pillows and cushions, and some of his clothes and towels. Now she spread them over the sand to make a floor.

She'd also neatly lined up the two portable ice-chests which the food was in, the picnic hamper, the first-aid kit he'd thrown in and a plastic box with an assortment of odds and ends, including a compass, a chart of Moreton Bay and a pack of cards. They had two drums of water, and all the bowls they'd been able to lay their hands on were outside catching rain.

She'd brought her tennis bag as well and had been delighted to think that she had a change of clothes as well as a small make-up kit and her brush.

But by three o'clock in the afternoon she ran out of energy abruptly and looked around the small, dry space, listened to the wind and the rain dripping down the canvas awning, glanced up at the overhang of rock, and dropped her face into her hands.

'Lie down, Honor,' Ryan said quietly. 'There's no more you can do at the moment.'

'You must be exhausted, even more so than me,' she said huskily. 'You did far more last night.'

'I'm not a slip of a girl,' he said wryly, and unrolled a deckchair cushion for her.

She hesitated then curled up on it. 'I'm not exactly a slip of a girl either.'

'You know what I mean.' He sat down and leant back against the rock wall.

'I suppose so. And you seem to be extraordinarily good at this kind of thing. How come?'

He glanced at her but she was watching the canvas awning opposite him. 'Well, my father was a miner, as I told you—a coalminer from Ipswich—but he also enjoyed fossicking for sapphires and semiprecious stones out in the back of beyond.

'We used to camp out in school holidays with him. We had an old utility we used to load up with our gear, a couple of ancient tents, billies and so on.' He grimaced.

'Ever find anything?'

'Nothing much. We thought it was good fun as kids, though.'

'You've come a long way, haven't you?' she said drowsily.

'Yes.' His grey eyes rested on the weary, unconscious grace of her figure, curled up on the cushion, then he looked away deliberately. 'Did I ever tell you how I got interested in art?'

'No...'

'I was wondering what to buy my mother for Christmas when I was about fifteen. Didn't have much to spend so I was looking around a second-hand shop with a china figurine in mind—she used to like them— when I came across this little picture, an original oil of a soft, hazy landscape in a battered old frame, but I couldn't afford it.

'So I bought her a china cat but I couldn't get the picture out of my mind; it seemed to open a new world...of vision for me, probably because the coalfields of Ipswich are not the prettiest places on earth. I kept going back to look at it, holding my breath in case it had been sold—and one day it had. I swore then that I'd own some great art one day.'

'That's...lovely,' Honor said.

He laughed quietly and glanced at her again, to see her lashes close as she fell asleep.

Three hours later she sat up and stretched. It was dark outside, still raining, but a gas lamp illuminated their refuge. She turned to see Ryan tending the Primus stove. 'Oh, that's my job,' she said concernedly. 'Sorry.'

'Don't be. It's only tinned stew. We're a bit limited with this stove. Hungry?'

'Well, yes,' she said in some surprise, and went on, 'It's a miracle you had all this gear on board really.'

'I keep—kept,' he corrected himself, 'it on board for beach barbecues, talking of which, I'm only cursing myself that I didn't bring the barbecue itself; it would have given us much more scope.'

'In this rain?' she said wryly.

'It was a gas barbecue. It was also as heavy as hell. Would you like a drink before we eat? I threw in a bottle of brandy but we'll have to have it with water.'

'I'd love one.' She smiled. 'But I feel an absolute wreck.'

'You could always go out and have a shower in the rain. I suppose the one consolation,' he said as her eyes flew to his, 'is that it's not cold.'

'Yes. Well—' she accepted a plastic beaker from him '—seeing as I've only got one change of clothes, I might do that tomorrow.'

'I brought a couple of spare shirts.'

She said the first thing that came to mind. 'Who was the painter?'

He looked at her with a raised eyebrow.

'I mean—' she took a sip of brandy and water '—the one who inspired your interest in art.'

'Oh, that.' He put the lid on the pot of stew, turned

the stove off and resumed what seemed to be his favourite position, leaning back against the rock wall with his knees drawn up. 'Brad Oldfield. It was an early one of his, long before he achieved the fame and fortune he has today. Funnily enough, I've never been able to find it.'

'So...' She gazed at him, wide-eyed. 'Oh, it's such a small world! But you must have had good judgement even then.'

He grimaced. 'A lot of people with no judgement at all like Brad's work.'

'What did you think when you came to meet him?'

'It's a small world.' He grinned.

'How long were you married to her?' she heard herself say, and flushed faintly. 'Sorry—I don't know why I asked that,' she added awkwardly, not looking at him but examining the contents of her beaker critically.

'Perhaps it followed on naturally?' he suggested. 'Seven years.'

She looked up and forgot to feel awkward. 'Seven years! Don't tell me it was the seven-year itch? Surely you must have had some idea sooner that you weren't going to make it?'

'Yes. In fact I had an idea quite a lot sooner,' he said drily. 'But unless you really want to know...' He shrugged indifferently.

'I suppose I am curious,' she said after a long pause, but added, 'And there's not much else to do.'

He regarded her enigmatically, his lips twisting, then shrugged. 'We were young—I was twenty-five and she was eighteen when we met. I had just started Bailey Construction but it had been a long, hard slog. Even staying at school after fifteen had been a battle; my father by that time was unemployed and my mother's health was deteriorating.

'Sandra...' he paused '...came along at a time in my life when I desperately needed—I don't quite know how to put it—some comfort, I guess. I was tired of fencing with girls, I was tired of being poor, I was tired of—'

'Hang on—what do you mean, "fencing with girls"?'

'Well, there were the bright, trendy ones, the ones who slept with you because it was the done thing; there were the ones who slept with you and clung like limpets and started to talk babies...

'Sandra was different. You could almost say that she was a very well-brought-up, old-fashioned girl. She didn't seem to want to sleep with me, she was refined, she was restful.

'I didn't realise until it was too late,' he said deliberately, 'that sex frightened her and probably always would, that I could dominate her—and did in a way that made me hate myself sometimes, that there would be times when I wanted to rant and rave to her to try to force her out from behind that serene, sedate, refined façde which, ironically, had so intrigued me to begin with. Only it was no façde, it was just all there was to her.

'She couldn't comprehend the breadth of my ideas or vision; she was terrified when I took risks and expanded the business; I remember the day I bought the *Sandra-Lee*. I was thrilled and exhilarated but she was shocked and worried and, as it turned out, petrified of boats...

'Well, when I say there was nothing more to her I still sometimes hope to God that's not true.'

'What do you mean?' Honor said with a frown.

He looked past her. 'That I was simply the wrong man for her. That I secretly and not so secretly sometimes terrified her into that bland passivity because I'm not and probably never will be—' He stopped and shrugged.

'Anything but forceful, arrogant, brimming with life and raw energy,' she said drily. 'I hope she didn't frustrate you into terrifying her physically.'

He shot her an ironic glance. 'No. I may have many faults but a woman-basher I'm not. There are other ways of being diabolical, however.'

'I'm sure,' she murmured. 'Did she never fight back?'

'Not really. So I spent seven years of my life trying to subjugate all sorts of emotions and feeling like a heel when I couldn't. She spent seven years of her life trying desperately to keep up with me, trying to bear my children but failing in that too.'

'Then it was probably the kindest thing you could have done—to divorce her. Surely she must see that by now? It's—how many years on?'

'Eight. There are times when I think she does and times when—I wonder.'

'Why have you kept in touch?' she asked curiously.

He grimaced and sighed. 'Guilt, I suppose. She's a shareholder too. I mean, I wanted to make sure she would never want for anything.'

'Has she not fallen in love at all in that time? She's only—what, thirty-three?'

'She's had a couple of totally inappropriate affairs,' he said dispassionately.

'What about you?'

'Do you mean have I had some inappropriate affairs?' he asked with a smile twisting his lips.

'There are rumours of mistresses,' she stated baldly.

'You shouldn't believe all you hear, Honor. Nine tenths of it is pure speculation. There has only been one serious woman in my life since Sandra; she would have

died rather than be known as my mistress and after a
few years together we parted amicably, and she's since
got married.'

'I thought men—' Honor stopped.

'No, most men don't take easily to living like
monks—is that what you were going to say?' he queried.

'Well, yes.'

'Nor have I, but on the occasions I've succumbed it's
been with…laughter and a mutual sense of need. It has
never been a procession of women simply because I can
afford them or because I'm insatiable. Does that set your
mind at rest?' he enquired, with a mocking little glint in
his grey eyes.

She stared at him. 'It's when you say things like that
that I'm reminded I don't really like you,' she said
coolly after a moment.

'Oh, well, that's got to be an improvement,' he
drawled. 'I mean if you can forget it most of the time…'

'I didn't say that either…' She stopped as a curious
tearing noise made itself heard above the rain, then there
was a roar and a crash, the canvas awning bulged in-
wards and she flew to her feet as Ryan did the same.
'What?' she whispered fearfully.

He took her hand and felt her trembling and put an
arm around her. 'I think it's the tree from above the
overhang. The rain must have washed away the soil
around it. Don't worry, we're quite safe.'

'But what if we get…blocked in? What if there's an
avalanche sort of thing?'

'There's not the height above us, not enough earth and
rocks to do that, Honor,' he said steadily. 'Just one in-
convenient tree. Which I will go and deal with, or at
least do what I can, while you finish your drink.' And
he kissed her lightly but directly on the mouth and put

her away from him before he disappeared into the wet darkness.

Honor stared after him for a long moment.

'Can't do a lot tonight,' he said, coming back half an hour later, soaked to the skin, covered with mud, with his hair plastered to his head and water dripping off his eyelashes. 'But I climbed up the overhang to test it out— gingerly—' he smiled wryly '—and I think everything that could come down has.'

She regarded him equally wryly. 'And I think you'd better take that shower you mentioned earlier while I dish up dinner.'

'Will do.' He reached for a towel and dry clothes then looked at her. 'Uh…'

'Just give me a call when you're ready to get dressed and I'll turn my back,' she said serenely.

'Yes, ma'am,' he replied meekly, and left their refuge once more before she could take issue. But Honor was congratulating herself on handling things in an adult, no-nonsense manner which reflected the way she'd taken herself to task a bit earlier after the slightly stunning sensation of his kiss.

'I shouldn't have slept this afternoon,' she said a bit tensely, however, after they'd eaten and she'd tidied up, made coffee and was sitting wondering what on earth she could do.

Ryan was lying on the cushion, looking quite relaxed and staring at the rock ceiling with his hands behind his head. 'Why don't you tell me a bit about yourself?' he suggested.

'If you're suggesting I trade intimate secrets with you,' she said tartly, 'in exchange for those you—'

'Not at all,' he said gravely. 'Not that there was anything particularly intimate in what I told you.'

'I don't entirely agree but what do you suggest?'

'What got you started in art?'

She thought for a bit. 'It was always there,' she said a bit helplessly after a time. 'My earliest recollection of pleasure is of looking at a little painting I used to have in my bedroom, of a candle on a table in a silver, genie's lamp kind of candlestick. You know, the gravy-boat kind.'

'Did you ever try to paint yourself?'

'Yes, of course, but very ordinarily. Strangely enough, my creative talents are quite domestic. I love designing and making clothes, and cooking.'

She saw him raise an eyebrow. 'They never look home-made, your clothes.'

'Some of them aren't.'

'That burgundy silk dress with the spots on it?' he queried.

'It was—' She stopped abruptly and wondered why she felt hot.

'You're very good, Miss Lingard.' They were silent for about ten minutes until he said, '*Have* you ever contemplated marriage?'

She sighed. It could have been because she was marooned on an island somewhere in Moreton Bay in the midst of awful weather with a possibility of it getting worse but she suddenly decided to be honest. 'Yes. I can't imagine it working for me, though.'

He turned his head to look at her. 'Why?'

'I think I'm much too independent for one thing; I don't seem to have any maternal cravings and I'm— quite happy the way I am.'

'Have you ever lived with anyone?'

She cast him a speaking look but he was studying the rock ceiling again so she said coolly, 'No. But, as you so rightly assumed, I'm not inexperienced and I am able to make the judgement that I would be rather hard to live with.'

'That could change.'

She leant her head back. 'If the right man came along? Perhaps.' She shrugged. 'In the meantime I'll stay the way I am.'

'And what do *you* do when you're dying for a man, Honor?'

She laughed, but more to hide the inward jolt of anger and shock than because she was amused. 'It hasn't happened to me to the extent that I've had to do anything.'

'Tell me to what extent it has happened to you, then.'

'I—' She stopped. 'There are times,' she then said slowly and honestly, 'when I wonder what I'm missing but there are also times when I look around at my friends—not all of them but quite a large proportion— and wonder if I'm missing much at all. So many people do seem to marry,' she said with a faint frown, 'and so often regret it.'

'What are you like when you're in love, or don't you think you've ever been in love?'

'Perhaps you ought to ask the two men I thought I was in love with,' she said ironically, and added, 'Where is this leading?'

'Nowhere tonight. Forgive me, but I suddenly feel absolutely knackered. When you're ready for bed just roll out the other cushion,' he said courteously.

She clenched her fists. 'Would you like the light out?'

'No, it won't bother me.'

'Good,' she said. 'I thought I might play patience; it could even be helpful.'

He chuckled. 'What are you mad about now, Honor?'

'The way you start these things and then just dismiss me!'

But all he said sleepily was, 'I'll try to mend my ways.'

So she played patience for about an hour, then visited the bushes, creeping along under the lip of rock to avoid getting drenched and watching out for spiders—and God knew what else, she thought exasperatedly.

When she got back Ryan hadn't stirred; she stood for a long moment staring down at him, and found herself thinking, of all things, about true companionship with a man who was also your lover and how it was the one thing she hadn't been able to achieve, had wondered if it was possible to achieve.

Not with him, she mused. I've got the feeling that the habit of command comes just a little bit too easily, and whereas Sandra might have taken refuge in bland passivity I would fight like a she-devil…what am I thinking?

And she shook herself impatiently, rolled out the cushion, switched the gas lamp off and tried to compose herself for sleep.

It didn't come for several reasons. Last night they'd managed to sleep together on both cushions although it had still been different from sleeping on a well-sprung mattress. Last night, though, she hadn't been cold—not that she was freezing or anything now but it had cooled down after the drenched humidity of the day. Last night she'd been totally exhausted; she wasn't now.

So she tossed and turned for a couple of hours until he said out of the darkness, 'Honor, this isn't working.'

'Oh, sorry, did I wake you?' But she was entirely unrepentant. Instead she was filled with a rather burning sense of injustice that centred on one small fact—if he hadn't told Mark Markham the lie he had she wouldn't have been here, contending with all sorts of privations, not to mention the sheer frustration of Ryan Bailey himself. She wouldn't have been wearing the same clothes she'd worn for two days; she wouldn't have been anything other than her normal, cool, poised self.

'Yes, you did. What's wrong?'

'Nothing!' she marvelled. 'I quite enjoy being gritty with sand, having to be smothered in insect repellent so I don't get eaten alive; I love sleeping on what feels like a park bench, listening to what could be a full-blown cyclone heading this way and wondering if Markham is lurking out there somewhere if he's not at the bottom of the ocean—no, nothing, Mr Bailey.

'And there's something else,' she said quite irrationally, and sat up. 'You're probably occupying the headlines right now—I can just see it—MILLIONAIRE MISSING!' she said dramatically. 'What a field-day they'll have when the missing millionaire turns up with a woman—MILLIONAIRE FOUND WITH MYSTERY WOMAN IN TOW!'

'Then we'll just have to enlighten them as to who you are and how you came to be "in tow", won't we?' he said reasonably.

She snorted. 'I can just imagine everyone believing it,' she said contemptuously.

'Believe me, they will.'

But the thought of that annoyed her even more and she made another disgusted sound.

'Honor,' he said gravely, 'I'm about to do something to relieve your state of mind. Just don't take it the wrong way.' And he got up, switched on the torch and held down his hand to her.

'What do you mean?' she asked warily.

'I'm going to make us more comfortable, that's all. Get up like a good girl, will you?'

She stared at him mutinously, then got to her feet without his assistance. She watched while he put her cushion on top of his then selected a large, dry towel.

'We did it last night, we can do it tonight. Lie down. I have absolutely no intentions towards you other than getting you to relax so that you can go to sleep—and I can get some sleep,' he added wryly.

'Are you—proposing to—?' She stopped.

'Yes, do exactly what I did last night.'

She blushed bright red. 'That was different; I was distraught and overtired—'

'You're not exactly a model of serenity at the moment,' he said with irony and a glint of impatience. 'Come.'

He took her hand, switched off the torch, sat down and pulled her down beside him, covering her with the towel. 'You don't have to look at me; face the other way if you like—and I will do this.'

Which was to lie down, turn her to face the rock wall and align her against him with her back to him, his arm laid over her waist and the long, reassuring length of him behind her.

He also said, 'Why don't you count paintings or something like that? Think of all the ones you'd like to add to the collection—by the way, I've decided to add a bit of variety to it. Some sculptures and some—' she heard a tinge of humour come into his voice '—Papuan artefacts are about to come my way, I believe, but only on loan for exhibition purposes. Know anything about them?'

'No,' she said slowly but with a quickening of inter-

est, and they talked desultorily about them for a few
minutes until he fell silent and she realised that he'd
fallen asleep.

I feel…ridiculous, she thought. Not because I'm uncomfortable but because I *am* ridiculous. Because I
haven't known whether I'm on my head or my heels for
weeks, because I don't seem to bear much resemblance
to the Honor Lingard of old who was so much in control,
because I'm possessed of the urge to fight this man most
of the time and yet I can lie in his arms and feel safe.
How strange…

In the event she finally fell deeply and dreamlessly
asleep and awoke to find herself alone. She lay for a
moment or two, wondering what was different about this
day, then realised that it had stopped raining and there
was even sunshine—admittedly weak but, nevertheless,
it was sunshine—coming through the open end of the
awning. She leapt up excitedly.

He was swimming, she saw, off the beach. There was
only a tiny break in the low cloud cover but it was
enough to give her a feeling of exuberance and hope
and, without thinking twice, she pulled off her top and
trousers, ran down the beach in her bra and briefs, waded
in, then dived beneath the water joyously.

'What a relief!' she called out to him. 'That rain was
beginning to drive me mad!'

She swam strenuously for about half an hour, up and
down, parallel to the beach, and emerged glowing.

He was waiting for her with a towel, wearing only a
pair of shorts. 'Thanks,' she gasped, and wrapped it
round her. 'That was wonderful.' She ran her hands
through her hair.

'Here's what you do now,' he said. 'Wipe yourself

down with this cloth rinsed in fresh water and it will take most of the salt off.'

'You're an absolute godsend in these kinds of circumstances, Mr Bailey,' she said with a grin. 'I don't know what I'd do without you. Sorry,' she added lightly, 'that I was such a bore last night.'

'You weren't.'

'Well, for that,' she said impulsively, 'I'll cook you a bumper breakfast.

He left her alone to change into her fresh underwear and white tennis skirt and top. That done, she cooked ham steaks with tinned pineapple and fried eggs—the only two eggs that hadn't been broken in transit from the *Sandra-Lee.*

'How's that?' she asked as she handed him a plate.

'Great. Thank you.'

'What have you been doing?'

'Digging a large SOS into the sand which I thought we might fill with stones to make it stand out more.'

'We should fly some flags, make a bonfire, although I suppose everything is too wet as yet.'

'Yes, but the flags are a good idea.'

She stopped eating. 'Have you any idea where we are?'

He grimaced. 'Sorry to say—no. Visibility is still poor and I seem to be curiously disorientated even with the help of the compass. But after breakfast we can explore the island, which might give me a better idea. At least it's flying weather now.'

'Do you think it will last?' she asked anxiously.

He smiled slightly. 'Let's just cross our fingers.'

They laboured after breakfast to fill in the SOS and erect flags with bits of clothing tied to them. Then Ryan left her on the beach, where, he said, she would be more visible, while he climbed over the ridge to the other side of the island.

While he was away she saw two light aircraft in the distance and she ran up and down the beach waving a red towel, as they'd agreed upon, but the planes came no closer. And as the morning wore on it grew hotter and more humid and huge, boiling clouds hid the sun but brought no relief.

He came back after a couple of hours. 'Well, I know where we are. It's entirely uninhabited—one of the very few in Moreton Bay,' he said with irony. 'And it's going to rain again.'

'Did you see those planes?'

'Yep. Don't worry, there'll be others.'

There was one about an hour later as the rain held off and the heat grew—a rescue helicopter, complete with news crew aboard. As they watched it land Ryan took Honor's hand and said, 'Well, that's the end of this chapter of our lives. Now we can get on to the next.'

'What do you mean?' she said uncertainly.

'Dear Honor—' his lips twisted as he studied her '—I've been extremely circumspect on this benighted island because I didn't feel it was fair to you to be any other way. But back in civilisation I won't need to be, will I?'

She wrenched her hand free and surveyed him angrily. 'I might have known!'

He raised an amused eyebrow. 'That I could be a thorough gentleman?'

'That you never give up,' she retorted.

'Now I wonder why I expected you to thank me for the care I've taken of you since we got kidnapped, Miss Lingard,' he murmured, and turned to the approaching news crew.

CHAPTER FIVE

THE next morning Honor read the newspaper with several sensations, one of them a sense of disbelief concerning the past few days. Another sensation caused a little glint of anger to light her eyes as she read all about Ryan Bailey in an article below a grainy photo of the two of them on the beach which was clear enough to show that they were holding hands. It read:

Self-made millionaire Ryan Bailey was rescued yesterday together with his art curator Honor Lingard after being allegedly kidnapped and stranded on...

It went on to say that charges had been laid, that the *Sandra-Lee* had disappeared, then gave a résumé of Ryan's life and achievements.

She laid the paper down and, to distract herself, wondered about Mark Markham. So far he hadn't been located but her car had been discovered all intact beneath his carport.

As she reflected the phone rang. But after a few minutes of extraordinary conversation she banged it down then snatched it up, all set to do battle as it rang again. '*Yes.*'

'How are you, Honor?' Ryan said down the line.

'I'm furious,' she replied. 'I've just had an offer from

a magazine to buy my exclusive story—my story about being marooned on a deserted island with the state's most eligible millionaire,' she said with heavy sarcasm. 'I told you this would happen!'

He chuckled. 'It'll all die down in a couple of days, but why don't you come and stay with me in the meantime?'

'You must be mad!'

'It would be very peaceful here; I'm ex-directory for starters and I've got a security guard to keep the Press at bay.'

'But why would I...? I mean...I'm speechless,' she said shortly.

'Now that's something I've never actually known you to be, despite your threatening me with it a couple of times. How about having dinner with me tonight, then?'

'Ryan—' She stopped and sighed. 'Look, you gave me a week off work; let's just leave it at that.'

'Honor,' he said, and she recognised the different note in his voice—the one that was not to be trifled with. 'Either you let me give you dinner or I come round and have it with you.'

'I...I'll go away,' she said breathlessly.

'Fine. I'll do it when you come back.'

'Oh!' she groaned. 'Why am I even having this ridiculous conversation with you?'

'Because you're an extremely stubborn woman,' he said drily. 'But then I too can be stubborn. I'll send a car for you at seven.'

That day she had plenty of visitors—friends who were all absolutely intrigued by her adventures as well as a detective, who came, he said, just to go over the statement she'd made. What perturbed her, however, was the concern he expressed, once they'd done this, at her living alone for the time being.

'What do you mean?' she said sharply. 'Do you think Mark Markham's...what?'

'Well, I don't want to alarm you unnecessarily,' he said mildly, 'but we know a bit more about him now. He has a history of mental instability. And, according to one psychiatrist who treated him, he is subject to very irrational impulses.'

'I can vouch for that,' she said slowly, 'but, assuming he didn't drown in Moreton Bay, surely he would stay as far away as possible from me—from both of us now?'

'Well, according to the same medico, he's incredibly tenacious when it comes to his—er—grand schemes. So, while he might not be mad enough to try to tangle directly with Mr Bailey again, he could see *you* as a means of getting to him.'

'Have you spoken to Mr Bailey about this?' she asked after a moment.

'Yes, ma'am. I've just passed on the psychiatrist's report. Because it had occurred to us...' The detective paused then said delicately, 'Seeing as Mark Markham thinks that you and Mr Bailey are...close—' he looked down at the statement in his hand '—although you *assured* us you only pretended to be to conceal the fact that you were trying to free Mr Bailey at the time, it occurred to us all the same that *you* might appear to be a better bet to kidnap this time—on your own.'

'Oh, look!' Honor got up and paced around for a moment, as much to conceal her agitation as the faint tinge of colour that had come to her cheeks.

'I know it's probably a very long shot,' the detective then said consolingly. 'But, you see, we are dealing with someone who is a diagnosed schizophrenic, if not worse.'

He gestured meaningfully. 'And, while we hope to lay our hands on him in the shortest possible time, the storms we've had have put an enormous strain on us; there's an awful lot of damage round Brisbane and the bay and not only that but it makes any unusual occurrences look more normal and, well, it would be a help, Miss Lingard, if... Are there any friends or family you could stay with for a couple of weeks?'

'A couple of weeks!'

'That should do it,' he said with no trace of humour.

'I...I'll think about it,' she said.

He rose and smiled at her. 'Thank you, ma'am. Do let us know where you are. And in the meantime lock your doors.'

She took an age to get ready. She finally chose a chalk-blue silk georgette dress, A-line with a scooped neck and short sleeves, in a print of shadowy, creamy camellias. It came to mid-thigh, was cool and comfortable, and she wore low-heeled grey suede shoes. Thankfully the storms had passed; the cyclone off Gladstone had headed out into the Pacific and the weather over Brisbane was peaceful, if hot.

At seven o'clock precisely her doorbell rang but she got a sudden attack of nerves and didn't release the chain when she opened it. However, it was Warren and she was grateful to find that he'd come in an unremarkable Holden car—just in case the Press were still hounding her, he said. He drove her to the mansion on the river.

'Is this where we're having dinner?' she said exasperatedly as they turned into the street.

'Yes, Miss Lingard. Mr Bailey said to tell you that it's much more private than a restaurant.'

And what can you say to that? she thought, but with annoyance.

Ryan himself answered the door and ushered her immediately out on to a flagged terrace that ran alongside the pool. There was a glass-topped table set in one corner, with candles and some hibiscus blooms floating in a shallow crystal bowl; there was the scent of jasmine coming from a creeper that climbed the wall and the pool was lit with discreet underwater lights that turned the water to a pale, inviting aquamarine.

'Campari and soda,' he murmured, pulling out a chair for her and placing a tall frosted glass with its pinky red contents before her. 'I hope you don't mind dining here but I thought it might be—safer.'

Honor had said nothing since their gazes had clashed when he'd opened the door and, to be honest, she was amazed at the impact he had made on her only a bit more than twenty-four hours after she'd last seen him.

His tidied thick hair with those silver strands reminded her of how it had looked wet or ruffled and lying on his brow; there were no blue shadows on his jaw now; his body, tonight beneath a perfectly pressed Abelard checked sports shirt and navy twill trousers, was as strong as a tree and...

'What do you want with me?' she said abruptly as he sat down opposite. 'I'm tired of fencing with you—if you want to go to bed with me—'

'Isn't that what you'd like too, Honor?' he interrupted quietly. 'I think it would be more honest if you admitted that you're doing the fencing.'

'Yes, all right, I have thought about it,' she said with

cool composure, 'but I'm not going to do it. May I tell you why?'

'Of course,' he said gravely, and studied her shining cap of dark hair, her faint freckles, the determined line of her jaw, then the lovely line of her throat down to the scooped neck of her dress.

She took a breath. 'Sandra's uncle said to me that you and she were like a tiger and a lamb. You and I would be completely different but no better; we'd be impossible. I spend a lot of my time wanting to fight you. I'm sorry,' she said candidly, 'but that's the way it is.'

'And a lot of your time thinking about sleeping with me?'

'Not nearly as much,' she said shortly.

'That could change,' he said idly.

'Are you trying to say that all our discord would disappear once I'd been slept with and rendered all womanly and submissive? Don't bet on it, Ryan.'

His teeth gleamed white in a fleeting grin. 'I think you're more of a feminist than you give yourself credit for,' he murmured, and went on before she could take issue, 'No, I'm not talking about rendering you all—submissive. If I thought that was possible I probably wouldn't like you half so much.

'But I do think you could discover that a lot of this fighting energy you're consumed with turns out to be something else altogether.'

'I've thought that a couple of times before,' she said with a trace of unconscious bleakness.

He raised a wry eyebrow. 'Did you fight those men as well?'

'No,' she said hastily. 'I mean I thought that I would...I don't know, be made over, I guess—ready to surrender my independence and that kind of thing. It didn't happen and I happened to *like* them,' she said with unmistakable emphasis.

'Well, perhaps it's destined to happen differently for you. Drink up,' he said gently. 'Mary's about to serve the first course. I'm sorry we're eating so early but I have an early start tomorrow morning; I'm off to Port Moresby in Papua New Guinea for a couple of days.'

Honor stared at him, then said indignantly, 'You've done it again! How dare you do this to me all the time?'

'Do what? You've just told me that you won't sleep with me—what more is there to say? At the moment.'

'There are times when I not only don't like you, I hate you,' she said bitterly, and finished her drink.

'Well, there is something else we could have a fight about if you like,' he offered. '*Do* you have anyone you could go and stay with for a couple of weeks?'

'No! Well, I guess so,' she said more reasonably but still with supreme irritation. 'I just hate the thought of imposing on friends. And anyway, what if he does come after me? He's mad enough to kidnap a whole household of people, going on past experience.'

'Then you'd better come here, Honor— Ah, Mary, thank you.' He looked past her and rose to help the other woman with the trolley she was pushing.

Honor forced herself to eat half a delicious seafood crêpe before she trusted herself to respond. 'Is that why you asked me when you rang this morning?' she asked reservedly as she paused to take a sip of wine.

'Yes, I did think of it.'

'Why didn't you say so then?'

'I didn't want to alarm you unnecessarily,' he said thoughtfully.

'That's exactly what the policeman said,' she said tartly, 'and then proceeded to put the fear of God into me— Well, not exactly—' she looked irritable again '—but you know what I mean. However—' she waved Ryan to silence '—imagine what the magazines would offer me if I lived here for a couple of weeks.'

'With a bit of luck they may never know. But anyway, do you really care?' He eyed her enigmatically over the rim of his glass. 'Surely to be safe and free from the thought of Mark Markham pouncing on you is far more important?'

'Ah, but there's always the problem of you pouncing on me.'

There was a long, acute silence as they stared at each other, and to her consternation a telling blush rolled up her throat until he said drily at last, 'Perhaps we should strike that remark off the record, Honor.'

'I—'

'Nor do I intend to argue with you all night,' he continued. 'If you want to keep your job you'll stay here until Markham is apprehended. It so happens that there's plenty to do here at the moment—the Papuan artefacts have arrived; there are dozens of them but there's no catalogue, only some rambling notes that it will take a genius to unravel. Thank you, Mary,' he said once more as she arrived bearing a platter of roast lamb and rosemary. 'Could you get me the phone, please?'

'What are you doing?' Honor asked disbelievingly.

'You'll see.' He started to carve the lamb, but stopped when Mary trotted out once more with a mobile phone. He took a card from his pocket, rang up the detective who had been to see Honor and told him that, as arranged, she would be staying with him until further notice.

'Yes,' he said into the phone, 'I agree with you; it's the best solution; this place is like Fort Knox. Yes, I'll pass it on.' He switched the instrument off and looked at Honor. 'He said to tell you that you've made the right decision. Mary,' he added as she hovered with vegetables to serve, 'Honor will be staying here from tonight. Warren will take her home to collect her things tomorrow.'

'I've a guest room all set up, Mr Bailey,' Mary replied, and said warmly to Honor, 'It will be lovely to have you, Miss Lingard. And I'm sure you'll be happy not to have to worry about that nasty young man.'

Honor said nothing until she withdrew and Ryan said, 'Well?'

'You remind me of a steam-shovel, Ryan Bailey.'

'Is that all?' he queried, with a wicked glint lurking in his eyes.

'Rather than risk demeaning myself, yes,' she said coldly.

'It is only common sense, Honor,' he said as one might to a child. 'Nor need you worry about me; I've never yet pounced on any woman.'

She looked at him through her lashes, her mouth set. He raised his glass, stared at it meditatively, then said, 'Would *you* like to introduce a topic of conversation to accompany the rest of this delicious lamb?'

'Yes,' she said precisely. 'Do let us talk about the weather, Mr Bailey. Because I can't think of another thing I'd like to say to you.'

He laughed quietly then said, 'All right, whatever you like, but just one thing, Honor—don't cook up any mad schemes while I'm away; it would not only be juvenile and irresponsible but also quite femininely irrational. In other words I expect to find you here when I get back.'

'Oh, you will—just don't expect any joy from it.'

'You were much nicer marooned on an island with

me,' he said wryly, put his knife and fork together and stood up. 'If you'll excuse me I have some work to do. But I'm sure Mary has made a dessert for you. Good-night, Honor—do make yourself at home.' And he walked away.

Her bedroom was on the second floor and opened on to the veranda that ran right along the upper storey and overlooked the pool. It had its own *en-suite* bathroom, a queen-size bed with a rather lovely, old-fashioned floral bedspread of pink, yellow and tangerine poppies, and a close-pile velvety yellow carpet and curtains.

Mary had lent her a nightgown and the bathroom, all white marble, was stocked with a whole range of herb-scented products, a beautiful pale tortoiseshell-backed brush and comb and a poppy-pink seersucker robe with a tangerine trim.

None of this comforted Honor much as she lay in solitary state in the dark, prey to a curious ambivalence. On the one hand she was quite sure that she was right to be terribly wary of getting closer to Ryan, yet on the other she couldn't help wondering if there was an inevitability about it that made her feel helpless and... curious.

And, to make it all worse, she couldn't get her mind away from the thought of him sleeping only yards away.

Then, suddenly, she found herself wondering *why* she was so independent, and after a while came to the conclusion that it might be connected to her growing up with only one parent and a father who'd been an independent kind of man anyway.

Had the habit been formed thus? she mused. Had the lack of a loving adult relationship in her life left her, well, not knowing about such things, or even with an idealised idea of them?

But what kind of loving relationship could she have with Ryan? Would there always be a part of him that no woman could have? What if she *did* sleep with him and found herself hungering for more than he could give…? Why was she even thinking like this?

She woke very early in the morning and heard someone swimming and, while she knew it must be him, something drew her to have a look. So she enfolded herself in the pink robe and padded quietly out on to the veranda.

Ryan was powering up and down the pool, his dark head sleek, his broad shoulders brown, his hips narrow in pale blue trunks as the rising sun laid a sheen like lightly tinted mother-of-pearl on the river beyond.

She watched while he did fifty laps, then withdrew just as quietly as he hoisted his big, streamlined body out of the water with extraordinary lightness and grace. And then she went back to bed.

The three days when he was away turned, with Honor not knowing quite how, into a time of peace.

She worked during the day among the crates of Papuan artefacts in the library, carefully unpacking a selection of masks, weird and wonderful headgear, carvings, shells, weapons, utensils, basketry and the like while she debated how they should be mounted and presented. At the same time she worked on preparing an erudite description of each item and a general history of its background.

She was lucky enough to find a couple of books on the subject in Ryan's library and it was with a growing interest in the whole area of Melanesia that she made preparations for their exhibition.

At other times she swam, read, and was curiously drawn to Ryan's garden, with its riot of gardenias, agapanthus, bougainvillea, its native shrubs and trees like grevillea and melaleuca, and the rainbow lorikeets and other colourful, noisy birds that invaded the garden at times.

She got to know his house, which was cool while it was scorching outside, spacious, and uncluttered in a way that not only suited the climate but showed off his art collection beautifully. She also spent quite a bit of time with Mary in the kitchen—a gleaming masterpiece of modern technology—exchanging recipes.

She was bending over a crate in the library, lifting a mask from the wood-shavings it was packed in, when he came home. The first intimation of his presence was a sound at the doorway and she turned, her eyes widened and she laid the mask down carefully but could think of not a thing to say.

He was formally dressed in a suit and tie and his grey eyes roamed over her—over her short-sleeved, silky cream shirt, her fawn shorts and yellow leather belt, her long legs and flat fawn shoes, the golden bloom her skin had begun to acquire from the time she'd spent beside the pool—and she found the impact of his scrutiny quite simply unnerving.

It made her feel as if he was seeing beneath her clothes to the lines and curves of her figure, but, what was more, it aroused her so that she was achingly conscious of those lines and curves, of the lie of her silk shirt across her breasts, the slenderness of her waist under the yellow belt, the smoothness but sudden incredible sensitivity of her skin beneath her clothes.

He spoke first, just a simple question. 'Honor?' But the question was repeated in his eyes and she knew exactly what he was asking.

'I...' She licked her lips.

He came towards her slowly until he was right in front of her and she had to tilt her head to look into his eyes as she twisted her hands together. 'May I?' he said then, barely audibly.

But she couldn't speak as it dawned on her that, for the first time in her life, she was in the grip of a physical attraction so strong that she could find no words or deeds to break it, not even when he put his arms around her and started to kiss her deeply.

It was in fact a shocking sense of relief that claimed her and it went on to become an experience like no other. She was besieged not only by the intimacy of being kissed but of being held, by the sensation of her breasts touching his chest, by everything that was taut, strong and so overwhelmingly masculine about him and which, correspondingly, seemed to reach through to the core of her femininity.

When he lifted his head at last he kept her body resting against his as he looked levelly into her eyes and said softly, 'Are you going to slap my face now, Honor?'

She closed her eyes briefly, then said very quietly but proudly, 'No. Nor am I going to rush to bed with you despite the fact that that was—something I seemed to need and want.'

A little glint lit his eyes as he gazed down at her and moved his hands on her hips. A glint of admiration? she wondered.

He said, 'So be it,' and kissed her just lightly on the lips before he released her. 'You've been busy. What do you think of them?' He looked around, then picked up the mask.

'I'm getting really interested,' she confessed.

He put the mask down and strolled among the other things she'd unpacked. 'The minister is very keen that they be exhibited. I'm thinking of setting them up in ground-floor foyer of the building so that the public has easier access. There's also a full-time security guard downstairs.'

'Good idea, but you'll need glass cases. How is the minister?'

'He sent his regards and hopes you've recovered from being kidnapped.'

'Thank you. I gather you were there about the bridge?'

'Yes.'

'I know this may sound silly but have you actually ever built a bridge before?'

He glanced at her wryly. 'Several. Why?'

'I didn't know, that's all. I've only heard of you in the context of buildings.'

'My first big project was a bridge so I'm rather attached to them,' he reflected. 'This one will be quite a test, however, of logistics, especially since the site is extremely remote at the moment.'

'Why are they building a bridge, then?'

'Because of a significant gold deposit in the area. There'll be other companies involved but Bailey Construction is the managing company.'

'A feather in your cap?' she suggested quietly.

'I never count the feathers in my cap until the job is finished successfully. I'll take you up to see it one day, Honor. Look, I'm going to change and then I really feel I deserve a sundowner on the terrace. Care to join me?'

Their gazes caught and held until she said coolly, 'Yes. Thank you.'

But in the intervening minutes she thought, Is he so sure of me? Is *that* what he meant about taking me up to see his bridge?

Yet, perversely or not, sitting on the terrace with their drinks as the sun set, he made no mention of their passionate encounter in the library, said nothing remotely personal.

'No word of our friend Mark Markham?'

'No. He seems to have vanished. They did ring yesterday to assure me that they've put out an APB throughout Queensland and New South Wales,' she replied. 'I asked them about the *Sandra-Lee* but so far nothing there yet either.'

'Hmm...'

'You'll miss her, I guess.'

'Yes. But boats can be replaced. Would you like to watch the news before dinner? I've been a bit out of touch for the last few days.'

'Whatever you like...'

So that was what they did and then they had a quiet dinner, all in the same impersonal vein. Honor discovered that she felt like pinching herself. Was this the same man whom she had been unable resist only a few hours ago?

No...be honest with yourself, Honor, she thought. It's like a subtle form of torture, having taken that step—and now this. Is that what he's doing to me? Because of what I said about not going to bed with him?

But after dinner things did get a bit more personal.

'So,' he said as Mary served coffee, 'what do you do with your evenings, Honor?'

They were in a smaller lounge, with comfortable brown leather buttoned settees set at right angles to each other in front of a television set.

There were books and magazines on a low table, a state-of-the-art sound system in a painted cabinet, beautiful slatted cedar blinds at the windows, lovely rugs on the sealed slate floor—and the Sisley in pride of place above an exquisite old mahogany travelling chest with bound brass corners.

'Whatever my mood dictates,' she said slowly, her eyes on the Sisley. 'Sometimes I sew, sometimes I read. If there's anything good on television I watch it; if there's not I play music, write letters, do the odd chore—I guess what most people do with their evenings at home.'

She leant her head on her hand, propped on the arm of the settee, slipped her shoes off and tucked her feet beneath her in an unconscious reproduction of how she sat at home. 'I also play tennis two evenings a week.'

'Do you ever get lonely?' He was lying back with his long legs sprawled out and the remote control of the television in his hand.

'No, it hasn't been a problem. Why have you got that painting in here? I would have thought this was a rather private room—' She stopped abruptly.

He turned his head and grinned wryly at her. 'I took your words to heart,' he drawled, 'about not showing off my Sisley. This is also the living-room that I use most and therefore where I see it most. Well, I *was* tempted to hang it in my bedroom but I decided that might test my self-control a bit.'

Honor frowned, hesitated, then couldn't stop herself from taking the plunge. 'Do you really have that problem with regard to me?'

'Do you think I'd ever have brought up the subject of you in black lacy underwear if I didn't?' he countered.

She opened her mouth, closed it, then sent him a speaking look.

'For that matter, Honor, do you go about kissing men the way you kissed me unless you—"have that problem" with them?' he parodied amusedly.

'No,' she said shortly.

'So?'

'Nothing.' She glanced at him coolly.

'In other words,' he said with irony, 'you're still grappling with our differences.'

'Yes, I am,' she confessed, but managed to infuse some indifference into her voice.

'Well, I do hope you'll give me the odd progress report,' he murmured, and flicked on the television.

If it hadn't been for the fact that he got the start of an episode of *Inspector Morse*, to which Honor happened to be addicted, she would have got up and left him. Curiously, they managed to watch it companionably—he told her that he was a fan too.

Two hours later when it was over and she yawned, stood up and said that she thought she might go to bed he also stood up and accompanied her up the staircase. Her door came first on the upper landing.

'Goodnight,' she said, and tensed as he closed his fingers around her wrist.

'No, I'm not about to pounce on you, Honor,' he said drily as her eyes flew to his. 'I merely want to pose this question to you. Are you going to dole out—embraces as *you* see fit? Or are you going to admit that we're in this together, that I've strenuously avoided taking advantage of you when it would have been child's play to do otherwise—?'

'*Child's* play?' she said huskily, her eyes dark and wide.

'Oh, yes, Honor. But I'm not that kind of man and you're only kidding yourself if that's the misconception you're hiding behind,' he said, with a glint of mockery in his eyes. 'There,' he added with lethal gentleness as he dropped her wrist. 'I'll leave you with that thought to brood upon. Goodnight, my dear.'

'No, I will *not* brood,' she told herself as she leant back against her bedroom door, but she did. And she vividly remembered the two nights when they'd slept in each other's arms with the uncomfortable feeling that he might have been right. No, it wouldn't have been 'child's play' but if he'd done it right he might have been hard to resist in those circumstances...

Oh, hell, she thought hollowly, I'm getting myself into an awful mess. It's so much easier when I can be just plain angry with him!

As it happened she got that opportunity the very next day.

She only saw him briefly at breakfast, when she confirmed distantly, in answer to his query, that she had plenty to keep her occupied with the Papuan artefacts for the next couple of days, without having to venture out.

'Good. I'll be gone all day,' he replied.

To which she said nothing at all.

Then, in the late afternoon, Mary came to seek her out in the library and asked her to come and inspect the dining-room.

'Well, of course, but—why?' Honor asked.

'I've used a new colour scheme but I'm not quite sure

about it and with you being arty, Miss Lingard, I thought you could let me know if I've gone wrong.'

Honor looked faintly bewildered but got up obediently and followed Mary into the formal dining-room. It was set, she saw, for a dinner party, with a dark green damask cloth over the large round glass and forged-iron table; it was in fact set for eight people, and there were white napkins, a lovely white Royal Doulton dinner service and a shallow bowl of deep red roses in the centre.

'It looks lovely, Mary,' Honor said sincerely but slowly. 'Is it...? It's not for tonight, is it?' she added.

'Yes,' Mary said happily. 'I've placed you over here, Miss Lingard. Opposite Mr Bailey.'

Honor took a deep breath. 'Did he...did he say I was coming?'

'Why, yes! Didn't he tell you?'

Honor controlled her voice with an effort. 'No. No, he didn't.'

'Must have slipped his mind,' Mary said comfortably. 'He has such an awful lot to think about, doesn't he? But they're not arriving until seven-thirty so you've got plenty of time. Is there anything you'd like pressed or—?'

'No, thank you, Mary. Unfortunately I won't be coming; I'm so sorry to upset your table but I think I might just be dining out this evening!'

'Oh, no, you won't, Honor,' a voice said from right behind her.

She swung round, her eyes sparkling with anger. 'You cannot keep me a prisoner here, Ryan Bailey,' she said tautly. 'Nor can you advertise to all and sundry that I'm living here—how *dare* you?'

'Unfortunately *I* can't live like a recluse, Honor,' he said drily, 'and this dinner was arranged some time ago.

Also...' he paused and looked her up and down sardonically '...someone resembling Mark Markham has been
noticed skulking around your street, which is why you
won't be going anywhere tonight unless you're quite
mad.'

CHAPTER SIX

HONOR was alone in her bedroom, where she'd retreated precipitately, for precisely three minutes. Ryan didn't knock; he simply walked in and closed the door behind him.

She swung round from the glass door that led to the veranda where she'd angrily been surveying the view with her arms folded and surveyed him angrily instead.

He'd taken off his jacket, half rolled up his sleeves and loosened his navy blue tie but he still looked every inch a powerful and impressive man as he shoved his hands into his pockets, looked around, leant his broad shoulders against the wall and let his grey gaze rest on her enigmatically.

She said finally, 'You have no right just to walk in here even if it is your house!'

'I beg your pardon,' he answered sardonically, and added, 'Are you reacting like this because you're scared, Honor? I mean, to hear that we were right to worry about Markham from your point of view?'

'Of course I'm scared to think of him skulking about my street,' she replied scathingly. 'But no, fear was not my initial reaction nor the cause of it.

'I *told* you. I resent having it advertised to all and sundry that I am living in the house of the state's most eligible bachelor because, whatever you say and however you try to explain it, people always wonder about these things. I probably would myself—it's only human nature,' she finished pointedly.

'Honor,' he said deliberately, 'people are already speculating about us.'

'*Who*…? Oh, you mean that madman? He's only one and he *is*…' She trailed off abruptly. 'Who else?'

'Dear Honor,' he said quite kindly, 'I'm sure I can say with no fear of contradiction that the first time you stormed out of work we became the subject of gossip both in the office and, as you so rightly predicted after our being on television together, not to mention being kidnapped together, out of it. Besides which,' he pointed out with infuriating rationality, 'they're right.'

'But…'

'Right about the fact that we attract each other. You, in fact, are probably the only person who appears to doubt it.'

She clenched her teeth. 'On the contrary, at this moment *I* could be the only person who is right,' she said bitterly. 'But look here, whatever the speculation is, the moment it's known that I'm living here I will be forever branded as one of your women!'

'Or it might go the other way,' he suggested with a sudden, dry little smile.

'What do you mean?'

'I could be branded forever as one of your men.'

'Now that,' she said with utter scorn, 'is patently ridiculous!'

'Why?'

'Well…well, it's your house for one thing.'

'So you keep telling me,' he remarked, and raised a wry eyebrow at her. 'Is that all you can come up with?'

She made a disgusted sound and turned away irately.

'Besides which,' he went on, 'the six people I'm entertaining tonight are Japanese businessmen who are only in Australia for a week; their grasp of English is limited and I'd be very surprised if they decide to rush out and inform the world of what is really only a bit of local gossip—anyway, they're very polite people normally.

'You see, Honor, I too don't particularly want to advertise the fact that you're here—until Markham is apprehended, that is. Although, of course, this is probably where he'll assume you are eventually.'

Honor swung back. 'Why didn't you *say* so?' she demanded. 'Why—?'

'I always enjoy hearing you delivering yourself of your great wisdom on the subject of us,' he murmured with an oddly austere little smile. 'And there are times when it's hard to get a word in edgeways.'

'*Rubbish!*' she denied forcefully. 'You simply enjoy baiting me!'

'That too,' he conceded.

She gazed at him then sat down on the bed abruptly. 'I…you…I really don't know why I put up with you,' she said disjointedly and rubbed her face distractedly.

'Oh, yes, you do, Honor,' he said imperturbably. 'That apart, your options are very limited at the moment, so why don't you put on some finery and come down and join us? I believe you speak Japanese?'

'Fluently,' she said bitterly.

'Well, then, added to that, a couple of these men are art connoisseurs and are bringing me some Japanese silk paintings, which, incidentally, is why I thought you might just enjoy the evening and why I also thought it might relieve the tedium of your—incarceration here.'

She could feel the colour flooding her cheeks and she bowed her head, studied her hands, then looked directly at him and said huskily, 'Could you just go away, please? I can't...deal with you at the moment.'

He straightened. 'Well, there's one way we could deal much better with each other, Honor, but I'll leave that for another day. Are you coming down or not? You could always have your dinner up here in solitary, righteous state,' he finished with soft mockery.

Their gazes clashed, with quite some considerable spirit returning to Honor's. 'I'll come down,' she said defiantly.

'Good.' He smiled slightly and walked out, leaving her with the totally deflating feeling that she'd been taunted into agreeing, that she'd fallen for his ruse to make her join them.

Why am I such a fool? she marvelled. How it must amuse him to know he can do this to me!

As she got ready she heard him swimming but this time refused to look.

She was annoyed by the realisation that the only dress she'd brought that would be suitable for a dinner party was black. Not that its blackness suddenly offended her, nor did the dress itself—it was a beautiful black crêpe sheath with cut-away shoulders and a narrow neck band embroidered heavily with jet beads.

What did annoy her was that it required a strapless bra and the only strapless bra she had with her was black. In fact she had a matching pair of black lace and satin briefs to go with the bra, and if she wore stockings, depending on the weather, she would be wearing a black garter belt that also matched.

'Well, I'm damned if I'll wear stockings tonight,' she muttered to herself. 'It's far too hot for one thing.'

And for another? an inner voice queried unkindly. It answered itself equally unkindly. For another, lacy black garter belts and stockings will be a treat that Ryan Bailey won't...

'What am I *thinking*?' she wondered aloud.

Accordingly, she was in an extremely militant mood as she showered and washed her hair, then blow-dried it to a silken, dark, gleaming cap. It was a mood that got worse when, once in the bra and briefs, she caught sight of herself in the full-length bathroom mirror.

Nevertheless something caught and held her and she stood for a long moment with her hands on her hips as she surveyed her slender, curved figure, her long legs, considered her stature, and thought—because she just couldn't help herself—about Ryan's height and his tanned, powerful body and how they would match each other in bed...

They were thoughts which caused her to swallow as a wave of pure sensuality swept through her and caused her to turn away abruptly.

But they were something she couldn't forget and caused her to linger before going downstairs, pointlessly checking her make-up, which was discreet and perfect. Her lips were a glossy scarlet; her nails were perfectly manicured into short, gleaming ovals; her father's intricate gold signet ring, which she'd had made smaller so that she could wear it, was on her little finger.

She checked the line of her dress, which came to just above her knees, and her long, golden legs, her smart black kid shoes that were in the latest fashion—small platform soles, chunky heels and sling-backs—until, with a sigh, she knew that she would have to make the decision to go down or not, and went.

It was midnight when she bowed formally six times and then again until the Japanese businessmen, beaming in unison, retreated to the waiting stretch limousine that would return them to their hotel. And she stood at Ryan's side beneath his impressive portico in a splash of light until the car had turned down the dirveway out of sight.

Then he turned to her and said, 'A very successful evening, Honor. You were a great hit.'

'The life and soul of the party,' she said drily and wearily. 'I don't think I'll take up interpreting—it's an exhausting business. But when you say successful—there was no business discussed.'

'Ah, but there will be. Thank you for your efforts, incidentally.'

'Does that mean I've swung another bridge?' she queried with some irony.

He looked down at her. 'If you let me buy you a nightcap I'll tell you.'

'No, no more to drink,' she said decisively.

'Not alcohol, just something cool and refreshing. In fact I'm going to have another swim; it's as hot as hell.'

Honor hesitated and wondered which would be worse—lying upstairs alone on what was a stifling night, listening to him in the pool and longing to be cooling off herself, or being there with him. I suppose I could always close the doors and turn on the air-conditioning—and feel just as stifled, she mused.

'All right,' she said at last with a tinge of helplessness.

So they went upstairs where she changed out of her black dress, removed her black lacy underwear with an oddly ironic little glint in her eye and a sudden tremor in her hands, and donned her one-piece floral swimsuit.

She added the pink seersucker robe, picked up a towel and stood in the middle of the room for a moment, lost

in thought. Then she went softly downstairs and out on
to the terrace, which was bathed in white moonlight.

She was down first and she slipped into the pool and
revelled in the experience although the water couldn't
exactly have been described as cold. Ryan dived in a
few minutes later.

They didn't swim for long and when she climbed out
she let the faintest suggestion of a breeze play on her
wet skin for a couple of minutes before wrapping her
towel round her and sinking on to a lounger. Ryan did
the same and handed her a tall glass.

'Mango and pineapple juice,' he said lightly. 'Very
good for the complexion, I should imagine.'

'Thanks,' she murmured, and felt herself relaxing
slightly. It was hard not to as the aqua waters of the pool
gradually stopped lapping and she noticed the moon's
reflection in the quiet waters of the river beyond the
garden; the perfume of the jasmine creeper was carried
on the breeze.

'By the way, they've found the *Sandra-Lee* sub-
merged in about thirty metres of water.'

She glanced across at him and saw that his mouth was
set grimly. 'I'm sorry,' she said quietly. 'Does that mean
it can't be salvaged?'

'Yes. It's a funny thing; Sandra came to see me today
and when I told her she was quite upset.'

'But you said...'

'Yes, she never liked the boat, or any boat, but apparently she had liked it being named after her. She
said...it was like the cutting of the last tie.'

'I don't know what to say,' Honor said slowly.

'You don't have to say anything,' he replied.

'Then why did you tell me?'

'I didn't precisely. I—' he grimaced '—found myself

speaking my thoughts aloud. But, since I did, I'll continue. I hope that for her it is the last tie and that once she gets over being upset she'll finally feel free.

'What else was I going to tell you? Ah, yes—no, you didn't swing a bridge this evening but you might have put the last staple into a joint-venture contract with a Japanese consortium to build a marina and shopping village on the Sunshine Coast.'

He raised a wry eyebrow at her and added softly, 'Just think what we could achieve, you and I, on a—more permanent basis.'

Honor laid her head back and stared at the stars. 'I'll ignore that,' she said finally. 'Nor do I believe that I deserve the credit for achieving anything. I still don't think that business works that way so your premise that we could go far together is invalid anyway. Besides which, I thought you were going to leave this kind of thing for another day.'

'It is another day.' He glanced at his watch.

She said nothing as she sipped her drink, then a sudden thought struck her. 'Is...Sandra speculating about us?'

'Probably, although she hasn't said so. Honor...' he paused '...why don't you tell me your real reasons for this impasse between us? Is it Sandra?'

'No. Yes. I mean—' she took a breath to steady herself '—one can't help thinking of her and not only of her *feelings*, but in the context of what it would be like— living with you. You see, sometimes it's impossible—'

She stopped, realising that she was, for the first time perhaps, putting her doubts into a coherent, unemotional form.

'Sometimes it's impossible,' she said again, 'to separate the forceful, business dynamo you are from the man. So much so that one can't help wondering if that side of you ever switches off entirely and whether any woman wouldn't find herself—put into a compartment in your life, with a label on it, speaking metaphorically.'

She shrugged. 'Then there's me,' she said. 'But I've told you about me.'

'Assuming I am that way,' he said wryly, 'wouldn't an independent woman who valued her freedom find it an ideal situation?'

She sat up and turned to him. 'So you're not denying the charge?'

'I didn't say that. I'm merely—theorising.'

'Well, there's no point in theorising upon unknown factors,' she said tartly. 'Are you or aren't you that kind of man?'

He smiled at her ruefully, yet a different kind of amusement lurked in his eyes, directed *at* her, she felt. 'I don't know,' he said.

'Well, when you work it out, Ryan Bailey, do let me know, but if you think I'm going to risk f—' She stopped abruptly and bit her lip.

'Risk falling in love with me?' he suggested. 'You know, I'm tempted to think that those things happen irrespective of—all sorts of factors, known or unknown.'

'I wouldn't put your life on it in my case.'

He laughed softly and drawled, 'Just because you've chosen the wrong men up until now, Honor, it doesn't mean that you can direct your mind and heart away from love for the rest of your life.'

'It also doesn't mean it will be you,' she pointed out coolly enough, but couldn't help adding with a flash of resentment, 'Who's to say that they were so wrong? Who are *you* to say it particularly? You've never met them.'

'No, but I can just imagine them.'

'All right, go ahead and do it!'

He lifted a quizzical eyebrow at her expression of outrage. 'Just bear in mind that you did ask for it, Honor,' he murmured. 'Let's see…of an age with you more or less, cultured, been to all the right schools and given to frequenting that heart of Brisbane top society, Ballymore, where all those old-school-tie types play and watch rugby union.

'Handsome young men—that goes without saying. Talented and articulate, I've no doubt; I'd even go so far as to say in the legal profession, which would have been your milieu as well as the art world on account of your father—and, of course, while he was still alive you would have been quite a catch… How am I doing?'

But Honor was staring at him with her mouth compressed; indeed there was a white shade around it and a dangerous glitter in her dark eyes. *'Don't—'*

But he wouldn't let her finish. 'On the right track, I see,' he said gently yet mockingly. 'Nor have I finished, Honor, dear. Not that any of that would have mattered had they had the maturity to make you feel like a real woman whereas…' he paused and watched her for a moment '…what they did do was create within you a sense of dissatisfaction with yourself and them that only served to increase your high-minded, imperious way of dealing with men.'

She gasped. 'I'm not like that!'

'Are you saying that you never once thought you might have been too strong-minded for either of them?'

Her mouth opened; she closed it, then said bitterly, 'Are *you* saying I need a strong hand on the reins? Or something along those lines? I have to tell you that I despise that kind of jargon nearly as much as I despise *you*!'

'I knew you were more of a feminist than you believed,' he murmured with a faint grin. 'And no, what I'm saying is that you're bright, you're beautiful, you're extremely spirited and you're quite wasted on nice-looking, pleasant, charming young men who appear to have all the right credentials but not the essential one of being able to match you physically and mentally.'

'That's as good as saying it,' she returned disgustedly, and looked moodily out over the river.

'But right?' he suggested after a moment.

She sighed, then said shortly, 'I don't know how you did it and I hope I never find out that you've been digging around in my personal life—'

'I haven't.'

'Then I must be terribly transparent.'

He didn't reply.

She finished her drink and set the glass down on the terrace. 'And it surprises me, in the light of my transparency, not to mention inability to choose men—' she cast him a withering glance from beneath her lashes '—that you want to persist with me.'

'It shouldn't,' he said idly. 'For one thing I promised myself quite a few weeks ago that I would have you one day, Honor Lingard. For another, were we to go upstairs now, cool and slightly damp, to the same bed, that beautiful body of yours would come alive for me.

'You see, Honor, you want me nearly as much as I want you, and you would for a time turn it into a contest—there's nothing you like more than a bit of a challenge, and I'd be perfectly happy to humour you until we were both of the same mind—with quite a stunning outcome, I'm sure.'

She swung her legs over the side of the lounger and said in a low, intense voice, 'I hate the sound of that if you must know. It's…it's demeaning and…' She couldn't go on.

'No, it's not,' he said drily. 'It's the way you're made and the way I'm made. Do you really believe that making love is always a sweet, saccharine affair?'

'*No*, but I do believe… Look here!' She stood up abruptly, compelled to bitter honesty. 'I don't know what to believe if you really want to know. But I did make a bargain with myself once. I did decide that if I ever…gave myself to another man it would be an *all-or-nothing* affair. But if that kind of love of my life didn't come my way then…' She gestured.

'Honor—' he stood up himself '—how the hell are you going to know what it is if you barricade yourself in so implacably?'

'That's my a…that's my business.' She glared up at him.

'All right.' He looked amused. 'You don't have to be so defensive, you know.'

'Well, you're certainly not helping matters!'

'Because I haven't gone down on my knees and sworn undying love for you? Or,' he said after a moment, 'because I can read you so well? Incidentally—' he grimaced as her eyes were suddenly wide and stunned '—that's often a much better bet than a lot of emotional, sentimental declarations.'

She stared up at him for what seemed like an age. Then she said in a curiously hollow, husky voice, 'The thing is, I don't really know you much at all. No, don't say any more—I'm going to bed. Alone.'

'Well, if it's any consolation, Miss Lingard,' he replied ruefully, 'I'm going to have to have another swim before I try to—retire.'

Honor stopped sorting Papuan artefacts the next morning with a gesture of intense irritation and sat down. She leant her elbows on Ryan Bailey's desk and propped her chin in her hands, to think darkly that she couldn't even leave the country, which was the only way she'd feel safe from Mark Markham now, because her passport had expired.

That was something she'd meant to attend to at least a month ago so that it would be all shipshape for her approaching vacation to Fiji in about eight weeks—but had forgotten.

'That's what he's done to me,' she muttered under her breath. 'Not to mention making me want to curl up and die of embarrassment even to think he could know…how it was for me. How did he?'

'Penny for 'em?' a voice she knew said from the library doorway.

'Oh!' She turned. 'Mr Oldfield. What are you doing here?' she added less than graciously.

'My, my!' Brad Oldfield strolled into the room. 'Something's biting you, Miss Lingard. Let me guess—Ryan?'

'Now why should you think that?' she retorted frostily.

'Just sprang to mind! Told you he could be a tiger. Don't tell me you're still resisting him?' He clucked his tongue in a way that infuriated her.

'If he's—'

'He hasn't.'

'Then what do you know about it?' she demanded.

'Just my own idea that you could make a perfect mate

for him, that's all,' Brad said mischievously. 'Thought he'd tie it all up while you were kidnapped with him on that island, as a matter of fact.' He shook his shaggy grey head. 'But then Ryan really enjoys a fight!'

She flinched visibly, causing him to study her wryly but say, 'As to what I'm doing here, I've been invited to lunch.'

'Lunch?'

'Yes. It is Saturday and even business moguls tend to take half a day off.'

'That's true,' another voice said—Ryan. 'Had you forgotten it was Saturday, Honor?' he drawled as he too strolled into the library, wearing checked navy blue and green trousers and a navy sports shirt.

'As a matter of fact, yes,' she said baldly.

'Never mind,' he said consolingly. 'Do you play golf?'

'No.'

'I only ask because that's what Brad and I are doing after lunch and I thought you might enjoy an outing.' He lifted an eyebrow and considered. 'You could always drive the buggy.'

'Thank you, no,' she said formally. 'I think I might keep working.'

'Now, Ryan,' Brad said chidingly, 'it's obvious to my old eyes that you aren't handling things at all well! I'm surprised, old son, really surprised and—'

He stopped as Honor stood up precipitately. 'And I'm surprised at you, Brad Oldfield!' she said crisply. 'Not only was he once married to your *niece*, who is still pining for him by all accounts, but *I* have nothing whatsoever to do with you. Good day to you, gentlemen,' she added. 'I hope you lose all your golf balls!' and she swept out.

But she wasn't completely out before she heard Ryan say gravely, 'I don't think Honor will be lunching with us somehow.'

He's a monster, she thought a little wildly as she closed herself into her bedroom. I have to get away!

Accordingly she got out a card, waited with mounting impatience until she heard Ryan and Brad drive off, then called the detective in charge of the case… Yes, he said, there had been a sighting in her street of a man resembling Mark Markham acting a little strangely, but no, he regretted to say, they had not tracked him down as yet.

'All right.' She drew a deep breath. 'I'm just ringing you to tell you that I'm changing residences for a few days—no, you really don't need to worry; I'm going to stay at a hotel.' She told him which one. 'I'm sure their security is excellent there and I shan't be opening my door to anyone—well, for the weekend anyway. And I'll be in touch with you…on Monday morning definitely.'

She put the phone down resolutely and started to pack a small bag. Then she simply called a taxi, left a note for Mary telling *her* not to worry, was fortunate in that Mary was taking a nap and Warren was cleaning the pool so that she was able to operate the gates herself, and escaped.

Once installed in a room at the Hilton she breathed a sigh of relief, but realised that she'd been looking over her shoulder ever since she'd left the house, and that she felt exhausted and appallingly tense. So she lay on the bed and tried to watch television, which on a Saturday afternoon consisted of a lot of sport, including golf, and unwittingly fell asleep, and slept until it was dark.

The phone woke her. She stared at it blearily then picked it up and said, 'Yes?'

There were a couple of heavy breaths then a click that told her the call had been disconnected. I don't *believe* this, she thought as her heart started to pound and she sat up abruptly and fumbled with the buttons to call the switchboard. But all they could tell her was that it had been a male caller asking for her by her full name, and then they said there was another call for her.

'Hang on…no,' she said disjointedly, but was not heard, apparently, and then a familiar voice said down the line,

'Honor?'

'Oh, Ryan,' she breathed, almost weak with relief. 'Oh, thank goodness.'

'Honor—are you all right?' he asked curtly.

'Yes, yes, but—did you ring me a few minutes ago?'

'No. Why?'

'Well, I think Markham might have—'

'Honor, stay there; *don't* open your door to anyone until I get there.'

'But how will I know it's you?' she said shakily.

'I'll speak to you on the phone when I arrive and I'll get the management to come up with me and let me in. I'll be twenty minutes at the most.'

It was an unbearably long twenty minutes but finally he walked into her room with the manager and a policeman behind him. As she looked at him apprehensively, not knowing what to expect, his mouth, which had been set in a grim line, relaxed a bit and he said mildly, 'This is not the time for recriminations, my dear. Tell us what happened.'

'I feel terribly foolish,' Honor said an hour later, back once more in the mansion on the river.

They'd just arrived; they were standing beneath the

chandelier in the hallway, Honor's bag on the floor beside her. Mary had appeared and embraced her with genuine emotion then discreetly disappeared, leaving them alone for the first time since Ryan had arrived at the hotel.

'So you should,' he said expressionlessly.

A wave of colour crept up her throat and she looked away awkwardly.

'On the other hand,' he went on, 'I may have goaded you into it. I'm sorry.' Her eyes flew back to his and her lips worked but no sound came. 'Honor,' he said quietly, 'why are you making this so hard for us?' And he took her hand and drew her, unresisting, into his arms.

'Am I...?' Her voice shook. '*Am* I made that way?'

He kissed her hair. 'Unfortunately, I might be made that way too. What are we going to do about it?'

It was quite a few minutes before she answered—minutes when she rested against him. 'Could I have a bit more time?' she whispered.

'So long as you'll allow a bit more of this,' he replied, and tilted her chin so that he could kiss her deeply.

But, just as something inside her was urging total capitulation, just as she had started to revel in the closeness and feel mindless with desire, Mary coughed behind them.

She heard Ryan swear beneath his breath but he released her without haste and turned to look enquiringly at his housekeeper.

'It's someone from Port Moresby on the phone,' Mary said awkwardly. 'Says it's very urgent.'

CHAPTER SEVEN

WHEN Ryan came to find her about ten minutes later he was looking irritable. Honor was in her bedroom, unpacking her bag, and he closed the door and sat down on the bed. 'I'm beginning to regret this bridge.'

She looked at him with a query in her eyes. 'Don't tell me you have to pop up to Port Moresby tonight?'

'No, Sydney. There's a problem with one of the joint-venture companies. It could cost us a lot of money if it holds us up. I'm taking the last flight.'

'Do you…can't you delegate that kind of thing?'

'No, not this one.'

She opened a drawer, replaced her underwear in it, then hung up a pair of shorts and a skirt.

'Honor—are you worried about Markham?'

'Not as much as I was,' she murmured wryly. 'But he must have been watching this house and he must have followed the taxi—what I can't understand is why he left it a couple of hours before he called the hotel.'

'Possibly to lull you into a false sense of security. But look, now that he's showing his hand they're bound to catch up with him shortly.'

She shivered. 'I hope so. It was…a horrible feeling.'

He watched her for a moment. 'You really are safe here, you know. The police are putting on extra surveillance and I've hired a couple more security guards. So if you don't do anything silly…'

'Point taken.'

'Would you like to come with me?'

Surprise caused her to sit down on the other side of the bed. 'For one night?' she said foolishly.

'It may take two or three,' he said.

'I…I don't think so,' she said slowly, and then went on with more decision, 'No, I'll be fine here. I'm still up to my knees in Papuan artefacts,' she added with an attempt at humour.

He got up but only to come round the bed to draw her to her feet. 'I think you're right,' he murmured. 'We wouldn't be able to spend much time together. But you do believe that I wouldn't leave you here unless I was sure you'd be safe, don't you, Honor?'

'Yes,' she said huskily.

His lips twisted. 'What about the other bit?'

'The other…? Oh, that.' She coloured slightly.

'Yes, that. Are you prepared to allow me a bit more of this, in other words?' He drew his fingers down her cheek, tracing the tide of warmth in them, then outlined her mouth.

'A bit more—yes,' she said unsteadily, and wondered if he had any idea of how close she'd come to total capitulation.

'Well, I'll be careful not to overdo it,' he said gravely although his eyes were amused, and he took her in his arms but kissed her only briefly before he put her away from him. 'Which is going to take some doing.'

'Thank you—for being so understanding earlier as well.'

'My pleasure—' The phone beside her bed buzzed. 'That will be for me… OK, I'm off. I'll take it in my room. Look after yourself.' And he was gone.

*　　*　　*

She looked after herself quite conscientiously the next day. In fact she found it hard to persuade herself to leave the environs of the house. But she also had a lot of time to think and the net result of her thoughts was the acknowledgement that Ryan was probably going to get his way, and there didn't seem a lot she could, or wanted to, do about it, despite the unsolved problem of whether she could take the risk of falling in love with a man such as he.

Then, on the second day that he was away, two things happened in quick succession. First, Sandra Bailey came to call and Mary, looking awkward, led her into the library and left them together, saying that she would bring them coffee.

'Hello,' Honor said uncertainly.

'Hello, Honor,' Sandra replied quietly. 'I hope you don't mind me doing this. I virtually—' she grimaced '—had to be searched before I was allowed in.'

'Oh, that's because—well, I suppose you know why I'm here, Mrs Bailey.'

'Yes—please call me Sandra, Honor.' She looked around. 'This room turned out well although I disagreed with Ryan about the necessity for it.' She moved some packing material from a chair and sat down.

'So you lived here?' Honor heard herself say before she could stop herself.

'Only for a year. It really hasn't got much of my imprint but then…I didn't do very well at leaving any kind of an imprint at all on Ryan. My uncle tells me you're…"staving him off" were his words, actually. Ryan.'

She looked enquiringly at Honor out of pale, rather haunted blue eyes. Once again she was perfectly groomed and expensively dressed, and she looked younger than her thirty-three years; in fact there was something oddly girlish about her, Honor decided.

She said, 'Forgive me, Sandra, but your uncle should know better than to meddle in other people's affairs.'

'I know.' Sandra looked down and smoothed her skirt. 'To be honest, I think he's using you to make me, well, forget about Ryan once and for all.'

'But that's something you can't do?' Honor said after a moment.

'I thought I had,' Sandra said softly, then she straightened. 'Yes, I have. I know it couldn't work; it never really did.'

'Then why—' Honor hesitated but found that she had to ask the question '—are you doing this to yourself? I mean, leaving *me* out of it, and I'm certainly not, well, his mistress—why?'

'Because, you see,' Sandra said thoughtfully, 'sometimes I just can't get it out of my mind that *once* there was something about me that attracted him deeply. And I wonder then if I could only...find that person that was me again...

'Oh, you probably think I'm very foolish but that's the way it is. Only, when I see you...'

She shrugged and gestured. 'Oh, I do know how foolish it is. You seem so right for him, so much better for him. You're far more intelligent than I am; you're decisive and...everything I'm not. So perhaps Uncle Brad was right.

'Have I said something wrong?' She looked at Honor, wide-eyed.

For Honor was, quite unwittingly, looking appalled at the thought of this woman, or any woman for that matter, spending fifteen years of her life hopelessly in love with the one man who was quite wrong for her.

'No.' She gathered herself. 'Well, yes. Look, it's not a question of being better at all; I'm only different. And I'm not at all sure that I'm right for Ryan either or vice versa—but look, there's got to be a right man for you, Sandra. Oh—' she closed her eyes briefly '—how to say this so you can believe that I'm being impartial?'

'You mean you're trying to tell me how wrong I am for him?' Sandra smiled a wise, sad little smile. 'It's nothing new. But I sometimes think that there is no right woman for Ryan, you know. Because there are times when he just shuts off and you can't get through to him at all.

'I suppose, though, now that he's turned forty he'll be thinking about someone to leave all this to. It would be a pity…if there was no one.

'What I really came to tell you,' she added, and stood up, 'was that I knew this would happen one day, and you have my blessing, Honor.'

'Sandra.' She thought for a time because, if she were honest, she was a bit lost for words. 'Will you do me a favour?' she said suddenly.

'Of course.'

'Instead of thinking you're not right for him, *please* look at it this way for a change—that he simply wasn't the right one for *you*; that he wasn't *good* enough for you; he didn't know how to be quiet for you or to be gentle or to enjoy the kind of things you enjoy. He didn't understand your values; he didn't understand *you*.

'Don't let the fact that he's made millions,' she said intently, 'invest him with all sorts of virtues and wisdom which he doesn't possess. In fact he probably achieved a lot of it by riding over people like a steam-shovel. I don't admire him for that, and neither should you.'

Sandra stared at her, transfixed, but what she would

have said Honor was destined not to know because Mary rejoined them with news of another visitor.

'It's the police,' she said. 'I haven't made the coffee yet but—'

'Don't worry, I'm not staying,' Sandra murmured, coming to life. 'Goodbye, Honor.'

'Sandra—' But the older woman almost ran from the room. Honor closed her eyes and thought, What have I done now?

'Miss Lingard?'

'Uh—yes, Mary. Ask them to come in here if you wouldn't mind.

'Well, what's he been up to now?' she enquired, on a bright but brittle note, of the detective that Mary ushered into the library.

'I'm very happy to say that he's behind bars, ma'am,' he replied, 'but we would like you to pick him out from an identity parade. I believe Mr Bailey is out of town?'

Honor sat down abruptly. 'You mean you've finally caught him? What a relief!'

The detective grimaced. 'We didn't actually catch him. He—er—turned himself in.'

She stared at him then started to laugh. 'I'm sorry,' she said finally. 'Why did he do that?'

'He's more than a little mad, ma'am. He said all he wanted to do was get back to painting his great masterpieces. He also sent his apologies.'

She blinked a couple of times then said anxiously, 'I don't have to come face to face with him, do I? Now, I mean?'

'No, ma'am. We'll do a line-up but he won't be able to see you. It's just a formality.'

*   *   *

Nevertheless when Honor got back to the house she felt physically drained as well as curiously saddened by Mark Markham's docile eagerness to please and she found herself wondering, despite all the havoc and destruction he'd wrought, whether there was any cure for his mania.

Still, she thought, at least I'm not bound to this house any longer—and went suddenly still as all that had passed between her and Sandra that morning flooded back to her. And she discovered that she was suddenly possessed of an unease of mind and heart that there appeared to be only one solution to—to put a bit of space between herself and Ryan Bailey.

'Mr Bailey won't like this, Miss Lingard,' Mary said with concern. 'I felt bad enough as it was when you left the last time!'

'But this time there's no danger, Mary. And, really, I can come and go as I like.'

'I know that but, well…' Mary looked supremely worried. 'I know it's not my place to say it but it's a bit like running away from him sort of and—he might not like it.'

'He's going to have to put up with it, however,' Honor said drily but her gaze softened. 'I can't thank you enough for the way you've treated me, Mary, but, well, there it is—I just need to get away from him for a bit.'

'Is it…is it anything to do with Mrs Bailey?' Mary asked tentatively.

'No,' Honor lied, but was struck by a thought. 'I don't suppose it's any good asking you not to mention Mrs Bailey's visit? No, I thought not.' She answered her own question with a grimace as Mary looked stubborn suddenly. 'Forget I even mentioned it—'

'I know he's a hard man sometimes,' Mary overrode her doggedly, 'but he's not a bad man.'

'And I think he's very lucky to have someone as loyal as you, Mary,' Honor replied. 'Look, I won't just walk out this time; I'll leave him a note—but that's my last offer,' she said with an attempt at humour.

'Dear Ryan'... Honor chewed the end of her pen and decided that she didn't feel like addressing him thus; it didn't sound right. So she screwed up that bit of paper and decided not to address him at all. She wrote:

I'm taking a few days off; hope you don't mind. Now that Mr Markham is in custody I feel quite safe. Thank you very much for all you've done and, to be honest, as Mary said, it does seem a bit as if I'm running away from you, but I'd still rather be sure about what I feel for you than sorry. Regards...

She reread it a couple of times, grimaced at its inadequacies but, as a vision of Sandra Bailey's haunted blue eyes came to mind, tossed her head and sealed it into an envelope. And she left in a taxi again but this time with Mary's anxious expression also to mind and a feeling of guilt that she was unable to shake off.

But once home she thought, All the same, I'm not going to sit around here feeling guilty—as well as wondering what he's going to do. I will *really* go away for a few days, right now, in case he comes home today.

Accordingly, she booked herself into a seaside resort on the Sunshine Coast for three nights and drove herself up there that afternoon.

But as the next day wore on it became ironically and infuriatingly clear that she was not going to be able to resolve anything in her mind. Was he the kind of man who would always cut himself off and put business and making money first? Even if reason dictated that Sandra was her own worst enemy, how could she, Honor, live with the thought of her and her sadness at the back of her mind?

And, of course, she mused, there's always the bottom line that if things don't work for us I might end up all forlorn and... Is it really possible?

She stared unseeingly at the horizon and realised with an inward shiver that she was definitely afraid of that prospect. Which means? she wondered. Has it already happened? Have I already fallen in love, in other words? Is it not an amazing burden to be stuck up here, wondering what he's doing, what he's thinking?

And she jumped up, suddenly feeling incredibly stifled and discontented with the lovely surrounds of the resort, the beach and the ocean, feeling contemptuous of the pleasant, lazy two days that lay ahead of her and knowing that she couldn't spend one more hour doing nothing but grappling with her thoughts. She drove back to Brisbane that afternoon.

But there she was presented with another problem. What did she do now—go and see him, or simply go back to work the next morning? 'Or send him a letter of resignation and—leave the country?' she murmured aloud, but suddenly remembered her expired passport which caused her to mutter something unprintable, then toss her head and reach for the phone.

It was Mary she got, who told her rather primly that Mr Bailey was still in Sydney and he wasn't sure how much longer he would be away.

'Did he...was he...very angry?' she asked cautiously

at the same time as she castigated herself inwardly for sinking to these depths and wished devoutly that things could be more private between her and Ryan.

'He didn't say, Miss Lingard,' Mary answered, 'but he did mention that if you should get in touch it would be helpful to know if you'd got those masks and things to exhibition stage yet, because the man who sent them to him is due in Brisbane in about a fortnight and looking forward to seeing them on display. Some Minister or other from Papua New Guinea.'

For a second Honor was speechless. Mary continued after a polite pause, 'He got me and Warren to pack them up again and send them over to the office—he said to tell you that too.'

'Mary—'

'Oh, Miss Lingard—' Mary suddenly became much more human '—I did warn you, didn't I? You see, he's not the kind of man you can mess about with and, well, I saw with my own eyes that you and he...I mean—I shouldn't be saying this by rights but I do like you and...but, well...' She stopped agitatedly, then repeated herself. 'You just can't mess about with Mr Bailey.'

Oh, *can't* you? Honor thought but did not say. She said instead, with incredible control, 'Mary, I do appreciate your—concern. Thanks very much and don't worry about me.'

She put the phone down gently but picked up the phone book beside it and threw it across the room. Then she clenched her teeth and resolved upon a course of action that was, she told herself, probably insane but, all the same, it was about time that somebody taught Ryan Bailey a lesson and there was no one better to do it than herself.

*   *   *

She dressed with extra care the next morning, choosing a pale ginger linen dress, straight and double-breasted with short sleeves and a short skirt, a square neckline and two rows of gold buttons. With it she wore sheer flesh-coloured stockings and a pair of brown leather shoes with little wooden Cuban heels.

She painted her lips a bronzy pink and put a beautiful old rose-gold watch-chain round her neck. Her hair was dark, smooth and glossy, and her usually pale skin now golden enough so that her freckles hardly showed.

Smart but businesslike, she told her reflection, then wondered why it mattered. Because it does, she answered herself fiercely—and went off to work in the same mood.

Her reappearance at Bailey House caused quite a stir. Everyone she met stopped to ask her some question or other and welcome her back. What had it been like stuck on an island with Mr Bailey? was the most frequent question but she did register the fact that no one asked her what it had been like stuck in a house with Mr Bailey.

She could only assume that that hadn't been allowed to become common knowledge, which she was grateful for but a little cynical about. The only reason it hadn't might have been a security-orientated one, she mused at the same time as she resolutely ignored the scarcely veiled speculation that she saw in many eyes.

And she'd only been in her office for five minutes when Pam Myer rang. 'Honor! Welcome back.'

'Thanks, Pam. How did you know?'

'At least ten people have popped in to tell me.'

'I can imagine,' she said drily down the line. 'Uh—is there any problem about me being back?'

'Not at all. Why should there be?'

'I just wondered. I haven't seen Mr Bailey for a while.'

'He's in Sydney,' Pam confided. 'But he did ask me to let you know when you came back to work that he'd be very obliged if you could—'

'Get to work on the Papuan artefacts exhibition,' Honor completed for her. 'Do tell him I'm getting stuck *right* into it, Pam.'

'All right,' Pam said slowly as if she suspected the irony behind Honor's words but couldn't work out how to deal with it. And she finished the call by saying only, 'It's great to have you back safe and sound, Honor.'

'Thanks, Pam.' She put down the phone feeling a bit ashamed, then spent the whole day in the storeroom where the artefacts were, completing her catalogue.

At a quarter to five she decided to call it a day, gathered her papers and walked through the reception area back to her office, or would have done if Ryan hadn't come in through the outer doors, accompanied by Bill Fortune, right in her path so that she was forced to stop as they both stopped.

'Hello, Mr Bailey,' the receptionist said brightly into this sudden impasse. 'How was your trip?'

Ryan allowed his shockingly insolent grey gaze to rest on Honor for a second longer before turning to her and saying, 'Tiring, thanks, Heather. I see we have Miss Lingard returned to the fold.'

'Yes, she came back this morning,' the receptionist replied, but not as brightly as before—in fact with a degree of uncertainty in her voice and an awkward look on her face at his tone.

'How fortunate we are,' her boss said with gentle but lethal mockery. 'Well, Honor—' that smoky grey gaze returned to her '—if you'd give me fifteen minutes to wrap things up with Bill I'd like to see you in my office.'

Two things registered in her mind—a disturbing awareness of Ryan that for the life of her she couldn't believe could exist at the same time as she was so angry with him, and the determination that she was not going to be held to ransom. In other words, if he could bait her publicly like this she would respond in kind.

So she glanced at her watch coolly and said, 'Only if you'd care to pay me overtime, Mr Bailey. I'm due to knock off in fifteen minutes.'

'By all means,' he replied easily. 'I'd be interested to know how you value your—after-hours services, Miss Lingard. Quite highly, I should imagine,' he drawled, and allowed a glance of unmistakable calculation and intent to roam up and down her figure.

Bill closed his eyes and took a few embarrassed paces away. Heather allowed her mouth to drop open unbecomingly, and Honor stepped forward with every intention of slapping his face.

But no sooner had she raised her hand than she dropped it and said quite audibly, even sweetly, 'There are some things even you can't buy, Mr Bailey, and I just happen to be one of them.'

And for one short instant she had the pleasure of seeing pure anger in his eyes, but the enjoyment was short-lived as he said very quietly through his teeth, 'I can carry you scratching, kicking and biting to my office if you *like*, Honor, or you can come quietly. Bill, I'll see you tomorrow,' he said, briefly raising his voice, and turned back to Honor. 'Well?'

She discovered that she was shaking as the door closed behind them. 'You've got to be the biggest bastard I've ever met!' she accused, rounding on him with her fists clenched.

'I could return the compliment,' he said curtly. 'You're certainly one of the most difficult, contrary women I've ever met, if not a downright termagant. Or is it something else with you, Honor?' he said as he dumped his briefcase on his desk and shrugged his jacket off with rough impatience.

'What do you mean?' she demanded.

'Well, what do *you* mean by turning back up here for work your usual immaculate self?' he said with withering scorn and a raking grey glance.

'I don't understand...'

'Don't you? I think you do. How better to tease and torment the life out of a man—is that what you are— one of those eternal teases? The kind of woman who actually gets her thrills that way?' he said contemptuously.

She paled but replied vigorously, 'Oh, no, I'm not! That has got to be another of those hoary old, much cherished male beliefs—it's got to be the oldest and tritest!'

'I've told you before about these trite but true things,' he murmured with fleeting amusement, but his eyes hardened immediately. 'So what are you doing back here—trying to teach me some kind of a lesson?'

It was useless to deny it; the way her colour fluctuated told its own story so she set her teeth and said baldly, 'Yes.'

'This is interesting,' he murmured, and went round his desk to sprawl out in his chair. He loosened his tie. 'Do tell me what kind of lessons I need to be taught, Honor.'

She regarded him in a fairly raging kind of way for

several seconds then forced herself to think. 'Look here,' she said at last, and resolutely ignored the faint smile that twisted his lips, 'I was perfectly entitled to do what I did and I can't help it if I dented your pride, Ryan. On the other hand, when I discovered that I had, *obviously*, I thought, Oh, well, if it's back to employer and employee, so be it!'

'At the same time as you got yourself ready for a fight, *obviously*,' he said with ironic emphasis. 'Honor, I hate to say this, because it is another old truism, but I think you're in some danger of becoming a frustrated spinster, you know. And if you'd let me make love to you I'm sure I could prove that.

'But in the meantime, if you've fought me enough for one day, would you mind if I—retired behind the ropes? I'm a little weary.' He smiled at her blandly. 'But I'll try to be—er—fitter for our next encounter.'

'Well, I wouldn't count on it, Ryan,' she said in a low, choking voice, and swung on her heel.

But, weary or not, he must have risen swiftly because he reached her before she got to the door and pulled her unceremoniously into his arms, saying in quite a different voice, 'Or is it something else entirely, Honor? Are you the kind of woman who likes to be overpowered and taken against her will? At least, the kind of woman who persuades herself she has been so that she can then abrogate all responsibility in the matter?

She fought several reactions—horror that he could seriously think that of her, panic because she suddenly realised how afraid she was of him touching her now in case she gave herself away, and, still, a blazing sense of hostility.

But as the reflection of all these emotions chased through her eyes he laughed softly and murmured, 'Dear

Honor, for the next few minutes you can teach me or tease me, fight me or hate me, but there's one thing I know you don't hate and that's me kissing you.

'Which is why, if you'll forgive me, I find the rest of it a little hard to take. After all, it's not as if I've ever forced these kinds of attentions on you before—'

'But you're going to now!' she whispered.

'I doubt it,' he said briefly, and started to kiss her.

It got out of hand, just as she'd feared, much as she tried to resist him and resist her seemingly instinctive response to him. She found herself filled with a quivering sort of tension as she stood mutely in the circle of his arms, not knowing whether to bite, scratch and kick, knowing it would be useless anyway as well as terribly undignified.

And while all these thoughts chased through her mind his hands moved on her body and his mouth roamed at will from her shut lips down the side of her throat...

The tension in her became a different sort. It slowly refocused itself from centring on the sheer injustice of the situation to a kind of thirst and hunger that was both devastating yet undeniable. And she knew suddenly just how long it had been hovering at the back of her mind, resolutely buried even after his two previous embraces— since that first clash in this very office.

But the sheer power and force of it stunned her because it was as if she were an inexperienced girl with her first man, yet at the same time a woman who could give, if she chose, just the kind of delight which he was inflicting on her.

What if I do choose? she thought dimly. What if I can't then ever choose differently—what if I'm hooked on this, on him? It never even occurred to me that that might happen to me before—those two times I thought I was in love...

But even these compelling thoughts faded as he held her hard against him and, this time, her lips parted beneath the pressure of his as her thighs and hips were moulded to his, her breasts crushed against him and a wave of sheer desire flowed through her.

They broke apart briefly and she found herself leaning against the door, her head back, her breathing erratic, their gazes locked.

Then he put his hands on the door on either side of her and simply watched the way her breasts rose and fell beneath the ginger linen, and how a pulse beat at the base of her throat. And she felt her body answering for her as her pulses leapt, felt the way the tall, slim length of her seemed to be designed for this one man, seemed somehow to cry out to be his property...

She licked her lips and said barely audibly, 'I don't...altogether understand this so—'

'I know,' he answered equally quietly. 'Do you think I haven't always known?'

'What?' she whispered.

'That there was an untouched, rather naïve side to you, Honor Lingard, in this respect.'

'I—'

'No, we've said enough.' And he slid his hands down to cup her shoulders, then further down to her hips, and she knew it was going to happen—the very thing he'd suggested that first time—that he was going to slide her dress up and cradle her hips while she leant against the door, seemingly rooted to the spot.

He did just that while their eyes never left each other and her breathing grew more ragged and what she tried to say died on her lips because the feel of his hands, slipping beneath her briefs and under her suspenders, was so shockingly, rapturously intimate that she could only close her eyes and make a strange, husky little sound in her throat as every nerve-ending she possessed clamoured for more, and she felt herself grow warm and wet with desire.

'Honor?'

'Don't,' she gasped, and shuddered suddenly in an unmistakable release that left her totally stunned.

He withdrew his hands, smoothed her skirt down and searched her wide, supremely dazed eyes, and she thought he sighed. A terrible flood of embarrassment engulfed her so that she wrenched herself free, stared at him, panic-stricken, for a moment, then reached for the door before he could stop her and slipped round it.

Her only consolation was that there was no one about, and that he didn't attempt to follow her.

CHAPTER EIGHT

ONCE home Honor did something quite uncharacteristic. She poured herself a brandy and drank half of it before setting the glass down on her dining-table and taking several deep breaths.

Then she went and had a shower, put on a cool, silky robe patterned with pink and yellow fluffy chrysanthemums on a pale green background, and started to concoct a light meal. The one thing she could not do was force herself to *think*—beyond what her hands were doing.

Nor, for reasons that she would never be able to fathom, did it occur to her that it would be Ryan Bailey ringing her doorbell just as her omelette was rising beautifully. In fact she was quite sure it was a friend who'd left a note beneath the door while she'd been away to say that she'd call back another evening.

All the same, she was tempted to ignore the bell but knew she'd feel guilty because her lights were visible from the road and from the passageway. So she gritted her teeth and went to answer it, trying to think up an excuse she could make to send her away, but once again the words died on her lips as she saw who was silhouetted in her doorway.

'No...' It was a whispered, half-choked sound she made.

But he said unemotionally, 'Yes, Honor. We're going

to resolve this now. There was nothing *wrong* with what happened, nothing to be ashamed of, and I refuse to allow it to assume heaven alone knows what kind of proportions in your mind.' He took the door from her grasp, closed it, and took her straight into his arms. 'Because you see,' he murmured, into her hair, 'if I affect you that way it's nothing less than what you do to me.'

And five heart-stopping minutes later he finished kissing her—but only, he said, because there was a distinct smell of burning in the air.

'Oh, my omelette!' She gasped, and he released her and followed her into the kitchen where they surveyed the blackened mound in the pan together. It was he who switched the hotplate off and carried the pan to the sink, he who suggested with a faint smile that perhaps they could do with a drink. It was she who said self-consciously that she'd already got one.

'Then may I join you?' he asked wryly.

So she led him into the living-room, poured him a brandy and took up her own half-finished drink awkwardly.

'Come here,' he said quietly, sitting down on her sofa.

She hesitated, then went to sit down beside him.

'Why don't you talk to me, Honor?' he suggested. 'Say what's on your mind.'

She thought for a bit, her colour fluctuating, then said abruptly, 'I thought you sighed.' He raised an eyebrow at her. Pleating the silky fabric of her robe, she continued, 'After... And you didn't follow me.'

His lips twisted. '*I* thought you'd rather I didn't chase you round the office.'

'Much rather,' she agreed. 'But...' She shrugged.

'If I sighed,' he said after a moment, 'it was because

you were so stunned and…uncomprehending, that's all. It was not because I was in any way—disapproving.'

'I didn't think that,' she said tartly, then bit her lip.

He laid his head back. 'So it was yourself you disapproved of?'

She said nothing but got up and went to the window where she stared out into the darkness for a few minutes, taking the odd sip of her drink.

'I suppose so,' she said finally, and turned, with her chin up. 'Perhaps you're right; perhaps there is a rather foolish and naïve side of me, but it's not very comfortable to feel…'

He got up like a big, prowling panther and said softly, 'Honor, look, it's just this.' He took her glass out of her hand. 'It's the chemistry between us, the wonderful charge that goes off between a man and a woman who attract each other. If you don't admit one other thing at least admit this. And if you don't believe how involved I am, let me *show* you.'

Some minutes later he'd eased her robe off her shoulders and his lips were wandering at will over her bare skin. All she had on beneath the robe was a pair of panties.

'Freckles everywhere,' he commented lightly, cupping her shoulders.

'You know that,' she whispered. 'You've seen me in my bra and pants.'

'Only briefly.' He paused, then slipped the robe down further. The loosely tied sash came apart and the garment flowed open down the length of her. 'And never like this. But then I knew I wouldn't be disappointed.' And he gazed at her breasts for a long moment before lifting his eyes to hers. 'May I touch?'

Honor's lips parted because the request was unexpected and almost unbearably bittersweet—a light, humorous gesture from a big, powerful man which touched her heart... She closed her eyes and said very quietly, 'Yes. Please.'

'But before I do—you know where this has to lead, don't you, Honor?'

'To bed?' Her lashes flicked up and an oddly wry little glint lit her eyes. 'In that respect I've fought you about as far as I can go, Ryan.'

'I'm so relieved to hear you say that, Honor,' he replied gravely. 'I was beginning to acquire an inferiority complex.'

She chuckled, a deep little sound. 'That's something I find hard to believe.' But she sobered as they stared into each other's eyes. 'One thing.'

He took her hands and it was his turn to smile fleetingly. 'Can I guess? You're not about to commit yourself to anything beyond the moment?'

She coloured but her dark gaze remained steady. 'No.'

'That's what I thought—it's fine with me. Beggars can't be choosers, can they?'

He slid his big hands down her body beneath the robe and her breath jolted in her throat; at last she lifted her own hands and all of a sudden wound her arms round his neck, pressing her brow into his shoulder.

'I don't know who's really doing the begging—but the bedroom's that way,' she whispered.

She felt the laughter reverberating through his big frame, then he swept her into his arms, picked her up and carried her to the bedroom.

She lay on her bed where he placed her, after slipping off her robe, and closed her eyes as he undressed. Then he lay down beside her and said, 'We've done this a few times—lain in each other's arms.'

'Mmm—that island seems so long ago.'

'I know.' He stroked her.

'Do you think they'll charge him?'

'I doubt it.'

'You know, I don't know why it didn't strike me at the time—but there's a bit of Vincent Van Gogh in him—in his style as well as his red hair and his mental instability.'

'Perhaps that's who he was modelling himself on.'

She smiled and took an involuntary breath. 'That's... lovely.'

'It's lovely for me too. I—like your bedroom.'

She opened her eyes at last and looked around. It was a spacious room and she'd had the walls painted a chalky lavender-blue. The double bed, which had been her mother's and father's, had curved cherrywood ends and the bedlinen, coverlet and carpet were all in ivory.

There was a matching cherrywood dressing-table with a framed mirror, an exquisite walnut writing-table and a chair in front of the window, and behind the bed the whole wall was hung with paintings, prints and photos framed in gold. A brass hatstand stood in one corner with all her hats on it, like exotic fruit. The clothes she'd discarded that evening lay carelessly thrown over a cedar chest.

'It's not—cloying,' he said quietly, and continued to stroke her body.

'No,' she breathed. 'I always had a vision of a bed-room like this but opening on to a lovely garden. Ryan...' She closed her eyes again.

'Tell me if I'm doing anything wrong,' he murmured.

'It's not that,' she whispered, then turned and clung to him convulsively as he slid her pants over her thighs.

'What is it?'

'It's too nice,' she managed to say wryly.

'Well, it's exquisite for me.' He gathered her close and ran his hands down her back, then started to kiss her until she was breathless and quivering.

But that was as nothing to how she felt when he took one nipple between his teeth and bit it gently. She arched her body, drew up one leg and drew her fingers down his back urgently, saying hoarsely, 'Don't do that to me again…'

Then she bit her lip as she felt his hands on the pale, satiny flesh at the tops of her thighs.

'Not a chance,' he replied unevenly. 'I've had about all the abstinence I can stand.' And he placed her on her back, said very quietly, 'Forgive me, Honor,' and possessed her finally.

She woke several hours later and had the strange notion that she was floating above the bed, close to the ceiling, which caused her to gasp and Ryan to move sleepily beside her and hold her in his arms. 'What's wrong?'

'Nothing.' She buried her face against his shoulder.

'Tell me, Honor.'

So she told him and added, 'Is that the effect you have on me?'

He kissed the corner of her mouth. 'How about the effect you have on me?'

'Tell me…' she whispered.

'Well, I'm all set and rarin' to go again.'

'I…so you are…'

'Do you mind?'

'No, I don't mind…' And she accepted him into her body again with the same soaring result that was not new now but something that was…a kind of abandonment in her that she'd never known before, a kind of true, delicate, yet growingly unselfconscious acceptance of the things he did to her, a budding sense of equality that took her by surprise but didn't fade.

And when they lay, sated at last, in a tangle of arms and legs she felt a kind of fulfilment that was like nothing she'd ever known, and was increased by the thought of spending a whole night in his arms.

'Unfortunately,' he said after a while, 'I should go.'

She moved abruptly. 'No, don't. I...like sleeping with you.'

'It's not that I don't like sleeping with you but—'

'Then why?' She sat up, ran her fingers through her hair and looked imperiously down at him.

He lifted a hand and traced the blue veins that threaded beneath the skin of her breasts, then laid the back of his hand beneath their weight, bouncing them gently. 'Well, my car is parked right in front of this building for one thing, Miss Lingard,' he said wryly.

She took a breath. 'Oh.' She lay back.

'Which normally wouldn't mean much but...' He paused.

'We could become famous,' she said rather drily.

'Honor—'

'No, no.' She sat up again. 'I can imagine how I would feel, trailing out at the crack of dawn, on top of everything else.'

'I did tell you it could happen this way round, didn't I?'

She looked at him narrowly. 'I don't...'

'That I could become one of your men,' he said perfectly gravely. 'After all, this is your house.'

Her lips quirked. 'If you're trying to make me feel foolish, Ryan, you're succeeding. Famous last words,' she marvelled reminiscently, then sobered. 'What will we do?'

'Come back here.'

She subsided into his arms and he kissed her hair. 'How about taking it as it comes for a while?'

'All right.' But she wondered if he'd caught the faintly desolate note in her voice.

If he had he said nothing but held her gently and she had time to reflect that she was the one who had insisted that she should not be made to commit herself to any more, with no inkling at the time that later she was virtually going to beg him to stay the night with her...

She said suddenly, 'Do you still want me to work for you?'

'Not particularly—and I only say that, Honor,' he said as she tensed, 'in the context of being in the same office with you—that kind of thing—while we try to shield this from public scrutiny. Unless you *don't* mind—'

'I do,' she said very quietly. Then she made herself smile as she added, 'It would be much simpler if you were—ordinary. Perhaps—well, after the Papuan exhibition, anyway—perhaps I could work from home?'

'Why not?'

'I'll try to stay out of your way until then.'

'You won't succeed—'

'I mean in the office!'

'All right. But would you consider coming to spend the weekend with me?'

'Yes, Ryan,' she said softly. 'I don't think I could keep myself away,' she added honestly.

'How about having the strength of will, then, to banish me from this bed before I—change my mind?'

She groaned and hugged him urgently for a moment, then pushed the covers aside and got up. 'Never let it be said that I'm weak-willed. I'll have a quick shower first and make you some coffee.'

'Honor.' He caught her wrist.

'What?'

His remarkable grey eyes were lazy, she saw, but humorous. 'Nothing. I just couldn't resist the opportunity to have you bend over me with nothing on, my beautiful, strong-willed lover.'

She bent lower and kissed him lightly on the mouth. 'Then make the best of it because I'm going!' And she twisted free and ran to the bathroom.

The apartment was aromatic with coffee when he came out of the bedroom, doing up his tie.

Honor hadn't dressed again; she'd put her robe on and now poured the coffee quietly.

'Thanks,' he murmured as she handed him a cup. 'Are you all right?'

She raised her face to him and didn't know that she had faint blue shadows beneath her eyes and lines of weariness beside her mouth. 'Fine.'

Something touched his mouth—she couldn't have said what except that it wasn't humour. He said lightly, 'When can I see you again?'

'I'm not sure,' she said huskily. 'What is it now? Thursday—well, it soon will be.' She looked at her grandfather clock across the room.

'Would you come to the house on Saturday morning, then?' he suggested. 'I've got business dinners tomorrow and Friday night—unless...?' He raised an eyebrow at her.

For a moment she was almost unbearably tempted to say yes but something held her back. 'No. Thanks.'

'Or I could come here afterwards.'

She smiled mechanically and sipped her coffee for strength. 'Saturday.'

He picked up her free hand, formed it into a fist and kissed her knuckles. 'So be it—Saturday. Come as early as you can. I'm going to go now.'

'Goodbye,' she whispered.

But he would have none of that. He wrested her cup from her and took her in his arms. 'You know you wouldn't feel happy doing this any other way, don't you, Honor?' he said into her hair.

'Yes,' she answered shakily. 'Don't take any notice of me.'

'Then will you give me your word that you won't run out on me between now and Saturday?'

'I *didn't*—'

'Honor,' he said gently but firmly.

'All right…'

'Good, that's a promise; don't forget. Why don't you go back to bed?'

'I will. As soon as you've gone.'

'Incidentally, there's no earthly reason why we shouldn't communicate on the phone in the interim.' He stood her away and smiled into her eyes. 'I'll ring you tomorrow evening at six.'

'Yes… Oh, I feel like an idiot!' But she clung to him for a moment longer, then released herself and smiled wryly up at him. 'Off you go.'

She waited until she heard the Lamborghini start up, then she did go back to the crumpled bed, making no attempt to straighten it. And she folded her naked body into the sheets and placed her head on the pillow that still bore the imprint of his as if she could fold herself back into his arms, and lay for a while, staring into the dark, thinking now as she'd been unable to do earlier.

She thought of her own foolish refusal to see him over the next few days and how, quite contrary to its implication, she felt bereft and lonely, *deprived*—yes, deprived, she thought unhappily, because he was not there beside her.

What have I become? she wondered. Who would ever have thought Honor Lingard would come to this? Not I, she answered herself ironically. I was always the one who made space for myself, who never clung.

Is that what's going to happen to me from now on? That I'm going to have to accept *his* space? 'And watch him shut himself off from me?' she asked herself aloud, remembering Sandra all of a sudden with a little lurch of fear in her heart.

Then something else occurred to her—that he'd not mentioned Sandra's visit, and she wondered why. But finally she fell asleep with nothing resolved other than that she was a changed person...

It was an effort to get herself to work the next morning. She also thought she looked pale and heavy-eyed and, by a total *lack* of fortune, the first person she ran into was Bill Fortune.

'Honor!' He greeted her with a grin. 'Did you sock it to him last night?'

'I...not exactly,' she murmured, hardly pausing in her stride down the corridor towards her office at the same time as she marvelled at the fact that she'd quite forgotten, in the enormity of what had happened to her afterwards, the scene of the previous afternoon.

'Tell me more!' Bill kept up with her avidly.

She sighed and stopped. 'We've come to an agreement, Bill. That is, we've agreed to disagree about nearly everything except art.' She grimaced, and added, 'On these premises.'

'Good for you. I mean, while I admire the man tremendously, I like to see someone with a bit of spunk take him on. On the other hand…' he paused and looked at her searchingly '…don't fall in love with him, will you?'

She gasped.

'Because I happen to know,' he went on soberly, 'that he eats, sleeps and drinks business; he's really a machine, not a man. You see, I've been with him for a long time now—I *know*. I also know enough about the women around him to see the signs, although in your case it's certainly been more—enlivening than the usual get-him-to-the-altar-quick attitude.

'But I'll not say another word! See you, Honor.'

She shut herself into her office thankfully and wondered a little wildly about Bill. He was about Ryan's age, she guessed, married to a rather colourless woman with little style, and they had three or four children, she thought.

Her ponderings were interrupted by the phone and the caller proved to be someone from the distributors of the glass display-cases that she needed for the exhibition; the ensuing conversation helped to take her mind off things.

In fact she didn't stop one way or another until about four in the afternoon, and then she received another call in her office—from Pam this time…

'Honor, Mr Bailey has asked me to ask you if, providing you have a few minutes to spare, you'd mind seeing him in his office.'

'Now?' she said uncertainly.

'Uh-huh, but only if you're free.'

'All...all right.'

He was lounging behind his desk in his shirt-sleeves but he stood up as she came in and for a moment they just stared at each other across the wide expanse of his desk.

Then he said quietly, 'I couldn't wait until Saturday. I couldn't even wait to hear your voice on the phone.'

'Oh, Ryan.' Something like a shuddering sigh ran through her, then they were in each other's arms. 'I've missed you,' she said foolishly, rubbing her cheek against his shoulder.

'Good,' he said lightly. 'I mean, so long as I wasn't alone.'

'No. No.'

He kissed her deeply, then looked at her with a wicked little glint in his eye. 'I'd like to go a lot further but I shall desist—somehow or other.'

'You'd better!' she warned, but with a grin. 'It's bad enough as it is. What if Pam comes in?' She glanced apprehensively over her shoulder towards the door.

'Pam won't,' he said definitely. 'I've told her—no interruptions at all.'

'Well, that should add plenty of fuel to the flames,' she said ruefully.

'What do you mean?' He looked down at her narrowly.

She opened her mouth to tell him about Bill but decided not to and said only, 'People talking.'

He released her but then took her hand and led her to the Barcelona chairs, waited until she was seated, then said, 'Would it be such a disaster if our names got linked? Seeing that they more or less are anyway.'

She opened her mouth, closed it, then said, 'Would you sit down, Ryan? I feel as if I'm being towered over.'

He sat opposite her and pushed a few things round the table between them.

'No, I don't suppose so,' she said slowly. 'It's... almost impossible like this anyway.' Their gazes locked. 'But you yourself said last night that I wouldn't feel right doing things any other way.'

'I wondered if you might see things differently this morning.'

A little jolt ran through her, a suspicion that what had happened the night before might have been a test—which she'd failed miserably, she reminded herself. She'd virtually had to be prised off...

So what did he mean? She stared at the objects he'd moved around—two magazines, a chunky crystal ashtray and a small silver model of Bailey House—then raised her eyes to his abruptly.

'You're trying to tell me that I'm being ridiculous, aren't you?'

'To my mind there's nothing ridiculous about you at all, Honor. I wouldn't be sleeping with you, I wouldn't have been unable to resist seeing you now if there were. But, despite the unfortunate curiosity that anyone in a position like this generates, is it really anyone's business but our own? I'm not suggesting that we flaunt ourselves, precisely.'

She stared into his level grey eyes and wondered if he had any concept of what it might be like to be written up in the social columns as someone who had once had a liaison with Ryan Bailey.

'I don't do much socialising other than for business reasons, Honor,' he said then as if he could read her thoughts. 'And the Press well know it's useless to hound me.'

'Well, what are you suggesting?' she asked huskily after a long moment. 'That it doesn't matter if your Lamborghini spends many a night outside my apartment?'

'No. I'm suggesting you move in with me.'

Her lips parted.

'Because that way,' he said, 'we could spend as much time together as possible. It would be a way to minimise the dislocation caused by the inevitable time I have to spend out of town. It would mean that where it was practicable you could come with me. It would mean,' he said with a sudden, dry little smile, 'quite a bit to my sanity.'

'Ryan—' her voice shook '—this is a big step but—' She stopped abruptly as her eyes fell on his hands and with cruel clarity she remembered just what had happened to her in this office only yesterday.

Oh, God, be careful, she warned herself. Don't abandon all your *own* sanity. Remember Sandra, remember…Bill Fortune. *Is* this man a machine or not, however he makes love to you and makes you feel? What would you really be letting yourself in for? A…compartment in his life, labelled 'mistress'? There and convenient whenever he has the time?

But the next thought that popped into her mind really shook her. Why doesn't he ask me to marry him? Why this…?

'Ryan, no,' she said, and didn't realise that her face had paled, although his eyes had narrowed and it was a piercing scrutiny that she was now subjected to. 'Um…please, let me try to explain.'

'Why don't you start by telling me how you felt when I left you last night?' he suggested.

She bit her lip but some little spurt of spirit came to her aid. 'All right, I will. Bereft,' she said honestly, 'as well as foolish, which doesn't mean to say I enjoy being tested out like that.'

'Honor—'

'No. *This* now, on top of what happened last night, is just too much. So...' She paused and wondered why she hurt so much inside, but made herself go on. 'Here's my offer. You're right—it's no one's business but our own and I can't go back and pretend I should never have slept with you. I...it...was something that consumed me and still does.

'So I'm prepared not to go to ridiculous lengths to hide it now; it wouldn't be honest, anyway. But I won't move in with you yet. I mean...' She twisted her hands. 'Well, I mean—'

'That I need to prove myself a lot more before you'll do that? How?' he queried. 'In bed?'

A bright splash of colour washed over her cheeks. 'No,' she said tautly.

'Then how, Honor?' he persisted, with a faint look of amusement at the back of his eyes.

She closed her eyes briefly and wondered how you could *ask* a man whether any woman would ever really get through to him, whether, even, he'd decided it was time to provide heirs for his name and empire, which was one aspect of the situation she'd simply not allowed herself to think about until now.

'Honor?' he prompted with a sudden edge of impatience.

That did it, though. Her lashes flew up and her eyes

were dark and defiant. 'Tell you what, Ryan, I'll let you know when you've achieved it.'

'Are we fighting each other again, Honor?' he said politely.

'That depends on how you take my offer,' she responded.

'Well, do you mean—' he looked at her thoughtfully '—that you'd come to one of these dinners tonight or tomorrow night?'

'I...' What have I done? she wondered.

'There's surely nothing compromising about being my guest at a business dinner?' he murmured, with an oddly sardonic little look lurking in his eyes.

'What,' she said with an effort, 'do you think we would achieve through it, though?'

'We'd be together for one thing. We could go home together—yours *or* mine. You wouldn't be sitting at home—alone.'

'All right,' she said abruptly. 'Tomorrow night.'

'And that's your last offer?' he said, his lips twisting. '*Yes.*'

'My dear Honor,' he said very softly, 'as well as longing to undress you and—do several other things I won't specify but which perhaps you can imagine, I have to tell you that I admire your spirit very much.'

She twisted her hands in her lap and suddenly her shoulders slumped. 'Do you?' she said desolately.

He got up and drew her to her feet. 'Of course. Would it be too much to ask if you reciprocated just a small part of that?'

She stared up into his eyes as he cupped her shoulders then ran his hands down her arms. And she trembled and was overwhelmed by his proximity, by the memory of him lying in her bed, long, tanned and strong with his dark hair awry, by the feeling that she was there again, lying beside him with his hands on the pale fullness of her breasts...

'Yes,' she said very quietly. 'Well, there are some things I do admire about you extremely.'

'The way I make love to you?' he suggested with a wryly raised eyebrow.

'That too. No, I'm not going to elaborate,' she said a little shakily. 'I'll reserve my accolades for other moments, I think.'

He grinned suddenly. 'I can't wait. Will you come home with me on Friday night?'

'Yes...'

'I'll pick you up at seven. Would you do me a favour? It's a very dressy do, this. Black tie et cetera. Would *you* wear black?'

'I did once before,' she said, and could have bitten her tongue. 'But only because I didn't have anything else.'

'I know; what a waste. These are not Japanese business people, incidentally, so you won't have to work so hard—it's a dinner dance for an American trade delegation.'

'Well,' she said, trying to hold her composure, which was being sorely tested by the way his hands were roaming her body, 'what about something that requires black underwear anyway?'

'That will do,' he said gravely. 'Are we friends?' He took her hands.

'Yes...'

Honor wore a tight, low-necked lace dress the colour of ripe mulberries with big puffed sleeves. It was the kind of gown you had to be quite tall to carry off and all she wore with it were tiny pearl studs in her ears and a pearl and amethyst bracelet. She carried an evening bag of matching mulberry taffeta embroidered with seed-pearls.

She was studying herself tensely in the mirror when Ryan rang the bell. So she switched off all the lights on her way to the front door, picked up her overnight bag and was all set to go as she opened the door.

For a moment they just gazed at each other as she took in how at home he looked in a dinner suit, bow-tie and blinding white shirt, at home, well-groomed, distinguished and relaxed. Then a faint smile lit the back of his eyes as he said gravely, 'Aren't you going to ask me in, Honor?'

'No, well, I didn't think of it—have we time?'

'About ten minutes.'

'That's not long. Is there any point?'

'Certainly.' And he took her overnight bag from her, steered her back into the lounge and switched on a lamp. 'Time to greet you, time to study you—which is a bit like studying a work of art, incidentally,' he said softly, his gaze roaming down the outline of her figure, her shining cap of dark hair, the smooth pale golden skin of her neck.

'Thank you,' she answered a trace stiffly.

'Did you make it?'

'No. Ryan—'

'Am I allowed to touch?'

'Well—'

'Gingerly? I wouldn't muss your make-up or disturb your hair.' And he put his hands on her waist. 'Are you regretting this?' he added quietly.

'I...' She bit her lip. 'I don't really know—how did *you* know?'

'I can generally tell—when those beautiful, severe lips

are set in an autocratic line, when your nose looks particularly classic and sculptured, when your head is held high and your eyes are haughty—that something is bothering you, Honor.'

She blinked, then smiled ruefully. 'Do I really look like that?'

'You do. It was one of the things that attracted me to you in the first place. I had the feeling that I was going to be put firmly in my place.'

'I don't think I've ever succeeded in doing that!'

'It's the trying that counts,' he murmured. 'Mmm, you smell delicious too. Shalimar?'

She agreed wryly and suddenly put her hands on his lapels. 'You're…looking good too.'

'Thank you, ma'am. I've got the feeling that I'm going to pale into insignificance beside you, however.'

'I doubt if that'll ever happen either,' she said with a grin. 'Well, there, I do feel better now. Not that I was feeling bad, just tense, you know.'

'In case I was going to shout it out to the whole world that we are lovers? It's tempting but I won't. We'll just be dinner companions tonight, shall we? Friendly but aloof—and the world can make what the hell it likes of it. How does that sound?'

Honor raised an eyebrow. 'There are a lot of things to like about you sometimes, Ryan.'

'Thank you again, ma'am,' he said humbly, but this time with the most wicked little glint in his eye.

CHAPTER NINE

'How was that?'

'An enjoyable evening,' Honor murmured.

'You didn't warn me that you were such a hot dancer.'

'You weren't so bad yourself.'

They stood side by side on the upper veranda of Ryan's house. It was a still, hot night and the river slid past, showing itself to be broad and flowing swiftly now where the lights from both banks caught and reflected in its surface.

'Are you very tired?' he asked.

'I'm tired and I'm strung up again,' she answered after a few moments. 'I don't know why.'

'Because it wasn't possible,' he suggested, 'for us to remain aloof while we were dancing together?'

She closed her eyes and said simply, 'Yes. I don't know how I'll ever be able to be aloof from you again.'

'Well, that's one thing we don't have to try now.'

'No,' she whispered, and turned to him at last. 'Hold me, please, Ryan.'

'I was afraid of this,' he said ruefully some time later, after he'd released the zip of her mulberry dress and slid it down her body.

'What?'

'How black, lacy underwear would become you.'

'Oh.' She glanced down at herself, standing in the

middle of his softly lamplit bedroom. She stepped out of her dress and back into his arms, and a little gurgle of laughter caught at her throat. 'I was tempted to throw it all away once.'

'Don't tell me.' He moved her to arm's length and studied the pale glow of her skin through her bra, the bare sweep of her waist and the flare of her hips, which were girdled by a tiny, frivolous suspender belt and equally tiny briefs, his gaze lingering on the pale, bare skin before the long sweep of her black stockings began. 'Do you know what else attracted me to you?' he added.

'No, tell me.' She didn't move.

'That long, fluid stride of yours.' He put his hands on her buttocks. 'It seemed to promise all sorts of delight.'

'Did it, now?' she whispered, with a sudden glint of sheer wickedness in her own eyes. 'Then how about this?' And she bent to pick up her dress, smoothed it and strolled across the room to the bank of built-in wardrobes where she hung it up carefully. Then she returned across the room to come to stand in front of him.

He sank down on to the end of the bed and said ruefully, 'I thought you were tired.'

'I thought so too but suddenly I don't think I've felt less tired in my life,' she answered simply and honestly. 'This is what I feel like doing—don't know why; I've never done anything like this in my life before, not really.' Her lips twisted. 'I hope you don't mind.'

And, so saying, she released her bra and took it off almost absently, then her suspender belt and briefs, and finally, with each leg in turn poised delicately on the bed, rolled off her stockings. Only then did she look at him—a look that was neither coy nor in any way embarrassed but a serious, open enquiry.

He said something under his breath and reached for

her. 'Mind?' he said. 'How could I?' And he buried his head in her breasts and a little while later made love to her so comprehensively that she could barely move afterwards and he seemed totally disinclined to do so.

'I don't know what got into me,' she said with some amazement as she woke the next morning.

'Don't regret it whatever you do,' he replied.

'Do you think it was all that intimate dancing?'

'Perhaps but, whatever, I'm a fan,' he said, taking her firmly into his arms.

'Well, I'm a bit shaken,' she persisted. She had to smile into his eyes as she spoke her next thought aloud. 'You know, you look much more approachable like this—with your hair in your eyes and stubble on your jaw.' She traced the blue shadows on his jaw with her fingertip.

'I wouldn't have thought I was at all unapproachable last night,' he murmured, pressing the soft curves of her body closer to him.

'Something got into me last night—I'm not quite sure what; that's why I'm feeling a bit shaken.'

'Oh. It wasn't anything I did last night?'

'Well, you're obviously responsible for a certain, delicious kind of lethargy I feel.' She moved against him luxuriously. 'And I wouldn't be at all surprised if I've got a few bruises,' she added serenely. 'We both may have got a bit carried away but—'

'Should we have a look?' he queried gravely.

'No, we shouldn't. That could lead to further encounters of a like kind and I don't think I'm up to it. Do you know what I would like to do?'

'No. Tell me.'

'I'd like to have a dip in the pool and then a huge breakfast.'

'That could be arranged. What about the rest of the day?'

'What would you like to do?' She kissed him lightly on the lips.

'Nothing,' he said lazily. 'Other than be with you.'

So that was what they did and they retired rather early despite having done nothing much all day.

'How do you feel about encounters of—any kind now?' he queried as he closed the bedroom door.

'I feel—' she moved into his arms '—very ready to be loved and cherished.'

He smiled down at her. 'That sounds nice.'

'How do you feel?'

'Amazingly similar.' He started to unbutton her blouse. 'Amazingly,' he repeated as he stared down at her breasts beneath her bra—which this time was a white one but rather sheer so that the darker skin of her aureoles showed through. 'Do you always wear matching underwear?' he queried then as he undid her skirt and observed her briefs.

'No, not always. Sometimes I even wear good old Bonds cottontails.'

'They probably take on a new meaning with you in them.'

She laughed softly. 'All of me seems to have taken on a new meaning lately. You know, I never really perceived myself as—well, sexy. Now, I know you've told me that I was unawakened et cetera—' she tilted her chin at him and looked haughty for a moment, then smiled ruefully '—but perhaps you were right. Mind you, I guess the ultimate approbation still rests with you.'

'As to whether you're sexy or not?' he murmured, with a quizzically raised eyebrow.

'Uh-huh.'

'Extremely.'

'Is that all?'

'What more could I say? Am I not the man you seduced totally last night?'

'I think we both did a bit of that,' she said with a glinting little smile. 'Am I not the girl standing all but undressed in your arms—and loving it?' she added softly.

'Is that an invitation to get on with it?'

'No, you don't have to do a thing other than what you're already doing,' she returned gravely. 'I'm enjoying it very much.'

His teeth glinted white and he bent his head to kiss her. 'All the same, I'm going to have to get on with it— I'm seriously stricken with desire, you see.'

'Good.'

He laughed and picked her up, took her to the bed, and they made love, slept for a time, then she woke to feel him caressing her thighs. She stretched contentedly and felt his fingers wander gently through the dark, springy curls at the base of her stomach, and a slow smile curved her lips. 'Can I try something?' she murmured.

'Be my guest.'

A few minutes later he said, 'This is a very good idea, Honor. I'll even go further and say it's brilliant.'

She laughed softly as she lay on top of him, and traced some little lines beside his mouth with her fingertip. 'I read once that more women should adopt this position;

it gives them more freedom—or something to that effect.'

'And does it?'

She moved slightly. 'It certainly feels lovely.'

He groaned. 'I don't think you should do too much of that.'

'You don't like it?'

'I have the opposite problem with it, in point of fact.'

'Which is?'

He laughed up at her. 'You know very well what it is, Miss Lingard.'

'I have to say,' she commented perfectly seriously before her lips curved into a smile again, 'that I don't know how long I can last either!' And she gasped as he moulded her hips to his and within a few short minutes they climaxed together in a way that took her breath away.

'What shall we do tomorrow?' she said drowsily some time later after they'd showered and were back in bed together.

'How about a game of golf? I could give you some lessons.'

'Ah, I may have misled you there; I have in fact played golf.'

He grinned. 'I might have known. Tell me more.'

'I got my handicap down to eighteen once but that was a few years ago and I've only had the odd social game since then, but I do know my way around a golf course.'

'Well, why don't we drive down to Sanctuary Cove, have a round and then we could have lunch at the Hyatt or whichever restaurant you prefer? There is—I have to tell you there is an ulterior motive behind that scenario.'

'Oh?'

'Mmm. This village and marina on the Sunshine Coast will be something similar to Sanctuary Cove—no golf courses but along the same lines, and there's a boat I'm interested in down there. We could have a look at it.'

She was silent for a moment but only because she was suddenly delighted at the prospect of striding around a golf course with him. 'It sounds like a great idea,' she said. 'Can we stop and pick up my clubs on the way?'

'I can get Warren to pick them up first thing. Then we'll have an early start. Sleepy?'

'Very,' she whispered. 'In fact exhausted suddenly.'

'Go to sleep, then. Hell,' he added as the phone beside the bed buzzed. 'Look, I'll take it downstairs.' And he kissed her lightly and got up.

'Don't forget to come back,' she murmured, hardly able to keep her eyes open.

'I won't.'

But in fact she was fast asleep when he did come back, so she didn't know that he watched her for a while then sighed before he got in beside her.

And when she did wake, to a lemon and apricot dawn, he wasn't beside her but getting dressed.

She sat up, yawned delicately and stretched. 'I didn't realise that you meant this early,' she said with a grin. 'You should have woken me.'

'Honor—' he came and sat on the bed and took her hand '—I'm awfully sorry but something's come up. I need to be in Singapore this evening so I'm flying out in a couple of hours.'

If he'd rendered her breathless last night it was as

nothing, she thought dazedly, to how she felt now. A tide of disappointment seemed to be coursing through her veins so strongly that she actually wanted to kick and shout.

Don't *do* this to me, her heart seemed to be saying as she clenched her fist. Not now when I've fallen far deeper in love with you than I thought possible, when I've done things I never thought possible—don't prove to me *now* that you're a machine, not a man, when it's too late for me to go back...

'Honor,' he said gently, 'believe me, if I could change this I would but it's not possible unfortunately.'

'No...' She had some difficulty in unclenching her jaw. 'I mean, I believe you. So. No golf. Oh, well,' she tried to say brightly, 'another day perhaps.'

'Yes. There will be plenty of other days.'

'OK.' She pulled her hand free and got out of the other side of the bed. 'Why don't I come and see you off? Then Warren could drop me back home—I've just remembered that my club's having its tennis championships today. I think I'll be a late entry!'

'Honor—'

'No, Ryan, I'm fine,' she said firmly. 'These things can't be helped.'

'You could come with me.' He crossed over to where she was standing in her slim grey silk nightgown.

'I couldn't actually.' She grimaced. 'My passport has expired and although I've applied for a new one it's not back yet. How long will you be gone?'

'Not long. This is...' he paused '...this is something I have to sort out once and for all; it's rather vital to Bailey Construction—or I wouldn't be leaving you like this.' He put his hands on her waist.

She looked up into his eyes and wondered how well

she was veiling what was in her heart—the turmoil, the pain... 'I believe you,' she said lightly.

But at the airport it was a different story. She could suddenly no longer hide the strong emotion she felt. 'Hey,' she said just a shade unsteadily, 'anyone would think you were going for a lifetime.' She tried desperately to cover it with wry humour. 'I think I'll just say goodbye now instead of hanging around.' And she reached up to kiss him briefly. 'Look after yourself!'

'You too, Honor.' He took her into his arms and kissed her thoroughly and without haste, so that she was breathless and trembling when he let her go. 'I'll be in touch,' he said gently, and turned away.

What neither of them realised was that a very famous golfer had recently arrived at the international terminal and the Press were there to greet him. Nor did they realise that one cameraman had stifled a yawn, looked around boredly, then nearly dropped his camera as he saw Ryan Bailey in a passionate embrace with Honor Lingard, his art curator, whom he recognised because he'd been aboard the rescue helicopter a couple of weeks back...

Honor didn't play tennis that Sunday although at times she wished she had because she spent the day roaming around her apartment, unable to settle to anything but her torturous thoughts.

These ran along the lines of a churning recognition that she wanted nothing more than to spend the rest of her life with Ryan, that she wanted to be his wife, his lover, his friend, the mother of his children.

But she didn't think she could stand taking second place to Bailey Construction or seeing him cut himself off from her—or all the things she'd feared and wondered about and that people had told her about... Things that she'd apparently had proven to her that very morning.

But then she thought, Am I making a mountain out of a molehill? Men have to work—what am I asking for? A nine-to-five man? That's something I know he could never be, so no, I don't expect that. But to break up our first really precious time together, not to be able to send Bill or whoever because of a special occasion, not to delay going by just one day...

Is it because he *can't* delegate, because the habit of command is too strong? Or is it because no woman will ever mean that much to him? Oh, hell, how many times have I asked myself these questions? she wondered hollowly. And then there's still Sandra...

But, as it turned out, she got two shocks the next morning, and one of them directly concerned Sandra Bailey.

She was in her office when Bill Fortune came to see her.

'Hello, Bill,' she said briefly. 'Come to give me some more advice?'

He closed the door and looked at her seriously. 'Honor, you're making a big mistake,' he said quietly.

'Now look here, Bill,' she said tautly. 'It's got nothing to do with you. I really don't understand why—'

'Have you seen this?' He handed her a newspaper, folded to an inner page upon which was a photo of her and Ryan in each other's arms at the airport.

She stared at it, then dropped it on her desk with a thud. 'It's still got nothing to do with you!'

'Where was he going?'

'Singapore—why are you asking me?' she said with a sudden frown.

He grimaced. 'He's being more secretive than usual, that's all. Did he tell you why?'

'Not really, but it was business, as usual—' She stopped abruptly and couldn't help the faint tinge of colour that came to her cheeks. She said thoughtfully after a moment, 'Bill, what do you think Ryan would make of these little comments of yours?'

'If he were honest he'd probably agree with me,' he said wryly. 'Sandra's in the news too—no, not that paper.'

'Oh? Why?'

'She's getting married again.'

'What?' she whispered.

'Yes, I was surprised as well,' he remarked. 'I didn't think she'd ever get over Ryan. Maybe she hasn't.' He shrugged.

'What do you mean?'

'Well, she's marrying a guy five years younger than she is, who looks suspiciously like someone on the make to me—he's some sort of impoverished musician.'

Honor realised that she was staring at him with her mouth open and closed it with a snap.

'Still, you're right; it doesn't have anything to do with me. Did he say when he'd be back?'

'No.'

'You know, Honor,' he confided, 'there are times when it's very difficult to work for a man who is entirely self-sufficient. And I happen to know that Sandra found, to her cost, that it was impossible to be married to him.

'I don't know why I'm doing this,' he said then with a rueful little smile. 'I guess I like you, that's why.' And he walked out.

Honor sat down abruptly and for some reason recalled

that afternoon many weeks ago when she'd been witness to Ryan verbally demolishing Bill Fortune... Why am I thinking of it, though? she wondered. Why do I have the feeling that something's going on that I don't understand?

But after minutes of trying to puzzle it out her gaze fell on their picture in the paper and she read the caption again with distaste...

Did they fall in love when they were kidnapped together? It certainly seems as if Ryan Bailey and Honor Lingard are now more than art collector and curator.

Then she thought of Sandra, marrying a man five years her junior, as well as the other thing that Bill had said about him, and she closed her eyes and thought, What have I done?

But that night she was asking herself what *to* do, only to have the decision taken from her in a curious way— she got a call from Ryan quite late.

'Honor?'

'Yes, it's me. How are you?' she said because she could think of nothing else to say.

'Missing you. Did you win the tennis?'

'No. I didn't play after all. And I spent all day today working on the exhibition—it will be ready in a couple of days,' she said hastily.

'Good. When will your passport be ready?'

'Oh.' She paused. 'I'm not sure. I only put it in last week—uh—they said it would take a couple of weeks. Why?'

'I've decided to fly on to Tokyo. Since I'm over here

it will kill two birds with one stone. I thought you might join me but never mind. We can do it another time.'

'Yes… Ryan—'

'Honor, is something wrong?'

'Ryan,' she said a little desperately, 'do you know that Sandra is getting married?'

There was a short silence, then he swore. 'No. Who to?'

She told him all she knew. And she finished by saying, 'It seems rather sudden, doesn't it?'

'Extremely sudden,' he said briefly. 'Listen, I'll be on the next plane home. Bloody hell,' he then said roughly, 'I've got two meetings tomorrow so it will have to be the morning after. Honor—how did you know about this?'

'It was in some paper, apparently. I…' She thought of telling him about her encounter with Sandra but couldn't seem to find the courage to do so. 'I thought you'd want to know.'

'Only she could do something like this,' he said impatiently. 'Look, I have to go, unfortunately, but I'll call you as soon as I get in the day after tomorrow.'

She put the phone down a moment later and stared at it. Yes, she thought, only Sandra could do something like this, poor soul, but at least you're coming home for her…

And the next day she worked like a Trojan; in fact she worked late into the evening, but by the time she'd finished the exhibition of Papuan artefacts was set up and ready to go. And when she left the office she put a letter marked 'Private and Confidential' for Ryan on Pam's desk.

The next morning she was on a plane herself, but heading for North Queensland. She disembarked on Hamilton Island and caught the *Sun Goddess*, a sleek, fast boat that took her up the Whitsunday Passage to

Hayman Island, where she intended to bury her wounded spirit for as long as it took to recover from the decision she'd made to step out of Ryan Bailey's life forever.

Hayman Island was beautiful, as was the resort. Honor slept a lot for a couple of days. Then, when that eased her physically but didn't seem to be much of a balm to her soul, she took to walking and swimming—swimming round the huge, bougainvillea-surrounded pool and off the beach, and walking the rugged hill-tracks of the island, made even more strenuous by the midsummer heat of the tropics.

She eschewed all social contact and ate as simply as possible beneath the white sail sunshades of the coffee-shop that opened on to the beach, overlooking the bay and Bali Hi—as they called it on Hayman—a lovely little jewel of an island whose proper name was much more mundane—Black Island.

She even thought there was some significance in that—some symbol pertaining to herself. She likened it to the magical vista that loving Ryan had opened up for her, only for it to be dashed because she wanted more than she could have.

The only other thing she allowed to hold her interest, apart from the seemingly endless books she read from the library, were the works of art for which Hayman Island was renowned—paintings, sculptures and Ming vases.

But there came a time, after she'd been away for ten days and was still feeling empty and bereft, when she read a Brisbane paper, and she was rocked by two items.

The first was a simple report, below a photo among some other wedding photos, of the marriage of Sandra Bailey to one Michael Wentworth, who had long hair and round, wire-framed glasses. She lowered the paper and stared before her with stunned eyes for minutes.

The second shock was in the business section, which she was scanning to check her share prices—her father had left her a small portfolio. Before she got to the right page the name Fortune caught her eye. The gist of the article was that Bill Fortune had parted company with Ryan Bailey, and in mysterious circumstances, given the long term of his employment with Bailey Construction. It was to be hoped, the article went on to say, that this was no indication of any trouble within the firm, which had several significant construction projects under way.

Why? Honor asked herself. And why did he let Sandra marry someone just for the sake of it? What if there is trouble in the company? What if he's over-extended himself and he did have to go away? Did I walk out on him when things were really difficult? Why couldn't he have told me?

She stared unseeingly before her and, as had happened to her once before, she suddenly felt stifled. She looked around Hayman but its beauty and its elegance left her untouched as she suddenly felt slightly small and as if she'd been unforgivably preoccupied with herself and her needs.

She flew home the next morning. She went to the office late that afternoon, not because she wanted to but because that was where she was sure Ryan would be if he was in town, and because she failed to summon the courage to ring the house and get Mary.

Of course, I could wait or I could ring Pam and leave a message for him, she thought. Would he come, after what I wrote in the letter about disliking the way I'd changed into someone I didn't know any more or feel comfortable with? I think I'm going to have to swallow my pride just this once and go to him...

It was as she stepped into the foyer of Bailey House that she realised she'd made an awful mistake. There was a reception on; there were waiters dispensing champagne and canapés; there was the minister from Papua New Guinea, who bore down on her as she stood dazed for a moment.

He enfolded her delicate hand in his huge one and said, 'Miss Lingard! I'm so very glad you came. Although you've left Mr Bailey, I believe, I wanted to congratulate you on the sheer excellence of this exhibition, which is all your work, I'm told. It makes me very proud to see these ancient things of my country so proudly displayed and eloquently described!'

Honor swallowed and said weakly, 'It's been a pleasure, Minister.'

'I was just saying to Mr Bailey—ah, here he is. I was just saying that she's an extremely talented woman, Judge Lingard's daughter, was I not, Ryan?'

Their gazes clashed and Ryan looked her up and down as he had once before, with patent, searing insolence, before he said, 'Yes, you were. And I have to agree with you, Minister—she is talented. It's just a pity that she doesn't know how to make the best of her talents.'

'Now, now,' the minister said gaily, 'you're just cross because she's left you; I would be the same, I'm sure! But come, my children, please don't spoil my pleasure! Miss Lingard, there are a few people I would like you to meet.'

And he bore Honor off triumphantly. Nor would he allow her to leave his side until the official party left, whereupon she found herself beside Ryan, making formal farewells with a smile pinned on her face and the feeling that she was wound up like an over-taut spring.

'So, that's that,' Ryan said as the limousine drew out of the building forecourt, and he turned to smile down unpleasantly at her. 'Could you not resist an hour of triumph, Honor? Or have you come back to teach me another lesson?'

'I...' She licked her lips.

'I'm sure this isn't very gentlemanly,' he said thoughtfully after waiting with mocking politeness while she tried to speak, 'but do you remember what happened the last time you came back to lecture me, or teach me or hate me? I myself happen to have the clearest recollection of it,' he said gently.

CHAPTER TEN

HONOR was so incensed that she strode off and it took about five minutes for her to realise that she was walking in the opposite direction to where she'd parked her car. She swung round and stopped at a traffic light, and a blue Lamborghini slid into the kerb beside her.

'History repeats itself—get in, Honor,' Ryan said drily.

'No!'

'Look, either you get in or I get out and chase you down the street if necessary.'

'You *wouldn't*!'

'Oh, yes, I would—we have some unfinished business between us, Miss Lingard, but that's not the way I prefer to do things.' And so saying he switched off the engine and reached for the door-handle.

She said something unprintable and got in.

'Wise,' he commented, and started the engine again.

She flashed him a furious look and said through her teeth, 'Just don't take me home—to yours or mine. Because if you do you'll have to drag me kicking and screaming out of this car.'

'Is that how afraid you are of being in my home or yours? I wonder why?' he said sardonically, and added, 'OK, we'll choose some neutral territory for this little conflict.' And he drove to the restaurant where they'd first dined together.

'How appropriate,' she said coldly as they were shown to a table. 'But I'm not hungry so this is just a waste of time.'

He scrutinised her mockingly, taking in her navy blue georgette dress with little white flowers, a heart-shaped neckline, padded shoulders and buttons down the front, and said, 'You look to me as if you've lost weight, Honor. What have you been doing to yourself—taken up marathon-running to subdue your newly aroused libido?'

She slammed her bag on to the table and said in a low, intense voice, 'If you say one more word along those lines I'll hit you.'

'You're being ridiculous, Honor,' he replied coldly, 'not to mention creating a scene. Sit down.' He waited, his grey gaze harder and more compelling than she'd ever known it, and she glanced around, then sank down with a tinge of colour staining her cheeks.

He followed suit and ordered two brandies, the same meal as they'd had before and a bottle of wine to accompany it. 'Now,' he said when the deferential waiter left his side, 'would you like to tell me what you meant in that emotional, highly charged letter you left for me?'

She drank some brandy to steady her nerves. 'It wasn't emotional or highly charged, it was simply the truth. You're not a man, you are a machine. Business will always mean more to you than anything else and it did leave me feeling uncomfortable with myself to think that I might join the ranks of…Sandra for one, but I wouldn't be at all surprised if there were more.'

'So you did fall in love with me?'

'No, I fell in love with a mirage,' she said bitterly. 'And, while I would hesitate to accuse you of falling in love with me, perhaps I was a mirage to *you*—unfortunately I think I was one to myself.'

'What does that mean?' he asked quietly.

She sat back and nursed her drink. 'I didn't expect to feel like that; I didn't think I was capable of it,' she said at length. 'And you *did* say to me once that an independent woman who valued her freedom might be the solution for you.'

'You'll always be an independent woman, Honor.'

She glanced at him with considerable irony but decided not to pursue that point. 'Well, then, there was also the guilt about Sandra—why didn't you stop the wedding?' she asked abruptly.

'Tell me first why you feel so guilty about Sandra,' he said, his gaze suddenly narrowed. 'You agreed with me once that divorce was the best thing that could have happened to us.'

'That was before she told me herself how she still felt about you, and before I…lectured her on the subject,' she said drily.

'When was this?'

She sat up slowly and put her glass down. 'Didn't Mary tell you, after all?'

'Not that I recall.'

She swallowed. 'She came to the house the day I…well…'

'Ran away? The first time or…? There've been three such occasions now, haven't there?'

She stared at him haughtily. 'On one of the occasions you had to go away suddenly on *business*, as a matter of fact.'

'Ah. Yes, I remember.' He raised an eyebrow. 'And I haven't been quite honest with you—Sandra herself told me. But only when I did try to stop the wedding.'

'Go on,' she said after a long pause.

'Perhaps I should start at the beginning—Sandra's beginning,' he said evenly. 'Michael Wentworth is not an impoverished musician with connotations of gigs, drugs, clubs and bars et cetera. He's in fact a highly gifted classical flautist but he is five years younger than Sandra and he hasn't succeeded in making a lot of money yet.

'He's also an extremely vague, unhandy and unworldly man who is not very good at looking after himself, but he's deeply, quietly and shyly in love with her.'

'Go on,' Honor said again, but thought her voice sounded as if it came from a long way away this time.

'And to her consternation Sandra found herself reciprocating that emotion. But she couldn't reconcile herself to it because—' he gestured '—he was younger, because she had no confidence in herself, because...' he paused '...he wasn't me.'

'I think...I begin to see,' she said barely audibly.

'I hope you do,' he responded, 'seeing that what *you* said to her that day apparently achieved in a couple of minutes what I and some others had been trying to do for years.

'She said it was like a combination of a cataclysm and a blow on the head. She said it suddenly made her see how little she deserved anyone to love if she could only see herself as a reflection through them.

'It gave her the courage, she said, to tell the world and *me* to go to hell—the courage to go ahead and marry a younger man because she could be happy with him, she could be quiet with him, she could mother him— and that seems to be what she needs. I gave them my blessing.'

Honor brushed away a sudden tear and said huskily, 'That's such a weight off my mind.'

'Does it mean that you'll come back to me with a clear conscience?'

'No,' she whispered, and looked away as their food arrived.

He waited again until the waiter had departed but what he said next really stunned her. 'Because you'd rather believe Bill Fortune?'

'How...did you know?'

He smiled grimly. 'You may not realise this, Honor, but Bill has...left.'

'I know! That's one reason... But I don't understand...' She trailed off bewilderedly.

'One reason you came back?' he hazarded.

'Well...' But she couldn't go on.

'Then let me tell you about Bill, Honor,' he said drily. 'You may remember—it was the day all this started in fact—that I was extremely angry with Bill over three contracts that had been lost while I was overseas?' He sent her a glinting, ironic look of enquiry.

She nodded dazedly.

'Well, I didn't just leave it there. I dug around and dug around until I was fairly sure that the reason we'd lost those contracts was that someone had leaked details of our tender to the opposition.'

Her mouth fell open. 'Bill?'

'Yes. Unfortunately, I had to set him up to prove it.'

'So that's why—' she swallowed '—he said the things he did. I mean... And the last time I spoke to him I couldn't understand why he wanted to know where you were—from me.'

'He was obviously suspicious. The call I got that night—our last night,' he said drily, 'was from a Singaporean banker—a friend of mine. He had with him a man who could prove conclusively that Bill had walked into the little trap I'd set for him—a man who was not anxious to set foot outside Singapore, however, but was quite likely to have second thoughts and disappear.

'It was extremely important that I sort it out once and for all for reasons that I probably don't have to tell you. Look, don't let your food get cold,' he concluded, and picked up his own knife and fork.

'But why?' she asked after a couple of mouthfuls.

'Why did Bill do it? He made himself quite a tidy profit out of selling that information, but there was more involved. Bill, unhappily,' Ryan said with no emotion, 'came to envy and finally to hate me. At least, that's what he told me when I confronted him.

'He also told me that he'd done his darnedest to "queer my pitch" with you, as he put it. And he added that he believed he'd been successful, which—' he stopped eating and looked right into Honor's eyes '—in the light of your letter and your flight, was hard not to believe, dear Honor.'

'Why did he come to hate you so much?' she said a little desperately after a moment.

'Ah.' He directed her a look full of cynical amusement. 'A quick-thinking broadside, Honor?'

'I don't know what you mean.'

'Yes, you do. That was a calculated shot to try to make me out to be some sort of monster who alienated a long-time employee with my high-handed ways—if not worse. Well, I may have been high-handed but I was always scrupulously fair and I always rewarded genuine effort more than generously,' he observed, and added as she choked on a mouthful of steak, 'Have some wine.'

She did, then said coldly, 'You do remind me of a steam-shovel at times, though, Ryan—I may have mentioned it before.'

'Do I now—in bed, for example?'

'That's…' She took another sip of wine and glared at him.

'Hitting below the belt?' he suggested softly with a raised eyebrow. 'I seem to remember doing nothing much at all one night; that prompted you to parade for me, then take your clothes off for me—'

'*Stop* it,' she whispered, going hot and cold. 'How… how can you fight so…so—?

'Dirty?' he said gently.

'Yes! Is it any wonder—?'

But he interrupted her again, 'No, the wonder of it is, Honor, that when you're in my bed you're quite… happy—one could say blissfully happy. It's when you're out of it that you fight me and run away from me, *even*,' he said with chilling, unmistakable scorn, 'after I've knocked down all your objections like a row of ninepins.

'But let's put this on another footing—why don't you marry me? We could spend a lot more time in bed in those circumstances.'

'And fight each other every inch of the way while we're out of it? No, thanks, Ryan. And—I'm going. Don't, just don't follow me!'

'Honor…' he studied her thoughtfully as she stood up jerkily '…no, I won't, but I'll tell you this much—we may fight from time to time but I can't see any other woman affecting me the way you do, and I can't see you doing the things you do for me for anyone else. Who knows? It all might just have turned me from a machine into a man.

'But there it is—I'm only sorry that I can't instantly make myself over into whatever kind of vision you have, but—well, good luck, my dear. Perhaps one day you'll be able to look back and think it's better to have loved and lost than—the other.'

And he stood up politely, waiting with no more than a dispassionate query in his eyes as she fought with angry tears, then turned on her heel and walked out.

If only he weren't so unpleasant and cutting sometimes, Honor found herself thinking the next day as she lay on her bed in the middle of the afternoon with a pounding headache.

'If only I didn't feel like dying and could stop wondering if I've made an awful mistake,' she said out loud, and sat up impatiently, hitching the pillows up behind her and folding her hands around her knees.

'If only I didn't keep thinking of the way he made love to me and remembering that in bed he wasn't like a steam-shovel at all but something so different, so... I can't even put it into words. If only I didn't feel more bereft now than I've ever felt in my life!'

She stared across the room and reminded herself of how he'd asked her to marry him, but even that didn't restore the black anger she'd felt at the time. Why in fact is all that rightful emotion seeping away, leaving me feeling so cold and empty and sick? she wondered.

She got up because only one answer presented itself to her, and roamed around the apartment for a while. Then she made herself a cup of tea and took it back to bed with the paper she had delivered daily. Once again—this time because nothing else interested her— she turned to the share-market section. And on the opposite page an article did catch her eye because it concerned Bailey Construction...

It was, it turned out, a Press release from Ryan to the effect that the parting of ways with Bill Fortune had been a mutual decision, that he wished Bill, his wife and his family everything of the best and thanked him for all the services he had performed for Bailey Construction.

Honor read and reread it, then closed her eyes. But five minutes later she got up again and ran herself a bath. As she dressed after it, in thin white pyjama-style trousers and a loose cornflower-blue top, she saw with some surprise that it was pouring with rain outside.

I don't even know what the weather's doing, she thought as she slipped on her white rope-soled shoes—I truly don't know...whether I'm coming or going.

But after staring at nothing for a long time she suddenly squared her shoulders and looked around for her car keys.

It was Mary who answered, whose disembodied voice said that, yes, Mr Bailey was in and that she would release the gates. It was Mary who stood at the front door waiting for her and told her, with a slightly anxious look on her face, that Mr Bailey was in the second sitting-room, and that Honor should go right through.

So she did. Ryan was standing at the windows overlooking the wet, darkening garden with a drink in his hand—just standing there with his other hand shoved into his trouser pocket and an unusually weary set to his shoulders. Nor did he turn until she cleared her throat, and then, when his eyes came to rest on her, they widened in surprise.

'She d-didn't tell you it was me?' Honor stammered.

'Mary? She didn't tell me it was anyone.'

'Well—do you mind?'

'You seem to have an ally in Mary, Honor,' he replied, and shrugged. 'As to whether I mind, time will tell, no doubt. Can I get you a drink?' He raised an eyebrow at her. He was wearing a long-sleeved white shirt with grey stripes but he'd loosened his tie.

'No...no, thank you. I came to—well, to try to explain some things.'

He surveyed her unemotionally for a long moment. Then he murmured, 'Be my guest. Do sit down.'

'I think I'd rather stand.'

'Very well.' But he sat down himself on one of the leather couches.

Honor clenched her fists briefly and felt her heart pound uncomfortably; she swallowed, then said abruptly, 'Why did you give out that Press release about Bill?'

He shrugged. 'He's got a wife and four kids.'

She turned away, found herself in front of the Sisley and studied it for a long moment. Then she turned back and said with more composure, 'That's what I came to talk about.'

'Bill's family?'

'No. I've always felt I didn't know you very well but when I stopped to think about it today I found the opposite was true. It was your Press release that made me see it.'

'Forgive me but I don't quite understand,' he said drily.

'Well, it made me realise,' she said slowly, 'that even though you can be high-handed with people you... well...' She paused. 'Not many men would care for an ex-wife the way you did Sandra. Not many men would allow Bill Fortune to walk away unscathed after what he did, because he has a wife and four children. Then there's Pam, whom you took the time to help escape from a horrible relationship—'

'I did very little,' he said, with a grimace. 'Don't tell me she's…?' He looked up at her enquiringly.

'She would slay dragons for you,' she said simply. 'Then there's me…'

'What about you, Honor?'

She moved suddenly and sat down at right angles to him. 'There's the way you took care of me when we got kidnapped. And the way you didn't take advantage of me when it would, perhaps, have been ''child's play''.'

'So?'

'Ryan… So, you see, I discovered that I knew a lot more about you than I realised, but in a way that makes it worse.' She stopped, then started again. 'Do you know what happened to me the morning you went to Singapore?'

He said nothing but his grey gaze was deep and intent.

'I wanted to scream and shout; I could have killed you,' she whispered. 'I was *so* disappointed.'

She thought that he sighed, then he held out his hand to her. She rose after a long, tense moment and went to sit beside him, and he put his arm round her shoulders. Suddenly she discovered that she was crying.

'Being away from you is like some form of torture,' she wept, 'but to find myself hating you for it, and hating myself because I'm probably being unreasonable but don't seem able to convince myself that I'm entirely so, is worse. *That's* what I meant when I said I was uncomfortable with myself, only ''uncomfortable'' is a mild term for it.'

'Honor.' He held her shaking body close and kissed her hair.

'No, let me finish… So I went away but that was awful too. I tried to persuade myself that I could cope but in my heart I knew I couldn't. I tried to tell myself that if you ever wanted to marry me, then I could be happy with what you could give—I could be a careful, loving wife, a social asset, a good mother, and it wouldn't matter if you were away for all the children's sports days and birthdays and our wedding anniversaries, or just a game of golf, because the alternative was... worse.

'But, you see, I do know now that there are some things in myself I just can't control. That's...all,' she said, and laid her head on his shoulder.

'This was the last thing in the world a foolishly proud but obviously naïve person called Honor Lingard expected to happen to her, but there it is,' she added barely audibly, then said, 'No, that's not quite all; I still don't know whether you love me or whether you might have decided that time was marching on and you had no one to leave Bailey Construction to.'

'Who suggested that?'

'Sandra.'

'Can I tell you what Sandra told me to tell you, Honor?'

She mutely lifted her wet, tear-streaked face to his.

'She said that if she'd gone out and hand-picked someone for me it would have been you.'

'How....? She couldn't know—she barely knows me.'

'No, but she knows *me*, and she must have divined a bit about you. And can I tell you what would happen to Bailey Construction if I didn't marry you, Honor, and have our children to leave it to?'

'What?' she whispered.

'I would sell out of it.'

'R-Ryan!' she stammered. 'But...but...'

'I know,' he said, and pulled her into his arms. 'Look, if someone called Ryan Bailey had been told a few months back that any woman could mean to him what you do he wouldn't have believed them. But when I began to perceive what I felt about you I also began to perceive that you might be the one woman I couldn't have. And that rather threw me.

'Then, just when I thought I was getting through to you, I went and did something stupid like leaving you because—well, perhaps some habits die hard,' he said with self-directed mockery. 'But, you see, I have to confess, Honor, that I've been trying to guard myself against not being able to have you...just in case it did work out that way.'

'Oh...' she whispered on an indrawn breath.

'Only,' he went on with that same mockery, 'when I thought I'd finally lost you I couldn't believe the black bitterness that engulfed me, which was probably why I went on the attack the way I did last night.

'I'm sorry, my love, truly sorry for the things I said. As a matter of fact, before you walked in just now I was remembering the way you made love to me, the way you took your clothes off that night for me, and was feeling like cutting my throat because I thought I'd killed all we had in several ways.'

'Ryan—'

'No, let me finish,' he said gently. 'I *had* wondered about a love like this—a woman who aroused you, who you just knew you could never tire of, who...got into your soul; a woman who, just to see her walk down a corridor or have her sit in a chair in your office, made you think of making love to her, made you want to talk to her for hours, all those things...

'Then it started to happen for me with you, but there was an added dimension to it—I got the feeling that I was falling in love with a piece of marble. So there was the added—wonder of making you come alive to love, bringing all that wonderful fire and spirit to it only for me—and the fear,' he said very quietly, 'that I might not be the man to do it.

'And I suppose that along the years I'd lost faith in it happening, so I was not only a bit cynical when it did, but down all those years I'd got so used to compensating for the lack of it with other things—mostly work,' he said drily. 'Honor—'

'Ryan...Ryan,' she whispered with new tears in her eyes. 'Oh, God, is it really like that for you?'

'If you married me we'd have the rest of our lives to prove it but—'

'No.' She put her fingers to his mouth. 'I mean, you don't have to say any more.'

He kissed her fingers then drew them gently away. 'Yes, I do. I have to tell you that, despite all that, I probably won't change overnight, but—and this is also true—every time I have to be away from you will...make coming home something it's never been for me before.'

'So long as you mean that, so long as we can cut it down to the bare minimum, I'll be very brave,' she said softly. 'I love you. This—piece of marble has never felt less like one than she does now.'

'This—machine has never felt less like one either,' he replied, and started to kiss her deeply and urgently.

'Perhaps I shouldn't be doing this,' she said to him some time later.

'Why not?'

'Well, I don't know if this is what...careful wives do,' she said gravely. 'Not that I'm a wife yet but you know what I mean.'

'I'm sure it's exactly what careful wives do, assuming they care for their husbands. Is this not what you meant about being a careful wife?' he commented, gazing down at her golden, freckled body, the long sweep of her bare legs, her paler breasts and hips as she lay on his bed.

She smiled and smoothed her hands across his shoulders. 'Not exactly but if you don't mind…?'

He laughed then on a suddenly indrawn breath, gathered her close and said unevenly, 'When I'm with you like this it's like climbing snow-clad mountain peaks in the sunlight, riding across a blue sea through silver spray under a white sail, watching a moon lay a path of gold over still, deep water.'

'You say the loveliest things sometimes,' she said shakily.

'When will you marry me?'

'Tomorrow?'

He laughed. 'I'll see if I can arrange it.'

He arranged it for four days later but twelve months later he presided over a different ceremony—the christening of their first child, who at three months old gave every promise, Ryan told her mother, of being very much like her.

'What makes you say that?' Honor enquired as she watched the dark-haired little girl sleeping serenely in her crib once the celebrations were over.

'I can see her growing up with long legs, an imperious nature and giving me hell from time to time—I don't know why, she just has that look about her.'

Honor laughed. 'You have to admit it's quite a while since her mother gave you hell, though.'

He reached for her hand and drew her out of the nursery. 'Oh, I don't know,' he said softly, closing the door and taking her in his arms. 'Motherhood becomes you,' he added. 'And if you really want to know I've been going through hell all this long afternoon.'

'Ryan—' she took a sudden breath '—is it still moonlight and mountains and—all those things for you?'

'No,' he said, but as her eyes widened went on, 'It's more now. It's peace and certainty as well—although there are still times, so many of them in fact, when to see you walk across a room is to think of making love to you. Incidentally, that's what I'm going to do right now. Good, careful mothers, so I'm told, take the opportunity to rest when their babies do.'

'Rest?' she whispered, with a wicked little glint in her eyes. 'Are you not confusing mothers with good, careful wives?'

He kissed her lightly. 'See what I mean?'

'No...'

'You still give me hell.'

'On the other hand the thought of—some time alone with you, resting or whatever, is this mother and wife's idea of heaven,' she said gravely. 'Ryan, it's worked so well I sometimes can't believe it,' she added and her dark eyes were suddenly suspiciously bright.

'Do you think it would be safe to say that we were made for each other, Honor?' he asked, cupping her face and kissing the tears on her lashes.

'I think it would.' And she moved into his arms again and rested against him with a little sigh of pure pleasure.

The world's bestselling romance series.

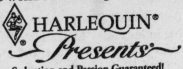

HARLEQUIN®
Presents

Seduction and Passion Guaranteed!

Introducing Jane Porter's exciting new series

**The Galván men: proud Argentine aristocrats...
who've chosen American rebels as their brides!**

IN DANTE'S DEBT
Harlequin Presents #2298

Count Dante Galván was ruthless—and though it broke Daisy's heart she had no alternative but to hand over control of her family's stud farm to him. She was in Dante's debt up to her ears! Daisy knew she was far too ordinary ever to become the count's wife— but could she resist his demands that she repay her dues in his bed?

On sale January 2003

LAZARO'S REVENGE
Harlequin Presents #2304

Lazaro Herrera has vowed revenge on Dante, his half brother, who refuses to acknowledge his existence. When Dante's sister-in-law Zoe arrives in Argentina, it seems the perfect opportunity. But the clash of Zoe's blond and blue-eyed beauty with his own smoldering dark looks creates a sexual force so strong that Lazaro's plan begins to fall apart....

On sale February 2003

Pick up a Harlequin Presents® novel and you will enter a world of spine-tingling passion and provocative, tantalizing romance!

Available wherever Harlequin books are sold.

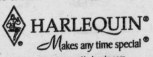

HARLEQUIN®
Makes any time special ®

Visit us at www.eHarlequin.com

HPGALVAN

International bestselling author

SANDRA MARTON

invites you to attend the

WEDDING *of the* YEAR

Glitz and glamour prevail in this volume
containing a trio of stories in which
three couples meet at a
high society wedding—and
soon find themselves
walking down the aisle!

Look for it in November 2002.

HARLEQUIN®
Makes any time special ®

Visit us at www.eHarlequin.com   BR3WOTY-R

FALL IN LOVE
THIS WINTER
WITH
HARLEQUIN BOOKS!

In October 2002 look for these special volumes
led by *USA TODAY* bestselling authors,
and receive MOULIN ROUGE on video*!

*Retail value of $14.98 U.S. Mail-in offer. Two proofs of purchase required.
Limited time offer. Offer expires 3/31/03.

See inside these books for details.

Own MOULIN ROUGE on video!

*This exciting promotion
is available at your
favorite retail outlet.*

Only from

HARLEQUIN®
Makes any time special ®

MOULIN ROUGE ©2002 Twentieth Century Fox Home Entertainment, Inc.
All rights reserved. "Twentieth Century Fox", "Fox" and their associated
logos are the property of Twentieth Century Fox Film Corporation.

Visit Harlequin at www.eHarlequin.com   PHNCP02R

This is the family reunion you've been waiting for!

TRUEBLOOD
Christmas

JASMINE CRESSWELL
TARA TAYLOR QUINN
& KATE HOFFMANN

deliver three brand new Trueblood, Texas stories.

After many years, Major Brad Henderson is released from prison, exonerated after almost thirty years for a crime he didn't commit. His mission: to be reunited with his three daughters. How to find them? Contact Dylan Garrett of the Finders Keepers Detective Agency!

Look for it in November 2002.

HARLEQUIN®
Makes any time special®

Visit us at www.eHarlequin.com

PHTBTCR

KATE HOFFMANN

brings readers a brand-new,
spin-off to her *Mighty Quinns* miniseries

REUNITED

Keely McLain Quinn had grown up an only child—so it
was a complete shock to learn that she had six older
brothers and a father who'd never known she existed!
But Keely's turmoil is just beginning, as she discovers
the man she's fallen in love with is determined to
destroy her newfound family.

*Look for REUNITED
in October 2002.*

HARLEQUIN®
Makes any time special®

Visit us at www.eHarlequin.com

PHR-R2

$ Saving Money $
Has Never Been
This Easy!

Just fill out and send in this form from any
October, November and December 2002 books
and we will send you a coupon booklet worth a
total savings of $20.00 off future purchases of
Harlequin and Silhouette books in 2003.

Yes! It's that easy!

I accept your incredible offer!
Please send me a coupon booklet:

Name (PLEASE PRINT)

Address _____ Apt. #

City _____ State/Prov. _____ Zip/Postal Code

In a typical month, how many
Harlequin and Silhouette novels do you read?

❏ 0-2   ❏ 3+

097KJKDNC7   097KJKDNDP

Please send this form to:
   In the U.S.: Harlequin Books, P.O. Box 9071, Buffalo, NY 14269-9071
   In Canada: Harlequin Books, P.O. Box 609, Fort Erie, Ontario L2A 5X3

Allow 4-6 weeks for delivery. Limit one coupon booklet per household. Must be
postmarked no later than January 15, 2003.

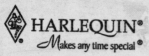

HARLEQUIN®
Makes any time special ®

Silhouette®
Where love comes alive™

© 2002 Harlequin Enterprises Limited   PHQ402

HEAT UP YOUR HOLIDAY SEASON BY SPENDING TIME
WITH THREE IRRESISTIBLE MEN...

Latin Lovers

A *brand-new* collection from
New York Times Bestselling Author

PENNY JORDAN
LYNNE GRAHAM
LUCY GORDON

Three handsome Mediterranean men are about to propose
seasonal seductions—and mistletoe marriages—in these
sensational stories by three of your favorite authors.

Look for it in stores—October 2002.

HARLEQUIN®
Makes any time special®

Visit us at www.eHarlequin.com

PHLL

S0-BRA-250

The Truth About
SUN *Exposure*

The Benefits and Dangers Revealed

PETER LAMAS

Strength
& Honor

BRONZE
BOW PUB.

The information in this book is for educational purposes only and is not recommended as a means of diagnosing or treating an illness. Neither the publisher nor author is engaged in rendering professional advice or services to the individual reader. All matters regarding physical and mental health should be supervised by a health practitioner knowledgeable in treating that particular condition. Neither the author nor the publisher shall be liable or responsible for any loss, injury, or damage allegedly arising from any information or suggestion in this book.

The Truth About Sun Exposure
Copyright © 2003 Peter Lamas
All Scripture quotations, unless otherwise indicated, are taken from the *Holy Bible, New International Version*®. NIV®.
Copyright © 1973, 1978, 1984 by International Bible Society.
Used by permission of Zondervan Publishing House. All rights reserved.
ISBN 1-932458-06-9
Published by Bronze Bow Publishing, Inc.,
2600 East 26th Street, Minneapolis, MN 55406.
You can reach us on the Internet at
WWW.BRONZEBOWPUBLISHING.COM
Literary development and cover/interior design by Koechel Peterson & Associates, Inc., Minneapolis, Minnesota.
Manufactured in the United States of America

CONTENTS

BOOKS BY PETER LAMAS

Beauty & Health Glossary
Beauty Basics
Dying to Be Beautiful
The Truth About Sun Exposure
Ultimate Anti-Aging Secrets

ABOUT THE AUTHOR

PETER LAMAS is Founder and Chairman of Lamas Beauty International, one of the fastest growing and respected natural beauty products manufacturers in the United States. He has been a major force in the beauty industry for more than 30 years. Peter's career began in New York City as an apprentice to trailblazers Vidal Sassoon and Paul Mitchell, providing the opportunity to work with some of the most famous and beautiful women of our time. His expertise in the areas of hair care, skin care, and makeup has given him a client list that reads like a *who's who of celebrities*.

His work has spanned numerous films, television, video, and print projects, including designing the gorgeous makeup used on the set of the epic film, *Titanic*. Peter has worked with the great names in fashion and beauty photography, including Richard Avedon, Irving Penn, and Francesco Scavullo. His work has been seen in photo shoots in leading magazines, such as *Vogue, Harper's Bazaar, Glamour,* and *Mademoiselle*.

Peter regularly appears on television and in the media in North and South America, Europe, and Asia. He travels extensively across the globe, speaking to women of many different cultures about how they can realize their potential to be beautiful both inside and out, especially educating them about the facts and myths on beauty products.

Cuban born Peter Lamas immigrated to New

York in 1961. Several years later, while pursuing a career as a commercial artist, Peter decided to finance his education by doing hair and makeup. As a result, he discovered he not only had a flair for doing hair and makeup, but he truly enjoyed helping each client look her best.

Peter's life has been dedicated to helping women feel good about themselves, by helping them realize their vast potential for personal beauty. To him, beauty is not just about the perfect haircut or makeup; it's about the full package. He can make just about any woman look absolutely stunning; but if she doesn't feel beautiful, she won't be. Beauty is very personal, and contrary to the cliché "that beauty is in the eye of the beholder," he came to realize that it is also in the eye of the possessor, because what makes us truly attractive to others is the projection of our self-esteem. Grace, confidence, and personality play a major role in attractiveness.

Peter's web site, www.lamasbeauty.com, is one of the largest women's beauty and health information resources on the Internet, through which he and a host of contributing writers keep women and men informed on important beauty and health topics.

Mr. Lamas is an innovative product developer in the cosmetics industry and recently received the distinguished honor from *Health Magazine* for developing the "Best Moisturizer of the Year." You can learn more about Peter's company, Lamas Beauty International, by visiting www.lamasbeauty.com or emailing him directly at peterlamas@lamasbeauty.com.

INTRODUCTION

And God said, "Let there be light." —GENESIS 1:3

SINCE the creation of planet earth, mankind has lived under the constant exposure to sunlight and ultraviolet light. If one studies the benefits of sunlight, it is evident just how good it is for our health and wellness. For centuries, natural healers and medical practitioners treated certain illnesses by exposure to direct sunlight. Heliotherapy, as it is called, has used the sunlight to treat rickets (a bone disease), tuberculosis (a lung disease), wounds, and help people regain strength after an illness.

Today, we also know that the positive benefits derived from sunlight must be balanced. As with all the "good" things of creation, abuse of any of them is destructive. Modern science has shown that sunlight and environmental exposure are the chief causes of premature aging of the skin. Since the skin is the largest organ of the body, sun damage thus affects your whole body. In fact, few beauty issues have raised more concerns than the effect of sunlight, in the short and long term, on the health, beauty, and well-being of our skin. And scientists are still finding new reasons to be concerned about overexposure to sunlight—

whether it's the kind we're all exposed to every day or the intense kind we get in the summer when we are outdoors or on the beach for hours at a time.

This book is a primer on many different areas of concern when it comes to you, your skin, and the sun. It's important to know the facts about sun exposure and what you can do to limit the damage the sun does to your skin—and even more important, to your children's skin, while they are at the age most vulnerable to sun damage.

The good news is that thanks to today's technology and what we now know about prevention, much can be done to prevent sun damage and maintain healthy younger-looking skin for life.

CHAPTER ONE

The Positive Effects
OF SUNLIGHT

WHILE the primary concern of this book is on how to protect yourself from the dangers of exposure to sunlight, it is important to not forget the health benefits of getting out into the sun. With more and more people spending most of their time under artificial lighting in offices and homes, it is possible to not get enough sunlight. And with today's warnings about overexposure to sunlight, we can become so fearful that we miss out on what we need for daily living.

BOOST YOUR SEROTONIN

Consider for a moment how much better you feel

when the sun is shining. Sunlight increases the production of the "feel good" brain chemical, serotonin, which improves your mood and helps drive back depression. This is why as the fall season turns over to winter, and the daylight hours shrink, many people suffer from Seasonal Affective Disorder (SAD)—a cyclic mood disorder caused by sunlight deprivation. While certain antidepressants that boost serotonin levels in the brain have become popular, sunlight also boosts serotonin. It also helps to control your sleep patterns and body temperature and to increase sex hormones.

BOOST YOUR VITAMIN D

Most people know about the positive benefits of sunlight on the production of Vitamin D, but here's a quick review. Vitamin D is a fat-soluble vitamin that promotes the body's absorption of calcium, which is essential for the normal development and maintenance of healthy teeth and bones. A lack of Vitamin D can be caused by a lack of it in your diet or by inadequate exposure to sunlight which helps the body make it. A lack of Vitamin D can lead to rickets or osteomalacia, a painful disease where the bones soften and are prone to bending and structural change.

MULTILEVEL BENEFITS

Other positive effects of sunlight include the treatment of chronic skin conditions such as acne, psoriasis, and eczema. It can help decrease blood pressure and lower your resting heart rate, lower cholesterol levels, increase cardiac output, and increase resistance to infections. Much of this is related to the role sunlight plays in helping the body make its own Vitamin D.

SUNLIGHT IS ESSENTIAL

The fact that overexposure to sunlight is damaging should not drive us to complete avoidance of it. To do that would be the equivalent of saying that because you burn your hand when you put it in a fire that you should toss your furnace out of your house. Sunlight is as important as vital nutrients to your body.

Before we move on to the importance of safeguarding the skin, we begin with a look at the complexity of our skin—its function, structure, problems, and solutions.

CHAPTER TWO

Skin 101

THE skin, perhaps more than any other aspect of our body, effectively reflects our life and experience. Yet it is also the most vulnerable. The skin is continually threatened by the ravages of time and the unpredictable effects of the environment. Safeguarding its health and appearance, at every age, is extremely important for all of us, women and men alike.

The psychological effects of changes in our appearance, and especially the aging process, determine our state of mind as powerfully as physical changes are reflected in the body. Our looks are a fundamental part of our sense of self. And, at best, they provide us with a sense of confidence and well-being in our personal and social relations. Thanks to today's scientific advances in technology and what research has learned about the functioning of skin, the ability to take care of one's skin and maintain its fitness has become possible for everyone, not just the privileged, wealthy few.

THE SKIN

Your birthday suit—do you know how special it is? Everyone's skin is the same, yet quite different. Skin has a personality just like you do, although it's made up of basic elements all skins have in common.

The first step in learning to take care of your skin well—for life—is to know what you're dealing with: A wonderful, living, breathing organ that never stops changing, growing, or needing your attention and help to be beautiful.

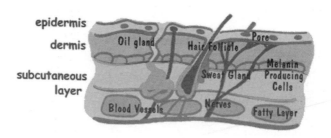

Skin is the largest organ of our body. It accounts for about 15 percent of our body weight, or approximately 6 pounds. What we see on the surface is just the beginning.

There are actually 3 essential skin layers:

- the epidermis—the skin you see.
- the dermis—the layers just below the surface.
- the subcutaneous layer—the innermost layer.

Like a team, each layer performs a specific, important function. Together the three layers form a protective barrier against the outside world to keep vital elements, such as moisture and heat, in, and the world out.

Your skin is intimately connected to your nervous system and emotions. It feels with you. Blushing, turning pale, or glowing, your skin reveals your most intense thoughts and emotions, and often your internal health is revealed in your skin color, texture, and general condition.

THE FIVE MOST IMPORTANT FUNCTIONS OF SKIN

- **Elimination.** All day, every day, skin removes toxins and debris as it sheds dead cells.
- **Secretion.** The skin's many sebaceous and sweat

glands help the body eliminate oil and perspiration.

- **Reproduction.** New cells are constantly being born through cell division in the basal skin layer. In young skin, on average, the process takes 28 days. But as we age, cell reproduction slows down. By the time we are 70 or 80 years old, new cells can take up to 37 days to develop.

- **Respiration.** Your skin can't live without oxygen. It is crucial to cell life and renewal. The skin gets its oxygen supply from oxygen-bearing blood circulating through the cells and by drawing it in from the air.

- **Moisture Control.** It's key to healthy, young-looking skin. Healthy skin maintains its moisture balance naturally. Moisturizers assist by adding even more moisture to the skin and locking it onto the surface. Firmness, suppleness, and smoothness are determined by your skin's moisture content.

THE PHYSIOLOGY OF SKIN

The Epidermis

The epidermis is the protective shield layer of your skin. It constantly renews itself by shedding old cells to make room for new. The epidermis is actually comprised of five sub layers. The two to know about are:

- **the strateum corneum**—the visible layer. Speed up the shedding process of this layer and voilà: better skin clarity, reduced appearance of fine lines and wrinkles.
- **the basal cell layer**—where new cells are born. Here amino acids, fatty acids, and other vital substances provided by the blood are transformed into new skin cells. These cells gradually move up to the strateum corneum in a 28-day cycle.

Within the basal cell layer are cells responsible for skin color. They produce the amount of melanin that creates your natural skin tone. Melanin also protects your skin against the sun. When you sun, even more melanin is produced, resulting in a tan, freckles, or the splotches we call "sun," "age," or "liver" spots. Sunning, in effect, puts your skin's melanin production into overdrive, trying to protect your skin from burning.

The Dermis

The dermis is the most important part of the skin's structure. It serves three important functions:

- It nourishes and supports the epidermis and helps it stay elastic and supple.
- It delivers nutrients to the epidermis through the circulatory system.
- It includes the cells that produce collagen and

elastin proteins that provide a support system of connective tissues that lend resiliency to the skin.

The dermis is also where deep wrinkles first form. It is the source of blood vessels, sebaceous and sweat glands, hair follicles, and pressure sensitive nerves that signal pain and touch. Waste products and carbon dioxide are eliminated from tissues, carried away by the circulating blood.

The Subcutaneous Layer

The subcutaneous layer is also called the "fatty layer." It is considerably thicker in women, thus giving the face a softer quality and finer texture than men's. As your skin ages, this layer diminishes, giving the face a more angular appearance. It is the "shock absorber" for the skin. The deeper hair follicles and sweat glands also originate here. It serves six important functions:

- Insulation and heat conservation
- A cushion against injury to bones
- Softens angles and creates pleasing curves
- Supports the upper layers, blood vessels, and nerves
- Acts like a nutrient reservoir
- Contains sensory and motor nerves that create our sense of touch

CHAPTER THREE

Sun . . . at Your Own RISK

WHAT is the most prevalent cancer among women between the ages of 25 and 29? Skin cancer, which is caused, in most cases, by sun exposure. We've all heard the warnings of dermatologists about the dangers of suntanning. But did you know that the incidence of melanoma—the most dangerous and often fatal form of skin cancer—has skyrocketed from 1 case in 1500 people to 1 in 75?

Fact: In the year 2003, the American Cancer Society estimated that out of the 54,200 people who would be diagnosed with melanoma, an estimated 7,600 people would die.

Fact: Melanoma is now the most prevalent cancer among women between the ages of 25 and 29. It is the second most prevalent cancer, after breast cancer, among women between the ages of 30 and 34.

Fact: Melanoma accounts for only 4 percent of all skin cancers detected, but a shocking 79 percent of all cancer deaths. If detected early, melanoma is almost always curable. However, it is much more likely than basal or squamous cell cancer to metastasize (spread) to other parts of the body.

Fact: Man or woman, 1 out of every 6 Americans will develop skin cancer during their lifetime. Overall, more men than women get skin cancers. But women, under the age of 40, develop them more frequently than men, possibly because of their suntanning habits.

THE MOST COMMON SYMPTOM OF SKIN CANCER

Doctors tell us to get a checkup if we notice a change in the size, shape, or color of a mole or freckle. But it's not the visible change of the mole that's most significant, but how deeply the change in the tissue has penetrated into the dermis. Anything deeper than 1.5 millimeters is serious because at that level melanoma can metastasize into your lymph nodes. Melanoma is fast and deadly. It can also metastasize through the blood to the brain, lungs, and in all your organs—anywhere in your body, in fact. It's a cancer that, if it has spread too far, is not successfully treated by chemotherapy, radiation, interferon, or any other known cancer treatment today.

WHO'S AT RISK FROM THE SUN?

Dermatologists say the light-skinned, fair-haired, and light-eyed are most at risk. Also, the very young and the very old, whose skin tends to be thinner and more fragile. And anyone with a family history of melanoma or other skin cancers should be vigilant about protection. There is also some evidence that women are more at risk for melanoma during pregnancy and postpartum, because melanocyte-stimulating hormones are secreted by the brain during that time and they may cause the skin to burn faster. Even dark-skinned African Americans are at risk, because skin cancer can occur on the lighter areas of palms and the soles of the feet.

WHY DOES THE SKIN TAN AT ALL?

Tanning is actually the skin's first defense against further damage. Our bodies contain the tanning pigment, melanin, to form a protective barrier so the sunlight cannot penetrate the lower layers of the skin where the DNA can get genetically mutated. Once it gets into the lower layers it can lead to precancerous and cancerous conditions. The more pigment our skin has naturally, the more protection it provides from burning. Scientists say that people living near the equator developed darker skins as a means of protection from the searing sunlight of those regions. But don't be complacent. Even people of Latin, African, or Mediterranean descent, with plenty of pigment in their skin, are showing up in doctors' offices these days with melanoma and sun-related skin problems.

SUN DAMAGE (PHOTOAGING) AND WRINKLES

The role of the sun cannot be overestimated as the most important cause of prematurely aging skin (called *photoaging*) and skin cancers. Overall, exposure to ultraviolet (referred to as UVA or UVB) radiation emanating from sunlight accounts for about 90 percent of the symptoms of premature skin aging, and most of these effects occur by age 18.

Sunlight consists of ultraviolet (referred to as UVA or UVB) radiation, which penetrates the layers of the skin. Both UVA and UVB rays cause damage leading to wrinkles, lower immunity against infection, aging skin disorders, and cancer. They appear to damage cells in different ways, however.

UVB radiation is the primary cause of sunburn. Because of its shorter wavelength, however, UVB primarily affects the outer skin layers. UVB appears to damage skin cells by directly bombarding the genetic material, *the DNA*, inside the skin cells.

UVA radiation is composed of longer wavelengths. They penetrate more deeply and efficiently into the inner skin layers and are responsible for tanning and allergic reactions to sunlight (such as from medication). The main damaging effect of UVA appears to be the promotion of the release of *oxidants*, also called oxygen-free radicals. These unstable particles are the result of many chemical processes in the body. In excess, however, they can damage cell membranes and interact with genetic material. They possibly contribute to the development of a number of skin disorders, including wrinkles and, more importantly, cancer. The large surface area of the skin makes it a prime target for oxidants.

THREE TYPES OF SUN-CAUSED SKIN CANCER

Basal cell carcinoma (non-melanoma cancer): 75 percent of all skin cancers. The survival rate after 5 years is 99 percent.

Squamous cell carcinoma (non-melanoma cancer): 20 percent of all skin cancers. The survival rate after 5 years is 95 percent.

Melanoma Skin Cancer (advanced malignant melanoma): 4 to 5 percent of all skin cancers, yet it represents 79 percent of all cancer deaths.

In 2003, an estimated over one million new cases of non-melanoma skin cancer will be diagnosed and 1,900 deaths will occur. In 2003, an estimated 54,200 new cases of melanoma cancer will be diagnosed and 7,600 deaths will occur.

WOMEN AND SKIN CANCER

Legs and Feet: Women develop three times as many melanomas and basal cell carcinomas on the legs as men.

Age Factors: More women than men under the age of 40 develop skin cancer.

Survival: Women have a better overall cure rate than men. Women tend to discover their skin cancers earlier, thus improving their chances for successful treatment.

MEN AND SKIN CANCER

Scalp and Ears: Men are two to three times more likely to develop cancer in these areas.

Face: Men are twice as likely to develop cancer on the left side of their faces. Note that when you drive, your left side is more exposed to light.

Nose: Men have one and a half times as many squamous carcinomas of the nose than women.

Chest, Back, and Shoulders: The prime areas for malignant melanoma in men. Men develop one and a half times as many melanomas on their backs as women.

Age Factors: More men over 50 will develop and die from malignant melanoma than women.

CHAPTER FOUR

Are You at Risk for SKIN CANCER?

TAKE THE TWO-MINUTE QUESTIONNAIRE. IT COULD SAVE YOUR LIFE.

Heredity and lifestyle play major roles in determining who gets skin cancer. To find out if you're in the high-risk group, ask yourself the following questions. Only one "yes" means you have a higher-than-average risk of developing skin cancer. The good news is that it is one of the most treatable of all cancers when detected early. Check your whole body every month, including in the armpits and between your toes. Have a dermatologist check you out head to toe once a year.

1. Family History: Has anyone in your family had skin cancer?

2. Ancestral Traits: Do you have Scandinavian or Celtic ancestors, fair or sensitive skin, blond or red hair, and/or blue or green eyes?

3. Mole Changes: Have you noticed any change in a mole or freckle—size, shape, color, or consistency? Any changes noticed in the skin around it, such as redness or swelling?

4. Large Moles: Do you have moles larger than a pencil eraser? Are they multicolored—blue, black, brown, tan, red, or pink? Do any have irregular borders? Do you have a lot of moles on your back?

5. Slow Healing: Do you have any open sores or wounds that refuse to heal or have been present for more than 2 weeks?

6. Discomfort: Do you have any spots or growths that repeatedly itch, hurt, crust over, scab, erode, or bleed?

7. Texture: Do you have a pearly, rough or unusual patch or lump on a high-risk area such as the lower part of the nose, or around the nose, eyes, or ears, on the ear itself, or on the center of the upper lip, the scalp, or temples?

8. Sunburn History: Did you experience at least one or two severe sunburns as a child or before the age of 18?

9. Short Hair: Do you have a short haircut that exposes your ears and the back of your neck?
10. Skip Sunscreen: Do you save it only for the summer or when you're skiing or on a sunny vacation spot?

CHAPTER FIVE

Sunproof Your CHILD

W<small>E</small> all need protection, regardless of heredity, sex, or age, but dermatologists say the young are at greatest risk because up to 80 percent of the damage caused by ultraviolet rays occurs before the age of 18. Why? Kids spend more time outdoors and in the sun. What's most disturbing about this exposure is that it takes decades for all the evidence to show up on the surface—in wrinkles, rough grainy texture, sagging, loss of firmness, and cancer. It's impossible to tell whether that basal cell carcinoma started last summer or 30 years ago in the family's backyard sandbox.

SIX EASY WAYS TO PROTECT YOUR KIDS

1. *Put a hat on.* Look for a wide brim and an

elastic chin strap for toddlers. This provides great protection against heat as well as sun exposure.

2. *Clothing considerations.* Diaper-only dressing may seem practical and cute, but it's too much exposure for baby skin. Loose-fitting, light-colored tees, tops, rompers, shorts, and pants are cool and comfy with better skin coverage by far. Be aware that up to 50 percent of ultraviolet rays can go through wet clothing, such as tee shirts worn for swimming.

3. *Make sunscreen a part of your child's daily grooming.* Don't wait till you get to the beach or playground and your child is too excited to stand still while you put it on!

4. *Use a sunblock specifically for kids.* Words to look for on the package include allergy tested, PABA free, formulated to be gentle enough for children's skin, and one that won't sting if it gets in the eyes. Waterproof is ideal if your child will be in and out of the water. Keep in mind that as much as 96 percent of ultraviolet rays can penetrate clear water.

5. *Sunglasses.* Older kids love the cool look. Buy sunglasses that are shatterproof and feature UVA and UVB protectant lenses.

6. *Have plenty of liquids on hand.* Kids get sweaty fast. Have plenty of water, juice, and other fluids handy to prevent dehydration. Reapply sunscreen often, because it gets diluted with perspiration.

CHAPTER SIX

Sunscreen and
SPF

THE first sunscreen was developed in 1928. In 1943, PABA (para-aminobenzoic acid) was discovered to be a powerful sun blocker. But it was not until 1978 that the Food and Drug Administration categorized sunscreens as drugs and began regulating them as such, so that the consumer could have some assurance of efficacy.

SPF

SPF stands for Sun Protective Factor, which sounds simpler than its explanation. The official explanation is that it is a number based on the minimal erythema dose or MED multiplied by the SPF number (the degree to which a sun cream, lotion, screen, or block provides protection against the sun). The MED number is the amount of sun exposure required to produce mild redness in the "average" skin.

Multiply your SPF number x 10 to find out how many minutes you can stay out in the sun without burning. If it takes 10 minutes to produce redness in the "average" skin (the MED number) and the SPF of your product is 15, it takes 10 x 15 = 150 minutes of sun exposure before your skin begins to show redness.

The SPF measurement guards against UVB exposure, but not always for UVA. You don't know when you're getting too much UVA rays because you don't see redness on your skin. UVA rays are sneakier. They penetrate and do their worst under the epidermis. SPF numbers are important to get a general sense of how much protection you're getting, but they are not the whole story.

Darker skins have lots more natural melanin in them—the determinant of pigment—and are more resistant to burning in general. But be wary anyway. You could be burning even though you don't see any visible redness. Palms and the soles of feet are vulnerable to sun damage, too.

TAN TODAY . . . BURN TOMORROW?

Keep in mind the many variables of sunlight. You may find yourself burning faster on the beach in high summer or the slopes in high winter than you will in your own backyard. Each 1,000-foot increase in elevation adds 4 percent to the intensity of the sunlight. A cool day with thin clouds may feel safe, but you're still getting from 60 to 80 percent of the ultraviolet rays. Don't assume that the amount of sun you could tolerate in Minnesota is the same as what you can handle on the beach in Mexico.

Have a few different levels of SPF protection on hand and adjust them to how your skin seems to be reacting today—not how it did a few years ago or even last summer. You change and so does your skin.

RX FOR SUN DAMAGE—
SUN AND SOME MEDICINE DON'T MIX

In this day of complex medications, some people may find themselves inexplicably reddening faster under the sun than they ever did before. For instance, users of Retin-A are routinely warned to avoid sun exposure because their skin becomes extra photosensitive and easily sunburned.

DON'T WASH YOUR PROTECTION AWAY

Look for a sunblock or screen that is not water-soluble. Even moderate perspiration can wash away protection, not to mention swimming and water sports. However, the newest products are water-resistant or even waterproof to allow for long-term, continuous water exposure without washing off. This is great news for swimmers and people who don't want to reapply sunblock or screen after every dip in the ocean or pool.

COMMONLY FOUND INGREDIENTS IN SUNSCREENS AND SUNBLOCKS

PABA: Although well known, it is not the best sunblock you can use. It only blocks UVB light, not UVA. It can cause contact dermatitis (irritation) on some people, and it stains clothing.

Cinnamates: They absorb UVB, but minimal UVA. They are insoluble in water, so they are used in waterproof sun protectors.

Salicylates: These were actually the first UVB sunscreens ever used, dating back to 1928. They only block UVB, but they are not water-soluble and are very stable and non-sensitizing.

Benzophenones: These block UVA and UVB light. But

they are water-soluble, so ordinary perspiration and water removes them.

Anthranilates: They provide multiple UVA blockage. Generally safe and stable, but they are oil-soluble, which means they will lose their effectiveness if you put an oil-rich lotion or cream or an oily suntan product over them.

Physical Agents: These are ingredients in your product that block UVA, UVB, visible light, and infrared radiation. White zinc oxide, for example, the lifeguard's friend, is an old-fashioned physical agent. Some of today's newer versions have reduced the particle size down considerably, so they are micro-fine and not so unsightly. In solution or lotion, a physical agent such as titanium oxide provides a broad protective barrier, yet is more cosmetically acceptable than the old formulas.

SUNSCREENS—THE FUTURE IS BRIGHT

New technology may include:

- Longer-lasting broader-range sunscreens.
- Using the body's own melanin to block burning.
- Vitamins A, C, and E to help protect and heal.
- Anti-aging ingredients that destroy free radicals—the unstable molecules released by our

skin when they're hit by sunlight and pollutants, leading to wrinkles and aging.

On a personal note, I'm very proud of a prestigious award I recently received. *Health Magazine* named the Lamas Beauty *Pro-Vita C Moisturizer SPF 15,* which I developed, as the "Best Moisturizer of the Year," after commissioning dermatologists across the United States to test a wide variety of moisturizers offered by cosmetics companies. The *Pro-Vita C Moisturizer SPF 15* was selected on the basis of its sun protective properties as well as unique blend of anti-aging ingredients.

CHAPTER SEVEN

Everyday Sun: Where Most Sun DAMAGE OCCURS

CONTRARY to what most people think, most sun damage and aging of your skin is caused by incidental exposure to everyday sunlight—not lengthy sunbathing—between the hours of 10 a.m. and 4 p.m. For example, people who walk or drive a lot get a surprising amount of UVA exposure in the course of their normal day. In addition, winter sunlight is as damaging as summer sunlight, yet few people think to put on sunscreen during the cold weather months. Aging caused by light exposure, called photoaging, is the biggest cause of facial wrinkles, crow's feet, grainy texture, freckles, and age spots.

Did you know that you could get sun damage just by sitting near a sunny window? UVA light is the culprit. Like all light, UVA penetrates glass and penetrates your skin—well past the epidermis and into the dermal layers you can't see. Although UVA rays only cause 1/1000th of the redness caused by UVB rays—the light primarily responsible for sunburn—they are even more damaging to your skin. Sitting by a window, even if you don't feel heat or redness, you can still be exposed to the skin-cancer-producing damage of UVA light exposure.

Unlike UVB light, which is strongest between 2 to 4 p.m., the sun emits the same amount of UVA light all day long. Some sunscreens are very good at blocking UVB light but are not as effective at blocking UVA. Read labels on your sunscreen carefully. You want a screen or block that does both. Without double protection, you could be staying out longer, thinking you're protected, but in fact, you're still giving your skin an overdose of UVA with all that additional sun time.

A quick look at the skin on the inside of your arm compared to the outside of the arm shows you the difference light exposure makes in skin quality.

What to do? Block. Block the sun whenever, wherever, and however. Thanks to today's sun care research, fueled by increasing concerns about aging, skin cancer, and the dangers of a thinning ozone layer, there are more ways to fight back against photoaging.

Not only will blocking the sun prevent burning and aging, it will also help control such common skin disorders as Porphyria, a condition that forms blisters on the hands and face when they are overexposed to light. Another concern that scientists are studying is the structural changes in skin cells caused by infrared radiation caused by everyday light exposure.

TANNING SALONS

Any credible dermatologist will tell you to avoid them completely. They are unregulated by any industry watch guard, so you have no assurance of what you're really being exposed to. The ultraviolet light you receive at any visit varies in intensity depending on the age of the bulb. Meaning, you could spend 10 minutes in a tanning bed one week and come out with a light glow, but the next visit you get burned in the same amount of time because the bulb was changed in the interim! The ultraviolet light from the tanning beds will damage healthy skin cells and deplete collagen levels and reduce elasticity. Collagen is what keeps the skin plump and firm—youthful looking. I call it the stuffing of the mattress. Once the collagen levels start depleting you will notice the skin becoming looser and the lines and wrinkles becoming more prominent.

THE OZONE AND SKIN

As has been clearly documented, the ozone layer is weaker and thinner than it used to be due to man-made pollution, and it's thinner over some areas of the earth than others. In the U.S., for example, sunlight has been measured to be 1 to 3 percent stronger than it was in 1978.

CHAPTER EIGHT

Repairing the
DAMAGE

IRONICALLY, Americans are pursuing the Fountain of Youth more avidly than ever, yet doing exactly what makes their skin age the fastest—exposing it to the sun. Since Coco Chanel first popularized suntans in the '20s, a sun-kissed glow has come to symbolize the good life of leisure, youth, and healthy living. It's the American Way to spend hours in the sun—on the beach, at the pool, on the tennis court, or even just working on the backyard garden. Outdoor living may be part of our lifestyle, but it's burning the life out of our skin.

Sun exposure causes a whopping 80 percent of the changes we characterize as "aging" in our skin.

THE SIGNS OF UVR—ULTRAVIOLET RADIATION DAMAGE (SUNLIGHT)

- Freckles
- Thinning or thickening of the skin
- Blotchy pigmentation
- Enlarged or broken blood vessels
- Loss of firmness
- Wrinkles and crow's feet
- Rough texture
- "Age" or "sun" spots
- Skin cancers

REPAIRING THE DAMAGE

Today's high-tech treatments can reverse the damage...to a degree. Here are the most effective treatments money can buy:

Laser Therapy

Laser therapy is the highest tech remedy for removing lines and wrinkles. Using high-beam light, doctors can vaporize wrinkles, age spots, and crow's feet in seconds.

Negatives: Lasers are good "erasers" for lines and dark spots, but they can't recontour skin that has lost its firmness. Some darker skins may show pigment changes. Sometimes touted as a quickie "lunch time" procedure, it rarely is. Depending on the degree of treatment and where it is, your skin is visibly red and raw for a week to 10 days.

Availability: Choose a dermatologist with an active laser practice.

Tretinoin—Vitamin A

Commonly called Retin-A, Tretinoin speeds up cell turnover, so younger, fresher skin emerges faster and evens out pigment irregularities. It lifts off the top layers of the skin to ease dryness and rough texture and soften visible lines. It stimulates collagen production to help replace collagen fibers broken by sun exposure. Originally used to treat acne, it is effective in smoothing the skin surface.

Negatives: Retin-A and the sun don't mix. Many people find it causes redness and irritation plus much greater sensitivity and faster burning even with moderate sun exposure.

Availability: The effective level of Retin-A you need for real improvement is available only by prescription. Usually in a cream or gel base, Johnson & Johnson's well-known Renova is a Retin-A treatment in an exceptionally rich cream to help counteract dryness and irritation, but it might aggravate oilier skins. For oily skin, gel-based Retin-A is a better choice. It combats acne as well as lines and wrinkles. Ignore the hype: Over-the-counter cosmetic products with Retin-A are too weak to offer much improvement.

Glycolic Acid

One of today's most popular treatments. It is recommended for resurfacing top layers of skin and easing lines and wrinkles. Glycolic acid is an alpha-hydroxy acid derived from sugar cane (other AHAs may derive from sugar-rich fruits). It quickly penetrates and loosens the "cement" that binds dead, old cells to the stratum corneum to permit the top layers of dead skin to shed evenly and rapidly. The new cells that emerge look fresher because they're younger and healthier. In a topical treatment using a cleanser or moisturizer, daily use smoothes the skin and evens out pigment irregularities, but to be effective you need a treatment that contains at least 10 percent glycolic acid.

Negatives: Irritation, burning, redness, and dryness.

Availability: The strongest glycolic "peels" are available at the dermatologist. These have a higher percentage of glycolic acid than is available over the counter. Peels can substantially help diminish fine wrinkles and age spots. If done weekly or biweekly for 6 to 12 consecutive sessions, increasing the strength gradually, the results, some doctors say, can be equivalent to a year's worth of nightly Retin-A. Weaker peels are available at many salons that also do some cosmetic resurfacing. Although cosmetic companies have jumped on the AHA bandwagon, most products you buy are too weak to achieve noticeable improvement beyond a little surface smoothing. To be effective they need to contain 10 percent or more glycolic acid or another AHA. Read labels and compare before you buy. Some of the best products are moderately priced drugstore brands.

Chemical Peels

Deeper penetrating and more intensive than glycolic acid, liquid chemical peels encourage even more shedding of dead or dry skin cells. After treatment, it typically takes a week to 10 days to reap their full benefits, which are a considerable reduction in acne scars, fine lines, age spots, and uneven textured areas. The best candidates for chemical peels are fair-skinned types with fine wrinkling or stubborn age spots to remove. Patients with darker skin, typically those with brown hair and eyes, may show irregular, blotchy pigmentation after a chemical peel.

Negatives: Skin is red and sensitive after treatment and should be treated carefully. Results are unpredictable with darker skins. Sun should definitely be avoided for up to 3 months after treatment.

Availability: Available only from dermatologists. Pick one who's well qualified in the procedure.

Dermabrasion

Once the best available treatments for serious skin damage, this mechanical abrading process is now reserved for extensive wrinkling, age spots, and problems such as precancerous crusts, called actinic keratoses, caused by the sun. It is very effective on the fine lines around the mouth and crow's feet.

Negatives: You'll leave the doctor's office bandaged and red, and your skin is not a pretty sight for 10 days to 2 weeks, so plan time off accordingly. No sun exposure for 3 to 6 months make this procedure best scheduled in the fall or early winter months. Like chemical peels, dermabrasion may result in uneven pigmentation if skin is dark or if only one part of the face is abraded.

Availability: Done only by a dermatologist. Pick one who's well experienced in dermabrasion.

Micro-Dermabrasion

The very latest in non-surgical, non-invasive

technology. It gives you immediate improvement by removing dead, flaking skin cells and stimulating the growth of fresh young skin cells and collagen. Like glycolic peels, the procedure is a real "lunch time" miracle, meaning there's no disruption to your normal activities afterward. Fine micro-crystals are vacuumed onto your skin by a technician through a hand-held device to polish the surface. In 10 to 30 minutes or so, your skin emerges with a pink glow. For serious problems such as acne scars, fine lines, scars, and melasma (over pigmentation or blotchiness), 2 to 12 visits are recommended. Micro-dermabrasion is safe and effective on all skin types and colors with excellent results reported, especially around the eyes, lips, and neck areas.

Negatives: Caucasian skin turns pink for a few days. All skins may feel a little sensitive. Some flaking will be noticed.

Availability: Dermatologists, skin-care salons, and day spas.

Collagen Injections

Collagen is one of today's most popular choices for wrinkle smoothing. Typically, it is injected via a very fine needle into fine or medium wrinkles on the forehead, eyes, lips, cheeks, and smile zones. Results show up in a week to 10 days, because the collagen plumps up tissue from underneath the surface and stimulates the skin's own production of collagen to plump up skin even farther.

Negatives: A collagen allergy test is a must before treatment. Results last on an average of 2 to 6 months, depending on the mobility of the areas treated and the amount injected. The very fine needle prevents most bruising, but some patients have slight bruising.

Availability: Only by a dermatologist. Pick one with an extensive cosmetic practice.

Botox

Quickly overtaking collagen injections in popularity, botox (the trade name of Botulinum Toxin Type A) is a purified toxin produced by the bacterium, clostridium botulinum. Pioneered in 1980 to treat "lazy eye" and uncontrolled eye blinking, botox has been used for wrinkles since 1989. Small doses, injected into facial muscles, especially in the forehead areas and between the eyes, paralyze the muscle and prevent it from contracting, so the lines above the muscle treated gradually fade away. It sounds scarier than it actually is. Injected via tiny needles into the skin, botox takes effect in 3 to 5 days and lasts from 3 to 5 months. Many doctors believe it is more effective than collagen in some areas of the face such as the forehead and around the eyes.

Negatives: Benefits are short-term, as the muscle action gradually returns. Some say botox injections are more painful than collagen injections. You may have a little bruising. A slight lowering of the eyelid may occur if botox is injected around the eyes or right above them—this is temporary. No permanent side effects have been reported from botox use.

Availability: Only by a dermatologist. Pick one with an extensive cosmetic practice.

Fat Injections

The dermatologist draws small amounts of fat from another part of your body and injects it under the grooves around your mouth, eyes, and between the brows. The big plus is that it's your own tissue, so your body won't experience any rejection or allergic reactions.

Negatives: Some say is more temporary than collagen with results lasting anywhere from 3 months to 3 years. And it means harvesting the fat from yet another part of your body to reinject into another—ouch!

Availability: Dermatologist only.

Electrocautery

After years of sun exposure, fine or broken veins may pop up or become more noticeable on the cheeks or around the nose. With a fine electric needle, the veins are cauterized to eliminate them. Three to 6 sessions may be required, but the procedure is uncomplicated and almost always very successful.

Negatives: Slightly uncomfortable for the second or two it takes to treat the vein. New veins must be treated as they occur. Some veins take several sessions to eliminate.

Availability: Through a dermatologist only.

Cryotherapy

Using liquid nitrogen or CO_2 slush, the dermatologist can remove dark age spots and very fine wrinkles. It is a subtle, non-invasive treatment that allows patients to wear makeup the same day.

Negatives: Several treatments may be required to achieve results.

Availability: Through a dermatologist only.

Facial Liposuction

Like liposuction for the body, facial liposuction firms and tightens sagging tissues. It is frequently used to restore a firm, smoothly contoured jaw line and correct the chin-neck angle back to a youthful 90 degrees.

Negatives: Liposuction is more of an operation than most of the other rejuvenating treatments and definitely not a "lunch time" procedure. Bruising is commonplace. If the skin is very loose, a surgical lift may be suggested along with liposuction to achieve the best results.

Availability: A cosmetic surgeon skilled in the procedure is highly recommended.

While the good news is that some of our bad behavior in the sun can be erased at the dermatologist's office, the best defense is still a good offense. Keep yourself and your children out of the sun when you can and use sunscreen when you are in the sun. When you think about it, it's not much to ask for a lifetime of looking younger and freedom from worries about serious skin problems.

CHAPTER NINE

The Art of SELF-TANNING

S ELF-TANNING has come a long way from the orangy, masky, phony looking versions of just a few years ago. Acceptance has grown tremendously, too. It used to be that people wouldn't admit they were faking it. Now it's offered in the best day spas and salons, and people pat themselves on the back for staying out of the sun and finding a new-tech way to get that golden glow.

NEVER SELF-TANNED?
HERE'S HOW TO GET GLOWING:

1. Pick the right brand for you, depending on whether you're fair skinned or darker skinned. Most

self-tanners come in two shades—light/medium or dark/deep. Be realistic and pick the one closest to your face, au natural, without a tan. When in doubt, pick the lightest version until you're confident about your color.

2. Get your skin ready. Self-tanners for the body have more pigment than ones for the face. Decide if you really want your face to be as dark as your body skin. Most spas and salons use a lighter version for the face for all but the darkest skinned clients.

3. The first thing a spa or salon does is give their clients a head-to-toe body sloughing with a mild exfoliating product. You should do the same. Dry areas will soak up more color than the rest of you and leave you looking blotchy. Be vigilant in the areas of your elbows, heels, and knees.

4. Once you've been scrubbed, your skin should be velvety smooth all over. Run your hands down your body. Any less-than-smooth areas need a little moisturizer to equalize them with the rest of you.

5. To prevent orangeade palms, before you start applying self-tanner, massage a pearl-sized dab of silicone-based hair product into your palm—one that controls frizzies is fine. This will block the self-tanner from being absorbed into your hands.

6. Self-tanner should be built up, layer by layer. Don't overdo it. If the tan turns out too light, you can

reapply later. Start with your feet and work your way up the body to your ears. Leave the tops of your hands until last.

7. Avoid getting self-tanner on lips, eyelids, brows, and nails.

8. When you're ready to do your hands, wash them first with soap and a nailbrush. Rinse carefully to avoid splashing water above the wrists and ruining the color you've already put on. Use a makeup sponge and apply self-tanner to your hands, one at a time, bending fingers to make sure the color gets into the creases. Let dry for 10 minutes, then do the other hand.

9. Your tan will last up to 7 days. To maintain color, just reapply every week. If your first coat is too light, simply reapply.

10. Keep your tan glowing all week by avoiding body scrubbers, Retin-A creams, anything with AHAs, BHAs, or glycolic acids—they all lift off the top layers of the skin and will alter your tan.

11. Don't save your self-tanner from one season to the next. Buy fresh to prevent ingredient breakdown and blotchy color.

12. Don't assume your tan is going to protect you from sun damage! Use sunscreen anytime you're out in the real thing!

CHAPTER TEN

The Stages of Your
SKIN'S LIFE

As efficient as skin is, it always needs help from you, the owner. That help includes:

- A regular regimen of daily cleansing and moisturizing
- A balanced, healthy diet
- Exercise
- Sleep
- Environmental protection

YEAR BY YEAR

Birthdays are inevitable, but a tired, worn, aged appearance isn't! With good lifelong care, much skin damage can be avoided or minimized. The good news: Its never too late to start to dramatically improve your skin's appearance now and years from now. The right skin habits can have dramatically beneficial effects on the skin despite time and the environment. The key is to avoid the sun as much as possible since sun—not time—is the primary cause of wrinkles and premature aging. Constantly exposed to the world and sunlight, the skin on your face always shows more wrinkling and damage than the skin of your body.

As you age, your skin undergoes significant changes. The cells divide more slowly, and the inner layer of skin (the dermis) starts to thin. Fat cells beneath the dermis begin to atrophy (diminish). The underlying network of elastin and collagen fibers, which provides scaffolding for the surface layers, loosens and unravels. Thus, your skin loses its elasticity. When pressed, it no longer springs back to its initial position but instead sags and forms furrows.

With aging, the sweat- and oil-secreting glands atrophy, depriving the skin of their protective water-lipid emulsions. The skin's ability to retain moisture then diminishes and it becomes dry and scaly. Frown lines (those between the eyebrows) and crow's feet (lines that radiate from the corners of the eyes) appear to develop because of permanent small muscle contractions. Habitual facial expressions also form characteristic lines. Gravity exacerbates the situation, contributing to the formation of jowls and drooping eyelids. Eyebrows, surprisingly, move up as a person ages, possibly because of forehead wrinkles. In addition, the ability of the skin to repair itself diminishes with age, so wounds are slower to heal.

YOUR SKIN IN ITS 20s

Pluses: Your skin glows with the radiant, fresh-faced look of youth. Cellular turnover is fast and efficient, usually in 28-day cycles. Estrogen and progesterone supply the oil that usually keeps 20s skin in perfect moisture balance. Collagen and elastin fibers are firm, smooth, and resilient, resulting in an equally soft, smooth skin texture. The fatty cushion is plump and gives the face softness.

Minuses: Even when you're young, burning the candle at both ends can result in puffy eyes, dehydration, and premature wrinkles. For many women, acne is still a concern. Sun exposure can make even skin in its youth dull, flaky, dehydrated, and reveal more damage later.

Solutions: An ounce of prevention is worth a pound

of cure. Wear a SPF 15 or higher sunscreen every day (not just on the beach). Have a twice a day cleansing routine to remove makeup thoroughly before bedtime and prevent bacteria and oil from building up and aggravating breakouts. Experiment with moisturizers, including oil-free versions, if you notice dryness. Eat a balanced diet and get plenty of exercise. Keep a watch on alcohol consumption. Don't smoke.

YOUR SKIN IN ITS 30s

Pluses: For many, the 30s are a prime time for their skin. Acne and excess oil production slow down. The skin may be perfectly balanced or only slightly on the dry side. The skin is clear, vital, glowing with health and vitality. Many women add sunscreen protection to their daily care, which is all to the good for the future.

Minuses: For others, age and environmental damage suddenly and clearly begin to show up in fine lines, crow's feet, capillary breaks, laugh lines, eyebrow grooves, and folds around the mouth. Cell turnover is slowing down, and the complexion may look dull or sallow. The production of new collagen fibers diminishes by about 1 percent a year while existing fibers twist and slacken.

Solutions: Many women first notice dehydration in their 30s. For most skins, unless they are oily or acne-prone, round-the-clock balanced moisturization is helpful. Frequent exfoliation boosts cell turnover and helps maintain a clear, fresh radiance.

YOUR SKIN IN ITS 40s

Pluses: By now, you know your skin. You have a more confident sense of what you need than ever before. You actually look better with less makeup than more. Time can only accent a great bone structure if you have it. If you've developed a good lifestyle and diet habits and avoided the sun in your 20s and 30s, you reap the rewards now.

Minuses: Your skin's ability to maintain optimum moisture on its own fades. Lines and wrinkles become more plentiful. Elastin fibers begin to thicken, which results in sagging and slackening, especially in the jaw area. Some crosshatching of lines and deepening expression lines between the eyes and across the forehead appear. Brown spots may pop up on cheeks or the backs of your hands. As menopause approaches, more dryness or oiliness may occur.

Solutions: A gentle cleanser that won't strip the skin of its natural level of sebum is ideal. A moisturizer with SPF 15 is recommended for day with a richer moisturizer/night treatment at night. Drink a minimum of eight 8-ounce glasses of water a day to plump skin and help eliminate toxins. If you've never taken vitamins, it's time to begin.

YOUR SKIN IN ITS 50s AND BEYOND

Pluses: If your skin had ups and downs in your 40s, it settles down after menopause. Most skin thrives on moisturizers and richer formulations and responds dramatically to the extra attention you can give. Many women get serious about diet and nutrition for the first time in their lives at this stage, which can help skin substantially now and years from now.

Minuses: As the fatty cushion thins, facial hollows can become more prominent. Under eye bags and slackening skin around the eyelids, nose, ears, and neck are common. Cell turnover and collagen and elastin fiber production continue to slow down. Facial bones—especially if you smoke—can shrink, causing all-around sagging. Overall, the skin is drier and less able to maintain moisture on its own.

Solutions: Sunscreen, SPF 15 or above, is recommended for daily use. Before bed, a rich moisturizer with alpha-hydroxy acids will gently exfoliate skin and boost cell turnover as it moisturizes. Avoid alcohol-based, moisture-depleting products. Diet, exercise, and nutrient supplementation are more important than ever.

CONCLUSION

Your entire life is lived inside your precious skin, so treat it with utmost loving care—the earlier in life the better. Realize that the needs of your skin change constantly—with weather, with the seasons, and especially with age. And realize that it's never too late to start caring for your skin. The most important thing you can do to safeguard it is to wear sunscreen and limit your time in the sun. Never ever allow your skin to be baked by sunlight. With the availability of excellent self-tanners today, you can still have a great looking tan without the damage!

> *"Beauty is in the eye of the beholder . . .*
> *but it is also in the eye of the possessor.*
> *What makes us truly attractive to others*
> *is the projection of our self-esteem."*
> —PETER LAMAS

PETER LAMAS is Founder of Lamas Beauty International as well as its principal product developer. Lamas Beauty International is one of the fastest growing and respected natural beauty products manufacturers in the United States. Their award-winning products are regarded as among the cleanest, purest, and most innovative in the beauty industry—products that are a synergy of *Beauty, Nature, and Science*. The company philosophy is to produce products that are safe, effective, free of harmful chemicals, environmentally friendly, and cruelty free. They insure that their products are free of animal ingredients and animal byproducts.

All of the Lamas Beauty International products can been seen and ordered from their web site, www.lamasbeauty.com. To contact them for a complete product catalog and order form or to place an order, please call toll free (888) 738-7621, Fax (713) 869-3266, or write:

LAMAS BEAUTY INTERNATIONAL
5535 Memorial Drive Ste. #F355
Houston, TX 77007

Lamas Beauty offers a full range of hair-care, body-care, and skin-care products. Some of the most recommended products include the following:

Pro-Vita C Vital Infusion Complex: Highly potent anti-aging cream that helps improve premature aging skin. Applied nightly, it defends, nourishes, and stimulates skin through a combination of three powerful antioxidants—*Vitamin C-Ester*, *Alpha Lipoic Acid*, and *DMAE* —all of which fight free radicals and help restore firm, supple, youthful-looking skin. Advanced delivery system encourages the skin's ability to regenerate, increases the skin's firmness and elasticity, minimizes the appearance of fine lines and wrinkles, and helps nurture mature skin.

Pro-Vita C Moisturizer SPF 15: Distinguished as "Product of the Year" by *Health Magazine*, as judged by dermatologists across the United States. A potent, multi-action formula to maximize protection during the day. Contains a high percentage of highly absorbable L-Ascorbic Vitamin C (one of nature's most powerful antioxidants), SPF 15 sunscreen protection against ultraviolet rays (UVA, UVB, and UVC rays), Hyaluronic Acid for intensive moisturizing, Vitamins A and E and Retinyl Palmitate (a derivative of wrinkle-smoothing Retin-A) in a unique delivery system.

Chinese Herb Stimulating Shampoo: A therapeutic special-care formula empowered with Chinese herbs used for centuries to promote healthy hair growth, stimulate and energize weak hair and scalp. Gently removes hair follicle-blocking sebum and debris that can slow growth and cause premature hair loss. This formula is mild and gentle and won't irritate, strip away color, or dehydrate hair or scalp. Helps alleviate dandruff and itchiness.

Firming & Brightening Eye Complex: Distinguished as "Product of the Year" by *DaySpa Magazine*. The major benefit of this anti-aging eye cream is its ability to lighten dark shadows and circles under the eyes through the unique natural ingredient, *Emblica*, which is extracted from the *Phyllanthus Emblica fruit* (a medicinal plant used in Ayurvedic medicine). Emblica has been shown to soften age signs, deep wrinkles, and lines as much as 68–90 percent in independent tests. Also provides intensive moisturization through Hyaluronic Acid, one of the most effective and expensive moisturizing ingredients available.

Unleash Your Greatness

AT BRONZE BOW PUBLISHING WE ARE COMMITTED

to helping you achieve your ultimate potential

in functional athletic strength, fitness, natural

muscular development, and all-around superb

health and youthfulness.

Our books, videos, newsletters, Web sites, and training seminars will bring you the very latest in scientifically validated information that has been carefully extracted and compiled from leading scientific, medical, health, nutritional, and fitness journals worldwide.

Our goal is to empower you! To arm you with the best possible knowledge in all facets of strength and personal development so that you can make the right choices that are appropriate for *you*.

Now, as always, **the difference between greatness and mediocrity** begins with a choice. It is said that knowledge is power. But that statement is a half truth. Knowledge is power only when it has been tested, proven, and applied to your life. At that point knowledge becomes wisdom, and in wisdom there truly is *power.* The power to help you choose wisely.

So join us as we bring you the finest in health-building information and natural strength-training strategies to help you reach your ultimate potential.

FOR INFORMATION ON ALL OUR EXCITING NEW SPORTS AND FITNESS PRODUCTS, CONTACT

BRONZE BOW PUBLISHING
2600 East 26th Street
Minneapolis, MN 55406

WEB SITES
www.bronzebowpublishing.com
www.masterlevelfitness.com

612.724.8200   Toll Free **866.724.8200**   FAX **612.724.899**

SO-BBY-151

10/24
STRAND PRICE
5.00

For all Families with a Teddy Bear

Publisher's Note

*The stories in this collection are reproduced in the form in which they appeared
upon first publication in the U.K. by George G. Harrap & Co. Ltd.
All spellings remain consistent with these original editions.*

KINGFISHER
Larousse Kingfisher Chambers Inc.
95 Madison Avenue
New York, New York 10016

First published in 2000
4 6 8 10 9 7 5

4TR/1000/THOM/(FR)/80MUN

The stories in this collection were first published by George G. Harrap & Co. Ltd.

Text and illustrations copyright © Joan G. Robinson,
1953, 1954, 1955, 1956, 1957, 1964

This selection copyright © Deborah Sheppard 1997

All rights reserved under International and
Pan-American Copyright Conventions

LIBRARY OF CONGRESS CATALOGING-IN-PUBLICATION DATA
Robinson, Joan G.
The Teddy Robinson storybook / by Joan G. Robinson.—1st [American] ed.
p.   cm.
Summary: Relates the adventures of a teddy bear and his owner.
ISBN 0-7534-5381-9
[1. Teddy bears—Fiction.] I. Title.

PZ7.R5664 Te 2000
[Fic]—dc21

99-058603

Printed in India

The
Teddy Robinson
Storybook

JOAN G. ROBINSON

NEW YORK

Contents

Teddy Robinson's Night Out

Teddy Robinson was a nice, big, comfortable, friendly teddy bear. He had light brown fur and kind brown eyes, and he belonged to a little girl called Deborah.

One Saturday afternoon Teddy Robinson and Deborah looked out of the window and saw that the sun was shining and the almond-tree in the garden was covered with pink blossom.

"That's nice," said Deborah. "We can play out there. We will make our house under the little pink tree, and you can get brown in the sun, Teddy Robinson."

So she took out a little tray with the dolls' tea set on it, and a blanket to sit on, and the toy telephone in case anyone rang them up, and she laid all the things out on the grass under the tree. Then she fetched a colouring book and some chalks for herself, and a book of nursery rhymes for Teddy Robinson.

Deborah lay on her tummy and coloured the whole of an elephant and half a Noah's ark, and Teddy Robinson stared hard at a picture of Humpty-Dumpty and tried to remember the words. He couldn't really read, but he loved pretending to.

He stared hard at a picture of Humpty-Dumpty

"Hump, hump, humpety-hump," he said to himself over and over again; and then, "Hump, hump, humpety-hump, Deborah's drawing an elephump."

"Oh, Teddy Robinson," said Deborah, "don't think so loud – I can't hear myself chalking." Then, seeing him still bending over his book, she said, "Poor boy, I expect you're tired. It's time for your rest now." And she laid him down flat on his back so that he could look up into the sky.

At that moment there was a loud *rat-tat* on the front door and a long ring on the doorbell. Deborah jumped up and ran indoors to see who it could be, and Teddy Robinson lay back and began to count the number of blossoms he could see in the almond-tree. He couldn't count more than four because he only had two arms and two legs to count on, so he counted up to four a great many times over, and then he began counting backwards, and the wrong way round, and any way round that he could think of, and sometimes he put words in between his counting, so that in the end it went something like this:

> *"One, two, three, four,*
> *someone knocking at the door.*
> *One, four, three, two,*
> *open the door and how d'you do?*
> *Four, two, three, one,*
> *isn't it nice to lie in the sun?*
> *One, two, four, three,*
> *underneath the almond-tree."*

And he was very happy counting and singing to himself for quite a long time.

9

Then Teddy Robinson noticed that the sun was going down and there were long shadows in the garden. It looked as if it must be getting near bedtime.

Deborah will come and fetch me soon, he thought; and he watched the birds flying home to their nests in the trees above him.

A blackbird flew quite close to him and whistled and chirped, "Goodnight, teddy bear."

"Goodnight, bird," said Teddy Robinson and waved an arm at him.

Then a snail came crawling past.

"Are you sleeping out tonight? That will be nice for you," he said. "Goodnight, teddy bear."

"Goodnight, snail," said Teddy Robinson, and he watched it crawl slowly away into the long grass.

She will come and fetch me soon, he thought. It must be getting quite late.

But Deborah didn't come and fetch him. Do you know why? She was fast asleep in bed!

This is what had happened. When she had run to see who was knocking at the front door, Deborah had found Uncle Michael standing on the doorstep. He had come in his new car, and he said there was just time to take her out for a ride if she came quickly, but she must hurry because he had to get into the town before teatime. There was only just time for Mummy to get Deborah's coat on and wave goodbye before they were off. They had come home ever so much later than they meant to because they had tea out in a shop, and then on the way home the new car had suddenly stopped and it took Uncle Michael a long time to find out what was wrong with it.

By the time they reached home Deborah was half-asleep, and Mummy had bundled her into bed before she had time to really wake up again and remember about Teddy Robinson still being in the garden.

He didn't know all this, of course, but he guessed something unusual must have happened to make Deborah forget about him.

Soon a little wind blew across the garden, and down fluttered some blossom from the almond-tree. It fell right in the middle of Teddy Robinson's tummy.

"Thank you," he said, "I like pink flowers for a blanket."

So the almond-tree shook its branches again, and more and more blossoms came tumbling down.

The garden tortoise came tramping slowly past.

"Hallo, teddy bear," he said. "Are you sleeping out? I hope you won't be cold. I felt a little breeze blowing up just now. I'm glad I've got my house with me."

*The garden tortoise
came tramping slowly past*

"But I have a fur coat," said Teddy Robinson, "and pink blossom for a blanket."

"So you have," said the tortoise. "That's lucky. Well, goodnight," and he drew his head into his shell and went to sleep close by.

The Next Door Kitten came padding softly through the grass and rubbed against him gently.

"You *are* out late," she said.

"Yes, I think I'm sleeping out tonight," said Teddy Robinson.

"Are you?" said the kitten. "You'll love that. I did it once. I'm going to do it a lot oftener when I'm older. Perhaps I'll stay out tonight."

But just then a window opened in the house next door and a voice called, "Puss! Puss! Puss! Come and have your fish! fish! fish!" and the kitten scampered off as fast as she could go.

Teddy Robinson heard the window shut down and then everything was quiet again.

The sky grew darker and darker blue, and soon the stars came out. Teddy Robinson lay and stared at them without blinking, and they twinkled and shone and winked at him as if they were surprised to see a teddy bear lying in the garden.

And after a while they began to sing to him, a very soft and sweet and far-away little song, to the tune of *Rock-a-Bye Baby*, and it went something like this:

"Rock-a-Bye Teddy, go to sleep soon.
We will be watching, so will the moon.
When you awake with dew on your paws
Down will come Debbie and take you indoors."

Teddy Robinson thought that was a lovely song, so when it was finished he sang one back to them. He sang it in a grunty voice because he was rather shy, and it went something like this:

"This is me
under the tree,
the bravest bear you ever did see.

13

> *All alone*
> *so brave I've grown,*
> *I'm camping out on my very own."*

The stars nodded and winked and twinkled to show that they liked Teddy Robinson's song, and then they sang *Rock-a-Bye Teddy* all over again, and he stared and stared at them until he fell asleep.

Very early in the morning a blackbird whistled, then another blackbird answered, and then all the birds in the garden opened their beaks and twittered and cheeped and sang. And Teddy Robinson woke up.

One of the blackbirds hopped up with a worm in his beak.

"Good morning, teddy bear," he said. "Would you like a worm for your breakfast?"

"Oh, no, thank you," said Teddy Robinson. "I don't usually bother about breakfast. Do eat it yourself."

"Thank you, I will," said the blackbird, and he gobbled it up and hopped off to find some more.

Then the snail came slipping past.

"Good morning, teddy bear," he said. "Did you sleep well?"

"Oh, yes, thank you," said Teddy Robinson.

"Would you like a worm for your breakfast?"

The Next Door Kitten came scampering up, purring.

"You lucky pur-r-son," she said as she rubbed against Teddy Robinson. "Your fur-r is damp but it was a pur-r-fect night for staying out. I didn't want to miss my fish supper last night, otherwise I'd have stayed with you. Pur-r-haps I will another night. Did you enjoy it?"

"Oh, yes," said Teddy Robinson. "You were quite right about sleeping out. It was lovely."

The tortoise poked his head out and blinked.

"Hallo," he said. "There's a lot of talking going on for so early in the morning. What is it all about? Oh,

15

She picked him up and hugged him.

good morning, bear. I'd forgotten you were here. I hope you had a comfortable night." And before Teddy Robinson could answer he had popped back inside his shell.

Then a moment later Teddy Robinson heard a little shuffling noise in the grass behind him, and there was Deborah out in the garden with bare feet, and in her pyjamas!

She picked him up and hugged him and kissed him and whispered to him very quietly, and then she ran through the wet grass and in at the kitchen door and up the stairs into her own room. A minute later she and Teddy Robinson were snuggled down in her warm little bed.

"You poor, poor boy," she whispered as she stroked his damp fur. "I never meant to leave you out all night. Oh, you poor, poor boy."

But Teddy Robinson whispered back, "I aren't a poor boy at all. I was camping out, and it was lovely." And then he tried to tell her all about the blackbird, and the snail, and the tortoise, and the kitten, and the stars. But because it was really so very early in the morning, and Deborah's bed was really so very warm and cosy, they both got drowsy; and before he had even got to the part about the stars singing their song to him both Teddy Robinson and Deborah were fast asleep.

And that is the end of the story about how Teddy Robinson stayed out all night.

Teddy Robinson Goes to the Toyshop

One day Teddy Robinson and Deborah were going with Mummy to a big toyshop. Deborah had ten shillings to spend. It had been sent to her at Christmas.

"You must help me choose my present, Teddy Robinson," said Deborah. "It will be nice for you to see all the toys."

"Yes," said Teddy Robinson. "You couldn't really manage without me. Shall I wear my best purple dress?"

"No," said Deborah, "your trousers will do. It isn't a party."

When they got to the toyshop there were so many things to look at that Deborah just couldn't make up her mind. Teddy Robinson got quite tired of being pushed up against the counter and squashed against ladies' shopping-baskets.

"Perhaps I'll have a glove-puppet," said Deborah.

"Then put me down for a bit," said Teddy Robinson. "I'm tired of being squashed, and I don't much care about glove-puppets anyway."

So Deborah sat Teddy Robinson down by a large dolls' house, and he sang a little song to himself while he was waiting. This is what he sang:

> *"See Saw,*
> *knock at the door,*
> *ask me in and shake my paw.*
> *How do you do? It's only me,*
> *it's half-past three,*
> *and I've come to tea."*

Teddy Robinson peeped through one of the upper windows of the dolls' house. A tiny little doll inside was sitting at a tiny little dressing-table. When she saw Teddy Robinson's big furry face looking in at the window she gave a tiny little scream. Then she said, in a tiny little, very cross voice:

"How dare you stare in at my window? How very rude of you!"

"I'm so sorry," said Teddy Robinson politely. "I'd no idea you were there. I was just looking to see if the windows were real or only painted on. I didn't

"How dare you stare in at my window?"

mean to look in your bedroom window."

The tiny little doll came over to the window of the dolls' house and looked out.

"That's the worst of living in a shop," she said. "Everybody comes poking about the house, and looking in at the windows, and asking how much you cost, and wanting to come inside and look round. Well, I'll tell you now – we cost a great deal of money, we're very dear indeed, and you *can't* come in and look round, so there!"

Then the tiny little doll made a rude face at Teddy Robinson, and pulled the tiny little muslin curtains across the tiny little windows so that he couldn't see inside any more.

"Dear me!" said Teddy Robinson to himself. "What a very cross lady! I'm sure *I* don't want to go in her house. I couldn't, anyway – I'm far too big. But it would have been politer if she'd asked me to, even though she could see I was too fat to get through the door."

Just then Deborah came over and picked Teddy Robinson up.

"I've decided I don't want a glove-puppet after all," she said, "so we're going to look at the dolls now."

So Deborah and Teddy Robinson and Mummy went to find the doll counter. On the way they passed dolls' prams, and scooters, and tricycles, and a little farther on they came to a toy motor-car with a big teddy bear sitting inside it.

"Oh, look!" said Deborah. "Isn't that lovely!"

"The dolls are over there," said Mummy, walking over to the counter.

"Listen, Teddy Robinson," said Deborah, "if I put you down here you can look at that bear in the car while I go and look at the dolls." And she put him down close to the car so that he wouldn't get walked on or knocked over, and ran off to join Mummy.

Teddy Robinson had a good look at the toy motor-car and the teddy bear sitting inside it. It was a beautiful car, very smart and shiny, and painted cream. The teddy bear inside it was very smart and shiny too. He had a blue satin bow at his neck, and pale golden fur which looked as though it had been brushed very carefully.

Teddy Robinson was surprised that he didn't seem at all excited to be sitting in such a beautiful car. He looked bored, and was leaning back against the driving-seat as if he couldn't even be bothered to sit up straight.

"Good afternoon," said Teddy Robinson. "I hope you don't mind me looking at your car?"

"Not at all, actually," said the bear in the car.

"Are you a shop bear?" asked Teddy Robinson.

"Yes, actually I am," said the bear.

"You've got a very fine car," said Teddy Robinson. "Are you going anywhere special in it?"

"No, actually I'm not at the moment," said the shop bear. "Don't lean against it, will you? It's a very expensive car, actually."

"No, I won't," said Teddy Robinson. "Why do you keep saying 'actually'?"

"Are you a shop bear?"

"It's only a way of making dull things sound more interesting," said the shop bear. "Anything else you want to know?"

"Yes," said Teddy Robinson. "Can you drive that car?"

"Actually, no," said the shop bear. Then, all of a sudden, he leaned over the driving-wheel and said in a quite different voice, "Look here, you're a nice chap – I don't mind your knowing. Don't tell, but it's all a pretend. This car doesn't belong to me at all, and I don't know how to drive it. They put me here just to make people look, and then they hope they'll buy the car."

"Fancy that!" said Teddy Robinson. "And I was thinking how lucky you were to have such a very fine car all of your own. You look so smart and handsome sitting inside it."

"Yes, I know," said the shop bear. "That's why they chose me to be the car salesman. But it's a dull life, really. If only I knew how to drive this car I'd drive right out of the shop one day and never come back."

"All the same," said Teddy Robinson, "it must be rather grand to be a car salesman."

"What are you?" asked the shop bear.

"Me? I'm a teddy bear. Don't I look like one?"

"Yes, of course," said the shop bear. "I meant, what is your job?"

Teddy Robinson had never been asked this question before, so he had to think hard for an answer.

"I suppose I'm what you'd call a Lady's Companion," he said. "I belong to that little girl over there. She isn't exactly a lady yet, but I expect she will be one day."

Just then Deborah ran back, so Teddy Robinson

had to say goodbye to the shop bear very quickly.

"You must come and see the dolls," said Deborah. "There aren't any nice ones for ten shillings, but some of them are simply beautiful just to look at."

She carried Teddy Robinson over to where Mummy was looking at a very large doll, dressed as a bride.

"Now just look at that one," said Deborah. "She's quite three times as big as you are, Teddy Robinson."

"And she can walk, and talk, and you can curl her hair," said the shop-lady who was standing by.

"She really is beautiful," said Mummy, looking at the price-ticket, "but we couldn't possibly buy her."

"Is she *very* dear, Mummy?" asked Deborah.

"Yes," said Mummy, "very dear indeed. She is five pounds."

"Dearer than me?" said Teddy Robinson.

"Oh, yes," said Deborah, "a lot dearer than you. She costs five whole pounds."

"Well," said Teddy Robinson, "if she costs five pounds I bet I cost a hundred pounds. Ask Mummy."

"Mummy," said Deborah, "how much did Teddy Robinson cost when he was new?"

"About twenty-nine and eleven, I think," said Mummy.

"Not as much as that doll?" said Deborah.

"Oh, no," said Mummy. "That doll is much dearer."

"Fancy that!" said Teddy Robinson to himself, and he felt half surprised and half cross to think he wasn't quite the dearest person in the whole world.

"I don't think it's much use our looking at dolls any more," said Mummy. "They're all so dear."

"Yes," said Deborah, "and I've just thought what I really would like to buy. Couldn't I have one of those dolls that are really hot-water bottles?"

"Why, yes," said Mummy. "What a good idea!"

So they all went along to the chemist's department, and there they saw three different kinds of hot-water-bottle dolls. There was a hot-water-bottle clown, and a hot-water-bottle Red-Riding-Hood, and a hot-water-bottle dog, bright blue with a pink bow.

Deborah picked up the blue dog.

"That's the one I want," she said. "Look, Teddy Robinson – do you like him?"

"Isn't he rather flat?" said Teddy Robinson.

"Yes, but he won't be when he's filled," said Deborah. "He's a dear – isn't he, Mummy?"

"Yes," said Mummy, "he really is."

"Everybody in this shop seems to be dear except me," said Teddy Robinson to himself. And he felt grumpy and sad; but nobody noticed him, because

"Isn't he rather flat?"

they were so busy looking at the blue dog, and paying for him, and watching him being put into a brown-paper bag.

All the way home Teddy Robinson went on feeling grumpy and sad. He thought about the doll dressed as a bride who was three times as big as he was.

"It isn't fair," he said to himself. "She didn't have to be three times as dear as me as well."

And he thought about the tiny little doll who

hadn't asked him into the dolls' house.

"She was a nasty, rude little doll," he said, "but she told me *she* was very dear too."

And he thought about the blue-dog hot-water bottle, who seemed to be coming home with them.

"Deborah and Mummy called *him* a dear, too. But I don't think he's a dear. I don't like him at all, and I hope he'll stay always inside that brown-paper bag."

But when they got home the blue dog was taken out of his brown-paper bag straight away. And when bedtime came something even worse happened. Teddy Robinson and Deborah got into bed as usual, and what should they find but the blue dog already there, lying right in the middle of the bed, and smiling up at them both, just as if he belonged there!

"*Look* at who's in our bed!" said Teddy Robinson to Deborah. "Make him get out."

"Of course he's in our bed," said Deborah. "That's what we bought him for, to keep us warm. Isn't he a dear?"

Teddy Robinson didn't say a word, he felt so cross. Deborah put her ear against his furry tummy.

"You're not *growling*, are you?" she said.

"Yes, I are!" shouted Teddy Robinson.

"But why?"

"Look at who's in our bed!"

"Because I don't like not being dear," said Teddy Robinson. "And if I aren't dear why do people always call me 'Dear Teddy Robinson' when they write to me?"

"But you *are* dear," said Deborah.

"No, I aren't," said Teddy Robinson; "and now I don't even *feel* dear any more. I just feel growly and grunty." And he told her all about what he had been thinking ever since they left the toyshop.

"But those are only dolls," said Deborah, "and this is only a hot-water bottle. You are my very dear

Teddy Robinson, and you're quite the dearest person in the whole world to me (not counting Daddy and Mummy and grown-ups, I mean)."

Teddy Robinson began to feel much better.

"Push the blue dog down by your feet, then," he said. "There isn't room for him up here."

So Deborah pushed the blue dog down, and Teddy Robinson cuddled beside her and thought how lucky he was not to be just a doll or a hot-water bottle.

Soon the blue dog made the bed so warm and cosy that Deborah fell asleep and Teddy Robinson began to get drowsy. He said, "Dear me, dear me," to himself, over and over again; and after a while he began to feel as if he loved everybody in the whole world. And soon his "Dear me's" turned into a sleepy little song which went like this:

> *"Dear me,*
> *dear me,*
> *how nice to be*
> *as dear*
> *a bear*
> *as dear old me.*
> *Dear you,*
> *dear him,*

counting flies, but they keep flying away."

"Silly boy," said Deborah.

"No," said Mummy, "he's not silly at all. He's reminded me that I must get some fly-papers from the grocer today. We don't want flies crawling about in the kitchen."

Teddy Robinson felt rather pleased.

"I like being busy," he said. "What else can I do?"

Deborah put the vase of flowers on the table beside him.

"You can smell these flowers for me," she said.

Teddy Robinson leaned forward with his nose against the flowers and smelled them.

When Daddy had found his newspaper and gone off to work, Mummy put some slices of bread under the grill on the cooker.

"We will have some toast," she said.

"And you can watch it, Teddy Robinson," said Deborah.

Just then the front-door bell rang, and Mummy went out to see who it was. Teddy Robinson and Deborah could hear Andrew's voice. He was saying something about a picnic this afternoon, and could Deborah come too?

"Oh!" said Deborah. "I must go and find out about this!" And she ran out into the hall.

Teddy Robinson stayed sitting on the kitchen table watching the toast. He could hear the others talking by the front door, and then he heard Mummy saying, "I think I'd better come over and talk to your mummy about it now." And after that everything was quiet.

Teddy Robinson felt very happy to be so busy. He stared hard at the toast and sang to himself as he watched it turning from white to golden brown and then from golden brown to black.

In a minute he heard a little snuffling noise coming from the half-open back door. The Puppy from over the Road was peeping into the kitchen. When he saw Teddy Robinson sitting on the table he wagged his tail and smiled, with his pink tongue hanging out.

"What's cooking?" he said.

"Toast," said Teddy Robinson. "Won't you come in? There's nobody at home but me."

"Oh, no, I mustn't," said the puppy. "I'm not house-trained yet. Are you?"

"Oh, yes," said Teddy Robinson. "I can do quite a lot of useful things in the house."

He began thinking quickly of all the useful things he could do; then he said, "I can watch toast, keep people company, smell flowers, time eggs, count flies,

~ watching the toast ~

or sit on things to keep them from blowing away.
Just at the minute I'm watching the toast."

"It makes an interesting smell, doesn't it?" said the
puppy, sniffing the air.

"Yes," said Teddy Robinson. "It makes a lot of
smoke too. That's what makes it so difficult to watch.
You can't see the toast for the smoke, but I've
managed to keep my eye on it nearly all the time. I've
been making up a little song about it:

"I'm watching the toast.
I don't want to boast,
but I'm better than most
at watching the toast.

It can bake, it can boil,
it can smoke, it can roast,
but I stick to my post.
I'm watching the toast."

"Jolly good song," said the puppy. "But, you know, it's really awfully smoky in here. If you don't mind I think I'll just go and practise barking at a cat or two until you've finished. Are you sure you won't come out too? Come and have a breath of fresh air."

"No, no," said Teddy Robinson. "I'll stick to my post until the others come back."

And at that moment the others did come back.

"Oh, dear!" cried Mummy. "Whatever's happened? Oh, of course – it's the toast! I'd forgotten all about it."

"But I didn't," said Teddy Robinson proudly. "I've been watching it all the time."

"It was because Andrew came and asked us to a picnic this afternoon," said Deborah. "Would you like to come too?"

"I'd much rather stay at home and keep house," said Teddy Robinson. "I like being busy. Isn't there something I could do that would be useful?"

"Yes," said Mummy, when Deborah asked her. "The grocery order is coming this afternoon. If Teddy Robinson likes to stay he can look after it for us until we come home. We'll ask the man to leave it on the step and risk it."

So it was decided that Deborah and Mummy should go to the picnic and Teddy Robinson should stay at home and keep house.

When they were all ready to go, Mummy wrote a notice which said, PLEASE LEAVE GROCERIES ON THE STEP, and Deborah wrote underneath it, TEDDY ROBINSON WILL LOOK AFTER THEM. Then they put the notice on the back-door step, and Teddy Robinson sat on it so that it wouldn't blow away.

Deborah kissed him goodbye, and Mummy shut the back door behind him. Teddy Robinson felt very pleased and important, and thought how jolly it was to be so busy that he hadn't even time to go to a picnic.

"I don't care *how* many people come and ask me to picnics or parties today," he said to himself. "I just can't go to any of them. I'm far too busy."

Nobody did come to ask Teddy Robinson to a party or a picnic, so after a while he settled down to have a nice, quiet think. His think was all about how lovely it would be if he had a little house all of his own, where he could be as busy as he liked. He had a picture in his mind of how he would open the door to the milkman, and ask the baker to leave one small brown, and invite people in for cups of tea. And he would leave his Wellington boots just outside the

He had a picture in his mind of how he would open the door to the milkman—

38

door (so as not to make the house muddy), and then say to people, "Excuse my boots, won't you?" So everybody would notice them, but nobody would think he was showing off about them. (Teddy Robinson hadn't got any Wellington boots, but he was always thinking how nice it would be if he had.)

He began singing to himself in a dreamy sort of way:

> "Good morning, baker. One small brown.
> How much is that to pay?
> Good morning, milkman. Just one pint,
> and how's your horse today?
>
> "Good afternoon. How nice of you
> to come and visit me.
> Step right inside (excuse my boots).
> I'll make a pot of tea."

A blackbird flew down and perched on the garden fence. He whistled once or twice, looked at Teddy Robinson with his head on one side, and then flew away again.

A minute later the grocer's boy opened the side gate and came up to the back door. He had a great big cardboard box in his arms.

When he had read the notice he put the big box on the step. Then he picked Teddy Robinson up and sat him on top of it. He grinned at him, then he walked off, whistling loudly and banging the side gate behind him.

The blackbird flew down on to the fence again.

"Was that you whistling?" he asked.

"No," said Teddy Robinson, it was the grocer's boy."

"Did you hear me whistle just now?" asked the blackbird.

"Yes," said Teddy Robinson.

"I did it to see if you were real or not," said the blackbird. "You were sitting so still I thought you couldn't be, so I whistled to find out. Why didn't you answer me?"

"I can't whistle," said Teddy Robinson, "and, anyway, I was thinking."

"What's in that box?" asked the blackbird. "Any breadcrumbs?"

Just then there was a scrambling, scuffling noise, and the Puppy from over the Road came lolloping round the corner. The blackbird flew away.

"Hallo," said the puppy. "What are you doing here?"

"I'm guarding the groceries," said Teddy Robinson.

"I'm guarding the groceries"

"Well, I never!" said the puppy. "You were making toast last time I saw you. You do work hard. Do you have to make beds as well?"

"No," said Teddy Robinson, "I couldn't make beds. I haven't got a hammer and nails. But I am very busy today."

"Why don't they take the groceries in?" asked the puppy.

"They've gone to a picnic," said Teddy Robinson. "I stayed behind to keep house. They decided to let the boy leave the groceries on the step and risk it."

"What's 'risk-it'?" said the puppy.

"I don't know," said Teddy Robinson, "but I like saying it, because it goes so nicely with biscuit."

"Got any biscuits in there?" asked the puppy, sniffing round the box.

"I'm not sure," said Teddy Robinson, "but you mustn't put your nose in the box."

"I was only sniffing," said the puppy.

"You mustn't sniff either," said Teddy Robinson. "It's a bad habit."

"What's 'habit'?" said the puppy.

"I don't know," said Teddy Robinson. "But it goes very nicely with rabbit."

Suddenly the back door opened behind him. The puppy scuttled away, and Teddy Robinson found that Deborah and Mummy had come home again.

"You did keep house well," said Mummy, as she carried him into the kitchen with the box of groceries.

"Don't you think he ought to have a present," said Deborah, "for being so good at housekeeping?"

"He really ought to have a house of his own," said Mummy. "Look – what about this?" She pointed to the big box. "You could make him a nice house out of that when it's empty. I'll help you to cut the windows out."

"Oh, *yes*," said Deborah, "that is exactly what he wants."

So after tea Deborah and Mummy got busy making a beautiful little house for Teddy Robinson. They made a door and two windows (one at the front and one at the back) and painted them green. Then Deborah made a hole in the lid of the box and stuck a cardboard chimney in it. Mummy painted a rambler-rose climbing up the wall. It looked very pretty.

"What would you like to call your house?" said Deborah. "Do you think Rose Cottage would be a nice name?"

"I'd rather it had my own name on it," said Teddy Robinson.

So Deborah painted TEDDY ROBINSON'S HOUSE over the door, and then it was all ready.

The next day Teddy Robinson's house was put out in the garden in the sunshine. He chose to have it close to the flower-bed at the edge of the lawn, and all day long he sat inside and waited for people to call on him. Deborah came to see him quite often, and every time she looked in at the window and said, "What are you doing now, Teddy Robinson?" he would say, "I'm just thinking about what to have for dinner," or "I'm just having a rest before getting tea."

"I never knew there was a house there"

The Puppy from over the Road came and called on him too. He sniffed at Teddy Robinson through the open window and admired him more than ever now that he had a house of his own.

And the garden tortoise came tramping out of the flower-bed and looked up at the house, saying, "Well, well, I never knew there was a house there!"

Then the Next Door Kitten came walking round on tiptoe. At first she didn't quite believe it was real. She was sniffing at the rambler-rose painted on the wall when Teddy Robinson looked out of the window and said, "Good afternoon."

The kitten purred with pleasure at seeing him.

"What a purr-r-rfect little house!" she said. "Is it really yours? You *are* a lucky purr-r-rson."

Teddy Robinson nodded and smiled at her from the window.

"Yes," he said, "it's my very own house. Aren't I lucky? It's just what I've always wanted – a little place all of my own."

And that is the end of the story about how
Teddy Robinson kept house.

– 4 –

Teddy Robinson Has a Birthday Party

One day Teddy Robinson said to Deborah, "You know, I've lived with you for years and years and years, and yet I've never had a birthday. Why haven't I?"

"I suppose it's because you came at Christmas," said Deborah, "so we've never thought about it. Would you like to have a birthday?"

"Oh, yes, please," said Teddy Robinson, "if you can spare one. And can I have a party?"

"Yes, I think it's a lovely idea," said Deborah. "When would you like your birthday to be?"

"Today?" said Teddy Robinson.

"No, not today," said Deborah. "There wouldn't be time to get a party ready. I shall have to ask Mummy about it. Besides, I haven't got a present for you."

"Tomorrow, then," said Teddy Robinson.

"All right," said Deborah. "We'll make it tomorrow. How old would you like to be?"

"A hundred," said Teddy Robinson.

"Don't be silly," said Deborah. "You can't be a hundred."

"Why not? I've been here about a hundred years, haven't I?"

"No, of course you haven't," said Deborah. "I know it seems a long while, but it's not as long as all that. I think you're about three or four. I'll ask Mummy."

Mummy thought it would be a good idea for Teddy Robinson to have a party.

"You can ask Philip and Mary-Anne to tea," she said, "and I'll make some things for you to eat. Would Teddy Robinson like a birthday cake?"

"Oh, *yes*," said Deborah, "with candles on. But how old is he?"

"I think he's three really," said Mummy, "but I'm afraid he'll have to be one tomorrow, because there's only one cake candle left in the box."

So everybody started getting ready for Teddy Robinson's birthday party.

Deborah bought him a little trumpet for three-pence and wrapped it up in pink tissue paper. Then she made a paper crown for him to wear on his head

She made a paper crown for him to wear.

(because he was going to be the birthday king). Mummy made the cake, and iced it, and wrote TEDDY on top with tiny silver balls. Then she made a lot of very small jellies in egg-cups. And Teddy Robinson sat and sang to himself all day long, and felt very proud and important, because he was going to have a birthday all of his own.

It was beautifully sunny the next day, so Deborah and Teddy Robinson decided they would have the party in the garden.

"We will have the little nursery-table under the almond-tree," said Deborah, "and you shall sit at the head, Teddy Robinson, and wear your purple dress and the birthday crown."

"Yes," he said, "that will be lovely."

"Now I must find something for us all to sit on,"

said Deborah. "I think my own little chair and stool will do for Mary-Anne and me, and the dolls will have to sit on the benches. Philip can have the toybox turned upside down."

"And will there be three chairs for me?" asked Teddy Robinson.

"No, not *three*," said Deborah. "Why ever should you want three?"

"But don't they always have three chairs for somebody special?"

"Oh, you mean three *cheers*," said Deborah. "That means three hoorays."

"Oh," said Teddy Robinson; "then can I have three hoorays if I can't have three chairs?"

"Yes, I expect so," said Deborah. "Now, don't interrupt me, because I want to get everything ready."

So Teddy Robinson sat and watched Deborah putting the chairs and benches out, and began singing his three hoorays, because he was so happy and excited.

> *"Hooray, hooray, hooray,*
> *my birthday party's today.*
> *You can come to tea*
> *at half-past three,*
> *and stay for ever, hooray."*

"Oh, don't say that," said Deborah. "It will all have to be cleared away and washed up afterwards, so we can't have people staying for ever."

"All right, then," said Teddy Robinson:

> *"Hooray, hooray, hooray,*
> *my birthday party's today.*
> *You can come to tea*
> *at half-past three,*
> *and stay until we tell you to go, unless*
> *somebody's fetching you."*

"Is that better?"

"Yes," said Deborah, but she wasn't really listening, because she was so busy thinking about where everybody was going to sit, and what she should use for a tablecloth, and whether there would be enough cups and saucers.

At half-past three the visitors arrived. The dolls were already sitting in their places, admiring the birthday cake with its one candle, and the little jellies, and the chocolate biscuits, and the piles of tiny sandwiches that Mummy had made.

And Teddy Robinson, wearing his best purple dress and his crown, was sitting on a high stool at the head of the table, and feeling like the King of all teddy bears.

admiring the birthday cake

"You do look grand," said Philip. "May I sit beside you?"

"Oh, yes," said Teddy Robinson, and felt very pleased at being asked. Philip gave him a small tin cow and some dolly mixture in a matchbox for his present.

"Oh, thank you," said Teddy Robinson. "I love cows, and Deborah loves dolly mixture. That *is* a good present."

Mary-Anne had brought Jacqueline with her. Jacqueline was her beautiful doll, who wore a pink silk dress and a frilly bonnet to match. Teddy Robinson was surprised to see that Jacqueline's eyes were shut, although she wasn't lying down.

Mary-Anne said, "Many happy returns of the day, Teddy Robinson. This is Jacqueline. Her eyes are

Nobody minded her eyes being shut.

shut, because she's rather tired today." ("They're stuck, really," she whispered to Deborah.) "But she is *so* looking forward to the party."

Jacqueline had such a beautiful smile that nobody minded her eyes being shut, and Teddy Robinson was very pleased when she was put to sit on his other side at the table.

"And this is Jacqueline's present to you," said Mary-Anne, and she put a little parcel down on the table in front of him. Inside was a beautiful little paper umbrella. It was red with a yellow frill all round the outside edge.

Teddy Robinson was very pleased indeed. "It's just what I was wanting," he said. "Can I have it up now?"

"Yes," said Deborah, "it can be a sunshade today."

52

And she opened it up for him. With a sunshade as well as a crown, Teddy Robinson felt grander than ever.

They had a lovely tea. Deborah poured the milk into the dolls' cups and saucers while Mary-Anne handed round the sandwiches, and Philip made everybody laugh by telling them funny stories.

Every time Teddy Robinson laughed, he fell sideways against Philip, and his crown went over one eye, and this made everyone laugh more than ever.

"Don't make him so excited," said Deborah. "You're making him behave badly." But Teddy Robinson just got jollier and jollier. He was having a

every time he laughed he fell sideways

wonderful time. He began singing:

> *"Ding, dong,*
> *this is the song*
> *I'll sing at my birthday tea.*
> *I'm glad you came,*
> *but all the same,*
> *the party's really for me . . ."*

"Teddy Robinson!" said Deborah. "What a rude thing to sing to your visitors!"

"Oh, sorry!" said he. "I didn't really mean that. All right, I won't sing. I'll ask you a riddle instead. When is a bear bare?"

"What does it mean?" asked the dolls. "It doesn't make sense."

"When he's got no fur on!" said Teddy Robinson, and laughed until he fell sideways again. As nobody else understood the riddle they didn't think it was funny, but they laughed like anything when Teddy Robinson fell sideways, because his crown fell over his eyes again, and the umbrella came down on top of his head.

When it was time for the birthday cake everyone sang *Happy Birthday to You*, and just for a minute Teddy Robinson forgot to feel jolly, and felt rather shy instead. But as soon as they had finished he got jollier than ever.

"I feel just like standing on my head," he said.

"Go on, then," said Philip. "I'll help you."

"No, don't," said Deborah. But Teddy Robinson was already standing on his head in the middle of the table with Philip holding on to him.

"*I feel just like standing on my head.*"

"Well done!" shouted Philip, as Teddy Robinson's fat, furry legs wobbled in the air. All the dolls laughed except Jacqueline, who couldn't see, because her eyes were shut, but she went on smiling all the time.

"Now I'll go head-over-heels!" said Teddy Robinson, and over he went.

"Mind the biscuits!" cried Mary-Anne, and took

them away just in time as Teddy Robinson came down with a bump that clattered all the cups and saucers. Everybody laughed and clapped except Deborah, who didn't like to see Teddy Robinson getting so rough.

"Do be careful!" she said. "Philip, put him back on his stool. Teddy Robinson, you really mustn't behave like that."

"All right, I won't do it again," said Teddy Robinson. "I'll sing about it instead." And then he began singing in a silly, squeaky little voice:

> *"The Birthday Bear,*
> *the Birthday Bear*
> *stood on his head*
> *with his legs in the air,*
> *and everyone laughed*
> *as the Bear with the crown*
> *went head-over-heels*
> *like a circus clown,*
> *and they laughed and laughed*
> *till he tumbled down.*
> *Hooray for the Birthday Bear!"*

He was so pleased with himself when he had sung this little song that he fell over backwards and disappeared out of sight under the table. Deborah pulled him out and brushed the cake-crumbs and dry leaves and little bits of jelly off his fur, then she sat him up at the table again.

"Don't be so silly," she said. "What ever will your visitors think?"

"They'll think I'm jolly funny," said Teddy Robinson, "though as a matter of fact, I didn't mean to fall over at all that time. I just leaned back, and there was nothing behind me, so I fell through it." Then he began singing again in the silly squeaky voice:

> *"Nothing was there,*
> *so the Birthday Bear*
> *leaned back, and fell right through it.*
> *Down with a smack*
> *he fell on his back!*
> *Wasn't he clever to do it?"*

Everybody started laughing again at this, so Teddy Robinson thought he would be funnier than ever. He leaned sideways against Jacqueline, so hard that she fell sideways against the doll next to her; and then they all went down like a lot of ninepins, and fell squeaking and giggling under the table.

Ex - and - shoff.

"I'm so sorry," said Deborah to Mary-Anne. "I'm afraid he's a little ex-and-shoff."

"What is that?" asked Mary-Anne.

"Excited and showing off," whispered Deborah, "but I don't want him to hear."

"I *did* hear!" shouted Teddy Robinson from under the table. "Ex-and-shoff yourself!"

Mary-Anne and Deborah took no notice of this, but Philip laughed. Deborah said, "I think it's your fault, Philip, that he's behaving so badly. You always laugh when he says something rude."

They picked up all the dolls from under the table, and when at last they were all sitting in their places again Deborah began handing round the chocolate biscuits. She put one on each plate, and each doll said "Thank you," but when she came to Teddy Robinson's place and looked up to speak to him she found she was looking at the back of his head.

"Teddy Robinson!" she said. "How dare you sit with your back to the table!"

"I'm not," said Teddy Robinson in a funny laughing voice.

"You are. Now, don't be so rude and silly. Turn round the other way, and put your feet under the table."

"My feet *are* under the table," said Teddy

"How dare you sit with your back to the table!"

Robinson, laughing more than ever.

Deborah lifted the cloth, and was very surprised to see that Teddy Robinson was quite right. His feet *were* under the table, but his face was still looking the other way, because his head was twisted right round from back to front.

"You *silly* boy!" she said, as she twisted it round again. "You deserve to get it stuck that way. Now, do behave yourself. You're not being funny at all."

"*We* think he is very funny," said one of the dolls politely.

"Thank you," said Teddy Robinson, and he bowed so low that this time he fell with his nose in the jam, and his crown fell off into the jellies.

"Now," said Deborah, when they had all finished laughing, "I think we'd better eat up the rest of the food before any more of it gets spilt or sat on."

So they finished up all the chocolate biscuits, and all the little jellies, and went on eating until there was nothing left but one tiny sandwich which nobody had any room for. Then, as it was time for the party to end, Philip said:

"Let's have three cheers for Teddy Robinson!"

Everyone shouted "Hip-Hip-Hooray" three times over; and Teddy Robinson bowed again (but this time he didn't fall over) and said, "Thank you for having me," because by now he was getting a bit muddled and had forgotten that it was his own party that he was enjoying so much.

And then everybody said "Goodbye," and "Thank you for having me," and "Thank you for coming," and "Wasn't it a lovely party," and Philip and Mary-Anne and Jacqueline went home, and the dolls went back to the toy-cupboard, and the party was really over.

Teddy Robinson, tired and happy, lay on the grass beside his birthday crown and umbrella. Deborah picked him up and carried him into the house.

"Well, Teddy Robinson," she said, "I hope you enjoyed your birthday party?"

"Oh, yes! It was the best one I ever had."

"It's a pity you didn't behave a *little* bit better," said Deborah. "You're getting a big boy now."

"Yes, but, after all, I was only *one* today, wasn't I?"

"Of *course* you were; I quite forgot!" said Deborah, and kissed him on the end of his nose.

And that is the end of the story about
Teddy Robinson's birthday party.

– 5 –

Teddy Robinson Goes to the Dancing-Class

One Saturday morning Teddy Robinson saw that Deborah was putting on her best dress.

"Where are we going?" he said.

"To a dancing-class," said Deborah, "to learn to dance. Won't it be fun?"

"What, me?"

"Yes, you can come too. Will you like that?"

"I don't think I'd better dance," said Teddy Robinson, "but I shall like to come and watch."

So he waited while Deborah put on her best socks and shoes, and had a red ribbon tied in her hair; then Deborah brushed his fur with the dolls' hair brush, and they were all ready to go.

"Oh, my shoes!" said Deborah. "Where are they?"

"On your feet," said Teddy Robinson, surprised.

"No, not these shoes," said Deborah. "I meant my dancing-shoes. I've got some new ones. They're very special – pink, with ribbons to keep them on."

"Well I never!" said Teddy Robinson. "You *have* gone grand and grown-up. Fancy having special shoes to dance in!"

Mummy had the new shoes all ready in a bag.

"You can see them when we get there," she said.

So they all set off, Mummy carrying the new shoes, Deborah hopping and skipping all the way, and Teddy Robinson singing to himself as he bounced up and down in her arms:

> *"Hoppity-skippity,*
> *rin-tin-tin –*
> *special shoes for dancing in,*
> *pink, with ribbons –*
> *well, fancy that!*
> *I'd dance myself if I wasn't so fat."*

When they got there Teddy Robinson stopped singing, and Deborah stopped hopping and skipping, and they followed Mummy into the cloakroom. Deborah changed into the new shoes, and had her hair brushed all over again; then they all went into the big hall.

Mary Jane was there, in a pale yellow dress with a frilly petticoat; and Caroline, with pink ribbons to match her party frock; and there was Andrew, in blue corduroy velvet trousers and shoes with silver buckles on them.

"Hallo, Teddy Robinson," said Andrew. "Have you come to dance?"

"Not today," said Teddy Robinson. "I didn't bring my shoes."

"He is going to watch," said Deborah, and she put him down on an empty chair in the front row. Then she ran off to talk to Mary Jane and Caroline.

All the mothers and aunties and nurses who had come to watch the class were chatting together in the rows of chairs behind Teddy Robinson, and on the chair next to him sat a large walkie-talkie doll, wearing a pink frilled dress with a ribbon sash. She was sitting up very straight, smiling and staring in front of her.

Teddy Robinson wondered whether to speak to her, but just then a lady came in and sat down at the piano, and a moment later the teacher, whose name was Miss Silver, came into the hall.

Teddy Robinson decided he had better not start talking now, as the class was about to begin. Instead he listened to all the mothers and aunties and nurses, who had all begun talking to the children at once, in busy, whispering voices.

"Stand up nicely, point your toes."

"Here's your hankie, blow your nose."

"Don't be shy now, do your best. Make it up and follow the rest."

"Where's your hankie? Did you blow?"

"There's the music. Off you go!"

Then the children all ran into the middle of the floor, and the dancing-class began.

Teddy Robinson, sitting tidily on his chair in the front row, thought how jolly it was to be one of the grown-ups who had come to watch, and how lucky he was to belong to the nicest little girl in the class.

"How pretty she looks in her new pink shoes and her red ribbon," he said to himself. "And how well she can dance already! She is doing it quite differently from all the others. When they are doing *hop, one-two-three* she is doing *one-two-three, hop, hop, hop,* and it looks so much jollier that way. She is the only one able to do it right. None of the others can keep up with her."

He smiled proudly as Deborah went dancing past, her eyes shining, her red ribbon flying.

A lady in the row behind whispered to someone else, "Who is that little girl with the red ribbon, the one who hops three times instead of once?"

The other lady whispered back, "I don't know.

She is new, you can see that – but isn't she enjoying herself? That's her teddy bear on the chair in front."

Teddy Robinson pretended he wasn't listening and hummed softly to himself in time to the music. He was pleased that other people had noticed Deborah too. He looked sideways at the walkie-talkie doll. She was still smiling, and watching the dancing carefully. Teddy Robinson was glad to think that she too was admiring Deborah.

When the music stopped and the children paused for breath Teddy Robinson turned to her.

"Aren't you dancing?" he asked.

"Aren't you dancing?"

"No," said the doll; "I walk and talk, but I don't dance. I've come to watch."

"I've come to watch too," said Teddy Robinson.

"I suppose you don't dance either?" said the doll, looking at Teddy Robinson's fat tummy.

"No, I sing," said Teddy Robinson.

"Ah, yes," said the doll, "you have the figure for it."

The children began dancing again, and the lady at the piano played such hoppity-skippity music that Teddy Robinson couldn't help joining in with a little song, very quietly to himself:

> *"Hoppity-skippity, one-two-three,*
> *The bestest dancer belongs to me.*
> *Oh, what a fortunate bear I be!*
> *Hoppity-skippity, one-two-three."*

The walkie-talkie doll turned to Teddy Robinson.

"How beautifully she dances!" she said. "I'm not surprised so many people have come to watch her."

"Thank you," said Teddy Robinson, bowing slightly, and feeling very proud. "Yes, she does dance well and this is her first lesson."

"Oh, no, it's not," said the doll. "I bring her every Saturday. She's had quite a number of lessons already."

"I beg your pardon," said Teddy Robinson. "Who are we talking about?"

"My little girl, Mary, of course," said the doll, "the one with the yellow curls."

"Oh," said Teddy Robinson, "I thought we were talking about my little girl, Deborah, the one with the red ribbon."

The doll didn't seem to hear. She was staring at the children with a fixed smile. Miss Silver was arranging them in two rows, the girls on one side, the boys on the other.

Teddy Robinson and the walkie-talkie doll both kept their eyes fixed on the girls' row.

"She looks so pretty, doesn't she?" said the doll. "I do admire her dress, don't you?"

"Yes," said Teddy Robinson, looking at Deborah.

"That pale blue suits her so well," said the doll.

"Thank you," said Teddy Robinson, "I'm glad you like it; but it isn't pale blue – it's white."

"Oh no, it's pale blue," said the doll. "I helped her mother to choose it myself."

Teddy Robinson looked puzzled.

"Are you talking about the little girl with the red hair-ribbon?" he asked.

"No, of course not," said the doll. "Why should I be? I'm talking about Mary."

"Whoever is Mary?" said Teddy Robinson.

"The little girl we have all come to watch," said the doll. "*My* little girl. We've been talking about her all the time."

"*I* haven't," said Teddy Robinson. "I've been talking about Deborah."

"Deborah?" said the doll. "Whoever is Deborah?"

"What a silly creature this doll is!" said Teddy Robinson to himself. "She doesn't seem able to keep her mind on the class at all." And he decided not to bother about talking to her any more. Instead he listened to Miss Silver, who was teaching the boys and girls how to bow and curtsy to each other.

"I must watch this carefully," said Teddy Robinson to himself. "I should like to know how to bow properly – it might come in handy at any time. I might be asked to tea at Buckingham Palace or happen to meet the Queen out shopping one day, and I should look very silly if I didn't know how to make my bow properly."

As the boys all bowed from the waist Teddy Robinson leaned forward on his chair.

"Lower!" cried Miss Silver.

The boys all bowed lower, and Teddy Robinson leaned forward as far as he could; but he went just a little too far, and a moment later he fell head over heels on to the floor. Luckily, no one knew he had been practising his bow, they just thought he had toppled off his chair by mistake, as anyone might – so they took no notice of him.

Then it was the girls' turn to curtsy. The line of little girls wobbled and wavered, and Deborah wobbled so much that she too fell on the floor. But after three tries she did manage to curtsy without falling over, and Teddy Robinson was very proud of her.

"Never mind," said Miss Silver, as she said good-bye to them at the end of the class. "You did very well for a first time. You can't expect to learn to dance in one lesson. But you did enjoy it, didn't you?"

"Oh, yes!" said Deborah. "It was lovely."

"What did she mean?" said Teddy Robinson, as soon as they were outside. "I thought you danced better than anybody."

"Oh, no," said Deborah. "I think I was doing it all wrong, but it *was* fun. I'm glad we're going again next Saturday."

"Well I never!" said Teddy Robinson. "I quite thought you were the only one doing it right. Never mind. Did you see when I fell off the chair? That was me trying to bow. I don't think I did it very well either."

"You did very well for a first time too," said

Deborah. "You can't expect to learn to bow in one lesson. We must practise together at home, though. You can learn to bow to me while I practise doing my curtsy."

"That will be very nice," said Teddy Robinson. "Then next time we shan't both end up on the floor."

That night Teddy Robinson had a most Beautiful Dream. He dreamt he was in a very large theatre, with red velvet curtains, tied with large golden tassels, on each side of the stage.

Every seat in the theatre was full; Teddy Robinson himself was sitting in the middle of the front row, and all the people were watching Deborah, who was dancing all alone on the stage in her new pink dancing-shoes. She was dressed like a princess, in a frilly white dress with a red sash, and she had a silver crown on her head.

The orchestra was playing sweetly, and Deborah was dancing so beautifully that soon everyone was whispering and asking who she was.

Teddy Robinson heard someone behind him saying, "She belongs to that handsome bear in the front row, the one in the velvet suit and lace collar."

Teddy Robinson looked round, but couldn't see any bear in a velvet suit and lace collar. Then he

"She belongs to that handsome bear in the front row."

looked down and saw that instead of his ordinary trousers he was wearing a suit of beautiful blue velvet, with a large lace collar fastened at the neck with a silver pin. And in his lap was a bunch of roses tied with silver ribbon.

"Goodness gracious, they must have meant me!" he thought, and felt his fur tingling with pleasure and excitement.

As the music finished and Deborah came to the front of the stage to curtsy, Teddy Robinson felt

He felt himself floating through the air

himself floating through the air with his bunch of roses, and a moment later he landed lightly on the stage beside her. A murmur went up from the audience, "Ah, here is Teddy Robinson himself!"

Folding one paw neatly across his tummy, he bowed low to Deborah. Then, as she took the roses from him and they both bowed and curtsyed again, everyone in the theatre clapped so loudly that Teddy Robinson woke up and found he was in bed beside Deborah.

At first he was so surprised that he could hardly believe he was really at home in bed, but just then

bowed and curtsyed together

Deborah woke up too. She rolled over, smiling, with her eyes shut, and said, "Oh, Teddy Robinson, I've just had such a Beautiful Dream! I must tell you all about it."

So she did. And the funny thing was that Deborah had dreamt exactly the same dream as Teddy Robinson. She remembered every bit of it.

And that is the end of the story about
how Teddy Robinson went to the dancing-class.

– 6 –

Teddy Robinson and the Teddy-Bear Brooch

One day a letter came for Deborah and Teddy Robinson. It was from Auntie Sue, and it said:

DEAR DEBORAH AND TEDDY ROBINSON,
   Please tell Mummy I shall be coming to tea with you all tomorrow. I hope you will like the little brooch.

And pinned to a card inside the letter was a dear little teddy-bear brooch. It was pink with silver eyes, and Deborah thought it was very beautiful. She gave the letter to Mummy to read and pinned the brooch on the front of her dress.

"Wasn't there anything for me?" asked Teddy Robinson. Deborah looked inside the envelope again.

"No," she said, "there's nothing else."

"Oh," said Teddy Robinson. "Then can I have

the envelope? It will make me a soldier's hat."

So Deborah put the envelope on his head. Then Teddy Robinson said, "Fetch me the wooden horse, please. It's time I went on duty. I'm going to guard the palace."

So Deborah fetched the wooden horse.

"And I want a sentry-box, please," said Teddy Robinson.

"I haven't got a sentry-box," said Deborah. "Will the toy-box do?"

"Yes, if you stand it up on end," said Teddy Robinson.

So Deborah emptied the toy-box and stood it up on end. Then she put the wooden horse inside, and Teddy Robinson sat on its back with the envelope on his head. He didn't really feel like playing soldiers at all, but he wanted to sit somewhere quietly and not be talked to for a while.

"Do you *really* like it in there?" asked Deborah, peeping in at him.

"Yes, thank you," said Teddy Robinson, "but you mustn't talk to me. I'm on duty."

So Deborah went off to play by herself, and Teddy Robinson sat on the wooden horse and began thinking about why he was feeling so quiet. He knew it was something to do with the teddy-

"Do you really _like_ it in there?"

bear brooch.

He began mumbling to himself in a gentle, grumbling growl:

" Fancy *her sending a brooch with a bear!*
 It isn't polite and it isn't fair.
 There's a bear here already
 who lives in the house.
 Why couldn't *she send her a brooch*
   with a mouse?
 Or a brooch with a dog?
 Or a brooch with a cat?
 Nobody'd ever *feel hurt at that.*
 But a brooch with a bear
 isn't fair
 on the bear
 who lives in the house,
 and who's always *been there.*"

Teddy Robinson went on mumbling to himself and getting more and more grumbly and growly. He was feeling very cross with Auntie Sue, so he said all the nasty things he could think of, for quite a long while. Then he ended up by saying:

"*When* she *gets a present I only hope*
"*that all* she *gets is an envelope.*"

"*Fancy* her sending a brooch with a bear!"

After that he began to feel quite sorry for Auntie Sue, and much better himself.

He heard Mummy come out into the garden and say to Deborah, "Hallo! Why ever have you emptied the toy-box and stood it up on end like that?"

And he heard Deborah say, "Hush! Teddy Robinson's inside. He says he's guarding the palace, but I think he's sad about something."

"Oh, well," said Mummy, "bring him with you. I

was going to ask if you would like to help make a fruit jelly for Auntie Sue tomorrow."

"Oh, yes," said Deborah. "Teddy Robinson can sit on the kitchen table and watch. He always likes that."

She bent down and peeped inside the toy-box.

"Have you finished guarding the palace yet, Teddy Robinson?"

"Yes, I'm just coming off duty this minute," said Teddy Robinson. "Help me down."

Deborah helped him down, and together they went into the kitchen. Mummy had poured some pink jelly into a bowl, and she gave Deborah some cherries and slices of banana on a plate.

"Drop them into the jelly, one at a time," said Mummy. "It's still rather soft and runny, but tomorrow it will be set beautifully, with the fruit inside it."

So Deborah knelt on a chair and dropped the pieces of fruit carefully into the bowl, and Teddy Robinson sat on the kitchen table and said "Plop" every time she dropped a cherry in, and "Bang" every time she dropped a slice of banana in. He always liked helping when Deborah was working with Mummy in the kitchen.

Every time Deborah leaned forward to look in the bowl, Teddy Robinson saw the teddy-bear brooch on her dress, its silver eyes shining and winking in the sunlight. He tried not to look, because he didn't want to feel cross again; but it was so pretty it was difficult not to notice it.

And then Teddy Robinson saw that the pin of the brooch had come undone, and every time Deborah moved it was sliding a little way farther out of her dress. He held his breath, waiting to see what would happen, and a moment later it slipped out and fell with a gentle *plop* right into the middle of the jelly-bowl!

Deborah was saying something to Mummy at the minute, so she did not notice. Teddy Robinson wondered if he ought to tell her, but it seemed a pity to remind her about it.

"After all, she's still got me," he said to himself. "She didn't really need another teddy bear."

He looked down into the bowl, but there was no sign of the teddy-bear brooch. If it was there it was well hidden among all the cherries and banana slices. Teddy Robinson was glad to think it had gone.

Deborah dropped the last slice of banana into the bowl.

"There," she said, "it's all finished. You forgot to say 'Bang', Teddy Robinson."

"Bang," said Teddy Robinson. "Do you feel as if

He looked down into the bowl

you'd lost something?"

"No," said Deborah. "Do you?"

"No," said Teddy Robinson. "At least, if I have I'm glad I've lost it."

"You *are* a funny boy," said Deborah. "I don't know what you're talking about."

Teddy Robinson began to feel very jolly now that the teddy-bear brooch had gone. He kept singing funny little songs, and asking Deborah silly riddles, and making her laugh, so that it wasn't until after tea that she suddenly noticed she had lost it.

"Oh dear! Wherever can it be?" she said. "It must have fallen off while we were playing. Help me look for it, Teddy Robinson."

They couldn't find it anywhere.

So Teddy Robinson and Deborah looked under chairs and under tables and all through the toy-cupboard, but, of course, they couldn't find it anywhere.

Teddy Robinson began to sing:

> *"Oh, where, oh, where*
> *is the Broochy Bear?*
> *First look here,*
> *and then look there.*
> *I can't see him anywhere.*
> *He's lost! He's lost! The Broochy Bear!"*

"You sound as if you're glad he's lost," said Deborah. "Why are you so jolly?"

"Because I'm jolly sorry," said Teddy Robinson.

"Oh, don't be so silly," said Deborah. "Let's go and ask Mummy."

But Mummy hadn't seen the teddy-bear brooch anywhere either. "He must be somewhere about," she said. "You'll just have to go on looking."

"But we've looked everywhere – haven't we, Teddy Robinson?"

"Well, we haven't looked everywhere," he said, "because we haven't looked on top of the roof, or under the floor, or up the chimney, but we did look in quite a lot of places."

"But I haven't been on top of the roof, or under the floor, or up the chimney," said Deborah.

"No," said Teddy Robinson, "but you haven't been in the jelly either."

"What are you talking about?" said Deborah. "And why are you so jolly? I don't see anything to feel so happy about."

The next day Auntie Sue came at teatime, as she had promised. She was very pleased to see everybody, and because she was his friend as well, Teddy Robinson was allowed to sit up at the table. He had a chair with three cushions on it, so he was high enough to have quite a nice view of everything.

There were sandwiches and cakes and chocolate biscuits, and in the middle of the table was the fruit jelly. It had set beautifully, and Mummy had turned it out on to a glass dish.

Deborah pointed it out to Auntie Sue.

"Teddy Robinson and I helped to make that," she said.

"Did you really?" said Auntie Sue. "How very clever of you both!"

She turned to smile at them, and then she said:

"Why isn't Teddy Robinson wearing his brooch? Didn't he like it?"

"Oh!" said Deborah. "Was it for him? How dreadful! I thought it was for me, and I pinned it on the front of my dress, and now I've lost it. I can't think where it is."

"It's sure to turn up soon," said Mummy. "We know it's somewhere in the house." Then she and Auntie Sue started talking together about grown-up things.

"Never mind, Teddy Robinson," whispered Deborah. "I'm sure we shall find him again soon."

"The trouble is he mayn't be there any more to find," said Teddy Robinson.

"Where?" asked Deborah.

"Where he was yesterday when we couldn't find him," said Teddy Robinson. "I'm afraid he may have melted."

"What ever do you mean?" said Deborah. "Do you know where he is? If you do I wish you'd tell me."

"Well," said Teddy Robinson, "think of something round and pink, with a lot of banana in it, that's on the table, and when you've guessed what I mean I'll tell you."

"Something round and pink with a lot of banana in it?" said Deborah. "Can you mean the jelly?"

"Yes," said Teddy Robinson. "Don't look now, but I *think* the teddy-bear brooch is inside that."

"Good gracious!" said Deborah. "How ever did that happen?"

"He fell out of your dress when you were dropping the fruit in it," said Teddy Robinson. "I saw the pin was undone and I didn't tell you, because I wanted you to lose him."

"But why?" asked Deborah.

"Because you'd already got me, and I didn't think you needed another bear," said Teddy Robinson.

"Oh, you silly boy!" said Deborah. "How could you think I'd ever love a silly little teddy bear on a brooch as much as I love you?"

"Think of something round and pink" —

Teddy Robinson was very pleased to hear Deborah say this.

"But you mustn't call him silly," he said. "He's mine now, and he's really rather special. I do hope he hasn't melted. Ask Mummy to start serving the jelly, then perhaps we'll find him."

So Mummy began to serve the jelly, and a moment later what should she find but the little teddy-bear brooch, all among the cherries and slices of banana! She was very surprised.

"How ever did he get there?" she said.

"He fell in when I was dropping the fruit in," said Deborah. "Teddy Robinson has just told me so."

"Well, fancy that!" said Auntie Sue. "So he can

have his brooch after all."

Then they washed the teddy-bear brooch, and dried him, and he was pinned on to Teddy Robinson's trouser-strap; and Teddy Robinson said "Thank you" to Auntie Sue for such a nice present. He was very pleased, because the teddy-bear brooch looked as good as new. He hadn't melted a bit, and his silver eyes still sparkled and shone, just as if he'd never been inside a jelly at all.

And that is the end of the story about
Teddy Robinson and the teddy-bear brooch.

Teddy Robinson
is Brave

One day Teddy Robinson woke up in the morning feeling very brave and jolly. Even before Deborah was awake he began singing a little song, telling himself all about how brave he was. It went like this:

"Jolly brave me,
jolly brave me,
the bravest bear
you ever did see;

as brave as a lion
or tiger could be,
as brave as a dragon –
oh, jolly brave me!"

And by the time Deborah woke up he was

beginning to think he was quite the bravest bear in the whole world.

"Whatever is all this shouting and puffing and blowing?" asked Deborah, opening her eyes sleepily.

"Me fighting a dragon," said Teddy Robinson, puffing out his chest:

> *"Bang, bang, bang, you're dead,*
> *sang the Brave Bear on the bed.*
> *The dragon trembled, sobbed, and sighed,*
> *'Oh, save my life!' he cried . . . and died."*

"You see? I killed him!" said Teddy Robinson.

"But I don't see any dragon," said Deborah.

"No, he's gone now," said Teddy Robinson. "Shall we get up? It's quite safe."

Halfway through the morning the phone-bell rang. Mummy was busy, so Deborah lifted the receiver, but before she had time to say "hallo" Teddy Robinson said, "I'll take it! It may be someone ringing up to ask me to fight a dragon." And he said, "Hallo," in a deep, brave growl.

"Hallo," said Daddy's voice, "that's Teddy Robinson, isn't it? How are you?"

"I'm better, thank you," said Teddy Robinson.

"Oh, I didn't know you'd been ill," said Daddy.

"I haven't," said Teddy Robinson.

"Then how can you be better?" said Daddy.

"I'm not better than ill," said Teddy Robinson. "I'm better than better."

"I see," said Daddy. "Now, will you tell Mummy I shall be back early today? And listen, I have a plan—"

"This isn't really me talking," said Teddy Robinson. "It's Deborah. Did you know?"

"I guessed it might be," said Daddy. "But it's you I want to talk to. How would you like to meet me for tea at Black's farm – and bring Deborah too, of course?"

"Will there be a dragon there?" asked Teddy Robinson.

"A what?" said Daddy.

Deborah pushed Teddy Robinson's nose away from the phone and talked to Daddy herself. "Oh, yes!" she said. "It would be lovely. Hold on and I'll fetch Mummy."

When Mummy had finished talking to Daddy and deciding where they should meet she said, "Won't that be nice? It's a long while since we had a walk in the country."

"Will you like it, Teddy Robinson?" asked Deborah.

"I'm just wondering," said Teddy Robinson. "A walk in the country seems rather a soppy way for a Big Brave Bear to spend the afternoon."

"Nonsense," said Deborah. "Daddy is much bigger and braver than you, and he doesn't think so. Shall I ask Andrew to come with us?"

"Not if he brings Spotty," said Teddy Robinson.

"No," said Deborah, "we'll ask him to bring someone else instead."

Andrew said he would like to come, and he would bring his clockwork mouse, who was small and easy to carry.

"A walk in the country will do her good," said

Andrew. "She had rather a fright yesterday with a cat who thought she was real and chased her under the sofa."

So after dinner they all set off.

Deborah and Andrew were excited to be going into the country. Teddy Robinson was still feeling very jolly and big and brave, but Mouse was a little trembly. She had really had quite a fright with the cat the day before.

"Are you sure we shan't run into danger?" she kept asking.

"Don't you worry," said Teddy Robinson. "I'm quite brave enough for two of us and I'll look after you. There's no need to worry while you're with me."

"Thank you," said Mouse. "I'm sure I shall be quite safe with such a big, brave bear as you. I was only thinking – suppose it should thunder?"

"Well, what if it did ?" said Teddy Robinson. "*I* shouldn't mind. I love thunder."

"Or what if we should meet some cows?" said Mouse.

"Well, what if we did?" said Teddy Robinson. "*I* aren't frightened of cows. I should just walk bravely past and stare at them fiercely." He began singing:

"Three cheers for me,
for jolly brave me.
Oh, what a jolly brave bear I be!"

Mouse said, "Hip, hip, hooray," three times over in a high, quavering voice. Then she said, "Oh, yes – certainly, and I know now how brave you are. A fly settled on your nose while you were singing, and you never even blinked."

"Pooh! That's nothing," said Teddy Robinson. "I killed a dragon before breakfast."

"Whatever is Teddy Robinson talking about?" said Andrew to Deborah. "What's the matter with him today?"

"I really don't know," said Deborah. "He woke up like it. I'm afraid he's showing off."

When they got out into the open country Mouse and Teddy Robinson were put into Mummy's basket so that Andrew and Deborah could run about freely. They had a lovely time.

But soon a large black cloud came up, and there was a low rumbling noise in the distance.

"Oo-err," said Mouse, "I'm sure that's thunder. Are you frightened of thunder, Teddy Robinson?"

"What, me? I should hope not!" said Teddy Robinson. (There was another low rumble.) "No – I hope not. Yes – I very much hope not."

Deborah and Andrew came running up, saying, "Look at that big black cloud!"

"Yes," said Mummy, "I don't much like the look of it."

"Deborah," said Teddy Robinson, "are you frightened of thunder?"

"Mummy," said Deborah, "are you?"

"No," said Mummy, "but I think we ought to get under cover as soon as possible."

Deborah turned to Teddy Robinson, "Not much," she said, "but we ought to get under cover as soon as possible."

Teddy Robinson turned to Mouse, "No, I aren't frightened of thunder," he said, "but I've decided we ought to get under cover as soon as possible."

Then they all began to run.

It wasn't a very bad storm and it hardly rained at all, but Mummy thought they had better hurry.

"We will take a short cut through this field," she said.

"Oo-err," said Mouse, "but there are cows in that field. Do you like cows, Teddy Robinson?"

"Oh, yes," said Teddy Robinson, "I think I like cows. I'll just find out. Deborah, do you like cows?"

"Mummy," said Deborah, "do you like cows?"

"Oh, yes," said Mummy, "of course I do. They are dear, gentle animals, and they give us milk. Don't you like them?"

"Oh, yes," said Deborah, "I like them too. Don't you, Teddy Robinson?"

"Oh, yes," said Teddy Robinson, "I like them very much. At least, I hope I do."

He turned to Mouse. "Of course I like cows," he said. "I'd forgotten for the minute how much I like them. They give us dear, gentle milk. Don't you like them?"

"Yes – I do if you do," said Mouse.

"Oh, I *love* cows," said Teddy Robinson.

"So do I," said Deborah.

"So do I," said Mouse, in a high, trembly voice.

"But I think," said Teddy Robinson, "I think it would be kinder if we all went *round* the field instead of walking though it. We don't want to disturb the poor, dear cows, do we?"

"Oh, no, we don't want to disturb them," said Deborah. "Let's go round by the hedge, then we can look for blackberries. *Please,* Mummy, let's go round by the hedge!"

So they all hurried round the edge of the field (much too quickly to look for blackberries) until they came to the gate on the other side. The cows watched them pass.

"I didn't see you staring at them fiercely," said Mouse to Teddy Robinson, as they went through into the lane.

"How could I? There wasn't time, with everyone running so fast," said Teddy Robinson.

They crossed the lane, and there on the far side of another field they saw Black's farm.

"Come along," said Mummy, "we'll climb over the gate and cut across this field. I expect Daddy will be waiting."

Halfway across the field a cow that they hadn't seen rose from its knees and came walking towards them.

"Oo-err," said Mouse, "run!"

The cow began galloping.

"Oh, dear!" said Teddy Robinson. "Why did you tell it to run?"

"It's all right," said Mummy, "there's nothing to be frightened of."

But Deborah said, "Run, Mummy!" And Andrew said, "Yes, let's run!" And before they had time to think about it they were all running as fast as they could.

Mouse and Teddy Robinson bounced up and down inside the basket until they were quite out of

"I didn't see you staring at them fiercely"

breath, and then all of a sudden a dreadful thing happened. Teddy Robinson bounced so high that he never came down in the basket at all. He came down in the grass, and there were Mummy and Deborah and Andrew still running farther and farther away from him towards the gate on the other side of the field. And the cow was coming nearer and nearer, puffing and galloping and snorting through its nose.

Poor Teddy Robinson! He couldn't do anything

"Eat me now and get it over"

but just lie there and wait for it. He had forgotten all about how to be brave.

"And to think it was only this morning I killed a dragon!" he said to himself. "Or did I? Perhaps it was only a pretend dragon, after all. Yes, now I come to think of it, I'm sure it was only a pretend dragon. But this is a terribly real cow – I can feel its hooves shaking the ground. Oh, my goodness, here it comes!"

The cow came thundering up, then bent its head down and sniffed at Teddy Robinson.

"Please don't wait," said Teddy Robinson. "Eat me now and get it over."

"Mm-m-merr!" said the cow. "Must I?"

"Don't you want to?" said Teddy Robinson. "I thought that was what you were coming for."

"No," said the cow, "I was only coming to see who you were. Mm-m-merr! What a funny little cow you are. I never saw a cow like you before."

"I'm not a little cow," said Teddy Robinson. "I'm a middling-sized teddy bear."

"Why are you looking at me with your eyes crossed?" said the cow.

"I'm not. I'm staring at you fiercely."

"Mm-m-merr," said the cow. "I shouldn't if I were you. The wind might change and they might get stuck."

"Why don't you say Moo?" said Teddy Robinson.

"Because I'm a country cow. Only storybook cows say Moo, not real cows."

"Fancy that!" said Teddy Robinson. "And are you fierce?"

"Terribly fierce," said the cow.

Teddy Robinson trembled all over again.

"Yes," said the cow, "I eat grass and lie in the sun and look at the buttercups. . . ."

"I don't call that very fierce," said Teddy Robinson.

"Well, I'm sorry," said the cow, "but that's all the fierce I know how to be. I told you I'm a country cow. I'm only used to a quiet life."

"Well, thank goodness for that!" said Teddy Robinson. "Now tell me about life in the country."

"Mm-m-merr," said the cow, "it's very quiet, very quiet indeed. Listen to it."

Teddy Robinson listened, and all he could hear was the sound of the grasses rustling in the breeze, and the cow breathing gently through its nose.

"Yes," he said, "it is very quiet, ve-ry qui-et, ve-ry . . ." and a moment later he was asleep.

It seemed hours later that Farmer Black found him in the field, and he was taken into the farm-house. And there were Deborah and Daddy and Mummy and Andrew and Mouse, all waiting for him, and all terribly glad to see him again.

"Oh, dear Teddy Robinson!" cried Deborah, "I *am* so glad you're not lost. And *what* a brave bear you are! I am sorry I said you were showing off."

"Yes, he really is brave," said Andrew to Daddy. "We all ran away, and only Teddy Robinson was

102

brave enough to face the cow all by himself."

"And stare at him fiercely," squeaked Mouse.

Then Daddy said Teddy Robinson ought to have a medal, and he made one out of a silver milk-bottle top, and Deborah pinned it on to his braces, and everyone said, "Three cheers for Teddy Robinson, our Best Big Brave Brown Bear!"

*And that is the end of the story about how
Teddy Robinson was brave.*

– 8 –

Teddy Robinson Has a Holiday

One day in summer it was very, very hot. Teddy Robinson sat on the window-sill in Deborah's room and said to himself, "Phew! Phew! I wish I could take my fur coat off. It *is* a hot day!"

Deborah came running in from the garden to fetch her sun hat. When she saw Teddy Robinson sitting all humpy and hot on the window-sill she said, "Never mind, poor boy. You'll be cooler when you have your holiday."

"Are I going to have a holiday?" said Teddy Robinson.

"Yes, of course you are," said Deborah.

"When will it come?" said Teddy Robinson.

"Very soon now," said Deborah, and she ran out into the garden again.

Teddy Robinson sat and thought about this for a long while. He knew he had heard the word 'holiday' before, but he just could not remember what it meant.

"Now, I wonder what a holiday can be," he said to himself. "She said I would be cooler when I had it. Is it a teddy bear's sun-suit perhaps? Or a little umbrella? Or could it be a long, cold drink in a glass with a straw? And she said it would come very soon. But how will it come? Will it come in a box tied up with ribbon? Or on a tray? Or will the postman bring it in a parcel? Or will it just come walking in all by itself?"

Teddy Robinson didn't know the answer to any of these questions, so he began singing a little song to himself.

> *"I'm going to have a holiday,*
> *a holiday,*
> *a holiday.*
> *I'm going to have a holiday.*
> *How lucky I shall be.*
>
> *What ever is a holiday,*
> *a holiday,*
> *a holiday?*
> *What ever is a holiday?*
> *I'll have to wait and see."*

"Yes," he said to himself, "I'll have to wait and see. I'll ask Deborah about it tomorrow."

But when tomorrow came all sorts of exciting things began to happen, so Teddy Robinson forgot to ask Deborah after all.

Daddy brought a big trunk down from the attic, and Mummy began packing it with clothes and shoes, and Deborah turned everything out of her toy-cupboard on to the floor, and began looking for her bucket and spade.

"What's going to happen?" asked Teddy Robinson. "Are we going away?"

"Yes, of course we are," said Deborah. "We're going to the seaside. I told you yesterday."

"How funny. I didn't know," said Teddy Robinson.

"That's why everything is going in the trunk," said Deborah. "To go to the seaside!"

"Us too?" said Teddy Robinson.

"No," said Deborah. "We shall go in a train. Now, be a good boy and help me tidy up all these toys. I've found my bucket and spade."

So together they tidied up the toys. Then they said goodbye to all the dolls and put them to bed in the toy-cupboard.

At last there was nothing left on the floor at all,

except one tiny little round glass thing that Teddy Robinson found lying close beside him. It was about as big as a sixpence, and was a beautiful golden brown colour, with a black blob in the middle.

He showed it to Deborah.

"Now, I wonder what ever that can be," she said. "It can't be a bead, because it hasn't got a hole through the middle."

"Now I wonder what ever that can be"

"And it can't be a marble," said Teddy Robinson, "because it's flat on one side."

"Perhaps it's a sweet," said Deborah.

"Suck it and see," said Teddy Robinson.

"I mustn't suck it in case it's poison," said Deborah. So she licked it instead.

"No," she said, "it isn't a sweet, because it hasn't got any taste."

"It's very pretty," said Teddy Robinson. "Shall we keep it?"

"Yes," said Deborah. "It's too pretty to throw away. I wish I could think what it is, though. I'm sure I've seen it before somewhere, but I can't remember where."

"That's funny," said Teddy Robinson. "I was thinking just the same thing."

Before they went to bed that night they dropped the pretty little round thing (that wasn't a marble, and wasn't a bead, and wasn't a sweet) through the slot in Deborah's money-box.

"That will be a safe place to keep it," said Deborah.

And the very next day they all went away to the seaside.

Teddy Robinson enjoyed the ride in the train very much, because he was allowed to sit in the rack and look after the luggage. And Deborah enjoyed it very much, because they had a picnic dinner in the train, and it was so lovely to be able to look out of the window and watch the cows in the fields and eat a hard-boiled egg in her fingers at the same time.

It wasn't until they were quite half-way there that

things began to go wrong.

Daddy lifted Teddy Robinson down from the rack. He was just going to give him to Deborah when he looked at him closely and said, "Hallo, old man, what's happened to your other eye?"

"Oh dear," said Mummy. "Is it loose? I shall have to sew it on again before it gets lost."

"No, it isn't here," said Daddy.

"Oh dear! Oh dear!" said Deborah. "Let me see. Oh, you poor boy! What are we to do? Wherever can it be?"

They all began looking round the railway carriage and in the corners of the seats, but the other eye was nowhere to be seen.

Deborah lifted Teddy Robinson on to her lap to comfort him and looked sadly into his one eye. Suddenly she said, "Teddy Robinson! Do you remember the pretty little round glass thing we found yesterday?"

"The thing that wasn't a bead, and wasn't a marble, and wasn't a sweet?" said Teddy Robinson.

"Yes," said Deborah. "Well, that was your eye! This one is just the same. Fancy my not knowing it when I saw it!"

"And it's in the money-box," said Teddy Robinson sadly.

"Oh dear, so it is!" said Deborah. "What ever shall we do?"

"Stop the train!" said Teddy Robinson. "We must go home and fetch it at once."

But they couldn't stop the train. Daddy and Mummy both said they couldn't. So Teddy Robinson sat in the corner seat and grumbled to himself quietly while Deborah tried to comfort him by telling him about the nice time he was going to have at the seaside.

"We'll go down to the beach every day," she said, "and you shall come with me. Don't mind about

"Stop the train!"

your eye too much. You shall have it as soon as we get home."

"But I can't go down to the beach with only one eye," said Teddy Robinson.

"Yes, you can," said Deborah. "No one will notice."

"No, I can't," said Teddy Robinson. "There will be other children on the beach. If I can't go with two eyes I won't go at all."

"Oh, Teddy Robinson," said Deborah. "What am I to do with you?"

"I know!" said Daddy. "Make him into a pirate. Pirates always wear a patch over one eye. Then no one will know."

"Yes," said Mummy. "What a good idea! And he can wear my red-and-white spotted handkerchief round his head."

"And he can wear curtain rings for ear-rings," said Deborah. "Yes, that *is* a good idea."

Teddy Robinson began to feel much happier, and by the time the train came into the station his one eye was twinkling as usual, and he felt as pleased as Deborah to think they were really at the seaside at last.

As soon as breakfast was over the next morning Teddy Robinson and Deborah got ready to go down to the beach.

Deborah wore shorts and a T-shirt, and Teddy Robinson wore his trousers and no shirt. Mummy fixed the patch over his eye, and hung two gold curtain rings over his ears with pieces of cotton. Then she tied her red-and-white spotted handkerchief round his head.

"There, now," she said; "doesn't he look exactly like a pirate?" And she called Daddy to come and see.

"My word!" said Daddy. "I hope he won't frighten everybody away!"

On the way down to the beach Teddy Robinson said to Deborah, "Do I really look like a pirate?"

"Yes," said Deborah, "you really do."

"What *is* a pirate?" asked Teddy Robinson.

"He's a fierce robber man who lives in a ship," said Deborah.

"Oh, goody! I love being fierce," said Teddy Robinson. "And who do I rob?"

"Other people who live in other ships," said Deborah.

"That will be very nice," said Teddy Robinson. "I hope there will be plenty of other people in other ships there."

But when they got down to the beach they found that the other people were mostly sitting about in deckchairs or walking about on the sands.

"I can't very well rob people who're sitting in deckchairs, can I?" said Teddy Robinson. "And I don't think I should look quite right sitting in one myself."

So Daddy and Deborah made a big sandcastle down by the edge of the sea, and when it was finished they sat Teddy Robinson on top of it.

"There," said Deborah. "Your ship has been wrecked and sunk to the bottom of the sea, but you are safe on a desert island all of your own. Now you don't mind if I go and play with the other children, do you?"

Teddy Robinson didn't mind a bit. When Deborah had gone he sat on top of his sandcastle island and looked out to sea, feeling very fierce and brave.

He watched the seagulls flying and diving over the waves. After a while one of them came flying round and swooped down quite close to his head, screaming at him. It sounded very fierce, but Teddy Robinson didn't mind because he was feeling fierce too.

"Who are you-ou-ou?" screamed the seagull. "And what are you doing here?"

"I'm a pirate," shouted Teddy Robinson, "and I'm not afraid of you, even if you do scream at me. This is my very own island, and you can't come on it."

"I'm not afraid of you even if you do scream at me"

The seagull screamed at him again and flew away.

Then a crab came waddling round the sandcastle island. It walked sideways and looked up at Teddy Robinson with cross black eyes.

"Who are you?" said the crab. "And what are you doing on my beach?"

"I'm a pirate," roared Teddy Robinson in a big, brave bear's voice, "and I'm not afraid of you, even if you do walk sideways and stare at me with a cross face. And this is *my* island, so you can't come on it unless I invite you."

"Are you going to invite me?" said the crab.

"Not unless you stop looking so cross," said Teddy Robinson.

"Then I shan't come," said the crab. "If I want to be cross I *shall* be cross, and even a pirate can't stop me."

And he scuttled away into the sand.

Teddy Robinson felt very happy indeed. There was nothing he liked better than spending a beautiful, fierce morning all by himself at the seaside.

He began singing about it as loudly as he could.

"*Look at me*
beside the sea,
the one-eyed pirate bear!

It looked up at him with cross black eyes

*You'll never be
as fierce as me,
so fight me if you dare!"*

Just then a big black dog came running down the beach and began barking loudly at Teddy Robinson.

"Woof! Woof! What are you doing?" he barked.

"I'm a pirate on a desert island," shouted Teddy Robinson, "and you can't frighten me, even if you do bark at me so rudely."

"Woof! Woof!" barked the dog. "You certainly are on an island. Look, there's water all round you."

"Good gracious, so there is!" said Teddy Robinson. "However did that happen?"

"I expect the tide came up when you weren't looking," said the big black dog. "Woof! Woof! Shall I save you?"

"No, thank you," said Teddy Robinson. "Pirates don't need to be saved. But thank you for telling me."

He was just beginning to wonder how he was going to get back to the beach all by himself when Deborah came running up and paddled out to the castle to fetch him.

"Oh, Teddy Robinson!" she said. "I heard the dog barking, and I got quite a fright when I saw you sitting

"You certainly are on an island!"

with the water all round you. Were you frightened when you saw the tide was coming up?"

"Of course I weren't," said Teddy Robinson. "Pirates aren't frightened. I was just looking out to sea with my one brave eye and I never even noticed it. You know, I'm very fond of my other eye, but I'm rather glad we left it at home after all. I do so like being a pirate at the seaside. Can I have a castle to myself every day?"

"Yes, every day till we go home," said Deborah. "But next time we won't put it so near the edge of the water."

When at last the holiday was over and they all went home again Teddy Robinson was quite excited to find his other eye still inside Deborah's money-box, and to have it sewn on again. He and Deborah both felt as if they had been away for years and years, because everyone at home seemed so pleased to see them again.

"How big you've grown!" they all said to Deborah, and "How brown you are!" they all said to Teddy Robinson. "What a lovely holiday you must have had."

"Oh! My holiday!" said Teddy Robinson. "I'd forgotten all about it!"

"What do you mean?" said Deborah.

"Well, I never had it, did I?" said Teddy Robinson. "Did it come while we were at the seaside?"

"Of course it did," said Deborah. "That *was* your holiday – going to the seaside."

"Well, I never!" said Teddy Robinson. "Was it really? Oh, I *am* glad if *that* was my holiday. I never thought it would be anything as nice as that!"

And that is the end of the story about how
Teddy Robinson had a holiday.

– 9 –

Teddy Robinson Goes to Hospital

Once upon a time Teddy Robinson and Deborah went to hospital. They didn't know a bit what it was going to be like because neither of them had ever been before, so they were glad to have each other for company.

A kind nurse in a white cap and apron tucked them up in a little white bed in a big room called the ward, and while Mummy was in another room talking to the doctor they lay side by side and whispered to each other, and looked around to see what hospital was like.

There were a lot of other children in the ward as well. Some of them were in little white beds like Deborah and Teddy Robinson, and some of them were dressed and running around in soft bedroom slippers.

There were coloured pictures of nursery rhyme

people all round the walls, and quite close to Deborah's bed there was a big glass tank full of water with a lot of tiny fish swimming around inside. It was called an aquarium.

Teddy Robinson liked this, and so did Deborah. After a while they sat up so that they could see better, and they watched the fish swimming round and round until Mummy came in to say goodbye.

They were rather sad to say goodbye, but Mummy promised she would come and see them again next day, and when she had gone Deborah comforted Teddy Robinson, and Teddy Robinson comforted Deborah, and a nice kind nurse came and comforted them both, so they didn't need to be sad after all.

A little boy in the next bed said, "What's your name? I'm called Tommy. Would your bear like to talk to my horse?" And he pulled out a little brown felt horse from under the blanket and threw it over to Deborah's bed.

"His name's Cloppety," he said.

"Thank you," said Deborah. "My name is Deborah, and this is Teddy Robinson," and she sat them side by side with their noses close together so they could make friends with each other.

Teddy Robinson and Cloppety stared hard at

each other for quite a long while, then they began to talk quietly.

"Been here long?" asked Teddy Robinson.

"Been here long?"

"About a week," said Cloppety. "We're going home soon because Tommy's nearly better; he's getting up tomorrow. Why are you only wearing a vest?"

"I don't know," said Teddy Robinson. "Deborah forgot my trousers."

"What a pity," said Cloppety. "I had to leave my cart at home, so I know what it feels like. Are you happy here?"

"Yes," said Teddy Robinson, "I like watching the fish."

"So do I," said Cloppety.

When evening came and all the children were tucked up for the night it was very cosy in the ward. Little lights were left burning so that it was never quite dark, and Teddy Robinson and Deborah lay and watched the nurses going round to all the beds and cots and tucking up each of the children in turn. Cloppety had gone back to Tommy's bed, so they snuggled down together just as they did at home.

"Dear old boy," said Deborah. "I'm glad you're with me. Isn't Tommy a nice boy?"

"Yes," said Teddy Robinson, "and Cloppety's a nice horse."

And quite soon they were both fast asleep.

The next day Tommy was up, and running around in bedroom slippers like the other children who were nearly better, so for quite a lot of the day Cloppety stayed with Teddy Robinson, and Tommy came to see Deborah every now and then, and brought her toys and books from the hospital toy-cupboard.

Mummy came to see them, and she brought a red shoulder-bag with a zip-fastener for Deborah, and a real little nightshirt (made out of Deborah's old pyjamas) for Teddy Robinson. She also brought his old trousers that had got left behind by mistake.

123

They were very pleased. Deborah wore the shoulder-bag sitting up in bed, and Teddy Robinson put on his new nightie straight away.

"That's nice," said Cloppety, peeping over the bedclothes when Mummy had gone.

"Yes," said Teddy Robinson. "It's just what I was needing. Do you wish you had one?"

"Horses don't bother with nighties," said Cloppety. "I wish you could have seen my cart, though. It's green with yellow wheels, and the wheels really go round."

But Teddy Robinson wasn't listening. He was beginning to make up a little song in his head, all about his new nightie. And this is how it went:

> *"Highty tiddly ighty,*
> *a teddy bear wearing a nightie*
> *can feel he's dressed*
> *and looking his best*
> *(he couldn't do that in only a vest),*
> *highty tiddly ighty."*

In a few days the doctor said Deborah was better, and she was allowed to get up and run about the ward with the other children who were dressed; but Teddy Robinson still liked his nightie so much better than his vest and trousers that he decided he wasn't well enough to get up yet.

"Shall I dress you, too, Teddy Robinson?" asked Deborah.

"No, thank you," he said. "I think I'll stay in my nightie and sit on the pillow. I can watch you from there, and it will rest my legs."

The next day Tommy went home because he was quite well again, and Teddy Robinson and Deborah were quite sorry when he and Cloppety came to say goodbye. All the rest of that day his bed looked so empty that they didn't like looking at it.

"Never mind, Teddy Robinson," said Deborah. "We'll be going home ourselves soon." And they went off together to play with the other children.

Those who were up and nearly better had their meals at a little table at the other end of the ward, so it wasn't until after tea that Teddy Robinson and Deborah came back to their own bed. When they did they were surprised to see a new little girl lying in Tommy's bed.

"Hallo," said Deborah. "You weren't here before tea."

"No," said the little girl. "I've only just come, and I want to go home," and she looked as if she might be going to cry.

So Deborah said, "I expect you *will* go home soon. But it's nice here." And then she told her all about the hospital, and showed her the aquarium, and the little girl told her that her name was Betty, and soon they were quite like best friends.

"I wish I'd brought my doll," said Betty, looking at Teddy Robinson. "I came in a hurry and forgot her. Mummy's going to bring her tomorrow, but I want her now," and she looked as if she might cry again.

"You'd better have my teddy for a little while," said Deborah. "He's nice to cuddle if you're feeling sad. But don't cry all over his fur. He doesn't like it."

So Teddy Robinson got into bed beside Betty. He didn't talk to her because he was shy and didn't know her, but Betty seemed to like him and soon her eyes closed and she fell asleep hugging him.

When it was Deborah's bedtime she didn't like to take Teddy Robinson back in case she woke Betty, so she asked the nurse who came to tuck her up. The nurse went over to Betty's bed and looked at her and then she came back to Deborah.

"Would you mind very much if she kept him just for tonight?" she said. "She is fast asleep, and it seems such a pity to wake her. It would be awfully kind if you could lend him."

So Deborah said she would, and Teddy Robinson stayed where he was.

Deborah soon dropped off to sleep, but Teddy Robinson didn't. He lay in Betty's bed and watched the night-nurse who was writing at a little table, and looked at the fish swimming round and round in the aquarium, and then he began to sing to himself very softly, and after a while when he was sure that all the children were asleep he rolled over, tumbled gently out of bed, and rolled a little way across the floor.

At that moment a baby in a cot woke up and began to cry. The night-nurse stopped writing and came quickly down the ward to see who it was. As she passed Teddy Robinson her foot bumped against him and she nearly fell over him. She bent down and picked him up and then hurried on to comfort the crying baby.

As soon as the baby saw Teddy Robinson he stopped crying and said, "Teddy, teddy," so the nurse put Teddy Robinson inside the cot and let the baby hold him. But when she tried to take him back the baby started crying again, so after a while the nurse left him there, hoping he would help the baby go to sleep, and she went back to her writing.

But the baby didn't go to sleep. Instead he began pulling Teddy Robinson's arms and legs and ears, and poking his fingers in his eyes. Teddy Robinson didn't mind much because it didn't hurt him, but after a while the baby pulled his right ear so that it nearly came off, and instead of sticking up on top of his head like the other ear it hung down with only a thread of cotton holding it on.

"I bet I look silly," he said to himself. "I wonder what Deborah will say." And he felt rather sorry about it.

In the morning when the children all woke up Deborah and Betty didn't know wherever Teddy Robinson could be. They looked everywhere in both their beds, but of course they couldn't find him. So as soon as she was dressed Deborah began going round the ward looking at all the children's beds and peeping into all the babies' cots. And when she came to the cot where he was she could hardly believe it!

The baby was fast asleep at last, but there was poor Teddy Robinson peeping through the bars with one ear hanging right down over his eye.

"You poor old boy," she said. "What *are* you doing in there? You look as if you're in a cage. Wait a minute and I'll get you out."

She had to ask a nurse to lift him out of the cot, and then she hugged him and kissed him and carried him back to her own bed.

– peeping through the bars with one ear hanging right down –

"Oh, Teddy Robinson," she said, "how did you get there? And what *has* happened to your poor ear? It's only hanging on by one little piece of cotton."

"I think you'd better pull it off," said Teddy Robinson bravely, "otherwise I might lose it."

"All right," said Deborah, "and I'll keep it for you till we get home; then we'll ask Mummy to mend it."

Then she gave the ear a sharp little tug and off it came.

"You're a dear brave boy," said Deborah, and she kissed the place where it had been, and put the ear carefully away in her shoulder-bag.

When the night-nurse came round that evening and saw Teddy Robinson sitting on the pillow with only one ear she remembered what had happened the night before, and she told Deborah all about it; how she had nearly fallen over him and had given him to the baby to stop him crying.

"But I *am* sorry about his ear," she said.

"It's all right," said Deborah. "I've got it safely in my shoulder-bag, and we're going home tomorrow, so Mummy will mend it."

"I'm so glad," said the nurse. "I was wondering if he would like it bandaged."

Deborah knew that Teddy Robinson would simply love that, so she said, "Oh, yes, please!" And the nurse bandaged Teddy Robinson's head round and round with a piece of real hospital bandage. He didn't mind a bit that one eye got covered up at the same time, and when it was finished both Deborah and the nurse said he looked lovely.

Early next morning Teddy Robinson was dressed in his vest and trousers again, and his nightie was packed away with his ear in Deborah's shoulder-bag. Mummy came to fetch them, and they said goodbye to everybody, even the fish in the aquarium.

She bandaged his head

They were both very pleased to be going home again, and Teddy Robinson was specially pleased because he was going out with a real bandage on. He couldn't help hoping that everyone would notice it, because then they would all know that he had been in a real hospital!

And that is the end of the story about how Teddy Robinson went to hospital.

Teddy Robinson's Concert Party

One day Teddy Robinson was lying on his back in front of the fire with Deborah's cousin Philip. Suddenly Philip tickled him in the tummy and said, "I say, Teddy R! Let's make a surprise. I feel like doing something funny."

"Oh, so do I!" said Teddy Robinson. "Where's Deborah?"

"She's gone to ask Andrew and Mary-Anne to tea today," said Philip. "Let's think of something to do when they come."

"I suppose I couldn't have another birthday party?" said Teddy Robinson.

"No," said Philip. "We must think of something new. Couldn't we do some tricks?"

"I know!" said Teddy Robinson. "Ask them to sit down to listen to a story, and then when they're all waiting you just fly out of the window. That would be a jolly good trick!"

"But I can't fly." said Philip.

"Oh, no. Bother! We can't do that then."

"Think of something else," said Philip.

"Make faces at them," said Teddy Robinson.

"That wouldn't be funny enough to make them laugh."

"The face you're making now would make anyone laugh," said Teddy Robinson.

"I'm not making a face. This is my ordinary one."

"Well, it's different from usual," said Teddy Robinson.

"That's because I'm thinking. Don't be silly."

"Well, then," said Teddy Robinson, "don't let's try to be funny. Let's do something Sweet and Beautiful and a little bit Sad, like the Babes in the Wood."

"No," said Philip. "Let's have something jolly, even if we can't be funny. Think again."

"*I* know!" said Teddy Robinson. "I'll have a concert party!"

Philip thought this was a fine idea. When Deborah came back he and Teddy Robinson told her all about it.

"I'm going to sing songs," said Teddy Robinson, "and say pieces of poetry, and we'll have some refreshments, and then I'll do conjuring tricks."

"But what's Philip going to do?" asked Deborah.

"Help *me*," said Teddy Robinson. "It's *my* concert party."

"And are you going to make the refreshments too?"

"No," he said, "you know I can't do that; but you're going to be very kind, like you always are, and ask Mummy."

Mummy said, yes, she would make the refreshments. They could have raisins (six each) and chocolate biscuits (cut in halves) and dolly mixture (handed round in a bowl).

Philip began making the programme, and Teddy Robinson sat beside him and told him what to write. Deborah brought the dolls out of the toy-cupboard and tidied them up.

"You can be the audience." she said.

The stage was a great trouble, until Mummy had a good idea.

Why not turn the kitchen table on its side?" she said. "You can have it in here, just for the afternoon." She gave them some old curtains and a bunch of chrysanthemums.

"The flowers aren't very fresh," she said, "but you might use them for decoration. And you can hang the curtains on a string and tie the ends to the table-legs."

Teddy Robinson told him what to write—

While Philip and Deborah got the stage ready Teddy Robinson sat thinking hard about all the things he was going to do.

"Are you sure you don't want anyone else to do anything?" asked Deborah. "It's rather a lot for one."

"No, thank you," said Teddy Robinson; "but I might have Jacqueline in one scene. Is Mary-Anne bringing her?"

(Jacqueline was Mary-Anne's beautiful doll.)

"Yes," said Deborah, "and Andrew is bringing his toy dog, Spotty. You might use him too?"

"No," said Teddy Robinson. "He argues too much."

When Mary-Anne and Andrew arrived, with Jacqueline and the spotted dog, they found the stage all set up ready. The curtains were hung on a string across the front, and the bunch of flowers hung from the middle, just where the curtains met. (You will see in the picture how it looked.)

In front of the stage all the dolls were sitting in tidy rows, staring at the curtains, and waiting for the show to begin. A large notice was pinned to the door. It said:

TEDDY ROBINSON'S CONCERT PARTY
Programme

RECITATION, by Teddy Robinson

A SEEN FROM SLEEPING BEAUTY, by Teddy Robinson
 and Jacqueline (thought of by Teddy Robinson)

SONG, by Teddy Robinson

REFRESHMENTS, thought of by Teddy Robinson,
 handed round by Deborah, made by Mummy

CONJURING TRICKS, by the FAMOUS WIZARD
 T. NOSNIBOR (helped by Philip)

  Audience arranged by Deborah

  No smoking or shouting

Jacqueline was very surprised when Mary-Anne

told her that she was going to be on the stage. She hadn't been able to read the programme herself, because her eyes were shut.

"I'm afraid they're stuck again," whispered Mary-Anne to Deborah. "Will it matter?"

"Not a bit," said Deborah. "She's going to be the Sleeping Beauty."

Jacqueline was hustled behind the stage to where Philip and Teddy Robinson were waiting.

"You're on next," Teddy Robinson told her. "I'm first."

"We're ready to begin now," said Philip.

"About time, too," said the spotted dog, who was rather cross at not being asked to go on the stage as well.

"Hush!" said all the dolls. "They're going to begin."

Teddy Robinson came to the front of the curtain. He bowed low to the audience, then he said:

"Welcome.
　　"Ladies and gentlemen,
　　what a sight
　　to see you sitting here tonight!
　　I'm pleased to see you
　　every one,
　　so clap your hardest when I've done—"

He bowed low to the audience.

This wasn't really the end of the poem, but as everyone started clapping their hardest straight away Teddy Robinson leaned back against the curtain and waited for them to finish. But he had forgotten there was nothing behind the curtain, so a moment later he fell through and disappeared out of sight.

The audience didn't know this was a mistake. Everyone clapped harder than ever, so nobody heard Teddy Robinson saying, in a rather cross voice, "But I haven't finished yet! There's another verse."

"Never mind," said Philip. "Let's do the next scene."

Teddy Robinson's head came out from between the curtains.

"The next scene is Sleeping Beauty," he said, "and please don't clap *till the end.*"

After a little waiting Deborah pulled the curtains aside. This was the first time the audence had seen the whole stage, and everyone said, "Oo-oh, isn't it pretty!"

On a pink cushion lay Jacqueline, fast asleep and looking very beautiful. There were two or three ferns in pots, arranged to look like trees, and some leaves from the garden were sprinkled about on the ground. On the other side stood the wooden horse, and on

A scene from Sleeping Beauty

his back, looking very proud and princely, sat Teddy Robinson. He was wearing the dolls' Red-Riding-Hood cloak (with the hood tucked inside), and a beret with a long curly feather (from one of Mummy's old hats) on his head. He also had a sword (cut out of cardboard) and socks rolled down to look like boots.

"How handsome he is!" said all the dolls.

"Huh!" said the spotted dog. "I think he looks soppy."

The horse began to move slowly across the stage towards Jacqueline. Philip was pulling it on a string from the other side; but the string hardly showed at

(thought of by Teddy Robinson)

141

all, so it looked very real. The dolls all wanted to clap, but they remembered just in time and didn't. The horse, with Teddy Robinson on its back, moved slowly forward until its front wheels came up against the edge of the pink cushion. Then it gave a jerk, and Teddy Robinson fell headlong over its neck and landed beside Jacqueline, with his nose buried in the cushion.

Everyone waited to see what was going to happen next, but nothing happened. They went on waiting. At last Teddy Robinson said, in a muffled, squeaky voice, "It's the end. For goodness sake, clap! I'm suffocating."

Deborah pulled the curtains quickly, and the audience clapped hard.

After a good deal of whispering behind the stage Teddy Robinson's head came out again from between the curtains.

"Ladies and gentlemen," he said, "as you never seem to know when it's the end of anything I'll tell you when to clap next time. The next scene is The Bear in the Wood."

His head disappeared, but shot out again a moment later.

"You can clap now while you're waiting," he said.

When the curtains parted once more Jacqueline

and the cushion had gone, but the leaves and ferns were still there. Teddy Robinson sat under the largest fern. He began singing:

> *"I'm a poor teddy bear,*
> *growing thinner and thinner.*
> *I haven't any Deborah*
> *to give me any dinner."*

The audience loved this. They laughed loudly, because Teddy Robinson looked so very fat and cosy that they thought he was trying to be funny. But Teddy Robinson had meant it to be a sad song. He went on:

> *"I'm lost in a wood*
> *where the trees are thick and high.*
> *If someone doesn't find me*
> *I might lie down and die."*

"Oh dear!" said one of the dolls. "Let me find him! I think he means it."

Teddy Robinson turned to the audience and said:

> *"I hope you won't get worried*
> *at this sad, sad song.*
> *I'm lying down to die now,*
> *but I shan't stay dead for long."*

143

He then lay down in the middle of the stage, and Philip emptied a basketful of leaves over him. Teddy Robinson sang the last verse,

"With only leaves to cover me
and grass beneath my head,
that is the end of the Bear in the Wood,
and now I'm really dead. You can clap now."

The audience clapped and cheered. Some of them thought it was sad, and some of them thought it was funny, but they all loved it. After that it was time for the refreshments.

Philip and Teddy Robinson, behind the curtains, were busy clearing away the leaves and ferns.

"How is it going?" whispered Teddy Robinson.

Philip peeped through the curtain.

"I think it's going jolly well," he said. "They seem to be enjoying the refreshments like anything."

When all was ready, and the last raisin had been eaten, Deborah drew the curtains for the Famous Wizard Nosnibor.

Teddy Robinson was sitting in the middle of the stage. He had a tall white paper hat on his head, and another hat (one of Daddy's) lay on a little table beside him.

"Why is he wearing a dunce's hat?" asked the spotted dog in a loud voice.

"He isn't," whispered Deborah. "It's a wizard's hat."

"Hush!" said all the dolls. "He's going to begin."

Philip handed him a stick covered with silver paper.

"This is my magic wand," said Teddy Robinson in a deep voice, "and I am the famous Wizard Nosnibor."

Then he waved the wand over the hat on the table, and said:

> *"Abracadabra,*
> *titfer-tat.*
> *You'll find a rabbit*
> *inside the hat!"*

Philip lifted up the hat, and there, underneath it, sat Deborah's stuffed rabbit. All the dolls clapped and said:

"What a wonderful trick!"

But the spotted dog said, "I know how he did that one. He put the rabbit there before we started."

"Hush!" said the dolls. "He's going to do another trick!"

Philip put two little bowls on the ground in front of Teddy Robinson. One was red and the other was white. He turned them both upside down, then he put a marble under the red bowl.

"Which bowl is the marble under?" said Teddy Robinson.

"The red one," everybody shouted.

Teddy Robinson waved his magic wand over the two bowls and said:

> *"Roll, little marble,*
> *roll, roll, roll.*
> *Choose for yourself*
> *your favourite bowl."*

"Oh, *I* know that trick!" shouted the spotted dog. "I saw a man do it at a party. The marble's gone under the other bowl, the white one. *That's* not a new trick!"

Teddy Robinson waited, looking mysterious and important. Philip lifted up the white bowl. There was nothing there. Then he lifted up the red bowl. There was the marble!

"You see," said Teddy Robinson, "it *is* a new trick."

The dolls clapped even harder and cried, "Oh, *isn't* he clever!"

But the spotted dog kept saying, over and over again, "It *wasn't* a new trick. Look here, listen to me—"

The Famous Wizard Nosnibor

"Andrew," said Deborah, "if you can't keep Spotty quiet I think you'd better take him away."

"Oh, all right," said Andrew. "I'll keep him quiet."

"Now," said Teddy Robinson, "if you've all finished clapping I'll show you my next trick."

"*I* wasn't clapping," said the spotted dog.

"This trick," said Teddy Robinson, "is called The Magic Flowers."

Philip laid a small bunch of flowers on the left-hand side of the stage. Teddy Robinson waved his magic wand and said,

147

"Snip-snap-snorum, fiddle-de-dee,
hokum-pokum, one-two-three.
Magic Flowers on the floor,
come to Wizard Nosnibor!"

The bunch of flowers began moving slowly across the floor all by itself. The audience clapped and cheered.

Teddy Robinson waved his magic wand once more, and then the biggest and best surprise of all happened. The bunch of chrysanthemums hanging above his head suddenly fell straight down into his lap, and at the same minute the curtains fell down on top of him, covering everything except his nose and one eye. The audience cheered louder than ever.

Teddy Robinson said, "THE END," very slowly and loudly, and bowed beneath the curtains.

There was a great deal of noise after this. The audience was still clapping and cheering, and Philip was shouting, "Hooray for the Famous Wizard!" And Mary-Anne was telling everybody it was the nicest concert party she had ever seen. Only Spotty was still arguing.

"I don't believe there *is* such a person as the Wizard Nosnibor," he said.

"If some people could read other people's names

backwards," said Teddy Robinson, "they wouldn't think they were quite so clever."

Much later on, when it was all over, Deborah said, "Teddy Robinson, that *was* a lovely concert party!"

"Yes, wasn't it?" said Teddy Robinson.

"Do tell me how you did the Magic Flowers," said Deborah.

"A piece of black cotton was tied on them," said Teddy Robinson. "Philip pulled it."

"But how did you get the other flowers and the curtains to fall down at exactly the right minute?"

"I'll tell you a secret," said Teddy Robinson. "I didn't. I think the string broke. You couldn't have been more surprised than I was. Don't tell anyone, will you?"

And that is the end of the story about
Teddy Robinson's concert party.

Teddy Robinson and the Beautiful Present

One day Teddy Robinson and Deborah went to Granny's house for the afternoon.

After tea Granny gave Deborah a little round tin, full of soapy stuff, and a piece of bent wire, round at one end and straight at the other end.

"What is it for?" asked Deborah.

"It's for blowing bubbles," said Granny. "I'll show you how to do it." And she dipped the end of the wire into the tin, and then blew gently through it into the air. A whole stream of bubbles flew out into the room.

"Oh!" exclaimed Deborah. "What a Beautiful Present!"

"It will keep you happy till Daddy comes to fetch you," said Granny, and she went away to tidy up the tea things.

Teddy Robinson sat in Granny's armchair and

watched Deborah blowing the bubbles. They were very pretty.

"Can I have one?" he asked.

Deborah blew a bubble at him, and it landed on his arm.

"Oh, thank you," he said. "Can I keep it?"

But before Deborah could say yes, the bubble had made a tiny little splutter and burst.

"Well, I'm blowed!" said Teddy Robinson. "That one's gone. Blow me another!"

So Deborah blew another. This one landed on his foot. But again it spluttered and burst.

"More!" said Teddy Robinson. So Deborah blew a whole stream of bubbles, and they landed all over

– they landed all over him –

him: one on his ear, one on his toe, five or six on his arms and legs, and one on the very end of his nose. But, one by one, they all spluttered and burst. Teddy Robinson's fur was damp where the bubbles had been, and he felt rather cross.

"The ones you give me aren't any good," he said. "They all burst."

"They are meant to burst," said Deborah.

"Then what's the good of them?" said Teddy Robinson.

"Just to look beautiful, for a minute," said Deborah.

"I think that's silly," said Teddy Robinson. "If I couldn't look beautiful for more than a minute without bursting, I wouldn't bother to look beautiful at all. Stop blowing bubbles and play with me instead."

"No, said Deborah. "I can play with you any time. I want to play with my beautiful bubbles just now. Don't bother me, there's a good boy."

So Teddy Robinson sat and sang to himself while he watched Deborah blowing bubbles.

> *"The trouble*
> *with a bubble*
> *is the way it isn't there*
> *the minute that you've blown it*

and thrown it
in the air.
It's a pity,
when you're pretty,
to disappear in air.
I'm glad I'm not a bubble;
I'd rather be a bear."

When it was time to go home Daddy came to fetch them on his bicycle. Deborah ran to show him the Beautiful Present.

"Show me how it works when we get home," said Daddy. "We must hurry now, because Mummy is waiting for us."

So Teddy Robinson and Deborah said goodbye to Granny, and Daddy took them out to the gate where his bicycle was waiting. He popped Teddy Robinson into the basket on the front, then he lifted Deborah up into the little seat at the back, just behind him.

"You carry my Beautiful Present, Daddy," said Deborah. So Daddy put it in his pocket. Then off they all went.

Teddy Robinson loved riding in the bicycle basket. The wind whistled in his fur, and he sang to himself all the way home:

"Head over heels,
how nice it feels,
a basket-y ride
on bicycle wheels."

It was beginning to get dark, and the lights were going on in all the houses when at last they reached home.

"Now run in quickly," said Daddy, as he lifted Deborah down from her little seat. "Here are your bubbles," he said, and he took Granny's present out of his pocket.

Deborah ran in at the front door where Mummy was waiting. Teddy Robinson heard her calling as she ran, "Look, Mummy – I've got such a Beautiful Present!" Then the front door shut behind them.

Daddy wheeled the bicycle round the side of the house to the tool-shed. He opened the door and pushed the bicycle inside, leaning it up against the wall. Then he went out again and shut the door behind him.

"Oh, dear!" said Teddy Robinson. "They've forgotten I'm still in the basket. I expect they'll come back and fetch me later."

But they didn't come back and fetch him, because Daddy had quite forgotten that he had put Teddy

Robinson in the basket, and Deborah thought she must have left him at Granny's house. So she went to bed thinking that Granny would be bringing him back tomorrow.

It was very dark in the tool-shed, and very quiet.

Teddy Robinson smoothed his fur and pulled up his braces, and sang a little song to keep himself company:

> *"Oh, my fur and braces!*
> *How dark it is at night*
> *sitting in the tool-shed*
> *without electric light!*
>
> *Sitting in the tool-shed,*
> *with no one here but me.*
> *Oh, my fur and braces,*
> *what a funny place to be!"*

He rather liked the bit about the fur and braces, so he sang it again. Then he stopped singing and listened to the quietness instead. And after a while he found that it wasn't really quiet at all in the tool-shed. All sorts of little noises and rustlings were going on, very tiny little noises that he wouldn't have noticed if everything else hadn't been so quiet.

—it hung just in front of his nose

First he heard the bustling of a lot of little ear-wigs running to and fro under a pile of logs in the corner. Then he heard the panting of a crowd of tiny ants who were struggling across the floor with a long twig they were carrying. Then he heard the sigh of a little moth as it shook its wings and fluttered about the windowpane. Teddy Robinson was glad to think he wasn't all by himself in the tool-shed after all.

Suddenly something came dropping down from the ceiling on a long, thin thread and hung just in front of his nose. It made one or two funny faces at him, then pulled itself up again and disappeared out of sight. Teddy Robinson was so frightened that he nearly fell out of the bicycle basket. But then he realized that it was only a spider.

What a pity, he thought. I'd have said Good Evening if I'd known it was coming.

A moment later he felt a gentle plop on top of his head and knew that the spider had come down again. This time he wasn't frightened, only surprised.

It seemed rather silly to say Good Evening to someone who was sitting on top of his head, so Teddy Robinson began singing again, in his smallest voice, just to let the spider know he was there.

"Oh, my fur and braces!
You did give me a fright,
making funny faces
in the middle of the night!

Hanging from the ceiling
by a tiny silver thread,
what a funny feeling
when you landed on my head!"

The spider crawled across the front of Teddy Robinson's head and looked down into one of his eyes.

"I say," he said. "I do beg your pardon. I didn't know it was your head I'd landed on. And when I came down the first time I'd no idea I was making faces at you. I was simply looking for somewhere to spin a web. I'm sorry I frightened you."

"That's all right," said Teddy Robinson.

"I believe I do make funny faces when I'm thinking," said the spider. "I often seem to frighten people without meaning to. Have you heard about Miss Muffet? Well, I gave her such a fright that they've been making a song about it ever since; but it was quite by mistake, you know."

Teddy Robinson began to feel rather sorry for the spider who was always frightening people without meaning to, so he said, "Well, *I'm* not frightened of you. I'm pleased to see you."

"Have you come to live here?" asked the spider.

"Oh, I hope not," said Teddy Robinson. "I mean I'm really only here by mistake. Deborah's sure to come and find me in the morning. She wouldn't have forgotten me tonight if she hadn't been given a Beautiful Present."

"What was it?" asked the spider.

"Bubbles," said Teddy Robinson. "They were very

pretty, but they kept bursting."

"And did you have a Beautiful Present too?"

"No," said Teddy Robinson sadly.

"What a shame," said the spider. "You know, I could make you a Beautiful Present myself. It wouldn't last very long, but it would last longer than a bubble."

"Could you really?" said Teddy Robinson.

"Yes," said the spider. "I could spin a web for you. I make rather beautiful webs, and they look lovely with the light shining on them."

"Oh, thank you," said Teddy Robinson. "I should like that. Will I be able to take it away with me?"

"Yes," said the spider. "But I must be careful not to join it to the wall or it will break when you move."

"And don't join it to the bicycle basket either, will you?" said Teddy Robinson. "I don't usually live in that."

"I see," said the spider. "Well, I will start at your ear, and go down here, and along here, and I'll catch the thread to your foot if you're sure that doesn't tickle you?"

"Yes, that will be very nice," said Teddy Robinson. "Shall I sing to you while you work?"

"Oh, do," said the spider. "I love music while I work."

So Teddy Robinson began singing:

*"Spin, little spider, spin,
in and out and in."*

And as he sang he heard a gentle whirring noise quite close to his ear, and knew that the spider had started spinning the web that was to be his Beautiful Present.

Soon the gentle noise of the spider spinning made Teddy Robinson so drowsy that he forgot to sing any more, and a little while afterwards he fell fast asleep.

It was morning when he woke up again. Someone was just opening the tool-shed door, and as the sunshine came streaming in Teddy Robinson could see the silver thread of the spider's web reaching right down to his toes. He kept very still so as not to break it.

Daddy had come to fetch his bicycle. As soon as he saw Teddy Robinson he called Deborah. She *was* surprised to see him.

"I thought we'd left you at Granny's!" she said. "Oh, you poor boy!"

"Yes, but look what he's got!" said Daddy.

"Oh, how lovely!" said Deborah, and she called

—*reaching right down* ... *to his toes*

Mummy to come and see. And Mummy and Daddy and Deborah all crowded round the bicycle to look at Teddy Robinson and admire his beautiful web.

"A spider must have made it in the night," said Daddy.

"Look how it sparkles in the sun!" said Mummy.

"And Teddy Robinson has got a Beautiful Present all of his own!" said Deborah.

Then Teddy Robinson was lifted very carefully out of the bicycle basket, and Deborah carried him into the house, holding him in front of her with both hands, so as not to break a single thread of the web.

"What happened to *your* Beautiful Present?" asked Teddy Robinson.

"It's finished. I threw away the tin," said Deborah. "And where are all the bubbles?"

"Gone," said Deborah. "They all burst. Your web won't last for ever either. Nothing does."

"Except me," said Teddy Robinson. "It's a good thing *I* don't burst, isn't it?"

And that is the end of the story about
Teddy Robinson and the Beautiful Present.

– 12 –

Teddy Robinson Tries to Keep Up

One day Teddy Robinson was sitting in Deborah's window, looking across the road, when he suddenly saw something very odd. In the window of the house opposite he saw himself looking out.

"Fancy that," said Teddy Robinson, "I never knew I was reflected in that window." And he sat up a little straighter and began to admire himself quietly.

"My fur looks better than I thought," he said to himself. "The part that's been kissed away all round my nose hardly shows from here. And my trousers aren't too shabby at all. I'm really quite a handsome bear from a distance." And he was pleased to think the people over the road had such a fine view of him.

But a little later, when he looked across again, he had another surprise. He could see quite clearly in the reflection of the window opposite that he had a hat on. A large, round, red beret with a bobble on top.

"That's funny," he said to himself. "I don't remember Deborah putting my hat on. Anyway my hat doesn't look like that. Can she have bought me a new one, and put it on my head when I wasn't looking?" Just then Deborah came running in.

"Hallo," said Teddy Robinson. "Why have I got this hat on?"

"What hat?" said Deborah, surprised.

"Haven't I got a hat on?" said Teddy Robinson. "A large, round, red beret with a bobble on top?"

"No, of course you haven't," said Deborah, and she came over and looked at him closely.

"Look over there, then," said Teddy Robinson. "Isn't that me?" And haven't I got a hat on?"

Deborah looked. "Oh, that's funny!" she said. "They've got a teddy bear just like you! He's even got the same sort of trousers. I wonder why they put him up in the window."

"Was it to show off that hat?" said Teddy Robinson.

"Yes, perhaps it was," said Deborah. "That big girl, Pauline Jones, lives there. The one who goes to school and wears a uniform. That's her hat."

"It's a very nice hat," said Teddy Robinson.

– a large, round, red beret with a bobble on top.

"Yes," said Deborah, "but I wish the girl was nice too. She's not a bit friendly. Once when I took you out in the dolls' pram she stared hard, but she never even smiled at us. When *I* go to a big school with a uniform I shan't be like that. I'll say hallo to everybody, no matter how young they are."

Teddy Robinson stared across at the other bear.

"I'd better have my hat on," he said.

"Yes, they may as well see you've got one too," said Deborah, and she fetched his knitted bonnet.

"Where are my other hats?" said Teddy Robinson.

"You haven't any, you know that," said Deborah. "But this is lovely, it's a real baby's bonnet."

"Yes, I was afraid it was," said Teddy Robinson. "Can't you lend me one of yours?"

So Deborah fetched one of her own hats. It had poppies and corn round it, and ribbon streamers.

"That's much better!" said Teddy Robinson. "Now, haven't I got a paper sunshade as well?"

"Oh, yes!" said Deborah. "What fun!"

And a few minutes later Teddy Robinson was sitting proudly in the window, with Deborah's best hat on and his paper sunshade over his head.

—sitting proudly in the window

Deborah was just having tea when she heard Teddy Robinson shouting, "Can I have something to eat? That bear over the road has got an orange!"

She ran in with her slice of bread and butter. It had a big bite taken out of it. She propped it up on Teddy Robinson's paw against the window, then went back to finish her tea. But a moment later Teddy Robinson called out again.

"Hey! That Jones bear has got a bun now!"

Deborah ran in again, this time with a slice of cake in her hand. She propped it up on his other paw.

"Now are you happy?" she said.

"Oh, yes, thank you," said Teddy Robinson.

But when Deborah came back again after tea, Teddy Robinson was looking gloomy.

"*Now* what's the matter?" she said.

"I don't like tea with nothing to drink," said Teddy Robinson.

Deborah looked across at the other window and saw that the Jones bear now had a bottle of milk in front of him, with a straw sticking out of it.

"Oh dear," she said, "poor Teddy Robinson! I'd better get the dolls' tea set out."

And soon Teddy Robinson was sitting with his tea nicely laid out in front of him on a tray.

"This *is* fun!" said Deborah. "I do wonder who is

doing it. Surely it can't be that girl, Pauline, who never even says hallo?"

Teddy Robinson didn't know who it was either. He tried to keep watch to see if he could see anyone moving about, but somehow he always just missed it.

Next time he looked he saw that the milk bottle had gone, and the bear was now reading a book.

"Bring me a book, Deborah!" he shouted. "A big book. The biggest you can find!"

Deborah came running in with the telephone book and propped it up in front of him on the toy blackboard. It was very dull, with nothing but long lists of names in it, but luckily Teddy Robinson couldn't read, so he didn't know how bored he was. And it was fun trying to keep up with the other bear.

"He doesn't even know I can't read," he said, and chuckled to himself.

But by bedtime he was getting quite stiff.

"Thank goodness I can get down now," he said. Then he looked across at the other house. A big dolls' cot had just been put on the window sill!

"Oh, my goodness!" he said, "whatever next?" Then he shouted loudly, "A bed! Bring me a bed!"

Deborah came running. "What is it now?"

"I must have a bed!" said Teddy Robinson. "A bed

all to myself. At once!"

"That's not a very nice way to ask," said Deborah.

"Please, dear Deborah, may I have a bed all of my own?" said Teddy Robinson. "I can't possibly let that Jones bear know I haven't got one."

Deborah rummmaged in the toy-cupboard and pulled out an old dolls' bed. "It's too small," she said.

"And the bottom's fallen out," said Teddy Robinson.

"But it's all we've got," said Deborah.

"Then it'll have to do," said Teddy Robinson. "Put my nightie on quickly and squeeze me in."

So Deborah did. Then she covered him with a doll's blanket, put the telephone book underneath, to stop him falling through, and put him up on the sill.

"Are you comfy?" she said.

"No, thank you," said Teddy Robinson. "But at least I'm glad I've got a proper nightie, and don't have to go to bed in my trousers."

"I wonder if they can see it," said Deborah.

"Shall we hang my trousers up?" said Teddy Robinson. "Then they'll know I haven't got them on."

So Deborah found a dress hanger, and hung Teddy Robinson's trousers up in the window for everyone to see. And Teddy Robinson lay underneath and thought how funny they looked without him

*— and thought how funny they looked
without him inside them —*

inside them.

Then Deborah kissed him and got into her own bed. Usually Teddy Robinson slept there too. Sometimes he pushed his way down in the night until he was right at the bottom of the bed and as warm as toast. But tonight he was very cold. The blanket was far too small, and he couldn't move an inch.

He had a dreadful night.

When at last Deborah came for him in the morning, he was too stiff and sleepy to sit up straight.

But Deborah was very bright. She said, "Oh, do look! The Jones bear is having breakfast now!"

Sure enough, there he sat in the window with a big packet of cornflakes in front of him.

"I'd better have eggs and bacon then, hadn't I?" said Teddy Robinson, waking up.

"No," said Deborah, "let's pretend you had breakfast in bed. Then while I'm having mine, you can be thinking of something to do afterwards."

But when she came back after breakfast Teddy Robinson was sitting all humped up, and she could tell by the look of his back that he was feeling sad.

"Haven't you thought of anything?" she said.

"No," said Teddy Robinson, "and I'm not going to. I'm tired of trying to keep up with the Joneses. They go too quickly for me. Look over there now."

Deborah looked across and saw that the Jones bear was now wearing a shiny blue party dress with big puffed sleeves, and a blue satin ribbon, tied in a bow between the ears.

"Oh dear," she said, "we haven't anything as grand as that. Shall I put on your best purple dress?"

"No," said Teddy Robinson sadly. "Did you see what he's got beside him?"

Deborah looked again. "Oh! A dear little dolls' sewing machine! *Aren't* they lucky?"

"Turn me round," said Teddy Robinson. "I shan't look any more. I think he's showing off. I don't like bears who put on airs." And he began singing, with his back to the window.

> *"Teddy bears*
> *who put on airs*
> *are not the the bears for me.*
> *Bears are best*
> *not over-dressed —*
> *in pants, perhaps,*
> *or just a vest,*
> *but* not *the clothes you wear for best —*
> *they're better fat and free.*
>
> *A friendly, free-and-easy bear,*
> *a cosy, jolly, teasy bear*
> *is always welcome*
> *everywhere.*
> *Fair and furry,*
> *fat and free,*
> *that's the kind of bear to be.*
> *Like me."*

After that he stuck his tummy out again and began to feel better.

"Lift me down," he said to Deborah. "If that Jones bear only wants to see what things I've got, then he doesn't need to see *me* at all. We can leave all my things in the window for him to look at, and then go off on our own to a desert island and be very happy with nothing at all. Why didn't I think of it before?"

So quickly they arranged all his things in the window. They hung up his nightie, his best purple dress and his trousers on three little dress hangers. They hung his paper sunshade and his knitted bonnet from the window latch. Then they took a sheet of cardboard and Deborah wrote on it in big black letters,

GONE AWAY FROM IT ALL

and they propped it up in front of the window on the toy blackboard. Then they went away.

Hours later Teddy Robinson was lying on his back in the middle of a small round flower-bed in the garden. He had no clothes on at all, and a gentle breeze ruffled the fur on his tummy. He sighed happily, staring up at the lupins as they waved gently over his head, and sang to himself softly,

> *"Lucky bear,*
> *lucky bear,*
> *all alone*
> *and free as air.*
> *No more things*
> *to bother me,*
> *lucky me,*
> *lucky me.*
> *Free-and-easy,*
> *fat and free,*
> *what a lucky bear I be . . ."*

"All the same," he said to himself, "I wish I had somebody else to be all alone and lucky with. That Jones bear would have done, if only he hadn't been so proud, showing off with all his things."

Just then he heard Mummy calling to Deborah.

"Listen," she said, "I've just met Mrs Jones who lives opposite, and what do you think she said? She asked me why Teddy Robinson had gone away! I told her he hadn't, and she said, 'Well, that's funny, my Pauline said he had, and she's so sad about it.'"

"But why is she sad?" said Deborah.

"Mrs Jones says Pauline is very shy and finds it hard to make friends," said Mummy. "She's often seen you two together and wanted to talk to you, but she was too shy. Then when her birthday came she asked for a teddy bear like yours. Mrs Jones thought she was too old for it now she goes to a big school. But Pauline wanted it so much that she bought her one. And she says she has been so happy playing with you and Teddy Robinson, and she'd hoped you were going to be friends. Isn't it funny?"

Then Deborah told Mummy all about it. And a little later she went over to Pauline's house.

Teddy Robinson said, "Fancy that!" to himself three times over, and fell asleep in the sunshine.

When he woke up again, Deborah and Pauline were peering down at him through the lupins.

"There he is," said Deborah. "Don't tell, but this is his desert island. Let's put Teddy Jones down with him, then they can get to know each other."

So Teddy Jones had his party dress taken off and was put down beside Teddy Robinson. Then Pauline and Deborah ran off to play.

The two teddy bears lay on their backs and looked at each other sideways.

"Nice to lie down, isn't it?" said Teddy Robinson.

"*Very* nice," said Teddy Jones, with a cosy grunt.

"I must say I got a bit stiff sitting up in that window," said Teddy Robinson.

"So did I," said Teddy Jones. "This is a nice little place you've got here."

"Yes, it's my desert island," said Teddy Robinson. "Have you got one?"

"Oh, don't start all that again!" said Teddy Jones. "I'm worn out trying to keep up with you!"

"What!" said Teddy Robinson. "You can't be as worn out as I am. That's why I'm lying here. I nearly broke my back in that awful little bed."

"You may as well know I wasn't as comfortable as I looked," said Teddy Jones. "That cot was too small. I had a shocking night."

"*Did* you?" said Teddy Robinson. "Oh, I *am* glad! But I bet mine was worse; my bed had no bottom to it."

"Now I'll tell *you* something," said Teddy Jones. "That hat wasn't mine. I borrowed it."

"Mine wasn't mine either," said Teddy Robinson. "I only borrowed it to keep up with you."

"But why?" said Teddy Jones. "Fancy a proud sort

of chap like you trying to keep up with me!"

"*I'm* not a proud sort of chap," said Teddy Robinson. "I thought you were. I'm only me."

"And I'm only me," said Teddy Jones.

"Well now, isn't that nice?" said Teddy Robinson. "If you're only you and I'm only me, we don't have to bother any more."

"And we might even come to tea with each other instead?" said Teddy Jones.

we don't have to bother any more.

"Yes, of course!" said Teddy Robinson. "What a silly old sausage of a bear I am! I've been so busy trying to show off to you with all the things I haven't got, that I quite forgot to make friends with you. You come to tea with me today, and I'll come to tea with you tomorrow."

So they did.

And that is the end of the story about how Teddy Robinson tried to keep up with the Joneses.

– 13 –

Teddy Robinson
and the Band

One day Teddy Robinson and Deborah and Mummy all went off to spend the afternoon in the park.

When they got there Mummy found a comfortable seat to sit on and settled down to knit. Deborah and Teddy Robinson sat down on the other end of the seat and looked around to see what they could see.

Not far away some children were skipping on the grass. After she had watched them for a little while Deborah said, "I think I'd like to go and skip with those children, Teddy Robinson. You wouldn't mind staying here with Mummy, would you?

And Teddy Robinson said, "No, I don't mind. I don't care about skipping myself, but you go. I'll watch you."

So Deborah ran off to join the other children on the grass, and Teddy Robinson and Mummy stayed sitting on the seat in the sunshine.

Soon a lady came along, holding a very little boy by the hand. As soon as she saw Mummy the lady said, "Oh, how nice to meet you here!" And she sat down beside her and started talking, because she was a friend of hers.

The very little boy, whose name was James, stared hard and said nothing.

"Look, James, this is Teddy Robinson," said Mummy. "Perhaps you would like to sit up beside him and talk to him."

So James climbed up on the seat, and he and Teddy Robinson sat side by side and looked at each other, but neither of them said a word. They were both rather shy.

Mummy and the lady talked and talked and were very jolly together, but James and Teddy Robinson sat and did nothing and were rather dull together.

After a while James grew tired of sitting still, so he climbed down off the seat, and when nobody was looking he lifted Teddy Robinson down too, and toddled away with him.

"I hope you aren't going to lose us," said Teddy Robinson. But James said nothing at all.

They hadn't gone far before they came to some trees, and on the other side of the trees they saw a

—rather dull together—

bandstand with rows of chairs all round it. It was like a little round summerhouse, with open sides and a roof on top.

James and Teddy Robinson went over to look at it, and, as there was nobody there, they were able to go right up the steps and look inside. After that they ran in and out along the rows of empty chairs, until they came to the back row, just under the trees. Then James sat Teddy Robinson down on one of the

—just sitting there thinking

chairs, and sat himself down on the one next to him.

"I'm glad I've got a chair to myself," said Teddy Robinson. "It would be a pity to share one when there are so many."

But James didn't like sitting still for long. A moment later he got up again, and, forgetting all about Teddy Robinson, he ran back to the seat where Mummy and the lady were still talking. He was only a very little boy.

Teddy Robinson didn't mind at all. He felt rather grand sitting there all by himself on a chair of his own, with rows and rows of empty chairs standing all round him, and he began to think how nice it would be if someone should happen to pass by and notice him.

He looked up into the leafy branches over his head, so that people would think he was just sitting there thinking, and wouldn't guess that he had really been left there by mistake. And then he began thinking of all the things that people might say to each other when they saw him.

> "*Look over there!*
> *Look where?*
> *Why, there.*
> *Take care, don't stare,*
> *but alone on that chair*
> *there's a teddy bear!*
> *I do declare!*
> *A bear on a chair*
> *with his head in the air!*
> *How did he get there?*"

He said this to himself several times over, and then he went on:

> "You can see that he's thinking
> (not preening or prinking,
> or winking or blinking,
> or prowling or slinking,
> or eating or drinking),
> but just sitting thinking . . ."

But he didn't think this was very good, and anyway he was getting into rather a muddle with so much thinking about thinking. So he was quite pleased when suddenly there was a rustling in the leaves over his head, and a sparrow hopped along the branch nearest to him and stared down at him with bright, beady eyes.

"Good afternoon," chirped the sparrow. "Are you waiting for the music?"

"Good afternoon," said Teddy Robinson. "What music?"

"The band," said the sparrow. "I thought perhaps you had come to sing with the band. It always plays here in the afternoons."

"Oh," said Teddy Robinson, "how very nice that will be! I love singing."

"So do I," chirped the sparrow. "We all do. There are quite a lot of us up in this tree, and we sing with the band every afternoon. I really don't know how

"Are you waiting for the music?"

they would manage without us. I'm sure people would miss us if we didn't join in."

"How very jolly!" said Teddy Robinson. "When will the music begin?"

"Oh, very soon now," said the sparrow. "You'll see the chairs will soon begin to fill up, and then the band will arrive. Have you paid for your chair?"

"Oh, no," said Teddy Robinson. "Do I have to pay? I don't want to buy it, only to sit in it for a little while."

"Yes, but you have to pay just to sit in it," said the sparrow. "The ticket-man will be along in a minute. You'd better pretend to be asleep."

But Teddy Robinson was far too excited to pretend to be asleep. He was longing for the band to come and for the music to begin.

Before long one or two people came along and sat down in chairs near by; then two or three more people came, and after that more and more, until nearly all the rows of chairs were full. Several people looked as if they were just going to sit down in Teddy Robinson's chair, but they saw him just in time and moved on.

Then along came the ticket-man. Teddy Robinson began to feel rather worried when he saw all the people giving him money for their seats. But it was quite all right; the man came up to where he was sitting and stopped for a moment, then he smiled at Teddy Robinson and said, "I suppose it's no use asking *you* to buy a ticket," and went away.

Teddy Robinson was very glad.

"Was it all right?" asked the sparrow, peeping through the leaves.

"Yes," said Teddy Robinson. "I don't know how he knew I hadn't any money, but it's very nice for me, because now everyone will think I paid for my chair."

He sat up straighter than ever, and started to have a little think about how nice it was, to be sitting in a chair and looking as though you'd paid for it:

> *"Look at that bear!*
> *He's paid for a chair;*
> *no wonder he looks so grand;*
> *with his paws in his lap,*
> *what a sensible chap!*
> *He's waiting to hear the band."*

And then the band arrived. The men wore red and gold uniforms, and they climbed up the steps to the bandstand, carrying their trumpets and flutes and a great big drum.

"Here they come!" chirped the sparrow from the tree. "I must go and make sure the birds are all ready to start singing. Don't forget to join in yourself if you feel like it. Do you sing bass?"

"I don't know what that means," said Teddy Robinson.

"Rather deep and growly," said the sparrow.

"Oh, yes, I think perhaps I do," said Teddy Robinson.

"Good," said the sparrow. "We birds all sing soprano (that means rather high and twittery). We

could do with a good bass voice." And he flew back
into the tree again.

Then the band began to play.

The music went so fast that at first Teddy Robinson
hadn't time to think of any words for it, so he just
hummed happily to himself, and felt as if both he
and the chair were jigging up and down in time to
the music. Even the flies and bees began buzzing, and
the birds were chirping so merrily, and the band was
playing so loudly, that soon Teddy Robinson found
some words to sing after all. They went like this:

> *"Trill-trill-trill*
> *goes the man with the flute,*
> *and the man with the trumpet*
> *goes toot-toot-toot.*
> *Cheep-cheep-cheep*
> *go the birds in the trees,*
> *and buzz-buzz-buzz*
> *go the flies and the bees.*
> *Mmmm-mmmm-mmmm*
> *goes the teddy bear's hum,*
> *and boom-boom-boom*
> *goes the big bass drum."*

When the music stopped everyone clapped hard;

Then the band began to play.

but Teddy Robinson didn't clap, because, as he had been singing with the band, he was afraid it might look as if he were clapping himself.

He was just wondering whether he ought to get up and bow, as the leader of the band was doing, when he suddenly saw Deborah walking along between the rows of chairs.

She *was* surprised when she saw Teddy Robinson sitting among all the grown-up people.

"*However* did you get here?" she said. "And why didn't I know? And fancy you having a chair all to yourself!"

"What a pity you didn't come before!" said Teddy Robinson. "I've just been singing with the band. Did you hear everyone clapping?"

"Yes," said Deborah, "but I'd no idea they were clapping for you. I thought it was for the band."

"Me *and* the band," said Teddy Robinson, "and the sparrows as well. They've been singing quite beautifully."

"I *am* sorry I missed it," said Deborah. "I was skipping with the other children when somebody said the band had come, and I came over to see. I thought you were still sitting on the seat with Mummy."

"James and I got tired of it," said Teddy Robinson,

"so we came over here, and then James went back, so I stayed by myself. But you haven't missed all of it. Let's stay together and hear some more."

Then Teddy Robinson moved up so that Deborah could share his chair.

"I do think you're a clever bear," she said. "I always knew you could sing nicely, but I never thought I should find you singing with a proper band and with everyone clapping you!"

And that is the end of the story about
Teddy Robinson and the band.

-14-

Teddy Robinson
and Toby

One day Teddy Robinson and Deborah were just coming home from the shops when a lady called Mrs Peters came out of her house and gave Deborah a parcel.

"This is a present for your favourite doll," she said. "Open it when you get home."

"Oh, thank you," said Deborah. "What is it?"

"It's a surprise," said Mrs Peters. "I made it myself."

Deborah and Teddy Robinson ran home with the parcel.

"It's for you, Teddy Robinson," said Deborah. "I know you're not a doll, but you are my favourite, so it must be for you."

"I wonder what it is," said Teddy Robinson.

As soon as they got home Deborah undid the parcel. Inside the brown paper there was some white tissue paper, and inside the tissue paper lay a beautiful little ballet frock. It was white, with lots and lots of frills, and instead of sleeves it had shoulder straps with tiny pink roses sewn on them.

"Oh!" said Deborah. "It's just what I've always wanted – a dress with a skirt that really goes out. Oh, you *are* lucky!"

"But I'm not at all sure it's what *I've* always wanted," said Teddy Robinson. "I was rather hoping it would be a pair of Wellington boots."

"But you can't go to a party in Wellington boots," said Deborah.

"But I aren't going to a party," said Teddy Robinson.

"Yes, you are," said Deborah. At least, I am. I'm going to Caroline's party this afternoon, and now

"I'm not at all sure it's what *I've* always wanted"

you've got such a lovely dress you must come too."

"Was I invited?" said Teddy Robinson.

"Not really," said Deborah, "but that's the best of being a teddy bear – you can go to parties without being asked."

They tried on the dress, and it fitted Teddy Robinson perfectly. As soon as he saw the frilly skirt standing out all round him he felt so dainty and fairy-like that he forgot to be sorry any more that his surprise hadn't been a pair of Wellington boots.

"I see what you mean about a skirt that goes out all round," he said. "It does make you feel like dancing. Do you think if I practised I could learn to stand on one leg like a real ballet dancer?"

"I think you might," said Deborah. "Lean up against the window and see."

So Teddy Robinson stood on one leg, propped up against the window, and spent the rest of the morning thinking about how nice it was to be a ballet-dancing bear with roses on his braces. He rather hoped that people going by in the road outside might look up and see him.

"Perhaps they will think I am a famous dancing bear already," he said to himself, and he began making up a little song about it.

—a ballet-dancing bear with roses on his braces

"Look at that bear
in the window up there
with the roses all over his braces!

You can see at a glance
how well he can dance,
and how charmingly pretty his face is!

What a beautiful dress!
I should say, at a guess,
he has danced in a number of places."

195

"But they're not braces," said Deborah. "They're shoulder straps, and anyway you can't dance as well as all that, even if you are standing on one leg."

When it was time to get ready for Caroline's party Teddy Robinson suddenly felt shy.

"Perhaps I won't go after all," he said.

"Why ever not?" said Deborah.

"Well, I do feel a bit soppy," said Teddy Robinson. "And I'm so afraid someone may ask me to dance. I haven't really practised enough yet. I wouldn't mind if I had some Wellington boots to wear as well. Nobody would expect me to dance then."

"But even if you had," said Deborah, "you'd have to leave them in the bedroom with the hats and coats. Nobody ever wears Wellington boots with a ballet frock."

"Couldn't I stay in the bedroom with the hats and coats?" said Teddy Robinson.

"All right," said Deborah, "you can if you want to."

So when they got to Caroline's house they went upstairs to take off their things, then Deborah went downstairs to the party, and Teddy Robinson stayed sitting on the bed among all the hats and overcoats and mufflers. He recognized some of them and began to feel rather sorry to be missing the party.

"That's Mary-Anne's blue coat with the velvet on the collar," he said to himself. "I wonder if she's brought Jacqueline with her." (Jacqueline was Mary-Anne's beautiful doll.) "And that's Philip's duffel coat. I shall be sorry not to see him. And that's Andrew's overcoat and yellow muffler. Oh, dear, I wish I'd come in my trousers and braces, or my purple dress."

Just then there was a scuffling noise outside the door, and Caroline's little dog, whose name was Toby, came rushing into the room and scrambled under the bed.

Teddy Robinson was very surprised. He didn't like Toby much because he was rough and noisy and thought he was a lot cleverer than anyone else. Teddy Robinson wondered whether someone was chasing Toby and waited to see what would happen. But nothing happened. Nobody else came into the room, and Toby stayed under the bed without making a sound, so after a while Teddy Robinson forgot about him and began singing to himself quietly:

> *"Parties are jolly and noisy*
> *for children and musical chairs,*
> *but bedrooms are quiet and cosy*
> *for overcoats, mufflers, and bears."*

"Who's that singing?" barked Toby, coming out from under the bed. "Oh, it's you," he said when he saw Teddy Robinson looking down at him. "Are you allowed up there?"

"Yes, I think so," said Teddy Robinson.

"I suppose it's because you're a visitor," said Toby. "I'm never allowed on the beds. But, then, you're only a teddy bear. I'm glad I'm not a teddy bear. I don't think much of them myself. Caroline has one, but she likes me much better."

"Yes, but hers is only knitted," said Teddy Robinson. "I'm a real teddy bear."

"Are you?" said Toby. "I can't see much difference.

"Are you allowed up there?"

Why are you wearing that peculiar dress?"

Teddy Robinson didn't know what 'peculiar' meant, but he guessed it was something rude, so he said, "It's not. It's a ballet-dancer's dress, and it's very pretty."

"It's pretty peculiar, you mean," said Toby. "And why are you wearing a ballet-dancer's dress if you're not dancing?"

"I'm resting just now," said Teddy Robinson.

"Yes, I see you are," said Toby. "But why aren't you going to the party?"

Teddy Robinson didn't like to say "Mind your own business" in somebody else's house, so he didn't say anything. He thought Toby was very rude and wished he would go away. But Toby went on talking.

"I think it's silly," he said, "to come to a party all dressed up, and then to stay upstairs on the bed."

"And I think it's silly to leave a party and come upstairs to go *under* the bed," said Teddy Robinson. "Why are you hiding?"

"I shan't tell you, unless you'll tell me," said Toby.

"All right," said Teddy Robinson. "You say first."

"They're going to have crackers," said Toby, "and I don't like the noise."

"Oh, I love things that go off with a bang!" said Teddy Robinson.

"Then why are *you* up here?" said Toby.

"I was afraid they might ask me to dance," said Teddy Robinson.

Just then Deborah came running in, all excited.

"Teddy Robinson, you must come down!" she said. "We're having tea, and we're going to have crackers, and I've told everybody about your ballet frock, and they all want to see it."

"All right," said Teddy Robinson, "but they won't ask me to dance, will they?"

"No," said Deborah. "You can just sit beside me and watch the fun."

So Teddy Robinson went down with Deborah, and everybody admired his ballet frock and made a fuss of him, and as nobody asked him to dance he sat beside Deborah at the table and felt very happy and pleased to be there after all.

When they pulled the crackers and they went *bang! bang! bang!* Teddy Robinson thought about Toby the dog hiding under Caroline's bed, and felt rather sorry for him.

But it serves him right, he thought. He was very rude to me, and, after all, I was a visitor, even if I wasn't invited.

One of Deborah's crackers had a tiny little silver shoe inside it. She hung it on a piece of ribbon and tied it round Teddy Robinson's neck. Then she gave him all the cracker papers and the little pictures off the outsides of the crackers, and Teddy Robinson sat on them to keep them safe. He had a lovely time.

After tea, when the children got down to play games, Teddy Robinson was put to sit on top of the piano so that he could watch all the fun.

They played Blind Man's Buff, and Squeak, Piggy, Squeak; and then Caroline's auntie sat down at the piano and said, "Now we'll have Musical Bumps, and there'll be a prize for the last person in."

This was very exciting. All the children shouted and laughed and jumped while Caroline's auntie played the piano very loudly. Then she stopped suddenly, and all the children had to sit down very quickly on the floor. Whoever was the last to sit down was out of the game.

The louder Caroline's auntie played the more the piano shook, until Teddy Robinson, sitting on top of it, felt he was simply trembling with excitement. The children went *jumpety-jump*, and Auntie went *thumpety-thump*, and Teddy Robinson went *bumpety-bump*, until at last only Philip and Caroline were left in the game. All the other children were sitting on the floor watching.

"This is the last go!" said Auntie, and she began

playing *Pop Goes the Weasel*. When she got to the "Pop!" she went *crash* on the piano with both hands and stopped playing. At the same minute Teddy Robinson bumped so high off the piano that he fell right in the middle of the carpet.

Philip was so surprised that he forgot to sit down at all. Everyone clapped their hands, and Auntie said, "Well done, Teddy Robinson! I really think you ought to have the prize. That was a wonderful jump, and you certainly sat down before Caroline did."

the wonderful jump

Caroline said, "Yes, Teddy Robinson ought to have the prize." And everyone else said, "Yes! Yes! Teddy Robinson is the winner!"

So Caroline's auntie gave him the prize, which was a giant pencil, almost as tall as himself. Teddy Robinson was very pleased.

After that the children all went off to a treasure hunt in the dining-room. Teddy Robinson sat in the big armchair and waited for them. He had a paper hat on his head, the silver-shoe necklace round his neck, his giant pencil on his lap, and the pile of cracker papers all round him. He was feeling very happy.

In a minute the door opened a little way and Toby's nose came round the corner, very close to the floor.

"Have they finished the crackers yet?" he asked.

"Yes," said Teddy Robinson. "You can come in now. They're having a treasure hunt in the dining-room."

"Oh, *are* they?" said Toby, and his nose disappeared again very quickly.

"Well, now," said Teddy Robinson, "I wonder why he rushed away like that. I told him it was quite safe to come in."

In less than two minutes Toby was back, but this

time he didn't just poke his nose round the door. He came trotting into the room, wagging his tail and holding a little flat parcel in his mouth.

"What have you got there?" said Teddy Robinson.

Toby dropped his parcel carefully on the floor.

"I won it in the treasure hunt," he said. "It's chocolate. I'm a jolly clever chap. Those silly children were all looking and looking, but I didn't even bother to look. I just walked in and sniffed my way up to it in a minute. Fancy not being able to smell a bar of chocolate! Don't you wish you were as clever as me?"

"I don't think you've noticed what I've got up here in the chair," said Teddy Robinson.

Toby stood on his hind legs and looked into the chair.

"My word!" he said. "Wherever did you get all those things?"

"From the party, before you came down," said Teddy Robinson. "These are from the crackers, and this is a little silver shoe, and this is the prize I won for Musical Bumps."

"Well, I never!" said Toby, looking at him with round eyes. "You seem to be a jolly clever chap too. I'm sorry I said what I did about teddy bears, and I'm sorry I was so rude about your dress."

"That's all right," said Teddy Robinson. "You

"Wherever did you get all those things?"

were wrong about teddy bears, but, you know, I rather agree with you about the dress. It is a bit soppy. I didn't want to hurt Deborah's feelings by not wearing it, but I'm glad I did now or I shouldn't have come to this lovely party. And now that I've won this very fine pencil I'm not going to bother to be a ballet dancer after all. I shall write a book instead."

And that is the end of the story about
Teddy Robinson and Toby.

-15-

Teddy Robinson is Put in a Book

One day Teddy Robinson sat in the bookshelf in Deborah's room. He had his thinking face on and his head on one side, because he was thinking very hard.

Deborah came running in to look for him.

"Where are you, Teddy Robinson?" she said, looking under the bed.

"I'm up here," he said. "You can't see me because I'm in the bookshelf, so I probably look like a book."

Deborah looked up and saw him. "You don't look like anything but my dear, fat, funny old bear," she said. "What are you doing up there?"

"Writing a book," said Teddy Robinson.

"I don't see you writing," said Deborah.

"No," said Teddy Robinson. "You know I can't write really. But I'm thinking, and it's the thinking that counts."

"And what are you thinking?"

"Well, I'm thinking that when I've finished thinking it would be nice if you would do the writing for me. You can use the giant pencil that I won at the party."

"Yes, I will," said Deborah. "That's a good idea. Tell me what the book is to be about."

"I don't know yet," said Teddy Robinson. "Come back later, when I've had time to think, and I'll tell you."

So Deborah went away, and Teddy Robinson started thinking again. But he just couldn't think *what* to put in his book. He thought of all the other people he had seen writing in books, and he began remembering the sort of things they mumbled to themselves while they were writing.

...he just couldn't think *what* to put in his book

Mummy had a little book that she always wrote in before she went shopping, and her mumbling went something like this:

> "A joint of bread,
> a loaf of lamb,
> a pound of eggs
> and some new-laid jam . . ."

"Well, *that* doesn't make much sense," said Teddy Robinson to himself. Then he thought about the little book that Daddy sometimes wrote in when he came home at night. His mumbling went something like this:

> "One-and-six,
> and two to pay,
> add them up
> and take them away . . ."

"And that doesn't make sense either," said Teddy Robinson.

Then he remembered the little book that Auntie Sue used to write in when she was knitting. Her mumbling went like this:

> *"Two for purl*
> *and two for plain,*
> *turn them round*
> *and start again.*
> *Slip the stitch*
> *and let it go,*
> *drop the lot*
> *and end the row . . ."*

"That's no good either," thought Teddy Robinson. "It must be because they're grown-ups that they write such very dull books."

So then he thought about the books that Deborah liked to read to him. Their favourite was a book of nursery rhymes.

"All right," said Teddy Robinson to himself, "I'll write a book of nursery rhymes. Now, shall I start with

> *"Baa, baa, brown bear,*
> *Have you any wool?*

or

> *"Twinkle, twinkle, Teddy R.*
> *How I wonder what you are?"*

Just then Deborah came back and said, "Are you ready yet?"

"Listen," said Teddy Robinson. "How do you like this?

> "My *fur is brown, silly-silly.*
> Your *hair is green.*
> *When I am king, silly-silly,*
> *you shall be queen.*"

"Who are you calling silly?" said Deborah. "And my hair isn't green."

"What a pity," said Teddy Robinson, "because I could go on like that for ever."

"What do you really want to write about?" said Deborah. "What are you most interested in?"

"Me," said Teddy Robinson.

"Why, of course," said Deborah. "What a good idea! I know what we'll do. I'll put *you* in a book!"

"But would there be room for me between the pages? Shouldn't I get rather squashed?"

"No, I mean I'll make pictures and stories about you and put them in a book: then everyone will know about you and think how lucky I am to have such a beautiful bear."

"Oh, *yes*," said Teddy Robinson. "Will you have a

picture of me being a pirate?"

"Yes, and I'll tell about how you wanted to go to a party in a ballet frock and Wellington boots."

Deborah found the giant pencil in the toy-cupboard; then she went off to ask Mummy for enough paper to make a whole book. Mummy gave her a roll of drawer-paper.

While Deborah was away Teddy Robinson sat and thought about how jolly it was to be put in a book without having to bother to write it. He began to feel rather important and started talking loudly to the dolls inside the toy-cupboard.

"Wait till you see me in a book," he said. "Do you wish *you* were going in a book? *My* book is going to be the most beautiful and enormous book you ever saw. It will be made of red leather, with gold edges to the pages, and it will be as big as the garden gate."

"Don't be so silly," said Deborah, coming back with the paper. "It won't be anything of the sort, and you really mustn't talk like that or I shall wish I'd never thought of it. After all, lots of other bears have been in books before. What about Goldilocks? She had three of them."

"Yes," said Teddy Robinson, "but they were only pretend bears. It's different when you're a real bear. You can't help feeling proud."

Deborah began to unroll some of the paper and cut it up into pages for the book. But because the paper had been rolled up the pages were all curly and wouldn't lie flat. So Teddy Robinson sat on them to help flatten them out, and while he was waiting he sang a little song to himself, very quietly in case anyone should think he was showing off.

> *"There are books about horses,*
> *and books about dogs,*
> *and books about tadpoles,*
> *and books about frogs,*
> *and books about children;*
> *but wait till you see*
> *the wonderful, beautiful*
> *Book about Me."*

When the pages were flat enough Deborah folded them together like a real book. But some of them went crooked, so she had to cut the edges. Then the pages seemed too tall, so she cut the tops off them. Then they seemed too wide, so she cut the sides off them. But whichever way she cut them they kept on coming crooked, so in the end the book got smaller and smaller, and still it didn't look like a proper book at all.

"There's just one sheet left," said Teddy

—and still it didn't look like a proper book at all.

Robinson. "I'm sitting on it. Couldn't you put me in a newspaper instead?"

"No," said Deborah. "I want you in a book. I think we'd better go and ask Mummy about it."

But Mummy was busy hanging up curtains.

"I'm sorry I can't help you just now," she said, "but I don't think I should be much good at making a book anyway. Mr Vandyke Brown is the man you ought to ask. He's made lots and lots of books."

Teddy Robinson and Deborah both knew Mr Vandyke Brown because he lived in their road. He had white hair, and a very large black hat which he always took off whenever he met them out of doors. Teddy Robinson specially liked him because he always said, "And how are you, sir?" and shook his paw very politely after he'd finished saying "Good Morning" to Deborah.

"Let's go and see him now," whispered Teddy Robinson.

"Yes, I think we will," said Deborah.

So she brushed Teddy Robinson's fur, and off they went.

Mr Vandyke Brown opened the door himself when they rang the bell.

"Good morning," he said to Deborah. "What can I do for you? And how are you, sir?" he said to Teddy

Robinson, shaking him by the paw.

Deborah told him why they had come, and Mr Vandyke Brown looked hard at Teddy Robinson, with his head first on one side and then on the other. Then he said, "Yes, I see what you mean. He *would* look nice in a book. Come inside and let's talk about it."

So they all went indoors into Mr Vandyke Brown's sitting-room, which was very untidy and comfortable. Teddy Robinson sat on a little stool, Deborah sat in a large armchair, and Mr Vandyke Brown sat on a table and smiled at them both.

"Am I to do the pictures or the stories?" he asked.

"Well, it would be very nice if you'd do them both," said Deborah. "I could tell you the stories if you like."

"Yes," said Mr Vandyke Brown, thinking hard. "Now, what sort of pictures would you like?"

"What sort can we have?" asked Deborah.

"There are all sorts of different ways of making pictures," said Mr Vandyke Brown. "I wonder which would be best . . ."

"Ask him what sort of ways," whispered Teddy Robinson, leaning towards Deborah.

"Teddy Robinson wants to know what sort of ways," said Deborah.

—five little pictures of Teddy Robinson—

—one in wool,

one in chalk,

"Well," said Mr Vandyke Brown, "drawing them, or painting them, or embroidering them with wool on cards, or chalking them on pavements, or sticking little coloured pieces of paper on to a bigger piece of paper—"

"I don't think chalking them on pavements would do," said Deborah, "because we'd never be able to lift them off. But I think any of the others might be nice."

"I'll tell you what," said Mr Vandyke Brown. "I'll do one of each kind; then you can choose which you like best."

So Mr Vandyke Brown made five little pictures of Teddy Robinson; one in wool, one in chalk, one with

one with pen and ink,
one with paint,
and one with bits of sticky paper

pen and ink, one with paint, and one with little bits of sticky paper.

Teddy Robinson didn't like the sticky-paper one or the wool one because it made him look rather babyish, and Deborah didn't like the chalky one because it made him look smudgy and unbrushed, and neither of them liked the painted one because the colours were so queer. But they both loved the pen-and-ink one because it looked so like him.

"I'm glad you chose that one," said Mr Vandyke Brown. "I hoped you wouldn't choose the painted one, because those are the only colours left in my paint box. All the others seem to have dried up. And I hoped you wouldn't choose the chalky one, because

'Shall I look fierce?'

Or shall I stand on my head?'

He kept wondering how he ought to look

I always get chalk all over my clothes. And I hoped you wouldn't choose the sticky-paper one, because when I sneeze all the little bits of paper get blown away. And I *am* glad you didn't choose the wool one, because I'm very bad at threading needles."

Teddy Robinson didn't understand a word of all this, but he knew it was his very own book that was being talked about, so he sat quite still and tried to look ordinary. Really he was feeling rather shy.

He kept wondering how he ought to look when Mr Vandyke Brown started drawing him.

"Shall I look fierce?" he said to himself. "Or shall I do something clever, like standing on my head? Or shall I just pretend I don't know he's drawing me?"

"I do want a picture of him with his party face on," said Deborah.

"Very well," said Mr Vandyke Brown. "And while I'm drawing him, suppose you do some drawing too."

So he gave Deborah a piece of paper and a pencil, and Deborah drew a picture of Mr Vandyke Brown

The picture that Deborah drew

MISTER VANDYKE BROWN

while Mr Vandyke Brown drew a picture of Teddy Robinson. And Teddy Robinson did nothing at all. He decided it would be better if he just went on looking ordinary.

For a whole week after that Teddy Robinson and Deborah went every day to Mr Vandyke Brown's house, and by the end of the week there were pictures of Teddy Robinson lying all over the room, and pages and pages of stories.

"I think we've got enough now to fill a book," said Mr Vandyke Brown, picking up the pages off the chairs and tables.

"But they're all on different-sized pieces of paper," said Deborah. "How shall we sew them together to make a book?"

"I don't think we'll bother," said Mr Vandyke Brown. "I hate sewing. And, anyway, I've got a better idea. Tomorrow I'll take them all to my friend, the Publisher. He is a very clever man who knows all about how to make proper books. If he likes these he will make them into a real book, so that anyone who wants it can buy it."

"Can we come too?" asked Deborah.

"I don't see why not," said Mr Vandyke Brown, "if Mummy says so. But you'll have to be very quiet and wait downstairs."

—pictures of Teddy Robinson lying all over the room.

So the very next day Teddy Robinson and Deborah went on a bus with Mr Vandyke Brown all the way to town to see the Publisher. At least Mr Vandyke Brown went to see the Publisher, and Teddy Robinson and Deborah sat downstairs in a large room where a lady was busy packing up big parcels of books.

They were so quiet that they never said a word to each other all the time they were waiting, and it seemed a very long time indeed. But at last Mr Vandyke Brown came leaping down the stairs, smiling all over his face, and hustled them out into the street.

"What happened?" asked Deborah as they hurried along.

"Let's go and eat some ices," said Mr Vandyke Brown, "and I'll tell you all about it."

So they went into a teashop and ate ices with chocolate sauce while Mr Vandyke Brown told them what had happened.

"The Publisher was very kind," he said. "He likes the book very much. He laughed in all the right places, and he hopes you didn't hurt yourself, Teddy Robinson, when you fell off the piano."

"But where is the book?" asked Deborah.

"Oh, it won't be ready for a long while yet," said

Mr Vandyke Brown. "I'm afraid we shall have to wait weeks and weeks before it is ready. It always takes a long time to make a real book. Is Teddy Robinson disappointed?"

"I think he is rather," said Deborah. "But never mind."

"Dear me," said Mr Vandyke Brown, "how silly of me not to have thought of it before! Did he think I should come down with the finished book in my hand?"

"He did really," said Deborah. "But never mind."

"Excuse me just a minute," said Mr Vandyke Brown, and he jumped up and ran to the door. Just outside, a lady was selling bunches of violets. Mr Vandyke Brown bought one and came hurrying back. Then he took off his large black hat, bowed low to Teddy Robinson, and gave him the bunch of violets.

"Please accept these with my most grateful thanks," he said.

Teddy Robinson didn't know what he was talking about, but he was very pleased indeed, because he had never been given a bunch of flowers all of his own, and nobody had ever bowed to him before in quite such an important way.

Weeks and weeks later, when they had nearly

forgotten all about it, a parcel came addressed to Master Teddy Robinson, and there inside was *his* book. It wasn't made of red leather, and it wasn't nearly as big as the garden gate, but Teddy Robinson thought it was the nicest book he had ever seen, because it had his very own name on the cover.

And that is the end of the story about how
Teddy Robinson was put in a book.